GOLGOTHA

REMNANT TRILOGY BOOK ONE

Angela R. Watts

Copyright © 2021 Angela R. Watts

All rights reserved.

Angelarwatts.com

Published in the United States

Cover art: J Caleb Design

This is a work of fiction. All characters, places, and events portrayed in these stories are either products of the author's imagination or are used fictitiously. Any resemblance to actual persons, living or dead, events, or locales is coincidental

No part of this publication may be reproduced, distributed, or transmitted in any form or by any means, including photocopying, recording, or other electronic or mechanical methods, without prior written permission of the publisher, except in the case of brief quotations embodied in critical reviews and certain noncommercial uses permitted by copyright law.

Contents

MAP	VI
ALSO BY ANGELA...	VII
PRAISE FOR GOLGOTHA...	IX
DEDICATION	X
1. Chapter 1	1
2. Chapter 2	11
3. Chapter 3	19
4. Chapter 4	24
5. Chapter 5	30
6. Chapter 6	34
7. Chapter 7	43
8. Chapter 8	54
9. Chapter 9	61

10. Chapter 10	72
11. Chapter 11	77
12. Chapter 12	84
13. Chapter 13	91
14. Chapter 14	101
15. Chapter 15	110
16. Chapter 16	122
17. Chapter 17	130
18. Chapter 18	139
19. Chapter 19	149
20. Chapter 20	156
21. Chapter 21	166
22. Chapter 22	170
23. Chapter 23	181
24. Chapter 24	187
25. Chapter 25	196
26. Chapter 26	208
27. Chapter 27	217
28. Chapter 28	234
29. Chapter 29	239
30. Chapter 30	252
31. Chapter 31	259

32. Chapter 32 — 264
33. Chapter 33 — 269
34. Chapter 34 — 284
35. Chapter 35 — 291
36. Chapter 36 — 297
37. Chapter 37 — 302
38. Chapter 38 — 306
39. Chapter 39 — 317
40. Chapter 40 — 321
41. Chapter 41 — 330
42. Chapter 42 — 336
43. Chapter 43 — 345
44. Chapter 44 — 352
45. Chapter 45 — 362
46. Chapter 46 — 369
47. Chapter 47 — 379

Acknowledgments — 381

About Author — 382

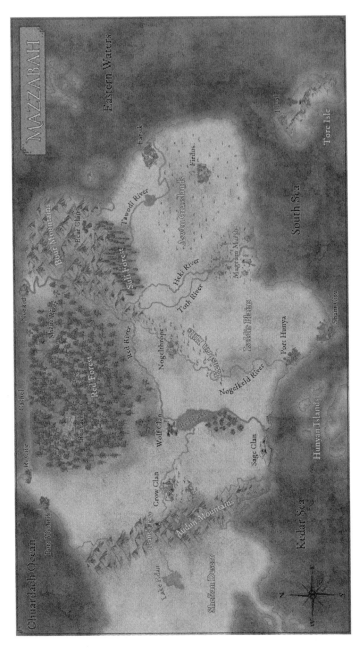

ALSO BY ANGELA...

THE INFIDEL BOOKS

Paradise Lost, The Infidel Books #0

The Divided Nation, The Infidel Books #1

The Grim Alliance, The Infidel Books #2

The Mercenary's Deception, The Infidel Books #3

The Blood Republic, The Infidel Books #4

Emmanuel, an Infidel Books short story prequel

Lockdown, an Infidel Books short story prequel

REMNANT TRILOGY

Golgotha

Tabor

WHISPERS OF HEAVEN

Seek

PRAISE FOR GOLGOTHA...

"Watts weaves a tale full of memorable characters and monsters in this epic struggle of dark versus light." — Emily Hayse, award-winning author of Seventh City

"GOLGOTHA is a gritty, hard-hitting, adventurous novel you don't want to miss!" — V. Romas Burton, award-winning author of Heartmender

"GOLGOTHA is a fantastic story I will look forward to re-reading for many years to come." — S.D. Howard, award-winning author of The City of Snow and Stars

"... You won't be able to breathe again until you've turned the last page." — Daniel Kuhnley, author of The Dark Heart Chronicles

"GOLGOTHA is as relentless as it is action-packed." — C.W. Briar, author of Whispers From the Depths

To Kody.
For being my partner in crime and letting me see if I could drag you across the floor like a corpse (for writing research).
Thanks for being my ride or die.

One

SOME PRINCES NEVER BECAME king. Some princes were lost in the histories, forgotten by the kingdom that once loved them, never to be mentioned again. The difference between kings and princes were a few well-held secrets. Prince Moray was a good secret keeper. He was also a capable wizard, which would help him greatly when he became king in a month.

If Buacach hadn't banned dark magic decades ago, he would not have to keep his magic secret. But he'd succeed. He always did.

Moray disliked visiting the kingdom streets. Peasants hurried about their day: workmen with carts of goods to sell in the town square, women trying to tame unruly children, dogs chasing down the couples weaving in and out of the cobblestone streets. Every time someone noticed Moray, they bowed briefly and moved on.

Moray rode his sleek black stallion, the cool autumn air biting his cheeks. The Buacach Kingdom was the wealthiest by far in Mazzabah, a melting pot of races and cultures, with his fine-blooded Goidelic heritage the king of them all. Even the most powerful of kingdoms, however, had to get their hands dirty to instill justice.

The solid hanging platform stood near the slums, close to the castle walls, farthest from the gated entrance. Most people didn't attend the hangings, which were cruel reminders of how many wicked people adulterated the world. They were also reminders of how well Moray's father ran his kingdom—maintaining order, no matter the consequence. *I'll have to be better than he is*, Moray thought. He watched the soldiers lead a thin man onto the platform, a small crowd looking on like hungry dogs.

The soldier spoke the usual babble by memory. Moray slowed his horse, watching the prisoner stand tall as the noose slipped over his head. The man wore nothing but rags, his pale arms visible—dark tattoos ran along his wrists and trailed to his chest. The marks of a magician. The marks of the damned.

Moray set his jaw. His father was a good king, but the magicians—ones like Moray—could help if the laws changed. Magic ought not to have been forbidden.

The soldiers stepped aside. The wizard never wavered, screaming past the gag in his mouth before the trapdoor was yanked beneath his feet. One jerk, and his frail neck snapped. Moray looked away, urging his stallion onward.

Pathetic. A true wizard would never die so easily. His spell ought to have saved him—if he had been strong enough, he would be alive.

One month, and it would all be his to rule. His father would step down, and Moray could bring justice.

He hitched his steed to the post outside of the small smithy. Sadon, the dark wizard who lived his life in seclusion, would arrive soon. Although Moray practiced, he had yet to reach Sadon's skills, but he would get there.

In Mazzabah, the line between good and evil was quite simple: magic was from Darkness, and Gifts were from Light.

Moray didn't have a Gift. Elohai had forgotten him, blessing his little brother, Finnigan, instead. Finnigan bore the skill of Energy—he could send fiery blasts or manipulate energy as he wished. These Gifts were from Elohai.

Or so they all claimed. Moray didn't believe Elohai cared about them. The Gifts were weak compared to the forbidden magics. Giftless and hungry for more, he'd naturally turned to the magics. The magics offered power, control, and skill. These were all necessary for a king. His parents would see that one day.

Sadon arrived on his paint horse, a breed from the Native tribes in the south, and hopped off. He rarely rode the mount but occasionally gave the animal some exercise like today.

"You're late," Moray said.

Sadon wasn't much older than Moray, but he hid his youthful stature and face with his gray cloak that covered him fully, regardless of where he was. Maybe it was to cover his long cloud-white hair so people didn't stare at him. Or perhaps he simply liked being known as the Phantom. Not many saw him, and those who called the "cloaked man" such a name were often ridiculed.

Sadon tied his horse, patted her strong neck, and headed into the smithy without a word.

Moray followed, locking the wooden door behind him. Sadon didn't have much of a temper. The two comrades teased incessantly, even when matters were serious and pressing. "Serpent got your tongue?"

Sadon found a lamp and lit it with some fire from his fingertip. The light illuminated the dank room, casting shadows on the old walls. He used the room occasionally to meet up with Moray, when he didn't want to teleport into the castle.

Moray wrinkled his nose at the smell of something rotting in the abandoned shack. "What is this meeting all about?"

"What do you think, *princess*?" Sadon opened a small trapdoor on the dusty floor, voice wry. He took great lengths to maintain privacy. Practicing black magic was punishable by death, and neither of them would take risks at getting caught. He crept down into the cellar, setting the lamp on the small, creaking table below.

Moray jumped down after him, shutting the trapdoor, fighting a sneeze.

"We're ready for Golgotha," Sadon said in a cool voice. He lowered his hood as a sign of respect, but that was all the respect he gave Moray. The wizard never bowed or used royal terms.

"We can open the portal?" Moray froze, zeal rising in his chest like kindled flames. To have the final game in sight after years of work caused his heart to race.

Sadon rolled his gray eyes. "Are you capable of not asking dumb questions?"

"When?"

Sadon shrugged, running a hand through his long, tangled hair. "I still believe that doing such a thing before you are on the throne is a poor choice. You must secure your role in the kingdom before we take action."

Moray paced. Sadon had actually found a way to open the portals after years of searching. "You speak of the dragon egg, about how I need the people's trust first?" He had not earned the egg's trust yet, but perhaps if he gained the kingdom's love, the egg would choose him.

Sadon watched him pace, pale face dull with boredom but his eyes sharp as a cat's. "You must be king, show the people you are trustworthy. When all eyes are not so keen, we put the plan into action."

The dragon egg sat in the castle, as it had for the past hundred years. Legend said that when the dragon's other half came to the throne, it would hatch and help bring Mazzabah to peace. Moray wasn't sure the thing would ever hatch. If he became king, he would definitely need the creature in his expedition to explore the second realm full of beasts and demons. But if the egg didn't hatch for him, Golgotha would be near un-survivable.

Golgotha, the second realm that had been split from Mazzabah after the Fall of the Species. Golgotha, the world of hell, a place that no fleshly human ought ever to enter or they would surely die.

Moray sighed. "If the dragon cannot pass through the portal, or if it doesn't choose me and hatch..."

Sadon scoffed. "Even if the thing doesn't hatch for you, we still can continue as planned. With the magics and with troops of soldiers that you can command, we stand a fair chance. I'll handle the rift."

"We need every advantage we can get." Moray didn't want to face Golgotha without at least a dragon on his side. It had been centuries since the last dragon hatched for a king.

"We can always try making it hatch," Sadon reminded him tersely.

"If it comes to that."

"You should be more concerned about making the kingdom like you." Sadon reclined in a creaky chair near the table.

"I might not be my little brother, but I have the kingdom's respect."

Prince Finnigan was adored by Buacach. He took the time to mingle with the peasants, helped do the grunt work in the kingdom, and offered hope and faith when anyone needed it. He believed in Elohai, just as their parents did, and despised the magics.

"Hmm." Sadon raised both eyebrows, changing the topic like he often did when a matter bored him. "How is the betrothal going?"

"The Wolf Clan wasn't thrilled to offer their youngest princess, but they've no choice if they want to keep the peace."

Moray thought of the Seven Tribes that were scattered across Mazzabah. A couple of the clans thirsted for war, while most simply tried to live peaceably. The Wolf Clan was somewhere in the balance—they had fought hard to gain their land and their freedom, yet sought peace and prosperity. They were handing their chief's youngest daughter, Princess Ama, as a peace offering to the Buacach Kingdom. If the clan kept alliance and trade with the kingdom, Buacach would protect them in return.

Sadon smirked. "Do you think you can handle the princess? The clans are awfully feisty people."

"As are the Goidelic. I can handle her."

Marriage was the last of Moray's concerns. The fact that he had to marry a stranger, keep her happy, have children with her—it was an outrageous part of being a king. Who had the time or energy for social appearances when he wanted to conquer the second realm? A wife was far too much work, and he had no interest in concubines. His grandfather and great-grandfather had practiced such a lifestyle, but his father, King Connall, was devoted to Queen Macha. Moray had no intentions to devote himself to anything but his work.

"I wouldn't be so sure. She could gut you in your sleep. I'll bet anything that she kills you on your wedding night." Sadon chuckled and ran a hand through his long hair that nearly reached his waist. "The Wolf Clan is not as placid as you think."

"You can't bet anything if I'm dead," Moray said dryly. "But that won't happen. The wedding ceremony is this month. Once it's over, I'll give it, what, three months of social appearances? The kingdom will probably calm down by then."

"If the dragon has not hatched by then, I make it hatch." Sadon stood. "Once all is calm, we send men into Golgotha."

Moray smiled. It was all his for the taking and the conquering. "Let it be."

Sadon pulled his hood up and climbed out of the cellar, Moray close behind. They left the smithy, with Sadon heading toward the wall of the kingdom. Moray guided his steed toward the Buacach castle.

The enormous cream-colored castle made of great stones and towers loomed over the greater half of the city. It stood as a beacon of hope, glory, and honor—three things that the kingdom stood for. Not for much longer, though. Once Moray got control, things would change for the better.

Moray rode his stallion into the castle stables, the stench of fresh hay and manure filling his nostrils. The damp atmosphere offered him comfort as he dismounted and allowed a stablehand boy to take the horse.

Moray slipped into the castle. As children, he and Finnigan had spent hours getting lost in the vast chambers, kitchens, washrooms, and secret doors. They'd gotten scolded but it hadn't stopped them. They'd only grown more cautious as to where they scampered into—one slipup had landed them in a servant's chamber, and they didn't want to repeat that horror.

As a man, Moray knew every crook and cranny of the castle. It was his home, but it held little sentimental value for him. He was far more interested in exploring Mazzabah and the second realm than staying home to rule peasants.

When he became king, the kingdom would be even more powerful than it was now. With Sadon at his side, who could stop them from creating a true empire?

Moray hurried through the halls, footsteps light on the marble floors, going straight to his chamber room. His servant, Graft, looked up from laying out Moray's dinner garb. Graft was a large black-skinned fellow from the deserts in the east and he was the closest thing Moray had to a true friend. The whole family considered him to be kin rather than a servant. Moray lived in competition against Finnigan, and for years, he'd worked to be better than his little brother. Even Sadon was Moray's workmate and ally. But Graft? Graft had always been loyal to a fault with no strings attached.

"Did you enjoy your ride?" Graft asked. He rarely showed emotion—no smiles, laughs, or jokes. Everything was dead serious to the man, who was only a year or two Moray's senior.

"Yes." Moray tore off his dusty tunic. Graft handed him a clean white one and Moray pulled it on, then grabbed a leather vest.

"Will you dine with the family?" Graft left Moray's clean pants on the bed and went to get his friend's shoes.

Moray sighed. "I already feel a headache coming on. Might as well make it worthwhile."

Graft loved Moray's family and treated Finnigan as a brother, as he had no blood kin of his own, but he simply had no clue how intolerable they all were. Their sweet talk and displays of affection—all of it was grating to Moray's nerves. He put up with it. They were family, after all. Moray might be a sinner and a magician, but he would still love his family. So long as Abaddon, his master, bid him to do so.

Two

— ◆ —

AMA HAD ALWAYS DREAMED of the type of love her parents shared. Chief Shaska, a kind-hearted man and a fierce warrior, led their clan with the heart of a wolf. Her mother led with stern love and compassion, always helping her father with the clan decisions. They were best friends and partners.

Ama would never have such a thing with Prince Moray. Watching her parents grieve over her choice to accept the betrothal hurt as much as it did to sign her soul over to a man she didn't know.

"I've no choice, Mama." Ama clasped her mother's worn hands. "If I don't marry Moray, our clan is at risk. Please don't cry." She fought back her own sobs, determined to be strong for her family and tribe. The Wolf Clan had fought for their freedom and for peace among the lands. If the Crow Clan, Moon Clan, or any other turned against them again, her people wouldn't survive. If the Buacach Kingdom kept a treaty with them, they could live in peace.

Ama was the only unmarried daughter. It was up to her to form that alliance.

As much as Ama longed for her soulmate, she longed for her people's happiness more. Creator made it clear that marriage was meant for love and nothing else. *Will You bless my marriage, even if I don't love Moray?* She was almost certain—almost—that she'd heard Creator tell her to go forth.

What else could she do?

Mama kissed Ama gently and pulled her into her arms. "If Creator has spoken to you, then so it shall be. We will always be home... we will always be here for you, my daughter." Her constant support anchored Ama like a solid rock while Ama tossed around in the sea of her fears and thoughts.

Ama breathed in the scent of her mother, the soft smell of smoked venison and cedar filling her nose. "I love you."

"I love you too."

They stepped outside to help the women cook over the open fires. Children raced around at play, a few bringing more firewood to help with preparing the meals. The Wolf Clan was centered on Creator. Thus, family was sacred.

Her family was all she'd ever known. Could she truly leave them? She watched the children for a moment, rubbing her light brown arm. *With Creator, I can do all things. Please, give me courage.* Fighting tears, Ama focused on grinding flour. In the morning, she would kiss goodbye her nieces, nephews, siblings, parents, grandparents—but tonight, they would celebrate and dance in the ways of their people.

Her father's words rang in her head: "There is no goodbye, only till we see each other again."

Would she see them again?

THE CLAN'S CELEBRATION CONSISTED of a great feast, games, and dancing. They worshipped and thanked Creator for their provisions, their home, and the treaty, though most of their hearts were heavy to let Ama go. She understood their torn spirits, but she refused to leave her clan brokenhearted.

So she danced.

The big drums throbbed in the night, the men never breaking the rhythm. Women sang and danced, and men joined in. They danced silly dances, which the children loved. They danced faster ones for the couples. Ama danced every dance she could, her heart overcome with joy over the music. She adored the music, the dances, the voices. How it could all be woven together and make something beyond beautiful left her breathless.

The people of the Buacach Kingdom, from what her older brother Etu had told her, didn't dance the way her people danced. If this was the last night she had to dance the way her heart desired, she wouldn't waste it. She wouldn't spend it thinking of how cruel Etu had been over her decision.

"Don't be selfish, Ama," he'd said. "It does not matter if you love the prince—would you deny your people a chance of life for your own personal gain?"

She shuddered softly as Etu's words rang in her head.

Hasa, the man she danced with, leaned closer and whispered into her ear, "Are you all right?"

Ama focused on her steps, scuffing dirt with her moccasins. "Yes."

"You've always been a poor liar, even since childhood." Hasa smirked, brown eyes studying her. "Is it Etu?"

"Keep your voice down." Ama looked away as they danced on, her left arm interlocked with his.

"Ah, it is. Has he been bullying you again?"

"I can handle myself."

"He should not treat you like a dog." Hasa shook his head. "You are a good woman."

"I have to do this for the clan, Hasa." Ama managed to keep her voice steady.

"The soul tie you are going to create with this stranger matters. It matters to you, to Creator, to all of us," Hasa whispered back.

Love and marriage were sacred things. They were not to be reckless over or ignored. But what could Ama do if not agree to marrying the prince?

"Pray Creator has mercy on me, then, Hasa," she said softly.

"You believe this is His will?" Hasa's tone grew tight. "Ama, you are my friend. If Creator has not told you—"

"He has." She was certain of that. Almost certain. Could she be entirely certain? *Perhaps I don't have enough faith.* "I am afraid, but I must do this."

Hasa looked down at her, his expression growing unreadable. "Very well, little sister. If Creator needs you elsewhere, I will not stand in His way... but let's enjoy tonight."

Ama smiled and squared her shoulders. Hasa had been her friend since they were young. Where she stayed far from the rock's edge, he had always inched closer for the view. Where she cried when she had disobeyed her parents' wishes, he had taken every beating with a small, satisfied look in his eyes. His troublemaking had grown worse in their teenhood years. At eighteen, they both faced the prospect of marriage, and while Ama had yearned for a soulmate, Hasa flirted with every girl in the clan.

Perhaps he would settle down while she was gone, or perhaps he would truly follow through with his intentions and join Etu's warriors. She didn't like the idea of risking either of them. Hasa was more of a brother to her than Etu.

Ama danced, focusing on the laughter of the dances, the strong voices of the singers, and the squeals of the zealous children. The bonfires cast a warm glow in the dark night. Every so often, she'd see her parents across the dancing grounds, but she never looked long. Despite their brave, loving expressions, she knew they feared for her.

Etu offered to dance with her as the music changed. Hasa begrudgingly moved away, dancing with another teenage girl. Ama danced with Etu to the soft music. Did her brother love her?

She loved her people. She was doing this for them. Etu was only trying to be a warrior and protect them all from battle.

But she wished he loved her.

Ama pushed the painful thoughts aside and focused on the beat of the drums.

Thump. Thump. Thump.

Her steps moved slow and steady alongside Etu's longer strides that he lessened so she could keep up.

Thump. Thump. Thump.

She took in the world around her. All of this would be gone from her tomorrow. Her family, her friends, her tent, her forest, her river, her freedom.

Ama had chosen to forgo it all. For her family, she would do anything.

DARKNESS ENGULFED AMA. SHE stood but could see nothing. Her bare feet touched the floor—a wooden floor—and she reached out, searching for a wall, something, anything. She hadn't a clue where she was, but a drive in her mind urged her forward.

Out. She had to get out.

She stumbled through the blackness until her hand hit something hard—a doorknob. Strange. Her people did not live in buildings with doors. Where was she? Ama twisted it, the heavy wooden door creaking, light pouring into the darkness. She grimaced and looked out.

A man stood in a large stone corridor. His broad shoulders shook softly. Ama couldn't see his face. As her eyes adjusted to the lightened hallway, she saw two bodies at the man's feet: a man with graying hair and a woman with long black hair. The man standing above them held a crown in either of his hands, but something dark dripped from his fingers.

Blood.

Ama tried speaking but nothing came out. The man lifted the crowns and stepped over the corpses. His powerful footsteps left a trail of blood as he walked away.

Ama moved closer and reached for the man and woman, a scream rising in her throat. She didn't know them. Didn't recognize who they were, or where she was. But her heart broke into a million pieces.

The man had killed them.

AMA FLINCHED AWAKE, BREATH catching in her throat. A thick animal fur covered her body, and she took in her familiar surroundings. She was safe in her family's tent. All was quiet, besides her father's snoring and an owl hooting outside.

She closed her eyes again, but the image of the two bodies and the strange man wouldn't leave her mind. Who were they? Crowns—the royalty of Buacach wore crowns, didn't they? She hadn't even married Moray and was already dreaming terrible things. Did this dream warn her of her future? Was she the woman bleeding out on the corridor floor? Would she die beside Moray, slaughtered like some animal?

She stopped her wild thoughts. The Gift of dreams was no small thing, and she had grown up with prophetic dreams. This one made her sick. It made her feel... weak. She hadn't been able to save the two people, hadn't stopped the killer, hadn't even spoken a word.

Ama gulped down the lump in her throat. No, she was looking into it too much, trying to assign meaning when there was none yet. She couldn't let her emotions take over and form horrid stories. Creator hadn't given her the dream to suffocate her with fear.

Then what did the dream warn her of? Who were the dead? And who killed them... and why?

Ama fell asleep without any understanding of the strange dream.

Three

FINNIGAN DIDN'T INTEND TO eavesdrop, but if there was one thing Moray ought to understand after twenty years in the castle with Finnigan, it was not to discuss anything in the corridors. Sound traveled well against the stone, and Finnigan liked knowing things.

Moray's voice came through the halls, hard like iron. "How many times do I have to tell you, Graft? They despise *me*, not the other way around."

Graft's voice followed softly. "They are your family. They love you, even if they do not understand your ways."

"My *ways*?" Moray scoffed. "You make me sound like a monster."

"You know me better than that." Graft never flinched or wavered.

Finnigan stayed out of sight. They were talking about Father, Mother, and him, no doubt. Moray could not stand them anymore. What had they done to deserve his disdain?

Biting his lip, Finnigan rounded the corner. "Oh!" He nearly ran into Moray and Graft both, a smirk on his face. "Sorry. I forgot about dinner. Amazing, how fast time can fly when you spend it outside these dreary castle walls."

Moray walked on, ignoring him. Finnigan was long since accustomed to Moray ignoring his existence, and he followed them. "How long will it take the princess to arrive? Seven days? Eight? You must be excited, brother." Finnigan didn't consider himself waiting for love, but if Elohai gave him a wife, hopefully she would be a nice one. For now, he was too busy to love anyone. Too many of the lords and ladies had miserable lives for the sake of stature and wealth. He wanted love instead of money, but it wasn't going how he'd like. Things rarely did.

"The trip is seven days, but who knows how long they will take on horseback. Anything could happen," Moray replied icily.

Finnigan frowned. "Could you give any more of a pessimistic answer?"

"Yes."

Graft intervened gently. "I am sure she is kind and beautiful. Every woman is, in her own unique way." He never spoke a harsh word over anyone, but Moray did enough of that for all three of them combined.

Finnigan felt bad for the Wolf Clan princess and hadn't even met her. She had to be kind, or completely reckless to agree to marrying Moray. Finnigan smiled at Graft, pushing his doubts aside. "Sure she is. They're well-bred people."

Finnigan had met many other people—the Kordreffs from their southeastern societies, the Sheftans from the desert like Graft, and countless others. The kingdom had many alliances, but Finnigan was most intrigued by the clans. Some of the tribes were violent and reclusive, but most of them were kind and brilliant. He wanted to better know them, even if he wouldn't be king, just to be their friend.

"Does it matter what she looks like?" Moray grumbled.

"No." Finnigan beamed. "We're just excited to see her."

Moray didn't look at him, jaw tight. "She's my wife. You best leave her alone."

"She will be my family too." Finnigan shook his head. "Am I not allowed to welcome her?" His brother was always jealous, always thinking his kindness was fake.

"Stay away from her," Moray snapped.

The jab hurt more than it should have. Finnigan rubbed his neck, voice quiet. "I'm not your enemy, Moray."

Moray didn't answer.

They ate dinner with the king and queen in the large dining hall, a large meal without guests. Finnigan spoke openly with his parents, enjoying the time well spent when they were all so often busy. They never spoke of politics over supper—it ruined King Connall's appetite—but the conversation slipped into small talk of magic. The king had been alerted that one of the men who helped trades with the Sheftans had tried the black magic.

"He must be punished," King Connall said with a sigh.

"But by death?" Queen Macha asked weakly. "Is it not time for that law to change?"

He frowned. "It is a solid law. It has limited the activity."

Executing magicians had always been a law they disagreed on. Queen Macha looked away, her graying hair curling around her round cheeks. Finnigan remembered when his parents had been vibrant with youth. Ruling the kingdom had zapped them of almost all of what had been, except their faith that Elohai would guide their every step.

Finnigan didn't know what to believe regarding the law. If he agreed with his father, then when they found out that Moray practiced, they would have to kill him. He had learned of his brother's magic over a year ago. It'd been accidental—Finnigan had been going to ask him something of little importance, and he'd seen Moray practicing in his room. Moray had quickly cleaned his mess, and Finnigan never let on that he'd noticed.

But he had. For over a year, he had chosen to ignore it. Surely, Moray would change his mind. Wouldn't he? Finnigan glanced at Moray, but his older brother showed no sign of interest in the conversation. Why would Moray choose to become a monster? What had the magicians ever done but mislead people, harm them, and do terrible things for power?

King Connall broke the silence. "I do not always enjoy justice, Macha. What was done cannot be undone."

Finnigan wrestled with his thoughts. *Stay silent for once in your life.* But doing so felt like he was signing his brother off to death. "Father, perhaps after this, the law ought to be changed. We can help such lost souls find Elohai instead of condemning them."

"There is a time for mercy and a time for justice." King Connall set his spoon down, running his fingers through his thick black-and-gray beard.

"If the law is neutral," Finnigan continued, "then Elohai could guide you in each case, Father. If a person is truly wicked, they may die. But if a person is not and Elohai says they have a chance, shouldn't we extend mercy as we are instructed?"

King Connall abided by Elohai's laws the best he could. If Finnigan wanted to save Moray, he needed the Letters on his side. But were they? Did Elohai not extend mercy to magicians of witchcraft and war?

He didn't know for certain yet, but he couldn't lose his brother.

King Connall studied Finnigan for a long moment. His piercing eyes softened. "I will pray about it, son. It would be a relief... but we shall see." The king had secured his kingdom for decades by a strong hand and a soft heart, but they all knew very well that everything could crumble with a few unbalanced choices.

Finnigan shot Moray a hopeful smile, but as usual, Moray looked away. Finnigan focused on chatting with his parents and forced his emotions aside. A smile was a perfect weapon because it hid any sign of internal damage.

Four

AMA RODE IN SILENCE with Etu, Hasa, and six of Etu's finest warriors. After three days of riding her mare, Usdi, Ama had little to do but pray and try to enjoy the time with her friends. She had grown up riding horses and doubted she could do much of it after she was wed. A small part of her held on to the hope she could do it anyway. She couldn't imagine life without spending time in the forest with Usdi.

On the sixth night, they approached the city of Buacach, the thick black sky hanging over the tall trees. The warriors carried lanterns to light the way along the small trail. Ama wasn't in the mood to talk, and obviously none of the men were either. She had visited Buacach only once, as a little girl, but she'd adored the woods surrounding it. The giant trees reached for the sky, like never-moving sentries for the whole world to see. *How deep their roots must go down, never yielding. They're strong where they've always been...*

Ama gulped hard. She already missed her family, her tribe, and her own sleeping pallet. Glancing at Etu, she let her mind wander once more. There'd been a time when she had admired her older brother, but she didn't know what she'd done to deserve his disgust. Did he truly want her gone from the clan?

She licked her lips and rubbed Usdi's fuzzy neck. Etu may have pushed her to make the decision, but she was the one who had agreed to it. Would Creator punish her? Perhaps He didn't care if her heart was trying to do good. Perhaps the laws meant more.

Etu led them to the giant iron gate that separated the kingdom from the wild. Guards lined the top of the large walls, barely visible in the dark despite the torches along the stone ledge. The men at the gate let the clan members inside.

"Welcome to the Buacach Kingdom. These men will lead you to the castle. Your horses will be cared for in the royal stables," one guard said, gesturing to a group of escorts on horseback.

Ama's insides churned but she followed Etu along. Usdi snorted, no doubt feeling Ama's hesitancy as she trailed after the others. Ama kept her head down. The guards in the watchtowers, the people in the street, the man she would marry... She didn't think she could trust any of them. Could she love them as Creator instructed? Her mind swam like a rushing, clashing river, her heart dragging across the rocks.

The escorts led them through the city, lanterns hanging from the buildings and lighting the cobblestone path. They stopped outside of the castle that towered above the kingdom. Even in the dark, Ama saw the castle's giant outline and a few glass-plated windows glowing with light. She would have a whole castle between her and the sky. Her chest constricted like a giant hand was wrapped around her heart.

The escorts dismounted, and one man spoke with Etu. Ama couldn't hear what they were saying. She glanced at the doors of the castle. A tall man ran out, dressed in plain garb, though it resembled some look of royalty. He slowed ever so slightly down the steps as he beamed at Ama, his blond curls dancing. "Hello! Welcome!"

Ama frowned at him, not dismounting. "Hello..."

"I'm Prince Finnigan. Please, just call me Finnigan. Ama, isn't it?" He stepped over, ignoring the warriors and the guards.

Ama studied him closely. "Yes, I am."

"Prince Moray is a bit preoccupied at the moment, but don't worry, you all have baths waiting and beds prepared." Finnigan smiled at her, then the warriors, dimples showing. "We are honored to have you here."

Ama almost asked where the king and queen were but quickly caught herself. They were probably busy, like Moray—her future husband who apparently had no more interest in her than she had in him.

Etu slipped off his stallion, and his warriors did the same. Hasa stepped over to Ama, though she needed no assistance as she got down.

"Prince Moray is busy?" Hasa asked coolly.

Finnigan's smile tightened. "I'm very sorry."

Some guards took the horses away. Etu bowed slightly to Finnigan, as the way of the Buacach were, but Finnigan stopped him.

"None of that, not with me. Come on inside." Finnigan, along with a few other guards, led the group into the castle.

Ama stayed beside Hasa as they followed. His sour expression made her stomach twist. She couldn't reassure him, so she kept silent. Finnigan gabbed like a bird with its head chopped off, talking about the grand architecture, then switching the topic and discussing their trip, then speaking of what they could expect in the morning. They were all invited to a morning breakfast with the royals.

Ama caught Hasa rolling his eyes at that. She bit back a smile. Finnigan was one of the few men she'd met that almost outmatched Hasa's talkative spirit.

Finnigan led them through corridors and stopped in front of one door, smiling at Ama with kind eyes. "This is your bed chamber, Princess Ama. I hope you get some well-deserved rest."

Etu frowned at her as if warning her to keep her mouth shut. Ama smiled at Finnigan, throat dry. "Thank you, Finnigan." She stepped into the room and shut the door behind her, heart hammering. Finally, she could be alone, find some peace.

She met the eyes of the servant standing near a large bath by the fireplace that took up half a chamber wall. She didn't need a servant! She could care for herself, and she wanted to be alone. What was this nonsense?

"Hello, Princess." The girl, no older than Ama, bowed low.

Ama winced. "Don't do that! Please, call me Ama. You don't have to bow. It is not the custom of my people." Perhaps she'd adjust to Buacach's customs, but there was no need to in the privacy of her room, was there?

The girl blinked. Her pale skin and black hair, wrapped in a tight bun, almost glowed in the warm light of the fire. "I am sorry—"

"Nothing to apologize for," Ama added, smiling. "What is your name?"

"Meili." She straightened ever so slightly. "Your bath is ready... Ama." A smile cracked her lips. "What a pretty name!"

Ama stepped over, forcing deep breaths. "Meili is also a beautiful name."

Meili turned to a small table nearby that was covered in soaps, oils, and towels. "You must be exhausted and sore from the trip. These will help soothe the aches."

"Would... would it be all right if I bathed alone?" Ama asked weakly.

Meili looked up, her small stature deflating. Her eyes filled with a strange look. Pity? Ama didn't want pity. "Of course, Ama. I'll be right outside. Please, if you need help with the oils, I can lend a hand."

"Of course." Ama didn't want to push the girl away; she just needed to be alone for a bit.

Meili left the room and Ama locked the door. She undressed, setting her soft leather dress aside, running her fingers over the colorful beads. She'd have to wear foreign dresses like the other women in Buacach. Such small changes made a world of difference. She laid her dagger and sheath, a sacred Gift from Creator, on top of the garments. Etu had a dagger similar to her own, both of them unlike any other blade known to anyone. They were kept secret from all people except the Wolf Clan.

Ama shoved her thoughts aside and stepped into the tub, the hot water loosening her muscles. She burst into tears. *Have mercy, Creator. Please. I'm alone. I'm afraid.*

Be not afraid, came the response.

What if I made a mistake? Ama asked. *I don't want to be punished.*

Ama thought of the strange dream with the bloody crowns and the foreign man. Was Creator warning her of her future as queen? She sank into the water and closed her eyes, the crackling fire masking her sobs.

Five

THE PROBLEM WITH HUMANITY was the never-ending drive to make things far more difficult than they needed to be. On top of this motivating force behind every person in existence, some people were merely stupid. Sadon sighed, reclining in the creaky wooden chair. The lord's quarters were lush and lavish, but the small room he allowed Sadon to teleport to wasn't much more than an oversized closet with a table and lantern.

Sadon had a problem. One he hadn't prepared for.

His master had warned him only last night of Ama's Gift. Dreams. Of all the blasted Gifts a soul could have! Why couldn't she wield Energy, like Finnigan? That couldn't hamper Sadon's plans. Dreams could ruin everything. If she were to suspect Moray—or anyone else—of foul play, it could cause trouble.

There were so many liabilities, so many outcomes, so many small details that could change the path ahead. It only took one person to change everything. And it was Sadon's job to ensure this plan didn't fail.

He took a slow breath and lit a pipe from his cloak pocket. Moray wouldn't expect anything. He was a strong magician, growing steadfast in the ways of the magic. But he wouldn't be king.

Sadon blew a ring of smoke and then closed his eyes. In just a short time, he would be the king's wizard. In a land where magic was cursed and Abaddon's finest were slaughtered at the hanging tree like dogs, Sadon would be the perfect example of what a man ought to look like.

He had come a long way from that pathetic slave boy who had panicked the first time he conducted a spell.

The door rattled open, and a man's voice came coolly. "Bit early, aren't you?"

"You're late. Everyone's always late." Sadon blew some more smoke.

A broad man stepped in with a smirk. "Let's begin. We still have a few details to discuss."

"Well, yes." Sadon rolled his eyes. "I didn't come to have tea with you for fun."

DREAMS WERE STRANGE THINGS. Always tattling, always fooling, always holding just a bit more than expected. Prophetic dreams, however, were nasty business. As a wizard, Sadon could manipulate dreams. He could enter a sleeping person's mind and correspond with them as if they were standing feet away from each other. With the black magic, a person could do almost anything.

But tonight, no amount of his magic could plague Ama's mind.

He couldn't even see her dreams. He couldn't break through to shift the dreams or frighten her. Sitting on the floor of his reclusive cabin, he mumbled under his breath and gave up.

Elohai protected her.

Harming a person protected by Elohai proved far more difficult than any other victim. He couldn't even get inside her mind.

This was a bigger problem than he expected. If he couldn't scare Ama into submission, who could? He didn't need some holy girl dismantling everything. What if she'd already had a telling dream?

Sadon sucked in a breath, calming down. Ama's weakness was her family and her clan. Surely, with so much at stake, she would keep silent, even if Elohai did warn her of something foul. He rubbed his temples and stood up from the floor of his cabin, blowing out the candles on the wooden table.

Of course, if she did cause trouble, the king would rein her in.

He got into bed, jaw tight as he stared into the darkness that engulfed him. He would be alert and he would warn Moray, just in case. There was no use in telling Barric about Ama's Gift. Sadon only had to fool Moray awhile longer, and then the plan would slip into place. Sadon would do his part in the path to better the kingdom.

I will make you proud, Master. I will do you well.

A few lives were worth losing for the sake of Abaddon's greater plan. Moray and Finnigan didn't deserve a fate in Golgotha, but it had to be done.

Not even an innocent princess would stand in his way. He would reach Golgotha, even if that meant his path toward the realm lay stained with blood. That would be a fitting way to show Abaddon he was capable of entering the realm of demons, where the creatures could be seen and smelled as clearly as if they were breathing bodies.

He'd proved his raw dedication for years. He closed his eyes, rubbing his hands through his hair. Zeal burned in his chest.

His master's reward was close now. So close. He would rule the demons that dwelled among the monsters. He would tame the beasts and damned creations.

Sadon smiled softly. Yes, that would be his fate. Abaddon had promised.

Six

FINNIGAN HURRIED THROUGH THE castle's stone corridors like a blind bat. He didn't mind gaining strange bruises from running into walls or missing tricky stair steps. He never heeded his father's suggestion of walking like a calm, graceful king at all times. Who had time for that?

Etu and the warriors hadn't been pleased by Moray's lack of appearance. Moray should've welcomed his betrothed, but Finnigan played intercessor. He didn't fault his parents so much—King Connall had a pressing matter with Lord Barric, who had come to the kingdom a month before the wedding ceremony for a visit to discuss some political matters. Lord Barric traveled often, but he grated Finnigan's nerves. He was a sickeningly charming lord, and Finnigan found him a bit overbearing, so he avoided him when possible.

Finnigan had to find Moray, then he'd check on his parents. The only problem was that he didn't know where his brother was. Moray hadn't told him where he'd be when the clan members arrived. Not that he communicated with Finnigan, ever.

He knocked on Moray's chamber door. "Moray?"

No response.

He rapped again. "Moray! Are you in there?"

The door opened, and Moray glowered at him, inches from his face. "What?"

"Ama is here." Finnigan set his jaw. "You missed their entry."

"A fact that will haunt my darkest nightmares." Moray pushed the door shut, but Finnigan shoved his boot in the way.

"What are you doing?"

"Working. Leave me alone."

Finnigan scowled at him, anger rising. "Your betrothed is here and you—"

"She'll wait till tomorrow to handle pleasantries. Go to bed, little prince." Moray slammed the door closed in Finnigan's face. The nickname had always grated on Finnigan's nerves, but he had bigger problems right now. He stormed down the hall but ran into Graft as he rounded the corner.

"Sorry, Graft." Finnigan's shoulders sagged.

Graft hesitated. "May I have a moment, Finnigan?" It'd taken years of adjusting, since he was used to being a servant and nothing more, but Graft finally saw Moray and Finnigan as if they were blood kin equals, like they always encouraged him to.

"Of course. Is something wrong?" Finnigan headed to his personal chambers, Graft on his heels.

"I am not sure."

"Oh..." Finnigan led him to his bed chambers quickly, curiosity piqued. Graft didn't talk much, especially not privately. Finnigan shut the door behind him, motioning for Graft to sit down on a cushioned chair. "Well?"

"It is about Moray," Graft said quietly.

"What about him?"

"He... has not been acting right." Graft kept his head down.

"You can tell me anything. We're all brothers. I've noticed he has been acting stranger than usual the past few months. Any clue why?" Finnigan paced near the fireplace. He hadn't asked Graft about his thoughts—he'd been too afraid of Graft's answers.

"I... I cannot say for certain."

"You've got a hunch?" Finnigan stopped in his tracks, unsure whether to share his suspicions. Graft was a kind soul. It would break him to know his best friend was interested in the black magic. Finnigan didn't have much proof anyway. He couldn't stir up strife.

"I... I think I may."

Finnigan rested a hand on Graft's broad shoulder. "So do I."

"You do?" Graft's eyes widened.

I'm Moray's brother. I'd best voice it first, Finnigan reasoned. "I think he's messing with the magics. I don't think he believes in Elohai's Gifts." The words stung, but Finnigan forced them out. "Of course, I could be wrong—"

"You aren't." Graft shook his head. "I know it is true, Finnigan."

"Does he know—"

"Nay, he has no idea I'm aware. He has kept it quiet, close to his chest."

Finnigan rubbed his jaw, mind whirling. So it was true. He'd need proof, but he couldn't get it. Moray would snap his neck if he poked his nose into this more. But he had to. If someone else found out, Moray would be ruined. "At least we know. I'll assume we're the only ones who know at the moment."

"If this is discovered, he will be destroyed," Graft whispered. "What do we do?"

"I... don't know," Finnigan admitted. "I've kept silent because I didn't want to make it worse."

"If the king finds out—"

"I've pushed him to change the law, but we shall see if it happens." Finnigan shook his head, throat dry. "We must warn Moray. He must stop while he can."

"He will not listen. He is hungry for power." Graft dropped his head in shame.

"That is his burden to carry, not yours." Finnigan patted Graft's strong arm and stared into the bright flames of the fireplace. "I'll speak with him tomorrow."

The thought of confronting Moray sent shivers up Finnigan's spine. He could not lose his brother to the darkness. He had to help him for the good of their kingdom too.

"Please... I do not want him angry with me," Graft forced, head still low.

"Don't feel guilty over speaking with me." Finnigan glanced over. "We cannot help him if we are clueless.

Things are better done with a team, yes?"

Graft straightened ever so slightly and nodded.

"He's my brother. I can handle him." Finnigan flashed a smile. He wouldn't let Graft see his concern. Not all of it. "Now, go on, get some rest. I think I know where he might be."

THE DRAGON EGG SAT in a small vault in the castle basement to collect dust for over a hundred years. Or, it would collect dust if it wasn't guarded and polished like an over-cherished piece of gold. Moray knew the history of every single artifact and item in the vault, but the egg held a special place in his heart.

The door opened with a soft creak, and he watched Finnigan creep in. Moray had avoided his brother for days now after bidding farewell to Etu and the warriors.

"Think it'll hatch?" Finnigan whispered, studying the egg. Thick, small scales covered the oval-shaped egg, which was white with brown marble etches flowing throughout.

"I don't know." Moray had tried everything the books said to boost the egg's desire to hatch for him when the time was ripe, but he honestly doubted the incantations and such were effective in this case. Without a dragon, Moray's conquering of Golgotha would be difficult. He'd still do it, but a dragon would benefit him—a weapon, a transportation vessel, and if the legends were true, even a means of opening the rift between the two realms. But the latter might just be lore. After the Split, Elohai had supposedly cast the legged serpents, the uncursed, to Mazzabah as friends to the peoples. He had cast the serpents, the cursed, into Golgotha to spend eternity.

Moray figured that far, far more had happened to cause the Split than just some naughty fork-tongued beasts. But the religious Letters were vague, and the scholars argued. Moray didn't have enough proof that something bigger had happened, so he didn't think of it anymore. Golgotha was still a realm, and it was still there for the taking. It reeked of power and resources. He wouldn't let beasts stop him from taking what Elohai had given them at the start.

"Moray?" Finnigan whispered again. "What are you thinking of?"

Moray tore his gaze from the egg, meeting Finnigan's eyes. "How ugly you are."

"Haha, amusing." Finnigan nudged him. "What if it hatches for *you*?"

"You've always been so obsessed over that egg," Moray said with a sigh. "You would sleep in this room, remember? When we were children, you were not sure if it might hatch at random, even if no king was enthroned."

Finnigan grinned sheepishly. "Legends are sometimes murky on small details. Anything can happen."

"It never hatched, and you still believe it will." Moray brushed some dust off his white tunic.

"You don't believe it will?" Finnigan asked in disbelief.

"Why would it?" Moray turned, heading for the door. "If you'll excuse me, I have a princess to woo."

"*Woo*?" Finnigan secured the vaulted room before chasing after Moray, footsteps heavy. Moray was the agile, silent cat of doom. Finnigan was the clumsy, loud mutt.

"Or at least earn an efficient level of common human decency." Moray nodded.

Finnigan groaned softly and walked alongside him. "That sounds more like you. It wouldn't kill you to *woo* Ama."

"Why bother?"

"Sh-she'll be your wife!"

"So?"

"Ama is in a foreign place, tons of information being shoved down her throat in a single month to prepare her for a lifetime of queenhood... You don't have any idea why she might appreciate love from her betrothed husband? You're not that daft." Finnigan nudged his arm hard.

"Allowing her to grow emotionally invested in this marriage would only upset her more," Moray said.

Finnigan grabbed his arm, stopping him sharply. "Ama is a believer. She wants to love you, Moray."

"She cannot," Moray said flatly. If anything, she'd been spending quite too much time with Finnigan since she'd arrived. Moray would have to fix that.

"Why not?"

"None of your business."

He was taking her heart into consideration by not loving her and allowing her harm. When he established his empire, all he would ask Ama for would be a son. He'd do anything to make sure she was not in pain for the nine months and birth it took to get an heir. He wouldn't abuse her or be unfaithful, so Ama couldn't perceive him as a monster. In time, she'd see he wasn't truly as wicked as the world painted magicians.

Finnigan didn't let go of Moray's arm, his eyes flashing with rage. "Would it kill you to be honest with me about anything?"

Moray always considered Finnigan as one of the least temperamental men he knew. Even saints had a line in the sand.

Finnigan knew. Moray could see it in his eyes.

"What does that mean, Finnigan?"

"You never talk with me anymore. We're supposed to be brothers—"

Moray shoved Finnigan back against the stone corridor wall, cutting him off. "I am going to be king! I do not have time for your childish games. You doubt my reasoning for my own betrothed? What's next, you doubt my ability to rule?" His voice burned, heat rising in his face.

Finnigan steadied himself, his breath hitching, but his rage didn't diminish. "You haven't given me reason to believe otherwise!"

"I have done everything for this kingdom! I will do far more than Father ever has!" Moray fumed as he held Finnigan's tunic collar.

In the Buacach tradition, if the king wished to hand off the throne to his heir before his death, he could. Moray had worked for years, earning that place and giving his father early retirement so he could live at peace instead of wearing himself to the bone. Finnigan wouldn't take that future from him.

"At what cost?" Finnigan whispered.

"Every king must make sacrifices. Isn't Elohai keen on sacrifices?" Moray smirked bitterly. "Stay out of my way, little prince. I will protect, defend, and better Buacach. I cannot do that if I am covered in leeches instead of backed up by real men."

He let go, turned his back on his little brother, and went inside his chambers. A small part of him, the paranoid part, wanted to pack up all of his hidden items he used during his rituals and incantations. If a soul found his magic possessions in his chambers, he'd be killed.

No one would find them. They hadn't thus far. Finnigan might have one of his hunches that something wrong was afoot, but he wouldn't tattle. Moray took a slow breath, shutting the chamber door behind him.

Seven

THE DAYS WORE ON, full of lessons, trying on new dresses, and more. Queen Macha was a gentle woman, but learning so much in a short time put Ama's nerves on edge. She needed and adored quiet time and being alone—she rarely got those luxurious things in the castle. She was always with someone, whether it was the queen, the queen's mini army of servants and helpers, or Meili, while Moray basically ignored her existence.

That evening, however, the queen told Ama she could explore the stables with escorts. Ama ignored the men as she hurried outside the castle, pulling her fur closer for warmth. She missed her traditional clothes, but the dress that Queen Macha had given her for riding closely resembled what Ama was accustomed to. The queen had custom-tailored it for Ama as a gift.

Queen Macha wasn't Mama, but she grew on Ama. Despite her prim and proper behavior, she apologized often for Moray's absence but never pushed too far, likely noticing Ama's lack of interest in talking about the eldest prince.

Ama slipped into the royal stables, cringing when the stablehands bowed upon her entry.

"Your mare is ready to ride," one of them said with a smile.

Ama's chest tightened. They had prepared Usdi for her? She didn't need anyone touching her—

Breathe. Be polite. "Oh, thank you."

His smile faded. "Is something wrong, Princess Ama?"

"No. Thank you."

"If you prefer to saddle your mare from now on, I will refrain."

"It is all right. Thank you." She smiled at him, moved by his kindness. Or simple courtesy. He couldn't treat her poorly, could he, since she was going to be queen. It was impossible to tell people's real motives in Buacach.

Ama hurried to Usdi in her stall. They had kept Usdi's blanket and saddle and had used them instead of the usual Buacach tack. Ama hugged Usdi gently as her mare nuzzled her.

The guards stayed in the stables but left her alone. Ama savored the silence, which was muddled only by the snickers and stomps of the horses. She stroked Usdi's long, thick mane, the tension of the past week falling off her shoulders.

A light voice came from behind her. "Are you excited for the wedding?"

Ama turned around tensely, catching herself short when she saw Finnigan leaning over the stable door. He flashed a big grin. "Sorry to scare you. You can hit me if you'd like. My face is strong enough to handle it."

She smiled. "Finnigan. Sorry."

"Going for a ride?" He nodded at Usdi. "I was just getting my stallion tacked up. Mind if I join you?" He pushed himself off the wooden stall door. "I know a nice path in the woods. I can shoo the guards off for you too."

Ama hesitated. "Should we ride alone?"

He smirked, unbothered by seemingly everything that crossed his path. "The guards will follow behind at a distance."

"All right." She trusted Finnigan the most out of all of them. He spent time with the servants, he helped the peasants in the kingdom, he told Ama stories of what he did out in the streets for his people. Meanwhile, Moray was more into politics and what made a strong kingdom rather than support the unfortunate. She trusted men like Finnigan. Men who sweated and bled for the good of their people. Men like her family and her clan.

Moray thought society was all brains and little brawn.

She couldn't agree.

Finnigan grinned and readied his stallion. Ama stroked Usdi's mane and neck, leaning against her, lost in thought. She watched one of the stablehands—a scrawny young boy with curly hair—as he entered the stables. One of the men barked an order at him. The boy ducked his head and hurried over to Finnigan, helping him tack the gray stallion. The boy helped the best he could, though his pale face and the bags under his eyes made Ama wonder if he felt all right. He coughed hard occasionally but focused on the horse.

Finnigan finished tightening the stallion's girth before ruffling the boy's hair. "Thank you, Peter. I think you best head home now. Get your mother to give you something for that cough, aye?"

Ama bit her lip as she watched. The boy smiled and hurried out of the stables.

"Who was that?" Ama asked, opening the stall door and leading Usdi out.

"Peter. He's a stable boy. Bright as a copper penny." Finnigan introduced Usdi and the stallion briefly, but neither horse minded the other much. They led the horses outside into the pale evening light.

Ama sucked in a gulp of fresh air, smiling. "Peter..." she repeated. "He likes you. It seems most of the kingdom does."

Finnigan shrugged the comment off. "Shall I help you mount?"

"Help yourself," Ama said, mounting Usdi with ease. "I have been on the back of a horse far more than you."

"Oh?" Finnigan laughed heartily as he jumped onto his stallion. "I've no doubt, Princess. Your people have an incredible bond with your herds, yes? My parents see my stallion and see a war animal. Nothing more." He adjusted the reins and smiled, then addressed the guards. "A few of you may follow, please, but the princess has had a long day. The queen has instructed me to teach her of the outside walls, so we will be going on a small ride."

The guards didn't appear worried, and a few mounted their own prepared steeds.

Finnigan smirked at Ama, heeled his horse on, and led her toward the wall. "I know a shortcut that leads out of the walls."

The capital of the Buacach Kingdom, named the same, was a large city, with the castle and the village enclosed within the walls. Ama loved the thought of escaping the busyness and greeting the outside world again.

"Oh?" Ama's brow furrowed as she let Usdi follow Finnigan. "There is more than one exit?"

He laughed. "The gate isn't the only way through or out. That's hardly safe."

"I am not accustomed to walls," she said tightly.

"Of course." Finnigan glanced back and nodded. "I'm sorry if I upset you."

Ama shook her head. "Thank you for taking me out here." She trusted no one and barely trusted Meili, but she could only keep things to herself for so long. Whether she liked it or not, she needed a friend. But she couldn't speak freely with anyone else. Especially not Moray.

"My pleasure. You could use a break." He watched the tiny path ahead.

"What do you mean?"

"You don't have to keep up any sort of act with me," he said. "I know this is all a great deal of change. A great deal of hardship."

"Your family is kind," Ama mustered. *But they are not mine.*

Finnigan eyed her. "Father is absent from near everything. Though his heart is in the right place, he is a busy man, and busy men hardly connect with what matters. Mother is preparing you to be queen in only a month, a job that takes a lifetime to achieve. Moray is..." he trailed off, eyes falling back to the road.

"Does he hate me?" Ama asked calmly.

"What?"

"Does your brother hate me?" She knew she was marrying a man who wouldn't love her. But if she'd done something to earn his hatred... She didn't know if she could truly live the rest of her life as a tool.

"No!" Finnigan blurted. "Goodness, no, Moray doesn't hate you. Believe me, I know what his hatred looks like."

"So he is indifferent toward me." Ama rubbed the leather reins in her hands absently.

"Well..." Finnigan groaned. "I suppose I cannot protect you from him, can I?"

Ama shook her head, her tightly braided hair giving her a headache. She hated wearing her hair up like Queen Macha insisted. "I know what I chose."

"Alliances have two sides," Finnigan said firmly. "You are doing this for your people, but Moray ought to..." he stopped again. "I am sorry, Ama. Your life has completely changed, and I can't imagine what it must be like. I wish we could have the alliance without sacrificing your life like this."

Ama steeled herself. "Do not speak that way. I am happy."

Finnigan straightened as if bracing himself. He said nothing more, and Ama wondered what went on in his head. Was he angry at her? Angry at Moray? Why would he care for her happiness?

Because he, unlike Moray, was a compassionate prince. She saw it daily in the way he cared for his people. She knew nothing about Moray. Nothing. What did he do in his spare time? What were his motives? What made him laugh? And why wouldn't he speak to her?

Ama pushed the thoughts away. "You'd best tell me of the surrounding forest. Or was that a cover story?"

"Er, both," Finnigan answered in a low voice so the guards trailing behind them couldn't hear. "I don't really think there's much to know about the Red Forest."

"Are there beasts?" she teased.

Finnigan shrugged, patting the stallion's strong neck. "A few, but they rarely attack unless provoked."

"What sort?"

"Great bears, a big fuzzy cat or two," he said with a smirk. "You people face more trouble with the wolves."

"They do not harm us." Ama thought of the wolf packs and sighed softly. She missed her clan. She missed her mother and father and...

"You'll see them again one day," Finnigan said gently.

Ama wouldn't see the wild world again. Moray would keep her in the castle. She didn't even know what he wanted—a quiet wife who bore his children? Or did he want nothing from her? Surely, he wanted at least a son, but Ama didn't know, hadn't the chance to ask, and didn't want to think about her future.

"You can return one day," Finnigan persisted. "I'll make sure of it. I'd like to visit your clan. Maybe you could give me a tour, like I'm giving you." He slowed slightly as they left the kingdom behind, the path ending at a small cluster of trees at the edge of the township.

Ama focused on the border wall made of thick black stone. As Finnigan had said, the grand gates were not the only entry and exit to the Buacach Kingdom. A large door—smaller than the grand gate but made of the same thick, strong metal—stood behind the trees. He beamed, leading his horse over. The guards up on the wall and in the watchtowers didn't so much as glance down at them but kept alert of what lay behind the wall.

Finnigan pushed open the door, obviously stronger than he looked. Not that she'd ever bothered looking.

"Where exactly are we going? Don't the beasts you spoke of come out at night? Could we see one?" Ama asked.

"You sound as if you want to!" Laughing, Finnigan mounted his horse again.

"It has been a long time since I've seen one of the bears!"

"If we see one, I'm afraid it won't be by happenstance, and I'll have to wrestle it off us, the hungry monstrosity." Finnigan led Ama and the guards through the wall.

"The guards would fight for you," Ama said dryly, casting a smirk at the guards trailing behind them. They didn't respond and kept their eyes on the towering trees that now engulfed them. Ama knew Prince Finnigan had more to worry about past the wall than cats and bears. Assassins had tried more than once to harm the royals. Who knew where they might hide in woods like these.

Finnigan guffawed and waved a hand at them, a small flicker of blue energy illuminating in his hand. "I can fight off a bear with my bare hands."

Ama gasped softly. "Is that your... Gift?" The words came out in a breath, excitement building in her chest. She had not known Creator had blessed Finnigan too.

Pulling his horse beside Ama's as they plodded along the narrow dirt path, Finnigan beamed. He showed her the blue energy burning in the palm of his right hand. "Aye. Impressed? It is a Gift from Elohai—like the ancient Gifts, only, well, modern." He chuckled. "Only certain individuals are blessed with such things, and wielding it is very draining, but when you are wise and ensure you're rooted in Elohai, He gives you strength to bear the Gift when it is needed. And every Gift is different, really, so Elohai knows how to help each person in their own weakness."

"And your Gift?" Ama asked. "Is it just fire?"

"It is less impressive now?" He laughed. "My Gift is strange. I have the ability of fire, yes, like a basic flame, and of energy. Fire is oftentimes a form of energy, so I'm able to control it in either capacity. I suppose there might be more to it, but I don't use it often enough."

Ama listened intently. Her Gift of dreams was comparable, and her people believed similar to what Finnigan explained. Only, the Gift of dreams was far different than wielding a fiery energy. Just as draining, though, she guessed. "Do you use it often?"

"No, only when it can help others." His gaze fell to the path ahead once more. "My father taught me the rules of wielding it at an early age. It has never been something I've taken lightly." His eyes flickered with something like grief, only briefly.

Ama didn't pry any more. "Tell me about the forest."

"The Red Forest is what you see. Trees, trees, a rock"—he gestured, fire diminishing from his hand—"a bird, no sky because of more trees..." He pointed east. "There are a few caves that way before the forest ends near the Bour River."

"Where do you usually ride?" Ama studied the trail that winded through the trees and bushes turning brown in the cool weather.

"Sometimes to the river, sometimes throughout whichever place suits my fancy." Finnigan shrugged. "It is a long ride to the river."

"Perhaps we can visit it another day." Ama didn't want the queen to grow frustrated with her if she took too long a ride. Right now, she couldn't afford to break any rules or ruffle any feathers. "This is a beautiful forest." Exactly what she needed after the weeks' worth of work.

"Isn't it?"

Finnigan studied the tree branches above. The forest blocked the setting sun, growing dark and eerie, but Ama didn't mind. While she found more comfort in the woods she'd grown up in, with open spaces and the sky never out of sight, this was the best she would get for who knew how long. She'd be grateful for it in all its strangeness.

They rode for a short while. Finnigan filled the silence with talk of the castle, the forest, the people. He asked her about her home as well. It hurt to talk about the Wolf Clan at first, but as she told him of her tribe, it became easier. When Finnigan asked questions about her family, she smiled genuinely for the first time since leaving her clan. He knew quite a bit about her culture, but she occasionally surprised him with details and stories.

As they headed back to the castle, the guards never far away, Finnigan changed the subject quietly. "It will all be well, Ama. Elohai will guide us." A pause. "You believe in Creator, yes?"

"Of course." Ama bit her tongue.

"There's not enough time to start talking of it now, but I'll ask Mother if we can do so soon. I'm eager to compare what is known of both omniscient beings. They sound so alike..." He trailed off. "I've a wild idea they might be the same."

Ama gulped hard, studying him. "Oh?"

"Your people have stories, and my people have Letters. We could always sit down and connect the pieces, explore what happened when the Split occurred."

The realms splitting had cast many people into the faraway corners of Mazzabah, resulting in different cultures, religions, and beliefs. It was a history that always fascinated Ama, but she had no access to any knowledge outside of the clan. Until now.

"I would like that," Ama said softly.

"Tomorrow, then, if I can wrestle you away from Mother's grasp."

Eight

"IT IS A PLEASURE to have you visiting with us, Lord Barric," Moray said courteously, having no pleasure at all regarding the husky, brown-eyed man before him.

Lord Barric and his wife ruled a large chunk of land right outside of the Red Forest, earning Buacach great wealth and well-trained soldiers. The benefits made up for the fact that Lord Barric was a miserable rat. Moray had no doubt the man worked out of his own selfish greed.

Lord Barric smiled softly. Despite being such an arrogant man, he wasn't loud or obnoxious in every way. "Thank you, Prince Moray."

Men from King Connall's counsel—generals from the knights and soldiers, and lords from King Connall's territory—gathered together to speak of the Crow Clan. The Crows lived in the desert lands, but they were nomads, always moving and often slaughtering the weak they ran across. They had not formed an alliance with anyone as far as Moray knew, and they were almost constantly at war with the other clans.

"As part of the betrothal, the Wolf Clan will become our ally. As winter approaches, Etu, the chief's eldest, has given word that the Crows intend to attack the Wolf Clan." King Connall's thick eyebrows furrowed, large jowls set in a frown. "We must help Etu prepare his warriors for the attack and send our men as aid. The Wolf Clan is precious to us as an ally." He didn't bother noting that the clan offered vast important trade: their furs, pottery, food, and knowledge of the land and clans could prove useful.

Lord Barric clasped his hands together and leaned on the oval wooden table in front of him, which the other men also had. "Allow me to send my own troops, my king! I have plenty of ready, strong men." It was no secret he had the best soldiers out of any of the lords. His soldiers often were more effective in battle and in defense than the king's knights.

A predicament Moray would have to fix when he became king. He bit back a sigh.

"We would appreciate that," King Connall said. "I will need everyone to be alert and have your own men prepared, just like always. We need to make this alliance last and protect our own as well."

Everyone agreed heartily. King Connall had earned a name for himself among all the land—a king who loved every soul who came across his path. They would all follow him wherever he led them.

Moray bit his lip. Would they follow him when he became king? All he had received were congratulations and excitement over his fate, but would they still see Connall as king? A silly concern. Now was no time for childish doubts. When a king passed on his throne, the kingdom respected the decision.

The meeting droned on and Moray listened, adding insight and input when it mattered. He couldn't wait till he was the one in control. He would lead the kingdom into a greater future.

IN THE SECLUSION OF the smithy's cellar, Moray sat down and glared at the wizard. "Why did you need to meet?"

"I missed your handsome face." Sadon sighed, sitting across from him and letting his hood fall. "C'mon, I know you missed me." He could tell Moray's patience was thin—no doubt from spending the day being a civil prince.

"What is this about?" Moray snapped.

Sadon smirked. "I've been keeping my eyes on Ama. I have bad news."

"What?"

"She's a steady believer of the faith." Sadon raised his eyebrows. "It is worse than I thought."

"She and I have come to a sort of agreement."

Sadon rolled his eyes, pushing his long white hair back with a smirk. "Oh, yes, I'm sure you'll keep your word." Not that he was really one to talk.

"It is none of your business."

"Am I not your counselor?"

"Wizard," Moray said tightly. "Hardly the same thing."

"You should know she has a Gift."

"A Gift?" Moray laughed and waved him off.

"Finnigan is Gifted. You know it is possible," Sadon argued. "This generation has lacked Gifted beings from the grand Creator, but there are still many of them." His voice dripped with sarcasm. It was just his luck that she stumbled right into his perfect plan.

"Ama is not one. She cannot heal or work the Energy as Finnigan can," Moray said.

Even Finnigan had kept his Gift quiet. No one knew, and the only time Finnigan used his Gift was when helping the civilians. He had once found an injured child roaming the streets. He had healed the little girl in the alleyway, making the lash marks on her back vanish, and took her into the castle. Now, she worked as Ama's right-hand servant girl.

"She has dreams."

"Dreams?" Moray leaned back, arms crossed against his chest.

"The master is especially interested in her soul." Sadon didn't bat an eye. "This is no laughing matter. I knew she believed, but I did not realize how deeply."

Moray set his jaw. "Her faith changes nothing in our plan. We must stay focused."

"She has dreams, Moray!" Sadon snarled. "You have no idea what this could do to us. If Elohai gives her a dream of us, of the Darkness, anything, and she speaks, we are ruined!" He needed to push Moray, test him, ensure he believed that Sadon was paying attention. If Moray thought he was slacking off in the final moments, things could go wrong. He had to prove he was on Moray's side—just for a bit longer.

"She won't!" Moray raised a hand. "Even if her Gift is that strong and she dreams of the truth, she won't dare speak anything. I've made sure of it."

Sadon cocked his head. "Give me a break, Moray. If this girl gets any idea what we're up to, she will run home and cry wolf. I know her type."

"What would her type be?" Moray demanded.

"She's a good-hearted person and far from a coward. If you underestimate her, she will destroy you." Sadon kept his voice low.

"She is not a prisoner. I cannot treat her as such," Moray said. He clenched his fists and stood, then paced in the musty cellar. It was a habit he shared with Finnigan. "If I act overbearing and she hasn't had a dream, then she'll see that something is wrong."

"You won't take the risk?" Sadon raised one eyebrow, jaw tight. "If she breathes a word, we are dead and the plan is destroyed. We've worked all this time, and for what? A Gifted girl will be our demise?"

"You are too paranoid. She won't act rashly. Her family is at risk anyway."

"Abaddon tells me otherwise," Sadon hissed. "He tells me we must end her life, Moray. Once the wedding is over, she must be eliminated before she causes havoc."

There, he'd said it. A drastic step but one Abaddon had made quite clear to Sadon. The girl had to be removed. She would stir trouble once the princes were gone—she'd make a fine queen but a terrible concubine. The last thing Sadon needed once Moray took over was drama between the women in the castle.

"I'll handle her. I will not kill her."

"How?"

Moray shook his head. "Trust me, she will not say a thing, even if she finds out. She started this mess to help her people, and she won't risk that over some black magic."

"Watch her." Sadon stood up and snatched his hood over his head. "If Master speaks again—"

"He may speak with me, if it is that important," Moray said, cutting him off. "I have pleased him enough to be spoken to, have I not?"

Moray absolutely adored their master. Sadon knew Moray's heart. There was no pleasure Moray truly treasured like knowing his master was happy with the work he was doing. Abaddon wanted Golgotha, and Moray would conquer it for him.

Only, Sadon knew Abaddon's wishes and knew Moray would not survive Golgotha.

Sadon scoffed. "I will see you before the wedding ceremony."

Soon, the next phase would begin. Sadon's years of hard work would bear immeasurable fruit. He would show Shafiq, the man who had broken him, just how far he had come since those tortured days in a cell as a mere child.

With some help, the kingdom would be his. Sadon would enter Golgotha as his master's servant. He'd be a wizard with absolute power, and the possibilities would be endless.

No one would get in his way—not even Moray, the man who considered him a friend. Enemies were far more trustworthy than friends. You were always ready for an enemy to do something against your favor. You let your guard down with a friend. That was far more dangerous.

Nine

MORAY CHANTED LOW AND soft in his bed chambers, the lantern glowing nearby. Something lay in his hands, but Ama couldn't see what. He stood alone but spoke as if someone heard. "What shall I do with her?"

No voice answered that Ama could hear, but Moray lifted his head. He met her gaze, eyes solid black.

AMA WOKE, HEART HAMMERING. In the darkness, with only the glow from the fire in the hearth, she stared at the ceiling. It was just a nightmare. Nothing to be upset over. It could mean anything. She'd never dreamed such a thing before. The dream of the dead couple and now this?

She sat up, the darkness in the corners of the big room weighing heavy on her. The fire burned steadily, shedding some light as she hopped out of bed. It was only a dream.

But she couldn't catch her breath, couldn't make her insides stop shaking.

Just a nightmare. No reason to get so upset.

Go, a voice said.

Ama hugged herself in front of the fire.

Go, the voice said again.

Go where, though? She couldn't go home. She had no reason to flee. It was just a nightmare.

But what if it wasn't? Moray could be practicing black magic. He showed no interest in Elohai, after all. He was power thirsty and—no. She was jumping to conclusions. It was just a bad dream.

Go forth.

Ama scowled. "Where do I go? I cannot flee home or tell my parents of my fears!" Especially not without proof that Moray was in the wrong, and he probably wasn't.

Then why had she had such a dream? She hadn't created Moray into a monster in her own head, had she?

Where do You want me to go, Creator?

No answer. She rubbed her eyes, forcing deep breaths. A short walk around the halls wouldn't hurt, would it? What else could she do? Leave? Fall asleep again?

She shook her head and pulled on her fur coat. Ama unlocked the chamber doors and peeped outside. The two guards standing outside the door glanced back at her in curious unison.

"Something wrong, Princess Ama?"

Yes. All of them calling her *Princess*.

"No," she said. "Just going to take a walk. May I be alone for a while? I will be right back."

The first guard, a stocky man with short blond hair, frowned. "We've got orders to stay with you—"

"But," the other man interjected, a bit thinner than his comrade, with curly black hair and a scar along his neck, "you may have some time to breathe." He watched her as if he could see past her placid expression. Were her jostled nerves that obvious?

"Thank you. I won't be long," Ama managed, slipping past them and walking down the hall, careful not to appear too eager to leave. She rounded the corner and kept her head up, the chilly hall sending a chill down her spine. Where was she going? Ama bit her lip and hurried on, rounding another corner. She went down a flight of short stairs, then found another unfamiliar corridor. She didn't care if she got lost. Not really. Not tonight.

Could she find Moray's chambers? They weren't on the same floor as her own, she knew that much. If Ama found him, what if she saw him doing what he'd done in the dream? With proof of his wrongdoings, she could take action, tell the king and queen, and go home to her clan. Perhaps when Creator had told her to come, He had wished her to help end the Darkness within the castle walls.

Ama sucked in a deep breath and walked on. Even if she roamed, she didn't know which chamber belonged to Moray.

She definitely couldn't ask a servant if one passed by—it wouldn't look right, the princess trying to find the prince's chambers. Ama almost laughed.

Rounding another corridor corner, Ama walked straight into someone. She grunted and jumped back. "S-sorry—"

"Ama," Finnigan said with a grin. "What are you doing out so late?" His grin faded as he studied her in the light from one of the hanging torches. "What's wrong?"

Ama frowned. "I'm... I'm just taking a walk. What about you?"

"A walk in a castle? Dreadfully boring," he said. "You look like you've seen a ghost. Is something the matter?"

Ama considered for a split second telling Finnigan about her nightmare. No, that was a foolish idea. Finnigan of all people wouldn't believe such a thing about his brother. "No. Just couldn't sleep."

Finnigan studied her, then smiled again. "Well, I'm going to the kitchen for a snack. Would you like to come with me?"

Ama nodded. Following him didn't seem like such a terrible idea.

He led her quickly through the halls. "I know this place inside and out. I can give you a map if you want to memorize it."

She smirked. "How did you know I was lost?"

"I used to get lost a lot too," he said with a laugh. "Moray made me a map. I do better when I can see something."

She walked behind him in silence. The dream still hovered in her mind.

Finnigan went down some stairs, around a few more corners, his steps quick. "There should be some chocolate cake waiting for us. Our cook always leaves me something sweet."

Ama followed, casting a few glances behind her as they walked, as if someone might be following. Moray's black eyes were ingrained in her head. "That is sweet."

Finnigan laughed. "Ah! You have a good sense of humor." He opened a wooden door, waving her in. "Welcome to the sacred land of food."

Ama stepped into the giant kitchen, immediately awestruck by the large iron ovens, the counters, the pantries overflowing with foods and barrels. It was a giant contrast to the way her people prepared and stored food. Her people never wasted any, yet she could smell spoiled potatoes somewhere from the pantry nearby.

Finnigan pulled a chair out from a table. "Take a seat."

She sat down, eyeing a small container on the table before her.

He grabbed two forks and sat across from her, opening the container. "Ah! Cake! Just as I expected."

Ama wasn't very hungry, but the cake did look delicious.

He offered her a fork, smiling. "Dig in."

Ama took a few bites and when her appetite returned, she relaxed. "Not bad."

"The best," he agreed. "Now, what were you doing, roaming about? I'm a very good listener."

Ama focused on chewing a big bite of chocolate cake, letting his words roll around in her head. On one hand, she knew he was a good listener, and it wouldn't hurt to say she'd had a nightmare but not clarify what sort. At least then he would know part of the truth. If she told him what the dream had been about, Finnigan wouldn't believe her. She had no proof, after all, and tossing around fearful assumptions would ruin things. "Just a nightmare," she said. She had no intentions of ever mentioning the dream she had had back at home.

"Me too." Finnigan nodded as if talking of the weather. "I had a dream that the dragon egg hatched, and the little beast clawed my face off."

Ama blinked. "Oh..."

"I was quite afraid," Finnigan said, chuckling. "But this chocolate cake is putting the nightmare at ease, I think. Mind if I ask what your nightmare was about?"

She couldn't just say *Moray*, and she couldn't speak of the Darkness. "Um, I would rather not," she mustered. "Nothing too serious."

"I'm sorry." He ate some more. "Nightmares are difficult."

"It is fine." Ama shifted in her seat, fighting the growing suspicion that he knew more than he let on.

"Ama?" Finnigan asked after a long moment of comfortable silence passed.

"Hmm?" She focused on the cake as an excuse not to talk, but she grew sick.

"Has Moray spoken to you?"

"About what?"

Finnigan glanced about the kitchen as if some great ghost might jump out at them—or Moray himself. "I cannot help but tell you a very serious matter, and while it may be untrue, I would rather speak like a fool than risk harm coming from my silence."

Ama stiffened. "I will not see you as a fool." She might, but it felt like the right thing to say.

"You know of the black magics?" Finnigan put his fork down, watching her intently.

The dream of Moray burned in her mind, but she maintained a composed posture. "Yes, of course. It is one of the things Queen Macha warned me of. My people were also well educated on the spirits and the Darkness." She suppressed a shudder. "We believe only Creator can help us in such a fight as one against principalities."

Finnigan nodded, working his jaw and studying his cake. "Yes, well, we agree."

"Why do you ask?"

"Practicing magic is forbidden in Buacach, as you know, and... it is punishable by death." He drew a weak breath. "If you were queen, and you had no proof someone was practicing but had enough to make assumptions for... certain things to add up... What would you do? Turn the person in to the court? Or speak with them first and try making them stop?" Finnigan ducked his head and waited for a response.

She didn't have any answer. Mulling the question over for a moment, with Moray lingering in her mind, she said, "It might depend on a few things."

"Like?"

"If they were repentant, if they had harmed anyone..." Ama sighed. "I do not know. Our laws are similar. A person learning religious secrets and aspiring to learn the ways of the spirits or magics is put to death in our clan. The Crows practice dark magic. They are dangerous."

"But what of mercy?" Finnigan mustered. "I believe justice should be solid, firm, unyielding, yes, as we all—

most of us—abide by... but does mercy have no role?"

"Our people are merciful," Ama said defensively. "We care for our women, our children, our men. No law is needlessly cruel."

He lifted a hand quickly. "No, no, I understand. Forgive me. But... but what if our people accepted just... a bit more mercy? Would that be of Elohai? Surely, He is a God of mercy?"

"When mercy is required." Ama gulped hard. *Will He have mercy on me for marrying without love? Didn't He lead me here?*

"We stick by the laws and never offer mercy." Finnigan shook his head. "That is no more of Elohai than only giving mercy. There must be a balance."

Ama sighed, rubbing her hands together, breathing in shakily. "When do we know what is Creator's will and what is our own?"

"Prayer. If we exercise both Elohai's justice and mercy, we will all be better off. Finding the balance and hearing His voice will not be easy, but I believe it must be done." Finnigan stopped short, eyes burning with vehemence. "I'm sorry..."

"I agree." Ama took some heart at his words. Maybe he was right. Maybe Creator did extend mercy, even when they deserved justice. "What makes you think of all of this?"

"Moray," Finnigan blurted. Immediately, his eyes grew wide and he gasped. "Not that—"

"Moray is practicing, isn't he?" Her heart sank like a rock in her chest. Surely, it had just been a bad dream, hadn't it?

Finnigan's eyes bulged again. He rubbed the back of his neck, forcing, "No! Well, no, I don't think so. Yes, he acts strange, and I've wondered, but no! There's no proof. And..."

Ama shook her head. "You do not have to defend your worries with me. Moray is a strange man. I... I wondered if there wasn't more to him, something hidden, but I worry it is for the worst."

Finnigan grimaced and eyed her. "What do you mean? Has he said anything to you?"

"Not much," she said. "But I had a nightmare about him. It was probably nothing but it felt... it felt like..." Ama stared down at the table, clasping her hands together tightly, trying to reassure herself she could say the truth. "I think Creator was trying to warn me." The Goidelic folk didn't think the same as her people, however, and she worried Finnigan might disregard her concern because it was based on so little.

"You had a nightmare of him?"

"Of him being a warlock." The words tasted sour on her tongue.

Finnigan ran his hand through his unruly hair. "I'm sorry."

"It was just—"

"I believe it is true." The prince's words were barely above a whisper.

Ama lifted her head, staring at him in dismay. "You believe me?"

"Aye. I think I've seen the same for myself. Only in small bits and pieces, never enough to know for certain." Finnigan glanced around the empty kitchen again.

"What... what will we do? Something must be done."

"This is my duty, my problem, Ama." Finnigan stood up, pacing on the worn, smooth wooden floors. His boots thumped, but he didn't try softening them. "I can handle it."

"It is wrong for a man practicing magic to become king, isn't it?" she asked.

It probably wasn't her place to say such a thing, but there, she'd said it. The court might hang Moray for his actions, or they might ignore it and Moray would marry her anyway. She shuddered at the thought. She'd never seen a hanging, and she never intended to.

"I will speak with him first." Finnigan hesitated. "Elohai is with me. He will guide me. If we want to try mercy... redemption... I believe now is the time to start trying."

"If Moray won't listen?" Ama shook her head, heart aching. She didn't love him, but she didn't want him dead. And she didn't want Finnigan hurt. If Moray lost his temper, he could hurt his brother.

Finnigan sighed. "I don't know. I've struggled finding an alternative for a while now. I don't have one."

"He cannot be king. Creator will not bless your kingdom"—Ama didn't say *our*—"if it is ruled by a dark heart."

While Finnigan didn't deny his brother's dark heart, his eyes fell heavy. "I know. I cannot turn Moray over to my father. It would break him. If the court finds out, my brother will die. If he repents, well, we can forget it ever happened and he can still be enthroned." His voice grew stronger, full of hope and zeal as he flashed a weak smile. "He'll change his mind."

"He will accuse us—"

"I won't be mentioning you," Finnigan cut in.

"He won't listen if you have nothing as proof."

"I must try." Finnigan stopped pacing and offered a real smile. "I am grateful you told me. I thought I was going insane. This is... a delicate, dangerous matter. I'm sorry it has harmed you."

"I am fine." Ama stood up, nodding solemnly. "I'm sorry, Finnigan."

She wasn't the only one with an older brother who despised them. Etu was dangerous, but he was also a practical man and revered Creator for the majority of the time, even if he twisted rules. He didn't belittle the demonic spirits or the Darkness. Ama didn't believe the same could be said about Moray.

But really, how much did she know? Even Finnigan didn't know Moray well. Maybe they would be wrong and things could continue as normal. Even though her life would never be as it was.

Ever.

"I'll lead you back to your chamber." Finnigan grabbed a small container of cake. "We'll give this to the guards as a token of our forgiveness for being annoying royals."

Ama chuckled and followed him out of the kitchen, overwhelmed with her thoughts.

Ten

FINNIGAN DIDN'T SEE MORAY much leading up to the wedding. He got the distinct nagging in his gut that this was done purposely. Every time he sought out his older brother, Moray was gone or busy. Finnigan tried visiting at nighttime, but Moray never let him in.

Moray was probably planning some grand, horrid scheme for his rule. Finnigan didn't like playing pessimist, but it was hard to deny that his brother was acting strangely.

And he didn't deserve Ama. Moray wouldn't talk to anyone, but he'd only met with Ama twice during the past week.

Finnigan hurried down the corridors, exhausted from his previous day spent helping some workers in the city. King Connall had long since stopped pressing that Finnigan focus on more political, court-centered matters. He could do whatever he liked.

But now, he had a specific goal in mind. One that was easy but foolish. *I'm nothing if not a fool at heart*, he thought. *Might as well be a useful one.*

If there was even a chance Moray was unfit for the throne, Finnigan had to handle the matter. The Buacach Kingdom deserved to be protected, defended, and cherished. If Moray had no desire for the throne besides to fulfill some greedy desire, Finnigan had to step in. Not that he wanted the throne for himself. Being king was a big job, a burden, and he was hardly leadership material. Perhaps King Connall could remain king for a while longer, till another decision was reached.

It wasn't that simple, though. If he thought of what must truly happen, he wouldn't act—and he knew he had to do something. For Moray's safety and the sake of their people.

Finnigan sneaked into Moray's chambers. The fire in the large hearth burned steadily. Not a thing was out of place—Moray's meticulous nature showed in his living quarters. Sighing, Finnigan strode across the room. He could hide in the closet. Or the cabinet. Or under the bed.

I'm an adult, he told himself. *I don't have to hide. I can sit right here till Moray comes.*

Finnigan gulped. Or he could just hide.

No, he wouldn't be a coward. He sat on a cushioned chair, watching the great clock tick, tock, tick, tock along. He got up, paced a minute, or maybe five. If Moray truly was practicing magic, he could look for anything troublesome.

Couldn't he?

The door opened, and Moray stepped in, freezing at the sight of Finnigan. "What are you doing in here?" he snapped. His hair was smoothed back, his clothes clean, and his face red with rage.

"Where have you been?" Finnigan asked. Moray didn't look like he'd been out riding or doing anything laborious. What had kept him busy the past week? The court and their father did not need him every single second. When Finnigan had asked, King Connall told him that Moray rarely joined them.

Moray glared at him. "How is that any of your business?"

"I've been looking for you, and you've been hiding from me." Finnigan crossed his arms.

"I have been busy helping the nobles and arranging things, Finnigan." Moray didn't budge from the door. "You should leave. I'm exhausted, and tomorrow is a big day."

Finnigan didn't see an ounce of excitement in Moray's eyes. If *he* were marrying Ama tomorrow—which he couldn't, he reminded himself—he wouldn't be able to sleep. "Not until we talk."

"Speak." Moray commanded as if talking at a mutt.

Clenching his fists and reining in his anger, Finnigan gathered his thoughts quickly. There was no good or easy way to tell his brother that he thought Moray was breaking rules and trying to be a wizard. "Moray, this has gone on long enough. I know you're practicing to be a wizard. It is illegal, it is wrong, and—"

Moray slammed the door shut behind him. In the blink of an eye, he crossed the room and grasped Finnigan by his shirt collar. "What the—"

"Let me finish!" Finnigan hissed. His heart hammered in his chest.

"What kind of bold assumption is that? You have the audacity—"

"I know it is true," Finnigan whispered, grabbing Moray's arm tightly. "You cannot lie and hide from me any longer. I cannot turn a blind eye."

"It is your assumption. You have no proof, do you?" Moray's cold eyes narrowed.

Finnigan considered bluffing, but that probably would only make things worse. "I don't need proof."

Moray laughed in his face but didn't slacken his grip. "No?"

"Stop, Moray. Please, stop this madness before it gets you killed. Whether your devil master takes your life when you mess up one too many times, or Father discovers your secret and has to hang you... stop it!" Finnigan shoved him back forcefully.

Moray snarled, eyes darkening. He pushed Finnigan back again. "Father will not hang me," he said, voice low. "My master loves me. More so than your Elohai ever has."

"That isn't true!" Finnigan said, gulping back fear. "Elohai loves you—*we* love you. I cannot stand by and let you ruin your soul, Moray. I won't!"

A smile danced on Moray's lips. "My soul is just fine. You should leave, Finnigan, because nothing will come of this conversation."

"No. I won't lose you." Finnigan stood fast, mind racing. If Moray didn't listen, what would he do? "You must stop this."

Moray shrugged. "I've done nothing wrong."

"You're practicing black magic. That is a crime punishable—"

"By death?" Moray grinned. "If you think I'm guilty, go on, then. Tell Father. Let the soldiers tie me up and let the crows peck my eyes out."

Finnigan's stomach churned. "Shut up!" He slapped Moray hard before he realized what he'd done. "You just shut up, Moray. You have no idea what you're doing. It is vile, it hurts everyone—"

Moray grabbed him by his shoulders even tighter, voice cold. "I know what I'm doing. I will be king, and I will rule and benefit my people. I will silence the men who get in my way. If you love our parents, our people..." He released Finnigan. "You will stay silent. Do not make this any more difficult than it must be. No one will believe you without facts anyway. You'd make a fool out of yourself and give Mother a heart attack."

Finnigan trembled with pure rage. This wasn't his brother. This wasn't the man he knew. "You are a fool."

"Perhaps. But the Darkness has a price, and the Light has no mercy for sinners. I will take my chances." Moray smiled softly, eyes glimmering as he met Finnigan's gaze.

"Very well." Finnigan straightened, but his insides churned like butter.

"Sleep well tonight, brother." Moray turned away, heading to his clothes that lay on the bed.

"I know you are a liar, and I will stop you. One day." Finnigan left the room. If he saw Moray's dark eyes or his smug smirk, he'd hit him again.

Eleven

THREE DAYS UNTIL THE wedding, and Ama's dislike toward the Buacach Kingdom had only grown.

Prince Moray kept to himself, and when he acknowledged Ama's existence, he spoke nothing of importance, as if she were a child who couldn't be trusted to voice her own thoughts. He wasn't as handsome as his brother, or perhaps he was and his sour personality ruined him. He had their mother's black hair and green eyes, while Finnigan had their father's gold hair and blue eyes.

Ama glanced sideways at Prince Moray, jaw tight. She and Finnigan had been in the library discussing the Letters when Moray had visited for a while. Discussing the likeness between Creator and Elohai—Ama was almost certain they were the same—with Moray present proved difficult. Even now, he spoke about matters she didn't care for, leading her toward her chambers as if she had nothing better to do but listen as he droned on about politics.

Being around Moray only made Ama wish for time spent with anyone else. Usually, that someone else was Queen Macha. The queen and a few women servants helped prepare Ama for her role as future queen. Queen Macha taught how the kingdom was ruled, the duties of a queen, and lessons of the kingdom's history, which varied drastically from Ama's clan.

Unable to handle it any longer, Ama stopped in her tracks and faced him. "Two weeks."

"What?" Moray blinked.

"You have treated me like a stranger for two weeks." There was no contempt or anger in her voice. "Yet you expect me to listen to you speak of the good of this kingdom? I haven't seen any sign that you care about Buacach."

Moray's eyes narrowed. "You've listened to Finnigan far too much. A blind man could see how much I love my people, Ama."

Ama clenched her fists. "Love? You have a thick mask, Moray, but a blind man could see past it."

Truth be told, she doubted that the whole kingdom suspected he was a liar or a traitor. Ama couldn't pinpoint why she thought Moray's reputation was a hoax. Her spirit constantly nagged her. He wasn't to be trusted. He didn't love them. But she needed proof.

"The whole kingdom loves me and would disagree with your ludicrous opinion." Moray smirked. "The fact that I do not smother you in flattery does not mean I do not care about Buacach. Kings are busy men."

He was guarded and reserved, but the things he did weren't for this kingdom, were they? Maybe she was only being paranoid and lonely. Maybe Creator wasn't trying to warn her.

Ama set her jaw and studied him. "Perhaps you should tell me what you expect of me."

Moray froze for a brief moment like she'd caught him off guard. She almost felt satisfaction over that. Almost.

He sighed. "I do not see you as anything less than my equal, but things will be simpler if you abide by the rules and stay quiet. You can be happy here. You can see your family at a later time. First and foremost, you are my other half, and we must maintain an image to the kingdoms, the tribes, the people all across Mazzabah. If we want control and alliances, we must be a good example of what this kingdom is capable of."

"And children?" Ama asked quietly, stomach twisting as she listened and fought off the urge to stab the prince with her dagger.

"No need for an heir for a long while. A child will help appearances but not for a few years." Moray shook his head, expression calm and collected. "I have no intentions to use or harm you, nor will I turn to any other besides you. I will respect your boundaries as your husband."

Ama clamped her jaw shut, her skin growing hot. "How honorable of you," she said coolly.

"I am offering you happiness and safety. I force nothing on you."

"It seems far too good to be true," she said. "You will break your word."

"Believe as you wish, but I will prove it to you." Moray shrugged, everything about his stance suggesting he truly didn't care what she thought.

"Your people's tradition on the wedding night, for the marriage to be final—you know what must be done." Ama kept her voice steady. The idea of bonding her soul to Moray scared her beyond belief, but what could she do? He was lying to her, giving her false hope as if she were a dumb child.

Moray laughed out loud before controlling himself. He leaned in and whispered, "No one will be watching us. I do not have to lie with you, Ama, for the world to see us as married. The certificate will be enough to bond us. Now, if you'd like to, I've no qualm with that, of course." His eyes glinted. "I know you are afraid. I know love means something to your people. I want to extend mercy. Do you accept it?"

Ama's hands shook slightly, but she kept them hidden in the folds of her blue dress as if Moray might notice. "Yes."

She didn't believe him. She had to steel herself for the inevitable—she was binding herself to someone she didn't love, and that would have hard consequences.

For my people, I must.

Moray pulled away and bowed. "Good night, Princess. Sleep well." He left, vanishing around the corner.

The guards remained outside, like usual, as Ama slipped into her chambers. Her feet ached from her new tight shoes. She stopped when she saw Meili laying out her nightgown. A tub of steaming water sat by the fireplace, and oils—the oils Ama had absently mentioned she preferred over others—sat on the bedside table.

"Meili... little sakura." Ama grinned tiredly, using the nickname Meili mentioned her father had used for her when she'd known him.

Meili beamed. "I thought you deserved a relaxing bath. I'll go and fetch—"

"No, no, you relax too. I don't need anything else." Ama began to undress, yawning. "Use some of the oils on yourself for a change. You deserve it." She hung her dress neatly in the large dresser.

Meili opened her mouth but shut it quickly, turning away to respect Ama's modesty.

"You can speak freely with me, Meili. Please."

"You act so strong, and you are so afraid. Why push the fear away?" Meili whispered. "It is all right to feel afraid or sad."

Ama bit her lip. "Hardly seems right to be afraid and sad when I made this choice for myself."

"Of course it is all right. You did this for your people, but your heart—it still matters."

"The heart is a wicked thing." Ama shook her head, staring into the fire as tears welled in her eyes.

Meili gaped. "It... it is?"

"The heart can want terrible things. I cannot follow it blindly." Ama closed her eyes. "What my head calls the good path, my heart weeps over, and I don't know if such feelings are all right or if Creator is ashamed of me."

"Creator..." Meili frowned. "You mean Elohai?"

"Creator and Elohai appear to be one and the same. The Letters sound so much like our stories... I couldn't find much that differed. It is fascinating that two different bodies of people might share the same Savior even though they hardly seem to relate."

She thought of Moray. Did he believe in Elohai or Creator? She doubted it. He had spoken like a scholar the entire conversation and recited from the Letters by memory, talking like it pained him. But when Finnigan spoke of Elohai, his eyes lit up, and he loved the truth.

"Finnigan speaks of him often, especially among the slaves and servants," Meili said gently. "Elohai sounds like a good Father."

Ama rubbed her arms, shivering. Finnigan had a heart of gold. "If He is Creator, then He is." She hadn't had much chance to speak about the subject deeply with anyone. Queen Macha had mentioned it and promised they would discuss it later. Ama was interested in their beliefs more than she was interested in proper dinner etiquette, but she could handle learning all of it in due time.

She couldn't afford to be overwhelmed. She had to let go of her homesickness. This was her life. Whether she liked it or not, she had to adjust. But repeating that mantra daily wasn't helping soothe her spirit. Praying, too, did little to comfort her.

"It is all right to grieve," Meili repeated firmly. "Your Creator may help us take the road that is difficult, but it doesn't mean He cannot wipe away our tears as we follow Him. I've loved so much the stories you tell me, Ama.

About Creator and the ways of your people. There's so much love... and freedom... and hope."

Ama stared down at the hot water engulfing her. Love, freedom, and hope. Then why did she feel so alone? Her chest tightened. "I love speaking with you, Meili. You are my only friend here."

Twelve

THE MORNING OF AMA'S wedding, Queen Macha and her ladies fussed and primped Ama to their hearts' content for at least two hours, maybe three—Ama couldn't keep up. She donned a rather puffy white wedding gown. Queen Macha promised it did wonders for her figure, but Ama preferred the dresses her people wore for their marriage ceremonies. Now wasn't the time for tears, however, so instead of thinking of all the things her clan did differently, she let herself shut down.

A better, stronger woman would have held her chin up and smiled through it all. She would have even enjoyed having her hair styled and oils doused on her. It was all she could do to keep her head up and smile and talk with the others, but she couldn't enjoy any of it as she thought of her husband-to-be.

Moray was a wizard. He loved the Darkness.

The world of black magic—the way of the warlocks and wizards, the way of the Darkness—was complex. Ama had been told stories when she was young. Her parents instilled a healthy, righteous view on the wicked ways of humans. Black magic was vile, and those who practiced were evil or misled, perhaps both. Such Darkness should never be meddled with. Ama had been warned countless times to never entertain ideas or interest in spells, enchantments, or any trinket of the warlocks. Although her clan hadn't been near such things often, her parents wanted her prepared if she were to ever leave them.

As her mind grew plagued with the memories and the fears of her future, she tried to focus on the reality occurring around her.

When the women finished preparing her, Ama walked with Queen Macha out of the room, silent as death. She had been told how the ceremony would go. She and Moray would be wed through what sounded like a long, serious, boring ceremony. The people would rejoice, and a grand feast would follow in the ballroom. The people would dance, but Ama would sit with Moray at the throne. When the festivities ended, she would go with Moray. The celebration would last three days, and Ama would hardly see any of it. She was a bit angered by this, but she truly didn't want to be part of the chaos either. She wanted silence. She wanted to be away from Moray.

She'd get nothing she wanted.

Queen Macha squeezed Ama's white-gloved hand. "Do not be afraid, dear. Elohai is in control, even when our path is unknown. Even when our hearts are afraid, trust in Him."

Ama sucked in a calm breath. "Yes, ma'am." Unlike usual, Queen Macha didn't remind her to call her "Mother."

How could she marry a warlock who worshipped evil? Black magic was intricate and vast. How could she love a man who dedicated himself to such things?

She couldn't do this.

They walked down the corridor, the ladies chatting and chittering like sparrows and chickadees. Ama tried ignoring them. Queen Macha's grip on her hand weakened, and the queen's steps faltered.

Ama grabbed her arm firmly, frowning. "Queen Macha, is something wrong?" She shoved her wedding veil up, studying the queen's pale face.

Queen Macha's eyes widened, and she clutched her chest, face pale as the dress Ama wore—and growing paler. Had she looked so sickly before? "I... I need to sit down. I'm sorry."

A strange heaviness came over the corridor as the women hushed. Ama held the queen tightly but could scarcely breathe. Two of the guards rushed over as their beloved queen collapsed. Ama strained to hold her upright, the ladies rushing to help. Queen Macha didn't move again.

"WHAT IS IT, FINN?" King Connall sighed, arms crossed over his chest, clearly annoyed that his youngest had dragged him into a secret compartment along the halls. Finnigan liked the secret holes, while he knew his father disliked being distracted from the ballroom overflowing with people that were waiting for his resignation.

Finnigan gulped. He had about a minute to get the story out. "Father, what I'm about to say isn't easy—"

"Spit it out, Son."

"Moray is practicing to become a wizard."

King Connall stared at him. His eyes didn't grow huge. His mouth didn't drop. Instead of surprise or horror, a flicker of grief came to his eyes. "You have proof?" His voice was quiet. Steady.

As if he knew.

"I... I don't, Father. I came in on him doing something strange once, but..." Finnigan shook his head. Would the lack of evidence give his father hope or break his spirit? Maybe Finnigan should have kept his mouth shut.

King Connall dropped his head, a gesture he rarely ever did, but in the safety of the tiny, mostly dark room, no one was around to see his weakness. "I am sorry, Finnigan. It should be you earning the throne today, not your brother."

The words slapped Finnigan in the face, rendering him nearly paralyzed.

"I have caught Moray in such actions too. He has a friend—a wizard, no doubt—teaching him. I do not know Moray's intentions, but I don't trust his heart. Not now, not anymore. I have prayed for Elohai to change him, but..." King Connall wiped a hand over his face. "I fear Moray has only grown worse. I should have warned him. I should have..."

"Father, there is still hope," Finnigan said quickly. He didn't want to see his father cry. Never again. Not after the time Finnigan had nearly frozen to death in a river during a hunting trip. They'd been unable to reach home after

Finnigan fell into the ice. They had made up camp, King Connall never leaving his young son's side, doing everything he could to save him. Finnigan still remembered hearing his father weep over his body. His young mind had made a stoic promise that he'd never make his hero cry again.

Yet here he stood, causing his father's tears once more. But it was because of Moray this time. It was his job to protect his mother and father. He had to.

King Connall squeezed his son's arm gently, kissing Finnigan on his forehead. "There is hope, Son. But the wedding... the wedding must be stopped. If Elohai has given me voices of warning, I would be a fool to ignore them any longer. You will marry Ama and be king, not Moray."

Finnigan struggled for breath. "But Father—"

"Moray will be respectfully moved away from the kingdom. I have a duty for him elsewhere. I will never end the life of my son. Elohai help me, I am not that strong." King Connall's voice broke, and he pushed the door open, letting a flood of light into the dusty nook. He stepped out but his knees buckled, and he fell.

"Father!" Finnigan lunged for him, grabbing him by his arms. "Father, what is it?"

King Connall clutched at his heart and gasped in pain. Finnigan pulled the thick robe away from his father's chest, yelling at the servants who rushed over. "Get help! Get a healer!"

They ran off. Finnigan focused on his father's face, holding him tight. "Hold on, Father. Please!" he choked out.

I hurt him. I put too much strain on his heart. This is all my fault!

"Finn?" A familiar voice echoed. Moray ran over, dropping beside him, grabbing their father's hand. "What is wrong?"

Finnigan sobbed uncontrollably. His body wouldn't move, the world stopped spinning, and his heart became as cold as the river he had almost drowned in as a child. He held his father close.

The light in the king's eyes shimmered and faded like a burning ember surrendering to the dark.

MORAY GRABBED HIS FATHER'S heavy body, overcome with rage. Finnigan sobbed on his knees like a child as the guards rushed to protect them and empty the hall, as if some unseen monster had killed their beloved king and all they knew to do was fight rashly.

Moray stared at the king's pale complexion. With steady hands, he closed his father's eyes and gently touched his weathered face.

Someone murdered him. Someone killed his father.

Who?

Moray glanced up at Finnigan and whispered, "Finn..."

Finnigan just wept and clutched their father's hand. His brother always had been attached to the king. Far more attached than he ought to have been.

Their father had been murdered. Moray knew he had to get up and go find who was responsible.

The killer would be long gone. Especially if King Connall had been poisoned, which was most likely, by the looks of it. Moray stood, desperate to move, to find the answer to the tragedy before he ever allowed the grief to catch him. A grieving person was a weakened one. Moray wanted to kill, wanted blood on his hands, wanted whoever did this to suffer.

The hall, the people, the body, it all faded. It whirled, morphing with a strange gray color, as if Moray plummeted down, down, down. His ears rang, and he reached out to catch himself, but he kept falling.

Down, down, down.

Colors surrounded him, engulfing his body like snakes contracting around his lungs.

A rift... Like the rifts to Golgotha.

He didn't scream. He didn't fight the vortex that surely could rip him apart.

After an eternity of falling, Moray hit the bottom of whatever lay at the other side of the portal. Everything turned to black, but his last thought slipped through his mind. *I hope Finnigan wasn't sent here with me.*

Thirteen

THE MOMENT AMA HAD taken Queen Macha into her arms, the queen had died. The soldiers and healers had taken the body for healing, but nothing came of it.

Ama sat with Meili in her own bed chambers. They'd gotten word from one guard, his voice ever so quiet, that the queen was gone, and then they'd been left alone.

Ama shook softly. She'd never seen someone die before. She'd killed game, she'd held sick children, she'd almost lost her father to an injury, but never something like this. *I'm weak. I should be strong.*

She steeled herself and stood. She'd changed into her old dress for the mere comfort of rubbing the beads on her skirt.

She needed answers. She had to figure out what had happened and what would happen next. Ama pushed the door open, whispering to the guards outside, "I'm finding Moray."

The guards stepped in her way. The man with the scar along his face shook his head. "Step inside now, Princess Ama. It is unsafe."

"Unsafe?" Ama blinked. "She was murdered?" The death had been strange and the queen a healthy woman. But who would murder her?

The guard didn't answer, shoving Ama back into the room rather roughly. The doors slammed shut, and something heavy slid outside the door.

Ama gasped. "They... they locked us in!" She lifted a fist to beat on the door but Meili rushed over, taking her arm.

"Ama," Meili whispered. "Something is wrong."

"The queen just died right in front of me. They won't let me out of my room to find anyone or see what's going on. Yes, something is wrong!"

"It... it must be..." Meili hesitated. "Ama, your life might be at stake. If our blessed queen, Elohai rest her soul, was... was murdered, then all of you royals might be in danger. You'd best stay here."

Ama didn't want to stay in her room. She wasn't afraid of being murdered. "Queen Macha was probably poisoned," she said quietly. "If I was, I'd be dead by now."

"Please, Ama. We cannot get out of here. Elohai will protect us." Meili squeezed her hand. Her gentle nature brought Ama's fear down a notch, but only because Ama realized how afraid Meili truly was.

Ama hugged her. "Sit, Meili. It will be all right."

Ama wiped at her eyes quickly. She'd shed enough tears for now. She could grieve later, after things were taken care of. For now, all she could safely do was pray that Creator would protect the others.

THE MASSIVE GRANDFATHER CLOCK droned on for hours. Ama sat silently on the bed with Meili, praying with all her heart: for mercy and protection for the castle and the royals.

Despite trying to drown herself in prayers, her head spun. Ama shivered slightly, standing to tend to the fire. She poked at it with the iron prod. Why had no one come? Where was Finnigan?

A soft thud and sliding sound from outside the wooden door made Ama jump to her senses. She gripped the iron prod, ready for anyone who might come through the door.

Lord Barric, a visiting noble Finnigan had mentioned before, stepped into the room. He wore his formal attire for the ceremony, but his expression grim. "Princess Ama, may I have a moment?" He glanced at Meili, eyes dark. Meili didn't budge.

Ama tilted her head at Lord Barric without wavering. "Where is the king?"

"The king is dead, Elohai rest his soul," Lord Barric said softly. "The princes, also, were poisoned. It is a tragedy, but I am afraid that the kingdom must be reined under control before chaos breaks loose."

Ama's chest tightened, and she struggled for breath. *Finnigan... no! It can't be true.*

"Get out," she snarled, lifting the prod. Guards stood behind Lord Barric, but she didn't care what they might do. "Get out, now!"

"Please calm down." Lord Barric gestured to Meili. "Leave now. I must speak to Princess Ama privately."

Meili stood up, trembling. She hesitated but gently nodded, then rushed past the guards.

They shut the door behind her, leaving the lord and the princess alone. Something in Lord Barric's eyes sent Ama off the edge.

"I know what you want from me," Ama said quietly. The hunger that lay in Lord Barric's eyes wasn't foreign to her. She had seen it in the eyes of one of her clan members, but she had stopped him that night before he had hurt her. The boy had been cast out of the tribe for good.

There would be no casting Lord Barric out. This kingdom knew no true justice.

"Due to the tragic passings—"

"You will receive nothing from me." Ama didn't step back, and she held the prod in her hand casually. Her blade was sheathed. She could reach for it, but he could take it if he expected her move. She needed every advantage she could get if she wanted to triumph over his ill intentions.

Lord Barric's expression grew cold as he stepped closer. "This will be much more beneficial if you do as you are told and listen closely, girl."

An image flashed in Ama's head. The man in the corridor, the blood-soaked crowns in his hands, the blood trail he left on the stone floor as he left the bodies.

The bodies. A man and a woman. King Connall and Queen Macha.

Ama's heart pounded as if a knife pierced through it. The air drained from her lungs. "You... you killed the royal family so you would get the throne."

How could she have forgotten that dream? How could she have been distracted by the chaos around her?

"That is a dangerous thing to say, Princess." Lord Barric's eyes narrowed, his demeanor changing. Ama was half his size, and he was doing all he could to intimidate her into submission.

Ama jutted her chin. "You and your wife will hang for this!" she hissed, grip on the prod tightening.

He moved closer, just out of reach of the prod. "You assume the court and nobles had nothing to do with this," he whispered. "The kingdom has suffered at the hands of Connall. He strove for alliances, to help others, to make trade beneficial to all of Mazzabah. But the people... the nobles... we want more." Lord Barric smoothed back his black hair. "Now, since no one will heed your words, listen closely."

Ama lunged, aiming the iron prod at Lord Barric's chest. He grabbed it and swiftly wrenched it free from her hands. In the same motion, he shoved her against the door, his chest against her back. He spoke low against her ear. "We will return to the ways of old. You have the honor of helping me replenish the royal line."

Ama struggled hard, fuming. "I'll kill myself before I ever let you touch me!"

"One wrong move, little girl, and I will end the alliance. I will trade the girls and boys of your clan as slaves. I will kill the chief, your precious father," he whispered.

Bile rose in Ama's throat, and she bit back a furious sob. She tried craning her neck to meet his gaze. She had to do as he said. He killed the royals, and the kingdom wouldn't stop him.

Who am I to end this? she questioned. *I am nobody.*

Lord Barric gently pulled her hair from its thick braid. "If we all work together, Buacach will become a great empire, as it was always meant to be. Enough of this pathetic government that Connall created." He smiled softly, growing quiet for a moment. "I am willing to keep the alliance with the Wolf Clan. Please don't make me regret the care I'll shed on your people."

King Connall had spent his entire life for the good of his people and foreigners. How could anyone from Buacach be on Barric's side? This couldn't be real. It was just another nightmare. Nothing more.

Ama shuddered as Lord Barric touched her body. "I will not endanger my clan." As if those words sealed her fate, Ama straightened. She would not fight yet—she couldn't risk it.

But she would not be afraid.

Lord Barric released her gently. "We must hurry. The ceremony will begin shortly." Instead of opening the door, he hastily removed his tunic.

Ama's insides lurched, and she fought the urge to vomit the light breakfast she'd had earlier. Her heart hammered so wildly she could feel her wrists throbbing. *I will kill him.*

One day, I will serve the royals justice. I will end the madness. I will protect my people. As a child of Creator, not as a victim.

She didn't cry or fight, entirely numb, terror seizing her heart as he undid her dress. Despite his zeal, Barric didn't get far into his sin.

A rough, mocking voice broke through the ringing in Ama's ears, almost a sing-song whisper. "Oi! Didn't your harlot mother ever teach you not to sleep with another man's betrothed, you little bastard?"

In the same instance, Lord Barric's heavy body was yanked off Ama. She scurried backward and jumped to her feet, diving for the dagger that lay hidden under her dress on the floor, not worried that she was clothed in just her undergarments.

A tall man, built like a tree and with a face like a bear, stood over Lord Barric. He smothered Barric's face with a rag. As Barric kicked and thrashed, the man sighed impatiently. Once Lord Barric passed out, the man pocketed the rag and said in a low voice, "Oi, Princess, get dressed. Preferably not the white gown that made Finnigan drool like a lovesick hound earlier. It'll be a dog to get blood outta later." He jumped away, sidling next to the closed door. "Hurry!"

Ama yanked on her dress and moccasins, then grabbed her deer-skin pouch that she kept on the bedside table. Once the dagger was securely tied around her waist, she whispered, "Who are you?"

The stranger put a finger to his lips. His face, past the stubble and mustache, was littered with scars—some old and white, some new and pink. "Shut up and follow me."

Still in shock from what had almost happened, Ama had no trouble obeying. The man opened the door, looked both ways, and dragged her behind him. He hurried nimbly like a cougar through the corridors.

The man must not have been one of the traitors Barric spoke of, which meant there were people who wanted the kingdom to be saved. But who was he, and why was he helping her?

He stopped suddenly, pushing a little against the stone wall just before the staircase. A large stone slid sideways silently. Ama gaped, but the man yanked her in. Then he pushed against the wall again from the inside, and it shut. The secret door led to a smaller low-hanging corridor. She struggled to see in the dark.

The man pulled her onward. Ama clamped her mouth shut and followed, her small legs barely keeping up with the man's long stride. He acted like he knew where he was going. She hoped he did. The castle was most likely in utter disarray. She didn't want to be seen by any hectic crowd or passersby. She just wanted to go home.

He led her around two corners, all the while silent as a ghost, before hurrying down a small, narrow flight of stairs. Breathing deeply, she descended the tiny stone steps. She didn't dare speak but wondered if the thick stone walls on either side of them could keep anyone beyond them from hearing. Better not to take the risk. She'd ask questions later, including how these tunnels were built.

If they made it out.

The man led her down three more flights of stairs. Licking her lips, Ama asked, "Are we underground?"

"Yes."

"Why?"

"There is a way out of here below the Red Forest. Now shut up."

Ama bit her lip but followed closely down the narrow passageway that smelled of dust, wet rock, and something dead. She clenched her fists and steadied her breathing. The adrenaline rush was at least being used now. She almost—almost—felt a strange sense of calm come over her as she focused on moving.

That calm shattered when a hooded figure materialized in the tunnel before them. "My condolences, Gunnar, but I need the girl."

Ama stifled a cry of surprise, staggering back. The hooded man hadn't been there before. People couldn't just appear out of thin air. Her chest grew heavy like some unseen force was pushing against her shoulders.

Black magic.

Gunnar pulled a dagger from his leather belt. "I'm getting paid good money to bring her to safety, wizard boy, so move."

The man laughed softly. "Either hand her over or vanish with her into Golgotha." He had no weapon, only a large, heavy-looking bag in his hand. "You're ugly enough, maybe the beasts will accept you as their own there."

"Golgotha!" Gunnar scoffed. "You really do live in la-la land, don't you? Move, vulture. I've got a bounty to earn."

"Very well."

The man whispered something. Gunnar lunged with the dagger tight in his grip. And disappeared.

Ama cried out, but the place where Gunnar had been was empty. How was he gone? "N-no! No! Bring him back!"

"Why would I do that?" The man stared at her from beneath his hood—she could feel his eyes boring into her.

Ama didn't back down, drawing her own colored dagger that glowed dark red, illuminating her face in the shadows. "Bring him back!"

"That dagger..." The wizard paused. "If you stay, you will wreak havoc. I'm sorry, but nothing may disrupt the plan further. Goodbye, Ama. Good luck."

He tossed the canvas bag at her. Ama caught it with a grunt, stepping backward, her foot catching on something heavy.

The wizard began whispering something in a foreign tongue. Ama ran forward, lifting the dagger high. She was inches away from plunging it into the wizard's heart before the tunnels fell away and she whirled into oblivion.

Fourteen

MORAY STARED UP INTO the face of a four-eyed beast. Hot foam and saliva dripped from the monster's jowls. It growled, a low sound from deep within its chest, and opened its maw wide, revealing rows and rows of jagged, sharp teeth.

Moray yelled and summoned his black magic, but before he could roll off his back, a blast of blue energy shot the creature off him. He jumped up. "Finn!"

Finnigan staggered forward, stepping behind Moray's back. A dozen creatures, resembling wolves but at least twice the size of any gray wolf that Moray knew of. The four-eyed beasts snarled and snapped their jaws, all foaming at the mouth. Their giant claws dug into the soft, thick dirt beneath them.

Two of the wolves attacked Finnigan head-on. Finnigan used his Gift with surprising skill, considering he rarely practiced—that Moray knew of.

Moray summoned magic, forcing black energy through the chest of three, four, five monsters. They lunged with their teeth bared and swiped with their claws. The black magic was easy to summon when one was in tune with Abaddon and the energy that could be contracted with simple spells or the force of the mind and body. Moray could wield it using either routine.

Finnigan shot fire from both hands, sweat dripping from his temples. Moray wrestled a creature to the forest floor as it grabbed him, sinking its claws into his shoulders. It bit at his throat, but he killed it with one blast. Using the black magic didn't drain Moray—but he knew that the fight would wipe Finnigan out.

In minutes, the dozen monsters lay scattered. Their black tongues lolled past their ugly teeth, their gold eyes glazed over. They reeked of death and burnt fur.

"What were those?" Finnigan demanded.

"Vakhtangs. The Farsiks spoke of them in the legends. Not much is known—those wizards didn't write down much." Moray panted, blood streaming from the gashes in his back. He stepped closer, examining one of the strange beasts. The monsters were rotting from the inside. Their thick, dark fur that stuck out was caked with dirt and sticks, and chunks of skin and flesh hung loose from their big skeletons. Moray nearly gagged.

Finnigan staggered beside him, eyes wide. "Oh, Elohai..."

"This is no time to panic. More will come. We must move." Moray turned his neck, swearing as pain flooded him.

"You're hurt," Finnigan choked out. "Here, let me—"

"I'm fine!" Moray snapped.

He was far from fine, though. He was in Golgotha—without Sadon, without his army, without a dragon. *Master, why have you forsaken me? Is this my punishment for not killing Ama as you wished?*

Finnigan grabbed his shoulder forcefully. Moray muffled a cry of anguish as his little brother healed the gash. Finnigan's eyes rolled into the back of his head, and he collapsed.

Panic filled Moray. Finnigan could heal without being drained of Energy—but Moray knew he'd never fought and healed all at once. He grabbed Finnigan and lowered him to the ground. "Finn!"

"I'm fine," Finnigan mumbled, but he didn't open his eyes.

"We must move. Vakhtangs run in packs of dozens, hundreds, maybe thousands." Moray glanced up at the thick black trees surrounding them like walls. He hadn't learned much of Golgotha because little was truly known besides legends and lore. That was the whole point of exploring it. But he had heard the legend of these creatures —if the lore was right, he and his brother didn't stand a chance.

Finnigan's body trembled but he sat up, pale as a ghost. Moray hauled him to his feet. "Lean on me," he said. "We have to keep moving."

They were two men, alone, with nothing but their skills and swords to survive in the second realm. Mortals were no match for the realm of bones.

Finnigan choked back a weak sob. "Where are we, Moray?" He stumbled on, weak as a kitten. No doubt he was still mentally stuck back in the castle hall, holding their dead father.

"Golgotha."

Moray dragged him through the woods. The giant black trees varied in size, some bigger than houses, some thin as a willow branch. They all tangled about each other and intertwined, blocking off parts of the forest and covering patches of the dirt ground.

No breeze ever ruffled the stark black branches. It smelled of rotting flesh and musty dirt, but nothing stood out besides the strange gnarly trees. He kept alert for more monsters. None came.

Moray's heart thumped in his chest and Finnigan panted as they walked, but nothing else startled the forest's chilling silence.

Who had sent them here? It couldn't have been Sadon— he was loyal. He would never do anything to compromise their plan or kill Moray. And Sadon swore no one else could open the portal.

Who was it, then? Was there the slightest chance that Moray's trust had been a mistake? Years of trusting that wizard, of learning his skills and formulating their plan to take over the realms... Why would Sadon ever betray him? There was nothing in Mazzabah that could have given him more control or money than their plan.

A low, long growl came from somewhere deep within the twisted branches and black shadows. Moray quickened his pace, though he knew they couldn't outrun any of those beasts. The only way through was to fight. How long could they last, fighting those things?

"Moray," Finnigan whispered. "Do you hear that?"

Moray bit back a tart reply. "Keep moving."

"We must fight."

"You're in no shape to fight, you weak—" Moray was cut short by another deep growl. Closer this time. Finnigan shook in Moray's grip but stood still, boots digging into the dirt.

A sinking feeling crept into Moray's stomach. He'd signed his soul over to the Darkness, and the beasts would rip out his throat in return? After all he had done to conquer Golgotha, he would die in it?

Even with Finnigan's Gift and Moray's magic, the vakhtangs were too big, had too much brute strength, too many teeth. There were too many of them.

Moray stood beside Finnigan and clenched his fist, whispering something. An ebb of dark energy engulfed his left hand.

The vakhtangs' claws never made a sound against the dirt. They crept around and through the thick branches. Saliva dripped from their broad jowls, their eyes burning with animalistic hunger. Moray lifted his fist, shooting the dark force toward the first two monsters. The energy ripped into their chests. The pungent smell of burnt flesh and hair tore through the air as the bodies dropped.

Five more jumped out of the darkness. Moray lifted a hand, summoning more black energy.

Finnigan beat him to it. He shot out blasts of his own blue energy into the hearts of two beasts. Moray fought off the other three until all that remained were limp, stench-ridden bodies. He stood frozen, eyes on the woods.

No more vakhtangs came.

Moray shuddered. "You all right?"

Finnigan's legs shook but he nodded. "We have... we have to keep moving. We have to get home."

Oh, lovely, Moray thought. *What should I tell him? That there is no way out? That I don't have enough power to get us home? That we're doomed unless Sadon saves us? What if I am wrong, and Sadon was the one who sent us here?*

He kept his mouth shut. He needed Finnigan to have hope and hold it together. "Finnigan, now is not the time to panic. Breathe."

Finnigan's sickly pale skin glistened with sweat, but Moray doubted his physical reaction was entirely due to the fighting. He was still in shock and couldn't fight forever. Moray trained for dire situations, trained himself to handle adrenaline and shock. Finnigan wasn't a soldier or a wizard.

"Do not tell me to stay calm! This is all your fault." Finnigan's voice rose with rage.

"How is this my fault?" Moray snarled. "I didn't kill our father! I didn't send us here!"

"You were going to, weren't you? Golgotha was in your plans, wasn't it?" Finnigan's eyes flashed. "You were going to send men here. You were going to play king!"

"I was going to help our people. I was going to explore the second realm for our benefit." Moray didn't back down. "Do not make me into some Darkness-obsessed monster, Finnigan! Not everyone who practices magic is lost to it! None of you could ever grasp such a simple concept."

Finnigan stumbled closer, shoving his finger into Moray's chest. "You are a fool! You have lost yourself and you don't even realize it."

"I had ambitions!" Moray said tightly. "What did you do? You helped the little poor children? Some prince you have been!"

A strange look came over Finnigan's face. Like he knew something Moray didn't. Like his heart shattered into a million pieces—again.

Before either of them could speak again, a soft, weary voice came from behind them. "Fighting among ourselves will only bring us harm, my brothers."

Moray spun on his heel in the soft dirt. "Graft?"

Graft stepped past a few large branches, head held high. His left arm was badly gashed, and scratches all over his exposed skin bled lightly. He came closer and forced a weak nod.

"What are you doing here?" Moray grabbed his arm. Graft was in the flesh—but he hadn't been with him and Finnigan at their father's death. Why was he here?

Finnigan pulled Graft into a tight hug—healing the wounds simultaneously. Graft held Finnigan up as his knees buckled.

Graft's eyes widened when the pain disappeared. "Finn! You should not—"

Moray moved closer. "You know Finn can heal, don't be a baby about it now! Tell us what happened."

Graft hesitated, voice small and heavy. "The... the king —"

"We know, we were there," Moray said sharply. "Why are you here?"

"The king and the queen are dead," Graft whispered, voice strained.

Silence. Moray's ears rang as he processed the words. Finnigan wept softly and stepped back, covering his face.

"Dead." Moray forced the word out, but it didn't make the truth any more real to him.

"Lord Barric murdered them," Graft continued, resting a comforting hand on Finnigan's arm. "I overheard him speaking with a man... a man in a cloak. I couldn't see his face, but they spoke of the murders and of Princess Ama." His voice dropped and he lowered his head, closing his eyes briefly.

Finnigan looked up, struggling to cover his sobs. "A-Ama? What did they say? What did they do to her?"

Moray tensed. He needed to stay in control and not panic. Even if everything he knew had changed while he was helpless in Golgotha.

"Lord Barric intended to make her his..."

"Concubine," Moray finished for Graft when the embarrassed brother trailed off. "He intends to take the throne with his wife, now that we are gone."

Moray knew Lord Barric was a rat, but this... He didn't expect him to be capable of murder or overthrowing his empire.

"The kingdom believes you are both dead," Graft whispered. "It is madness."

Finnigan hugged Graft again weakly, shaking. "We have to get back! Ama needs our help." As if a surge of energy hit his veins, he stood on his own.

Moray didn't let his thoughts linger on what Lord Barric would be doing with Ama. *I will kill him.*

To do so, they first had to escape Golgotha, which was impossible. He could not let his brothers know this. They would kill him if they learned the truth. "We must find a way out of here first," he said quietly.

Graft lifted his head. "Can it be done?"

Moray couldn't look into his brother's weary brown eyes and tell him the truth, so he said, "Yes. We have hope."

The Light would never prevail.

Fifteen

SCREE! SCREEE! SCREEEE!

Ama jerked upright, air rushing into her lungs as she gasped. The musty corridor, the rats scurrying along her feet, the hooded man—they all flooded through her mind as if she had dreamed it all a mere second before. A soft light burned her eyes and she looked around, the fresh smell of moss, dirt, and leaves filling her nostrils.

Screee!

Towering red trees surrounded her like a thousand giants glaring at her intrusion on their territory. Ama froze where she sat on the pine-like needles. It was like the Red Forest in Mazzabah, only greater.

Ama shivered. The image of the wizard in the corridor flashed through her mind. He had sent her here.

And the man who had saved her...

"Gunnar!" Ama yelled, scrambling to her feet on the soft dirt and needles. Nothing but the thick trees surrounded her, and their tops went on and on—she couldn't see them end. Dizziness clawing at her mind, Ama swayed and screamed again. "Gunnar!"

What if he was gone? Dead?

The *scree* sound was gone now, replaced by eerie silence that sent shivers down her spine. The wizard had said something about Golgotha. The second realm of death.

A big hand twisted around her shoulder and clamped over her mouth. Ama screamed again, muffled by the calloused hand, and she bit a finger. The hand let go.

"Shut up!" The vaguely familiar gruff, low voice of Gunnar.

"Gunnar!" Ama whirled around.

He stood before her, his scarred, stubbled face twisted in a scowl. "What the bloody hell is wrong with you?" he barked.

"Where are we?"

"Do I look like a fairy godfather to you? How should I know?" Gunnar kept his voice down, his dark eyes taking in their new surroundings. He handled the change much better than Ama—his expression never shifted from that of annoyance. "Oh, this is just... this is just brilliant!"

Ama bit her tongue, heart hammering in her chest. "We're in Golgotha, aren't we? That's what the wizard said." She whispered it just in case some wicked beast in the forest wouldn't hear her say it, like it might make it true if they heard.

Gunnar stormed away a few feet, touching one of the giant red trees. He swore again. "Doesn't look like any place I've been in Mazzabah."

Ama was engulfed by a heaviness as strange as the one that had settled over her when Queen Macha died. The air itself seemed to seal her up and crush her chest. "Gunnar?"

He kept swearing under his breath, taking in every detail of the forest he could find. If the legends were true—and there was obviously some weight to them, since this place even existed—then they were certainly doomed.

Ama looked up, but there was nothing pushing on her chest, of course. The air was clear and smelled like any forest ought to. *We are not doomed. We cannot be.*

Good and evil spirits roamed Mazzabah, but they rarely exposed themselves to the naked eye. If the legends held true, then Golgotha ought to be overflowing with wicked beings that were visible to the human eye and spirit.

Ama felt that something was wrong here, but she saw nothing. What if this realm was the same? How could they win against things they could not see?

Her hands shook. "Gunnar!" she repeated, voice louder, sharper.

"I am not your servant boy!" He faced her, red with rage, his hand on the hilt at his side. She'd noticed his small arsenal of weaponry while they were escaping the castle, but now she realized how useful the weapons would be. All Ama had was her pouch, dagger, and the heavy bag from the wizard that she'd dropped as soon as she'd woken up in this strange place.

Grimacing, she knelt, digging through the canvas sack. "We have food... water... all kinds of things. Look!"

Gunnar looked over the supplies. "The wizard didn't want us dead soon, huh? A blasted shame we can't give him a kiss for his merciful efforts in prolonging our miserable lives." His voice dripped with venomous sarcasm.

"We... we can make it." Ama stood and let him pick up the bag.

"We ain't getting out of here. Let's get that clear." He paused, eyeing the trees again. "We are not the first people to get sent here, and we won't be the last. Not a soul escapes the Place of Bones. Get that through your head right now, Princess, because I won't listen to you nag about false hopes for the rest of my unfortunate life." Gunnar turned away with a huff.

Anger flashed in Ama's chest and she lunged forward, shoving Gunnar hard. "How dare you give up so easily!" Despite her short height, the mercenary staggered a little at her push—he hadn't expected it.

He lifted a hand but didn't strike her. "How dare *me*?" he said with a snarl. "I saved your hide back in that castle! What about your lovely prince? Where was he?"

"Dead!" Ama screamed, tears burning her eyes now. She pictured Finnigan, his big grin, his wild mannerisms. She pictured Moray and how he had never had the chance to repent for what he had done. "They're dead!"

Gunnar scowled. "That's not my problem."

Ama clenched her fists, moments away from beating the man who'd saved her life. "What *is* your problem?" She couldn't think of the princes without breaking, and she couldn't break—not now. Ama wouldn't cry in front of Gunnar. They would survive, even if the legends said death was inevitable.

"I was hired to save you, and I'm obviously not getting paid now." Gunnar let out a low, mirthless laugh. "But I don't intend to die here without a good fight."

Ama set her jaw. "We can get home. We can't just live here forever!"

"We're dying here. No way around it." He was as stubborn as she was, but Ama didn't intend to back down. She couldn't survive without some hope, even if Gunnar refused to agree.

Maybe they would die here. Maybe she'd lose her mind. The invisible claw around her lungs kept constricting. What was wrong with this place?

"What's wrong with you?" Gunnar asked sharply. "You look sick."

"I am."

"Well, throw up in a bush and let's get moving. Can't let the shock get a hold of us. It's just a realm of death, can't be that bad." Gunnar turned away gruffly, mumbling under his breath.

Ama's legs wouldn't move. She had to pull herself together. Calm down. Focus on surviving.

They're dead. They're all dead.

You'll die too.

Hot tears ran down Ama's face. She gripped her dagger, closing her eyes. She could not break.

Gunnar stopped in his tracks. "Do you smell that?"

Ama opened her eyes to see him with his sword drawn. She stepped closer quickly, skin growing cold. The stench hit her, and her stomach lurched. "Smells like... like something rotting. Must be you."

Gunnar held a finger to his lips. She didn't see anything in the woods—did he think something was out there? There were probably hundreds of monsters in the woods. Creator only knew what lay hundreds of feet above them in the treetops. Ama unsheathed her dagger. She wouldn't die without a fight.

Four beady yellow eyes gleamed in the shadows. Gunnar waited, appearing calm as could be. Was he truly fearless? Even a mercenary felt fear at some point, didn't they?

The creature moved out of the shadows. Four eyes were embedded in a large wolf-like face, and the creature stalked on four legs ending in giant claws. Its immense rib cage sank low, tufts of fur and bloody flesh hanging off the bones.

Ama suppressed a scream, stomach twisting. The horrendous monster sniffed and jumped at Gunnar, saliva flying from its large mouth. Gunnar swung the sword with ease, beheading the rotting thing in one sweep. He laughed, eyeing the woods. "Wolves hunt in packs. Stay close, Princess."

"My name is *Ama*," she snapped. She readied her dagger, though she doubted it did much to the beasts. By the time they could get close enough for her to jab their eyes out, she'd be dead, but she wouldn't let Gunnar fight alone.

Two more of the beasts came from the left and three from the right. Gunnar pulled out a dagger and grinned wide. Three of the monsters attacked him at once, but in mere seconds, he had decapitated them. Their black blood, thick like tar, splattered Gunnar's street clothes.

The other monsters dove for Ama.

She jumped out of the way on shaky legs and stabbed the nearest four-eyed wolf in one of its eyes, but the beast jerked free. A howl roared from deep within its broad rib cage. Ama cried out, stumbled back. The second beast tackled its kin, throwing itself toward Ama.

Gunnar shoved her out of the way. His sword made one clean slice through both of the monsters' heads. "Run!"

Ama gripped her glowing dagger and ran through the woods. Small and large trails littered the forest, but none were worn enough for a human to travel quickly. She picked a small one and raced through it anyway, jumping over rocks and large branches.

A growl erupted from the thick, dark bushes on her left. The monster leapt out, hauling after Ama.

Gunnar ran and jumped between the monster and Ama. He shot the sword up into the monster's rib cage, too close for a good beheading. Black blood spurted from the wolf's body as Gunnar yanked the sword back out. "Ama, move those stubs! Let's go!"

Ama ran on, heart in her throat. She'd get him back later.

Screee!

There was the scream again! Ama glanced around but stumbled on the path. *Focus ahead. Run!*

Screee!

Ama gasped for breath, casting a brief look over her shoulder as she stopped where the trail abruptly ended. "Do you hear that?"

Gunnar scanned the forest, swearing. "Where's the trail? Trails don't just end!"

"Do you hear that screaming sound?" Ama insisted. She glanced behind them into the trees but saw nothing. The screaming sounded like it came from above. With countless trees, all hundreds of feet high, she might never find the source of the noise.

"What are you doing?" Gunnar growled. "We have to keep moving." He grabbed Ama by her arm, yanked her into the shrubbery.

She jerked away. "No, something is screaming, can't you hear it?"

"No!" Gunnar got in her face, eyes dark. She could tell he was in survival mode, like a soldier in the heat of battle, the whole world on his back and he had to keep moving. For warriors, moving meant survival, and stopping meant embracing certain death.

"I know we have to move, but this noise—"

"It's probably a trap, another monster, anything!" Gunnar shoved her off the path. "You wanna live? Go!"

Ama followed him into the forest, but something small and warm dropped from the trees and clung to her shoulder. A cry rose in her throat and the *screee* flooded her eardrums.

She reached around, and her hand hit something furry. A small round face with huge pink eyes stared back at her, with tiny gray curved teeth protruding from its mouth. Ama screamed again—but the little creature didn't bite her nose off. Instead, it wrapped around the back of her neck. It was small, about the size of a squirrel but with a long, slinky body.

Gunnar reached for the little creature, eyes wide. "Don't move!" When he grabbed it, the creature opened its tiny mouth—but this time, Ama heard nothing.

Gunnar yelled, staggering back a step and covering his ears. The creature stopped when he let go, curling its body closer to Ama. She couldn't breathe, expecting the fuzzy white creature to tear out her jugular. The thing watched Gunnar like a tiny guard dog.

"Ama—" Gunnar groaned, clutching his head.

"Did you hear it?" Ama asked shakily, clenching her hands into fists, controlling the urge to snatch the foreign animal off her shoulder and flee.

"It busted my eardrums!" Gunnar yelled. "What do you think?"

"Stop yelling!" She grabbed Gunnar's wrist. He snarled, face red with rage, his eyes furious as he studied the creature on her shoulder. It hissed at him but didn't scream again.

"I... I didn't hear it when you did. And you didn't hear it when I did," Ama mustered. "It doesn't make sense."

"You need to get it off." Gunnar still spoke too loudly.

Ama's neck hurt from looking down at the creature, but she slowly reached up and touched the fuzzy head. The creature didn't hiss, bite, or scream. It rubbed against her hand and its eyes fluttered.

"I've seen it all." Gunnar whispered something angrily in his native tongue before glancing back to the deep red trees. "It probably woke the whole forest."

"I don't think so." Ama gulped and gently cupped the animal to her chest, grinning. Her heart softened, as if all the weight and fear from before vanished.

"Put it down!" Gunnar kept a healthy distance. The creature glared at him briefly as if it might pounce. "Every creature in this cursed place is the enemy, Ama!"

She held no fear of the creature. Had she been fooled by the Darkness into thinking the creature was good? Jaw tightening, Ama studied the thing that rubbed against her. She mentally asked Creator if the little creature was wicked, but she didn't hear any answer.

Another low growl came from behind her. Heart lurching into her throat, she whirled around, gripping her dagger in her right hand. Three of the rotting beasts crept closer, snapping their jowls. What did they eat when they didn't have human meals?

Gunnar jumped in front of her, slicing the head off one beast when it attacked.

The tiny creature against Ama's breast opened its mouth wide, sharp teeth bared. She couldn't hear the cry, and since Gunnar didn't yell, he probably didn't either.

The other two beasts howled and screeched, slamming their heads at the ground in anguish. Ama's skin ran cold as roars tore from the rotting beasts' lungs. She moved backward, shaking. "G-Gunnar!"

He didn't move away, sword raised in case they attacked.

The creatures roared but collapsed, blood pouring from their furry, torn ears. Ama gaped in horror, staring down at the little creature in her arms that had done the lethal damage. The white fluff licked its teeth and practically beamed up at her.

"What the bloody mother-of-pearl was that?" Gunnar lowered his sword, which was covered in black blood. He moved closer but stared at the creature in utter dismay.

"It... it..." Ama cleared her throat. "She killed them. She didn't kill us!"

"She? I won't be kissing the rat on the mouth for it!" Gunnar growled. "Let her go."

"No," Ama said. She had prayed and it seemed that Creator had answered quite clearly. "She obviously isn't the same as the others. She saved us."

"Saved!" Gunnar guffawed. "I had the situation under control. I've killed more than you, and I don't need some pink-eyed rat to save me."

Ama frowned deeply, and against her chest the creature hissed at Gunnar. "Gunnar, I asked Creator if this"—she gulped, not sure what to call the thing in case it decided to bite her—"little one was safe or not, and it seems obvious she is. I won't get rid of her if she wants to stay with me."

"You've lost your mind." His scowl grew hard and his face expressionless. "This is Golgotha, Ama, not a damn pet shop! It is the second realm, and there is no good here."

Ama lifted her chin. "She stays with me if she wants."

"There is no good here!" Gunnar slammed the side of his left fist against a giant tree, sending bark flying. "All this place offers is death and heartbreak."

Ama gulped hard but didn't move away. "Mazzabah has evil creatures. If this place used to be joined, perhaps good creatures were trapped here too."

Why would Creator trap good things in hell? Why would He allow bad things to enter the land of His children?

Gunnar shook his head, dark hair streaked with the tar-like blood. He turned away and started back into the dark forest. "We must keep moving."

She followed close. "What do you think those wolf things were?"

Gunnar chuckled. "Let's call them rotwulves."

Ama rolled her eyes, but the lack of hope the man had made her blood boil. She would survive. She had her clan to save. Ama cupped the little creature close and prayed, her voice a soft whisper in the forest. Gunnar didn't tell her to be silent. Despite her prayers, she couldn't shake the feeling someone was watching her.

Sixteen

THE DARK FOREST WENT on forever, with the lack of sunlight and putrid air making Finnigan's lungs feel like tar. As the trio walked through the thick shrubs, thorns, and jagged rocks, Finnigan tried praying. Elohai created Golgotha, after all. There had to be a reason that He had sent them here.

Why, though?

It was not a question of self-pity, but of determination. Their mother and father were gone, but he and Moray could still save the kingdom. If they could escape...

He could process the deaths later.

Finnigan's mind drifted. Ama's fate was not finished—it was something happening while he wandered through Golgotha, but there was nothing he could do to save her. Somehow, he'd get back and he would save Ama in the end, before it was too late. *Please, Elohai, do not let her die.*

There had to be a way to get out. Elohai needed them to save the kingdom, but Finnigan had no idea how they would get back. Maybe there was no way out, and Moray was only giving them false hope.

They walked in silence. They didn't speak of the deaths. They didn't speak of Lord Barric's intentions with the kingdom or with Ama. They walked for hours that way. Moray might have been a wizard and probably knew more of Golgotha than Finnigan and Graft, but he spoke nothing of it. But Finnigan prayed hard and begged Elohai to get them home so he could slay Lord Barric with his bare hands.

AFTER HOURS OF WALKING and fighting off any beast that crossed their path—all three of them covered in black blood by the end of the day—the repetitive landscape ended.

Moray stumbled through the black branches first, reaching out with one hand to move the branches away. When nothing was there, he fell face first.

Finnigan jumped after him. "Moray!"

Graft pushed past the shrubs and into the clearing. With big arms that barely bulged, he yanked Moray out of the dust.

The black forest ended like someone had cut the trees off with a blade. Finnigan turned around to see what had replaced the rotting black behemoth trees.

Soft dirt squashed beneath his boots. A big, bright sun lay above them—even though the forest behind them hadn't much light at all. Finnigan stared at the flat land and slowly exhaled. "Moray... Graft... This is all wrong."

Across the acres of prairie, scraggly trees scattered the horizon, the landscape only muddled by an occasional boulder.

"It's Golgotha," Graft whispered.

Moray stared at the prairie. "The ecosystem just... cut off. Started something different..."

Finnigan cleared his throat, blood growing cold. "At least things cannot hide here." There was nothing in this landscape to hide behind or under.

"This place will have monsters. We must be alert." Graft had picked up a hefty branch from the forest, wielding it like a club. He'd killed a few beasts with some lucky blows and black blood speckled his forearms.

Finnigan patted Graft on the back. "We will be just fine. We can face anything!" A part of him meant it. They'd gotten through a whole day—surely it had been twelve hours—surviving those hideous beasts with sharp teeth and big claws. They only had some scratches and bruises showing for it. Somehow, they'd lost minimal blood and, of course, were not dead.

How long would the miracles last? Finnigan was running low on strength, his Gift draining him of strength but not of hope. "Faith will help us fight, and hope will carry us through."

Moray led them into the prairie without a word. Finnigan bit his lip and followed beside Graft, voice low. "Moray?"

Silence.

"We have all gone long enough without communicating."

"What is there to communicate?" Moray never looked back. "Our parents are dead. Our kingdom is taken over. Ama is being used like a dog. Which topic would you like to discuss first? How about the fact we are in the second realm, the Place of Bones, where we are certain to die before we ever get the chance to escape?"

"There's a chance we will get out and we will fight to take that chance. You said so yourself." Finnigan's heart pounded at the mention of his loved ones, but he wouldn't show it. Moray already thought he was weak. Finnigan wouldn't prove him right ever again.

"Yes," Moray said, tossing his head. "We will escape. I'll be sure of it. But Lord Barric will have us sent back again if we do not kill him."

Finnigan bit his lip. "Who sent us here, Moray?"

"If I knew, I would not have let it happen."

"You are lying to me."

"That's what you think I do best, is it not?"

Finnigan grabbed Moray's arm and yanked him to a stop. "We need to discuss this. We are princes. We must work together." His father's words flooded back to his mind.

"I may know who sent us here, but I will not throw around assumptions without proof. I will not have proof till we reach the kingdom again." Moray pushed him off, but it seemed he was too tired to give the gesture much effort.

"How do we get back, then? You know more of this place than you are letting on." Finnigan bit his tongue, struggling with his anger.

Moray thought for a long moment. Graft didn't speak but watched Moray with keen eyes. Graft could protect them with a mere club from monsters, but he couldn't protect the princes from themselves.

Finnigan would not lose this battle. He would not lose his kingdom, and he would not lose his brother.

Moray licked his lips. "We can escape. We must reach a large body of water, like an ocean, for me to perform the spell."

"Spell?" Finnigan's anger flashed, his tone clipped.

"Yes, spell." Moray rolled his eyes. "I am a wizard. I'm sure it shocks you to hear it. It doesn't matter if you know now, does it?"

Finnigan ignored his brother's heavy sarcasm. His heart hammered, and bile rose in his throat. He'd wanted to be wrong. "Should we count on a spell to get us out of here?"

"Would Elohai bless such a thing?" Graft asked softly.

Moray waved a dismissive hand. "I do not see Elohai doing anything to get us out. My master can provide. Now, let's move. This is a prairie, and we need a large body of water."

Graft shook his head. "Elohai is the only way."

But Moray didn't respond.

Finnigan started walking again, but his mind wandered. Moray was lying. Elohai could not bless the usage of a spell. He closed his eyes briefly and then focused on the land around him.

He could've believed that nothing horrid could lie in the grasses, but he thought of snakes, of birds, of the usual creatures that lay in "normal" prairies. Anything could be here. They had to be alert. They walked on and on and on—but the sun never moved. It sat in the center of the pale blue sky above.

After a couple of hours, Graft pointed it out. Finnigan almost wished he hadn't. "The sun has not moved. It has been at least two hours. Perhaps more."

"So?" Moray sighed. "It is Golgotha."

"The trees, the rocks, everything is all the same," Finnigan said, voice tight. "Look." He picked up one small pebble and then another. Both rocks were the same shade, same shape, same weight. "Identical. "

Graft's steps slowed. "The grass... all the same height. Something is very wrong, Moray. I feel it in my gut. This place is more wicked than the black forest."

"There are no monsters." Moray kept walking without slowing down, ignoring the strange details staring him in the face.

Finnigan's insides churned. "There is no greater monster than time. There is no greater danger than staying in the same place forever!" His voice ended in a shout, but it did not echo. He glanced down at the dirt, but there was no shadow. "Moray..."

How had they missed this?

Graft moved and stepped in front of Moray abruptly, his giant frame relaxed but solid. "Moray, please. There is something wrong."

"What do you suggest we do?" Moray shouted. "We must keep moving!"

Finnigan knew he was right. They couldn't progress if they went backward or if this place was just a trick of the mind. "I do not think this place is... is real."

Moray didn't laugh or scoff. "It is not."

Graft ran a hand over his bald head. "We must find a way that is more than flesh and blood to escape this place."

What if they never found a river or the sea, if Moray truly could help them? No, that was not right. Spells wouldn't help. Finnigan pushed his doubts away. "We pray!"

"Pray?" Moray scoffed. "We keep walking. A trap can only last so long."

"If it's a trap, we are being hunted." Graft frowned and glanced about. "We should pray. I do not think we can escape Golgotha by our blood alone."

Would Elohai help them here, even in a place of death? Even when they deserved to be killed? Finnigan hadn't helped his people. Moray was a wizard. The only one of them who deserved life was Graft.

Finnigan's chest ached. *I am sorry, Elohai. I am so sorry.*

"Go ahead," Moray said tightly. "Pray. Then we walk."

Finnigan hesitated before closing his eyes and bowing his head. A beast could have jumped out and killed him, but he would be vulnerable to Elohai. Voice soft, he prayed aloud. "Elohai, please guide us out of this place. It is wicked. I feel it in my spirit. This forest is a trap and we do not understand it, but if two of us feel this way, surely that is You speaking. Remove the blindfold from our eyes. Remove the illusion from our head. Show us the truth and let us out, in the name of Elohai."

Finnigan opened his eyes, lifted his head. The sun beat down on him and sweat trickled down his neck. The grass remained still at his feet.

Nothing.

Moray chuckled. "Let's walk."

Graft rested a gentle hand on Finnigan's shoulder, walking alongside him. "Elohai has a purpose for every detail, Finn. We will be all right."

Finnigan nodded but looked across the land. For a split moment, he saw the figure of a hooded man standing against the grass, yards away with a staff in his hand. Only for a moment, and the man was gone. A ripple of light lingered where he had stood.

Finnigan blinked.

He was seeing things. That could not be good.

Seventeen

AMA SPOKE GENTLY TO the little creature as they walked. Gunnar told her to shut up, but she replied that the creatures in the forest could most likely smell them first. As the hours passed, the forest did not grow darker, and Ama wondered where the slight light came from. Sunlight couldn't pass through the treetops so high above, but it was not pitch black. She could see Gunnar and a few yards around her at all times.

Some things were best not mulled over for too long.

The creature, Courage, fell asleep draped around Ama's shoulders. She named her Courage because if the wee thing could scream at some monsters and make them drop dead, so could she. Ama chose courage in the Place of Bones because her Creator had overcome death.

Though it didn't seem to become night or day, the temperature dropped. Ama shivered. "How are you not cold?" she whispered to the sleeping fluffball near her cheek.

Gunnar glanced back at her, steps never faltering. "You can hardly say three words to the man who saved you, but a big-eyed, fanged rat is worthy of your conversation?"

"She is prettier than you," Ama muttered.

"I heard that."

"How big do you think Golgotha is?"

"If the realms were split, I would say at least as big as Mazzabah. Kind of makes sense, but I ain't no bloody scholar," Gunnar said. He walked with his sword in his hand.

Ama fell silent. She missed Mazzabah already. She missed her father's strong arms when he hugged her, her mother's laughter as she told Ama stories, and the songs her people had sung around the campfires.

"Gunnar?"

No response.

"Gunnar?"

He walked a bit faster.

"Is something wrong?" Ama asked.

"Yes."

"What?"

"You're trying to talk to me."

Ama scoffed softly. "If you didn't want to talk with me, you should have left me with Lord Barric."

He said nothing.

"Who are you?" she asked.

"Me."

"Who sent you to save me?" Ama licked her lips.

"Etu."

Ama's steps almost faltered. "E-Etu?" The blood rushed from her face and she caught her breath. No... There was no possible way it was true.

Gunnar nodded. "Etu sent for me before the royals were murdered. I do not ask questions, but I assume he knew the murder would take place, knew you would need help soon."

"No..." It couldn't be. Etu couldn't have known that.

"Do not ask questions that you cannot handle the answers to, Princess."

"If he knew and did not stop it..."

"No one can stop such a thing," Gunnar replied. "Perhaps he just had a hunch."

"Someone could have stopped it!"

"Don't lose your emotions on me." He cast her a rebuking glare.

Ama walked faster, matching his stride. "I will not keep quiet so you can wallow in self-pity!"

Gunnar laughed. "All right. If you want me to talk, I'll talk." He placed a hand over his heart. "I haaaate you," he said in a sing-song voice. "Is that good enough for you? I hate all of you royals. I took Etu's job only for the money, and now I'm stuck in hell without a bloody coin to my name."

Ama's face flushed with heat. She wanted to shout at him, hit him, but she couldn't blame him. She had agreed to wed Moray for her people, been unknowingly caught up in some wild scheme, and then cast into Golgotha by a strange wizard. Almost as if this was the wizard's cruel way of showing mercy. Or perhaps it was a game. Finally, Ama sighed. "I'm sorry."

Gunnar glanced back with narrow eyes. "A woman never apologizes unless she is preparing for an attack."

"Scared of my dagger?" If she could've been outcast with someone else, she'd have chosen Finnigan. He would have been kind and hopeful. But she had to keep it together and get back, for her people. For Finnigan's people.

"You wish."

"Why take the job? Do you have family?" Ama couldn't let her thoughts wander. She'd focus on the matter at hand, which was getting to know the brusque individual who looked like a wolf on two feet.

Gunnar chuckled, a rough sound. "Ain't got any."

"Parents?"

"You're awfully pushy," he snapped.

Ama crossed her arms. "We're in Golgotha. Telling secrets won't kill us now."

"You tell one first."

"I miss my family." The words left her mouth before she could stop them. Grimacing, Ama held her breath. No doubt, Gunnar already viewed her as a weakling.

"At least they're alive. And that's not a secret."

"Yours aren't?" Ama asked.

He shook his head absently. "Dead."

She followed as closely as she could. "I am sorry."

No response.

"Where is your home?"

A scoff. "Used to be at sea. Ain't got one now."

"You're a sailor?"

"My father was. His ship disappeared when I was young." He cast her another brief look. "Ask me another question,

Princess, and the bounty price rises. I don't work with loudmouths."

THEY CAMPED AFTER A few more hours of walking. They had no supplies, but Ama was used to sleeping in the forest without a blanket. The pine needles made the hard ground bearable, but the cold bit deep into her bones.

Gunnar sat up to watch the camp. He said he would wake her in a few hours. She didn't want to think about being woken up. It made it harder bothering to sleep at all.

Ama imagined her family sleeping soundly in their tents. She imagined Finnigan's voice and laughter as they spoke of the Letters.

Courage rubbed Ama's cheek with her face and curled up against her neck tighter. Her little body offered little heat. Ama looked up across the small fire Gunnar had started. He had some supplies in his pants and a small shoulder pack— he had withdrawn only some flint and two pieces of hardtack he shared with her earlier. They weren't eating the supplies in the canvas bag but drank some out of the waterskins.

"Gunnar?" Ama whispered.

"I am not going to exchange body heat with you."

"How much do you know about this place?" she forced out, not entirely sure if she wanted an answer.

Gunnar sighed heavily. "Not too much. But the sailors had plenty of legends 'n' lore." His big shoulders slumped as he stoked the fire, never looking at her, the flames flickering in his dark eyes. "Some claimed that the ships lost to the seas found their way into Golgotha. There has never been rhyme or reason to the legends so I doubt anything is what we may expect. Who knows what is true and what is fiction?" His voice grew distant, like he had stopped listening to himself.

Ama gulped hard and watched the fire crackle, burning up the dead brush and sticks they'd gathered. "I know you think we're doomed, but... but I think Creator will help us return home, Gunnar. I do not believe He would forsake us here."

"I do not understand how you people believe in gods." Gunnar leaned back against a tree, stretching his long legs out. "Awful lot of headache it is, believing in things you can't see."

"You cannot see love, but still people love each other."

"I don't." Gunnar shook his shaggy head. "Lovely little try, Princess."

Ama kissed Courage's soft head. "Creator has kept us alive this long. That's a miracle."

"No," Gunnar said, his voice growing taut. "That's me with plenty of years of survival under my belt."

"Thank you for helping me escape, Gunnar." Ama didn't feel like arguing with him—it was like speaking with Etu— but she was grateful he had helped her run from Lord Barric. She didn't imagine what she might have been faced with—she'd thought about it all nonstop as they walked and couldn't handle it any longer. She would have been used, a failure to her family.

It looked bad, but she decided she was better off in Golgotha than if she'd been stuck as Barric's slave. Mostly. After all, if she survived and found some impossible way to escape, she could still save her family. Ama's insides twisted. The odds didn't look good, but she still had a chance.

Gunnar waved a big hand. "My pleasure. I only regret not cutting his—" He stopped mid-sentence, clearing his throat.

Ama smirked. "You don't have to clean your speech up for me, *princess*."

"You'd best sleep before I switch off with you." He rolled his eyes. "Sweet dreams of your prince."

"I don't have a prince."

"Finnigan seems terribly interested in you." Gunnar smirked.

Ama's throat tightened. "He is gone."

He shrugged slightly and said no more.

She closed her eyes again, the warmth of the fire finally engulfing her.

A LARGE WHITE SERPENT coiled in the forest trees above, its large golden eyes watching her as she slept. Its tail inched lower, lower, till it traced the ground near her leg. The tip of the scaly tail touched her leg and curved around her blade.

A man stood over her, moving closer as the snake's tail entwined around the blade hidden beneath her clothes. He spoke softly. "Hello, Princess. Do not be afraid. I am here to help you." His face was shadowed by a large dark hood, his cloak hiding any distinguishable features of his tall body.

Ama couldn't move. *Asleep—I'm asleep. Just a nightmare.*

"If you wish to return to your people and save them, follow me." His voice was gentle. Comforting. Strong. He extended a flawless hand toward her.

Ama's breath lodged in her throat. His words were familiar somehow. Safe and inviting. "W-who are you?"

"I am your master's servant," he said gently, never moving. The serpent's grip on the dagger tightened, and Ama reached for it. Her arm wouldn't move. Her whole body lay immobile in the dirt. Fear gripped her throat.

"Who are you?" Ama choked out again.

His voice darkened as he tilted his head. "I am the chosen who will free you from this place of death. I will save you if you follow me."

"Creator is my master," she whispered. "He did not send you."

The snake's tail wrapped around her waist, tighter, tighter. It slid up her chest, and Ama gasped for breath. The man stood still, pulling his hand away from her. "Then you will rot here. If you do not turn away, Ama, you will die here. Forgotten. A failure to your people."

AMA JERKED AWAKE AND sat up, eyes wide, breath shallow.

No snake. No man in a cloak. Her blade was still securely attached to her belt. The fire's light flickered across Ama's body as she relaxed.

"You all right?" came Gunnar's voice, only a few feet away. "You've still got a while to sleep." He didn't wait for any answer. It didn't take a scholar to understand that Golgotha offered nothing but nightmares.

Ama curled up again. Courage hissed at Gunnar softly, hiding in her arms. *Creator, what did the dream mean?*

Eighteen

"I DON'T THINK ANYTHING in this prairie is alive." Finnigan trudged after his brother. For three hours, they'd walked on without any break and without any conversation since his prayer had been ignored. He didn't understand why Elohai didn't remove the illusion from their minds, but they'd no choice but walk through it.

Graft cleared his throat. "I don't think so either."

"I wish we knew who or what is doing this." Finnigan clenched his fists. It was all fake. He felt it in his bones. The identical trees and rocks, the perfect grass, the never-moving sun—and not a single breeze ever relieved them. They found no water. The dehydration and hunger pangs were almost more than Finnigan could handle, but Graft and Moray didn't complain, so he didn't either.

Was anything in Golgotha real? Were they walking into some trap where they'd meet their death at the end of the prairie, or was there any end to the madness? Finnigan waited for a killer monster to jump out, but nothing came.

He knew he had to stop or he'd drive himself mad. He was already seeing strange men in the prairie.

Moray was still refusing to speak of what he knew—about who sent them here, about the magics, about everything. Finnigan hoped he'd break and do so soon. Moray may not have all the answers, but even some assumptions would help about now.

"We just need to reach water," Moray muttered.

"If there is no water?" Finnigan asked. "Maybe we should turn back and face the forest again."

"No use. We're dead either way if we don't find water. We've been here longer now anyway." Moray didn't look back, his tunic sticking to him with sweat.

A part of Finnigan almost missed the tangible beasts he could kill with his Gift. Not knowing what made him uneasy about this place was far worse than facing a clawed monster. His Gifts drained him, but he was able to bounce back relatively quickly. So far. He hadn't a clue if Moray's magic drained him.

As Finnigan prayed, he glanced at Graft. All the years they had been friends, Graft's calmness under any calamity never ceased to amaze. Finnigan had broken down when he'd come to Golgotha. He'd wept over his parents and Ama and his people—just thinking of them again made rage burn in his chest. Graft walked along unmoving, unafraid. Finnigan's heart eased ever so slightly. He had his brothers still, and that was enough.

They walked for at least another hour. Sweat poured from their faces and soaked their shirts. Without water, however, they slowed considerably. Without tools to dig, they couldn't do anything but walk, and Moray never suggested he use black magic to somehow summon water, so Finnigan figured he couldn't.

Ahead of him, Moray came to a complete halt. "Do you hear that?"

Finnigan ran into him, grunting, wiping sweat from his brow. "What?"

"It... It's gone." Moray glanced back at them. A vein in his neck bulged. "I keep hearing something, but it disappears just as quickly."

"Is it your conscience?" Finnigan smirked.

Moray hit him in the gut.

Graft moved between them, frowning deeply. "I hear it now."

"What?" Finnigan glanced around, but nothing had changed, not a single thing. Everything in the prairie remained the same.

"Shut up!" Moray hissed. "Listen!"

Finnigan clamped his jaw shut and strained to hear anything besides his own breathing.

"It's gone." Moray's shoulders sagged in defeat. The sun shone down in their faces. Between exhaustion—heat exhaustion and weariness from hours of nonstop moving—and lack of water, Finnigan's body begged him to stop and be still. Just for a minute.

The others must've had the same idea because they stood there under the sun, heads back, eyes closed. Finnigan didn't bother opening his eyes again. Just for a second. No monster could kill him in a split moment.

"Brothers..." Graft mumbled.

No answer.

"We should move. I hear it."

"I don't hear anything now," Moray said with a groan.

Finnigan rubbed his eyes. "We should take a break, Moray. Rest a little. We'll die without water and we'll die faster if we don't rest." Anger peeked through his exhaustion. Why had he followed Moray all this way? He should've argued they rest sooner. Sweat trickled down his neck and he wiped at it, scowling.

"I hear it coming closer." Graft's voice grew urgent. He gasped, shaking Finnigan's shoulders. "Wake up!"

"I'm awake!" Finnigan stepped sideways. "We must rest. We'll die from heat exhaustion."

"It isn't that hot," Moray said. "It's a prairie, not a desert."

"Snap out of it!" Graft begged. He shook Finnigan's arm again.

Finnigan opened his eyes and glared at Graft, but his anger dwindled. Graft's eyes grew wide with fright.

"I don't hear anything, Graft. What's wrong with you?" Finnigan looked up again. His chest tightened at Graft's fear. He'd not seen him so upset since... well, never.

"It is tricking us!" Graft whispered, voice trembling, eyes heavy with pure panic. He jerked Moray by his shoulders. "We must move!"

Moray shoved him off weakly. "Oh, ease off, Graft." He blinked as if he had been asleep and didn't understand what they'd been arguing over.

Something was wrong.

"W-we should move." Finnigan took a step. Another. His body moved like it weighed more than iron. His eyes drooped, and his mind grew foggier by the second.

A soft, dull whir. Almost like a buzzing bee. Far away at first, but he'd heard it.

"Do you—" Graft grabbed his arm.

"I hear it!" Finnigan couldn't see anything different around them. "Whatever it is, it must be a monster."

Moray shoved past them. "Keep moving. We'll kill it when we see it."

Finnigan couldn't shake the feeling that if Graft hadn't dragged them from that strange moment, they wouldn't be moving now. A trance... or just exhaustion? He stuck close to Graft's side as they moved onward, but his legs dragged through the grass.

"Moray..."

He didn't respond.

"Moray, something is wrong. Something..."

"Just walk!"

"I thought we were supposed to see the spirits in Golgotha!" Finnigan groaned. "There is nothing but monsters of flesh and bone, and now this? Where are the demons? Why can we see nothing?"

Whirrr.

Whirrrr.

Finnigan stopped in his tracks, glancing at Graft with a gulp. "Do you hear that?" they asked in unison.

"It's getting closer." Moray lifted his head to the sky again. "Sounds like it's coming from above."

The sound stopped for a few seconds, then came again, louder this time, clearer. A shadow trickled over them as something blocked the sun, but only for a moment. By then it was too late.

A large black creature dove out of the sky, plummeting toward them at an ungodly speed. Finnigan lifted both hands and forced bolts of blue energy toward the monstrosity. The creature rolled and missed the attack.

Moray jumped in front of Finnigan, snarling something, blackness surrounding his arms. He shot it at the monster that came closer. The monster skimmed over it.

"Move!" Graft shouted. He shoved Finnigan out of the way, and Moray ducked and rolled.

Two giant webbed wings sprang out of the creature's body. It stopped just above their heads, a gust of wind knocking them over. Moray shot another ball of blackness at the creature. It turned its malformed black head to face them, but it had no eyes. Curved white horns protruded from its bumpy head. For a split moment, it acted as if it saw Moray, but it shot back up into the sky.

Finnigan gasped for breath, summoning more energy. "What is that?"

"No idea, but it's hungry." Moray moved closer to his brothers, chest heaving. He always stayed calm under pressure, but the flicker in his eyes unnerved Finnigan.

The creature flew high into the pale sky. Moray and Finnigan both prepared themselves for another attack, or whatever the strange creature might do next. Graft gripped his makeshift club, standing tall beside his brothers, though Finnigan didn't think his weapon stood much of a chance.

Finnigan sucked in a breath as the creature dove toward them again. It moved with the agility and speed of a hawk. Moray sent his magic at it in one giant burst—but once again, the monster sped downward and around it. Finnigan lifted his hands. Blue energy burned through his veins and flooded the sky. The creature swerved one last time, unscathed.

The beast spread its great wings only a few feet above their heads. The gust of air stunned them, though Moray took his shot, sending another blast of black energy toward the monster's exposed smooth underbelly. The energy shot through its rotund belly. Opening its mouth wide, it revealed two large yellow fangs aimed right at Moray's head.

"Moray!" Energy burned from Finnigan's hands toward the creature's head.

A flash of brown. Moray fell sideways, pushed over by Graft before the monster could get his target. Dark red venom burst from the monster's fangs, splattering onto Graft's face. As soon as the monster unleashed the venom, it recoiled. The energy from Finnigan hit it at the same moment. It fell backward, flesh burning from Moray's magic, and the blast from Finnigan sending it prostrate.

Finnigan grabbed Graft as his brother fell face forward. His heavy weight pulled Finnigan down, but Moray helped him lower Graft onto the ground.

"Graft!" Finnigan held Graft tightly, heart twisting in horror as the venom vanished. Burn marks were the only signs left that showed the venom had touched him, as if it had seeped into Graft's skin in mere nanoseconds. The stench of burnt flesh filled Finnigan's nostrils, but he gripped his brother close to his body. A scream tore from Graft's throat. His body jerked and shook.

Moray faced the monster that lay twitching in the prairie grasses. He brought both arms up, aimed them at the writhing monster, and screamed a chant. A giant orb of darkness flew from his body and into the monster. Its head exploded, black blood splattering the prairie and Moray's clothes.

Finnigan held Graft, shaking hard. "M-Moray!" He tried healing Graft but nothing happened. He held Graft by either side of his face, focusing all of his Gift, all of his spirit, on removing the burns, but nothing changed. Graft sobbed in agony, large shoulders trembling with each one.

Moray dropped beside them, yanking Graft up into his arms, eyes wide with pure horror. "Graft, breathe. You'll be fine. Heal him, Finn!"

"I-I can't!" Finnigan choked out. He tried again, harder this time, sweat trickling down his flushed cheeks. The venom would not leave Graft's body. "It isn't working!"

Graft screamed, jerking against Moray. "Stop... stop, please..."

Finnigan pulled his hands away. "Just hold on!" *Elohai, show me how to save him! Stop the venom from going through his body.*

Moray cupped Graft's face gently, steadying him against himself. "You'll be fine. I'm going to carry you. We need to get moving." He spoke without hesitation, but Graft shook his head, gasping for air.

"No." Graft groaned. "No!"

"I am not leaving you in this hell," Moray whispered. "I will carry you till we get home."

"I'm *going* home!" Graft's legs jerked hard against the dirt. He grabbed Moray with one hand, his hand clutching at Moray's tunic, the veins in his arm swelling. "I..." He yelled in pain, then choked out, "Let me go."

"No." Moray tried standing up with him, but Graft's body seized and Finnigan helped hold him down. "No! Get up, Graft. We have to keep moving." Moray's voice rose with rage. "Get up!"

Tears ran down Graft's face, tracing the fresh burn marks. The veins in his neck bulged and sweat broke out on his forehead. Finnigan had never seen such a terrifying sight. And he could not save him.

"All pain must end..." Graft held on to Moray tightly, shaking uncontrollably. "L-let me go."

Finnigan reached and rested a hand on Graft's head. "You'll be just fine, Graft. Just fine. Just hold on." There had to be something they could do. Graft was big, strong, faithful. He couldn't leave them. They needed him.

But there was nothing to be done.

"All hearts... will be healed..." Graft breathed, but every breath sounded like rock dragging against rock. Tears streaked his cheeks. Moray held him against his chest, face taut with rage. "I love you both." A weak smile tugged on Graft's lips.

All hearts would be healed. Graft feared not even death. He would see his family again. One day, he'd see them. It was enough to comfort him. His body jerked, seized, and Finnigan held on to his free hand.

Finnigan kissed it again and again, but his brother's eyes rolled into the back of his head. Finnigan didn't let go of his hand, as if he could somehow tether him to the world, as if he could force him to hold on to life. Graft might have been ready to go home, but Finnigan was not ready for him to leave. *I need him here. I need him.*

Graft did not moan or cry again. He didn't open his eyes, shaking against Moray as the minutes dragged by. Moray whispered softly to him. "We will see you very soon, Graft. Don't be afraid. Don't be afraid, brother."

Graft fell limp after Moray spoke.

Moray's whole body caved in and he pulled Graft against him, rocking him back and forth. He heaved with body-racking sobs but never made a sound. Finnigan leaned against him, weeping into the crook of his brother's neck. Reality and nightmares faded into nothing as their other brother died.

Nineteen

MORAY HELD HIS BROTHER'S corpse till no more tears came. What God took the life of a good man?

This was all his fault. He never should have tried entering Golgotha. Graft had died saving him.

No. I had reason to come, I had reason to want this realm. I was going to do good. I am not a bad man.

He had gotten his brother killed.

Finnigan sat beside him. He'd pulled away from Graft's body and held his head in his hands. Praying to the God that let His servant die a brutal death.

Moray laid Graft's body to rest on the prairie floor. He folded Graft's hands. He had already closed his eyes but couldn't look at Graft's burnt face again. He would never hear his voice again, hear him laugh, tease him about stupid things, tell him he'd been so much more than a servant. Had he said it enough? Did Graft know he loved him as much as he loved Finnigan?

Moray stopped himself and pushed all emotion aside. He had to compartmentalize. Move on. Survive. He would handle Graft's death later, but right now he had to find a way out of here. Refusing to look at the corpse again, he nudged Finnigan's shoulder. "Let's move."

Finnigan didn't budge an inch. "No."

"No?"

"We... we have to bury him... or something."

"Do you have a shovel?" Moray asked sharply. "Neither of us can manipulate earth. We cannot bury him." The words tasted like acid in his mouth but they were true. "He saved us. We can honor him by doing good to that sacrifice. Let's move."

Finnigan sat there on the ground, his tear-soaked face smudged with dirt and sweat. "I can't move my legs, Moray," he said, voice hoarse.

"Get up!" Moray refused to extend pity or patience when Finnigan was wasting their only chance to survive. That was one of the basics of war—those that were in perpetual state of motion survived. It helped to have a plan, but sitting and crying when arrows were being shot at you didn't take much brain power either.

"I can't move!" Finnigan choked out, tears in his eyes. His broad shoulders were slumped in utter exhaustion. It'd never been like Finnigan to admit defeat.

"Trying to heal Graft drained you, didn't it?" Moray's rage subsided. The healing had not worked, but Finnigan had not stopped trying. "It could have killed you." Moray blinked. "Finnigan, it could have—"

"But it didn't," Finnigan mumbled.

"I am not so sure!" Moray knelt and studied his brother closely. Finnigan's skin was pale as a bleached bone, his eyes almost shut no matter how hard he struggled to keep them open, and he couldn't hold himself up. Moray held him tightly. "I'll carry you. Are you ready?"

"No. Don't move me." Finnigan grabbed his arm but his grip was weak. Moray shoved his hand off. "Y-you need to rest too." Finnigan's eyes closed and he slumped forward, body giving out like a falling tree. Moray caught him and held him, but his own eyelids drooped.

Moray fell backward, groaning in exertion as he pushed Finnigan into the dirt. Sweat trickled down his forehead. Sleep. Sleep would fix the exhaustion clawing at his bones.

"I can save you, Moray."

A voice. Soft, yet firm. Inviting, yet unfamiliar.

Moray lifted his throbbing head, face mingled with salt from sweat and tears. He blinked in the blinding sun. A man stood nearby in a white tunic, dark pants, and sandals, with a cloak over his broad shoulders. He held a tall black staff in one hand, the top of the staff shaped like a serpent's head. He smiled at Moray kindly, his weathered face clean-shaven. "I can save you, Moray. This land has taken one brother. It need not take another."

A follower of the magics, judging by his staff. Only the ancient teachers had borne such precious artifacts. Many of them had been lost, Sadon had said.

Moray's throat went dry as he fumbled for words. "Who are you?"

"A blessed believer in our master, Abaddon." The man smiled, dark eyes kind. "I can save you and your brother.

You must only fulfill the wishes of our master. He alone knows what is best for us. You have run from his will. He is a forgiving father—you may turn back."

Kill Ama. Abaddon's instructions plagued Moray's mind again. He straightened, muscles screaming in pain, taking a shaky breath. "You... you speak of his instruction to kill my betrothed?" His voice caught with rage. "Just how am I supposed to kill her now?"

The man chuckled. He stood a few feet away, not budging, as still as if he were part of the illusionary world around them. "It will be clear to you soon. I am your last hope. Kill the rat who despises your master before it is too late. I will then save you and your brother."

Moray set his jaw, indignation burning in his chest. "If I don't kill her?" It wasn't like he could—she was not here in Golgotha.

"Then I will be forbidden to save you, and you will die here." The man's response was simple.

"I am a follower of Abaddon. I am gifted in his magic!" Moray said with a snarl. "I can save us, without your help."

"You have disobeyed his will, and only sorrow shall follow you for your consequences." The man studied him for a long moment, a thin smile tugging his lips. "You are a strong man, Moray. You and I could do great things for these realms, but your loyalty to Abaddon must be tested to ensure you are trustworthy. You understand this."

"I have done nothing but please my father." Moray clenched his fists. This man was no one to accuse him of being a childish fool. He had disobeyed once—only once.

And Abaddon hadn't even given him a reason to destroy Ama.

"Make the wise decision, Moray, and the future we can create together will be endless. The people who have doubted you will be ants under your feet. But only if you follow the ways of our master. Only if you follow me."

Then he was gone.

Moray growled under his breath, falling against his brother. He would make Abaddon proud—and he needed no one. Sadon had failed him already. He did not need help from some illusion wizard with the nerve to tell him what to do. He only needed to follow Abaddon. But he wouldn't kill the girl.

He closed his eyes, and the world fell to black.

THEY HAD LEFT THE red forest behind over six hours ago, and Ama almost missed it. She wouldn't miss the rotwulves, though. There had not been many, but they'd been strange creatures, all acting as if they had minutes of life left and needed flesh to devour or else.

They'd run into other creatures in the forests, creatures like big cougars but with stripes and six legs. When Gunnar shed their blood, it had been as orange as a sunset sky.

Ama was grateful to leave the forest and its monsters behind, but she couldn't shake the feeling that the prairie ahead of them was worse. Courage seemed to sense it, too, whimpering against Ama's neck.

The trees, rocks, and grasses all stood peaceful against the brilliant horizon. The sun burned bright, and she wiped at her brow as sweat trickled from her temples.

"Gunnar?"

He grunted in his usual caveman manner.

She'd had conversations with rocks and babies that were more interactive. "Something feels wrong."

"I do not lead expeditions based on a woman's gut feelings."

"Maybe that's why you have so many scars."

"What was that?"

"Look around you. This prairie isn't right."

"Seems right to me." Gunnar kept walking through the grass and dirt. "Looks just like the prairie in Mazzabah, where the Crows live."

"It feels wrong!" Ama's gut nagged like a thousand claws were prodding, begging her to stop, pleading for her to be wise. She couldn't turn around. Yet, how could she move forward in this shadow of death? The sun was shining so brightly, and it all looked perfect.

"We keep moving. If it helps, pray to your God."

Gunnar spoke with disdain, but Ama sucked in a deep breath. She prayed long and hard. Her feet ached. After the hours of walking in the sun, her skin was growing tender and sore. Her eyes ached and she fought off weariness.

She wiped at her forehead again. Why were her hands so shaky? No, her legs were what was shaking. Ama watched the grass—none of it moved. Nothing moved except her and Gunnar.

Not even the sun moved.

Ama's head swam. Everything was supposed to move. Every forest had a steady throb of life: small creatures scuttling through the grass, the sun rising and falling, the breeze catching the trees. Every forest had *life*. This prairie land stood silent, almost fake, like a painter had etched it onto the side of a canvas and tossed Gunnar and Ama into the center of it.

Ama gasped. "It's... not real." *Creator, is this one of the illusions the legends spoke of?*

Gunnar walked on. One pace, two paces, three, and stopped in his tracks. "Something's in the air."

"Are you even listening to me—"

"Something's hunting us from the sky. Something's up there."

Ama glanced up, but the sun blinded her. "Huh?"

"You are right. The sun isn't real. It isn't the same as the one over the forest with the rotwulves." He paused. "I don't think this place is real."

Ama gulped. "Should I be more shocked by our predicament or you admitting I was right?"

"Follow me and stay close. Anything can happen out here." Gunnar continued walking, jaw tight. "If I say run, you run, no questions asked or blades drawn."

Ama glanced down at the colored dagger she'd already used more than once. Her arms were already aching from the fighting she'd done. "Don't go play hero again."

"Oh, I'm not playing hero. When we get out of here, your prince Finny is giving me my own bloody island." Gunnar smirked down at her before focusing intently on the task of staying alive when the whole realm wanted their blood.

Twenty

MORAY SAT IN A pit of vipers. They ran across his bare body and twirled around his limbs, their scales running over his flesh and soothing the aches deep within his weary muscles.

He saw the figure nearby, moaning softly as he knelt. "Father—"

"You will become king of Golgotha and Mazzabah. You will do so without the Light," Abaddon said, voice like ice.

"Of course, Father. What shall you have me do?" Moray relaxed as a thick snake pushed about his shoulders.

"This land belongs to me as Mazzabah does—but be cautious. Do not be fooled by the Light." His master's dark eyes burned into him.

"Of course." Moray bowed low.

"You have felt the oppression of the Darkness, and it has welcomed you, has it not?"

"Aye, it has."

"You have seen nothing of what the Light is capable of here. Do not be so foolish to think I have completely dominated this land, nor have you."

Those words pounded through Moray's being. "I will gain control."

"Obey me, or you shall die."

"What shall you have me do but rule?"

"Obey me," the voice repeated.

Kill Ama.

Follow me.

Rule the realms.

The dream cut out.

"DO YOU HEAR THAT?" Finnigan moaned, rolling over onto his side.

Ow.

Dirt…

Finnigan shot upright, blood rushing in his head. He spat out sand from his mouth and groaned, skin protesting being moved so abruptly. He glanced down at his arms, burned red in the sun. He was grateful he was mostly clothed, since it had been cold in Mazzabah, but the clothes also made him sweat. He felt like a wet fish in a dry, dusty boat.

The sound came again. Soft and steady, like something walking in the distance.

"Moray!" Finnigan snarled. He winced as he hit Moray's shoulders. His older brother slept beside him, face covered by his arms. "Do you hear that?"

"Silence?" Moray didn't stir.

"Something's there!"

As if realizing he was in the dirt under the pounding sun, Moray pushed himself up with a pained growl. "What?"

Finnigan strained to listen, breath catching. "V-voices! I hear voices!"

"Don't look so happy about that. We're in Golgotha. Those voices could be anything. It could be a hallucination. We've no idea how long we slept in this sun without water or food. Maybe it's been days." Moray's face tightened, and his brow furrowed. Hearing it all said aloud like that didn't exactly furnish hopes.

Finnigan got to his feet, swaying for a moment. "I'm gonna check it out." Drained from the fighting, walking, and healing, he shoved the exhaustion away. They'd be dead meat if they kept sleeping. He didn't want to think about how long they'd been asleep already. Underneath the never-moving sun, they'd die like shriveled raisins. Finnigan was too good-looking to shrivel up. Being ripped apart by a beast was more of a thunderous way to die, if he had the choice. He'd rather not die in general.

Still, he needed to know what was making that sound. The only creature they'd spotted in this illusionary world was the venom-spitting bat creature.

The steady sound continued, and Finnigan's eyes struggled. Everything blended into one—the trees, grass, and pale sky all smashed together into one unidentifiable image he couldn't make out. "Huh."

Moray sat up. "What do you see?"

Finnigan blinked, glancing back down. He could see Graft's body well enough. "Guess the sun is messing with my eyes. I can't see anything past three feet away," he said sheepishly, rubbing his eyes.

Moray stood up and looked across the fields, but he blinked. He swore softly. "I see two people."

"People?" Finnigan grabbed his arm. "Where?"

Moray gestured, but Finnigan's vision still blurred the landscape together. Finnigan groaned. "W-who is it? Who could be out here?"

Moray slowly pulled Finnigan back a step. "No clue. Might be survivors from sailor ships, like the legends said. Remember? The ships being cast here? But... I doubt they lasted this long." He inhaled, ducking behind some bushes with his brother. "Someone must have been sent in here behind us."

"We need to see who it is," Finnigan whispered, shoulders hunched. "Whomever it is, whatever is going on... we're dead men walking anyway." The words were true, as much as he hated them. Without water and food, they didn't have a chance of trudging much longer. The prairie didn't have any end in sight.

Moray met his gaze, sorrow and exhaustion heavy in his eyes, but a flicker of determination burned behind them. "All right." With all his might, he called out, "Hello!"

Finnigan struggled to see anything past the closest tree. "Well?"

"They're... coming toward us," Moray whispered. "I can't see their faces yet."

"Elohai, don't let this be a mistake," Finnigan prayed, hoping he wasn't too late.

"It's..." Moray froze. "It's a man. And Ama." The words fell off his tongue in a whisper. "This must be some hallucination. We're seeing things." He glanced up at the sky, but no bat-monster attacked.

Finnigan didn't feel any nagging in his gut, but he could just be in shock or hysteria. "A-Ama..." He shook his head and got up. He started running in the general direction Moray had pointed. He wouldn't die out here not taking this risk of seeing Ama again.

"Finn!" Ama's voice, a scream of surprise and joy. "Finnigan! Is it you?"

He ran weakly, staggering. His vision cleared enough so that he didn't make a head-dive into any rocks. "Ama!" Burning joy traveled through his belly into his chest. *It's real. She's real!*

He reached her, wrapping his arms around her with the little strength he had left, burying his burnt face against her shoulder. Her small frame sank against him.

"You're alive!" Ama squeezed him tightly. "Barric said... he said you were all dead!" The horror in her voice made Finnigan's heart shatter.

"Moray and I are alive." Finnigan held her firmly against his chest, arms trembling. "I-I thought you were with Lord Barric. He... he did this. He did all of this."

Ama didn't pull away. "Queen Macha—" She sobbed. "I'm sorry, Finnigan. I'm so sorry."

He stroked her back. He didn't dare tell her that their father was dead, too, and he didn't want her to see Graft's body. He didn't think she was weak enough to give up after seeing someone lost to Golgotha—but he did not want to see her weep again. "It's all right, Ama. We will get home. We will set everything right."

The big, gruff man stepped closer, eyeing Finnigan head to toe, his expression tight. "How long have you two been out here?" He lifted his head as Moray stepped over slowly.

"Who are you?" Moray snapped.

"I'm the merc who saved your princess." The man smirked at him.

Finnigan blinked, anger rising. "Who hired you? Did you—"

"Etu hired me." The man didn't bat an eyelash at Finnigan's disgust. "Now that we're all alive, we'd best get out of here." He rubbed a hand through his shaggy hair, sweat trickling down his neck.

Moray and Finnigan exchanged a cross glance of utter distrust. This person could be working with Barric or anyone, for that matter. Mercenaries were never loyal.

"Gunnar helped me," Ama said quietly. "We can trust him."

"How long have you been in this prairie?" Gunnar asked.

Moray hesitated. "We walked for about a day."

Gunnar grunted. "Did you ladies pass out in the sun?"

Ama stepped away from Finnigan, pulling a waterskin from her pouch. She offered it over, and he fought hard not to down it all in one gulp. The water brought him to his senses a little, but mostly his body craved more. He took a few sips and passed it to Moray, who did the same. Finnigan studied Ama over, eyes aching from the heat. A small furry creature was draped around her shoulders, watching him with big eyes.

"Ack!" Finnigan stepped back. "What—"

"This is Courage." Ama smirked, stroking the little fuzzy head. "She's a friend."

"A friend," Finnigan repeated.

"Every creature must be viewed as the enemy here." Moray stepped closer and grabbed Ama's arm. "What were you thinking?"

As soon as he touched Ama, the white creature opened its mouth wide, revealing sharp fangs and tiny teeth. Moray froze.

Ama straightened and calmly pulled free. "Courage senses emotions. I don't know why, but she is very protective of me. If she decides to scream, she somehow chooses who hears it. She's killed four-eyed wolves with her gift, so be careful."

"About busted my bloody eardrums out too." Gunnar crossed his arms over his big chest. "Can we discuss something more important than the rat?"

Finnigan scowled. A part of him wanted to take a moment to process all he had lost. But he had to move forward and save Ama and his people. "We don't know much more than you do."

"Sure you do." Gunnar eyed Moray. "Listen, I ain't cheap. Etu hired me for one job. I didn't sign up to gallivant across the second realm of hell and bones with a bunch of royals. When we return to Mazzabah, I expect my own island, at the very least."

"Cheap?" Finnigan repeated in disdain. He stepped closer, fists clenching as he snarled, "We're all in hell together and you expect us to owe you?"

Ama touched Finnigan's arm. "Please. We cannot argue now. We need to stop and try to understand what all has happened... from the beginning."

MORAY COULDN'T TELL THEM everything he knew, nor could he hide from the truth any longer. Not all of the truth anyway. Each of them recanted their part of the story. Moray and Finnigan had held their father as he'd breathed his last. Ama had been present when Queen Macha had died, then she'd been imprisoned until Gunnar had saved her from Barric's clutches. Gunnar had been hired shortly after news reached the outside of the deaths—he hinted that Etu had spies within the castle walls—and he'd saved Ama. They'd gotten to the underground when a wizard got rid of them.

It was then that all eyes turned to Moray. Thus far, he hadn't said a word about his magic or his training.

"You worked with that wizard who sent us all here. *He* sent us, didn't he?" Finnigan's expression grew hard, unreadable, like their father's used to when they'd gotten into trouble. Strange how such little details now held so much meaning.

Moray sighed. "Yes."

"And?" Ama demanded.

"His name is Sadon." Those who practiced black magic gave up their true names when they climbed the ranks. Moray hadn't, of course, nor had he insisted on knowing Sadon's real name. "We've worked together for over a year now."

It had been at least two years, if not more. Sadon had been the one to teach Moray to use the black magic, summon the energy with ease, chant the spells and incantations so flawlessly, and be in control at all times.

"What were you doing?" Finnigan asked coolly.

"I was training." Moray stretched his sore arm muscles.

"You wanted Golgotha as your own, didn't you? You were waiting for the dragon to hatch so you could have it on your side when you broke all hell loose." Finnigan's voice dropped, his eyes narrowing. His body shifted, and he lunged for Moray, snarling. "You—"

Gunnar jumped between them, shoving Finnigan back hard. Finnigan staggered and Ama grabbed his arm.

"Stop!" she shouted.

Finnigan struggled past Gunnar, face red with rage. Moray braced himself. "Listen, Finnigan. It is not what it seems. I didn't have selfish intentions!"

He wanted the glory, power, skills. He was not selfish if those things made him stronger. Only strong kings could lead unstoppable empires. Abaddon had told him he had one chance. He could not waste it, even if he didn't know what Abaddon wanted of him yet. Not anymore. Not entirely.

"Liar!" Finnigan snapped.

"I wanted to enter Golgotha but not to unleash hell!" Moray snapped back. "I wanted to better Mazzabah. I would not have started something I could not handle."

"You are a man!" Finnigan screamed at him. "You were never in control. No one can control the realms or the demons." He shoved Gunnar off and grabbed Moray by his shirt collar, shaking him. "You bloody fool!"

Moray didn't push him off. All of his grand plans and holy intentions had gotten their brother killed. He deserved Finnigan's rage. He deserved death. "I am sorry," he said.

Ama watched, eyes wide, whispering, "Creator, please forgive us."

"Oh, quit your praying!" Gunnar growled. "Elohai has abandoned us here. No going back now."

Finnigan released his iron-like grip on his brother. Moray lowered his eyes. He held no shame for his intentions, but the guilt from killing Graft suffocated him. His master had punished him. Graft was the one who took that punishment, even though he shouldn't have. If Moray had obeyed about killing Ama, perhaps all would've been well.

He licked his lips. Was it too late to do as his master bid? He said so himself, didn't he? But he spoke as if not even the Darkness could be trusted.

But the man, Abaddon's servant... Through that wizard, was Abaddon offering redemption?

"We'd best get moving," Gunnar muttered. "We have more to talk about, and the sun isn't setting anytime soon."

Twenty-One

LIFE WAS NOTHING BUT a web of lies. Every lie had just enough truth to make it strong enough to hold its place in the form. Every reality had another side. Sadon's passion lay in understanding both worlds. He lived among the reality people knew yet yearned for the unseen reality that was forbidden. For normal humans, such a calling would drive them mad, but not Sadon. The dreams of serpents and chants and murders he entertained at night did not drive him to delusion. They drove him to perfection.

His perfected plan wasn't the plan he shared with Moray.

Most of it had been the truth. Sadon hadn't put years of training and black magic wisdom into the prince for naught. He also didn't see Moray as fit to be king of their master's empire. Sadon was far closer to Abaddon than Moray was. Moray had failed to obey his master's warnings about Ama's dreams, and they had both paid for it.

Sadon tossed a few sliced carrots into his pot of boiling stew that sat over the fire. His reclusive cabin offered all he needed—safety, supplies, and a sense of coziness. While he teleported most everywhere so no one could trail him and find where he lived, he didn't use spells for all things. Making something without any Darkness involved was a mundane but rewarding task that gave him solitude.

Sadon stirred the vegetables and broth together. He grabbed some thyme and pepper from one of many shelves in the kitchen, giving the stew a healthy sprinkle of both. He stirred it again, tasted it, and smirked. "Perfect."

He cleaned up the messy kitchen, long white hair hanging around his bare shoulders. Thick scars covered his body, scars he was proud of. His chest and stomach were tattooed with a black marking—he was chosen. Elect. Powerful.

He would lead the Legion in the final war over the realms. Lord Barric was far more his equal than Moray had been. Abaddon would unleash Golgotha over Mazzabah and have complete control, conquering the realms Elohai had created for His glory. It was not the plan Moray knew, but it was the plan Sadon would die for.

He would make his master proud.

Tap, tap.

Sadon froze in the center of his kitchen. He scowled as he glanced around at the cabin, which was overflowing with thick plants, baskets of bones, carved furniture, flaming candles, and glowing lanterns. No one knew where he lived. He was miles and miles away from the kingdom. The clans hadn't even found him before.

And no one had ever knocked on his door.

Shafiq could not have possibly found him. Satisfied he would be able to handle whatever lay behind the door, Sadon tossed on a tunic and opened it.

A boy stood in the dirt, thin as a rail, his dark blond hair covering his eyes. He wore only pants, his bare torso littered with familiar scars—and the same mark Sadon had. The black ink had been etched into the boy's pale skin the same way it had in Sadon all those years ago.

Sadon grabbed the boy's scrawny shoulder, snatching him into the cabin. "Who are you?" he demanded. Shafiq was trying to find him and kill him, once and for all.

The boy trembled. "O-Oliver."

Sadon held him tightly, but the boy didn't fight back or lift his head. "Who sent you here?"

"N-no one—"

Sadon grabbed the boy's chin and stared into his eyes—white as snow. He was blind. Why would Shafiq train a cripple? "Tell me the truth. How did a blind boy stumble across my door if no one sent him here?"

"E-Elohai led me here." The boy trembled. "He... the man... I cannot say his name... I... I ran... Please do not send me back!"

Sadon considered the child's words for a long moment. "You are lying. You have come to kill me." He dragged the boy outside, pulling him toward the cellar. "Shafiq will have to come kill me himself. I will not harm a child unless my master bids me to."

He'd heard nothing of killing this boy. Years ago, that had been Sadon's weakness. He wouldn't hurt women or children, and for this reason, he had failed often.

Not anymore. He would harm whomever he had to in order to do his Father's will.

Oliver screamed and cried. "N-no! He'll come for me. Let me go!" He fought hard but didn't use any black magic. Sadon frowned, pushing the cellar open. In a swift motion, he tossed the blind boy into the dark hole.

"I will keep you safe. But you must obey me," Sadon called in a stern voice. He slammed the cellar door shut, the boy's sobs ringing in his ears.

You have chosen the perfect time to try and kill me, Shafiq. I shall show you how my master prefers me over you.

Twenty-Two

THE SUN NEVER SANK. Sweat trickled down Ama's temples, and her legs burned from exhaustion. Her body yearned for rest, a few more hours of sleep, but she reined those thoughts in. Golgotha was a place of turmoil. Not every battle would be against flesh and blood. She had to fight the invisible too.

Ama finally voiced her questions as they walked on. "Legend said that the demons here were visible to the eye. We're being attacked right now and we see nothing, just like in Mazzabah." She'd found slight relief from not seeing any spiritual manifestation thus far. The monsters didn't scare her. She could gouge their eyes out, slit their throats, and move on. Demons were cast out only by Creator's mercy.

"Perhaps, since this is an illusion, they have no need to show themselves," Moray suggested.

"I've felt them before in the forest, but they've not revealed themselves," Finnigan said. "The legends all swore that you could see a demon, a whole group of 'em, the moment upon entering the second realm."

"Demons can't be every place at once," Ama said quietly. "Can they?"

Moray sighed. "Not exactly."

"Then how can so many people be afraid if there is only one demon of fear?" Gunnar piped up coldly. "Isn't that what you people believe?"

"There can be more than one demon of fear, and more than one demon of any other manifestation," Moray scoffed. "But one specific spirit cannot be in two places at once."

"Only Elohai can be omnipresent," Finnigan agreed. "Which leads us to a problem. If the demons aren't scattered all over Golgotha like they're supposed to, where are they?"

Ama rubbed her arms as they walked, glancing at Moray. He seemed to know more about Golgotha than they did, or at least he'd studied more than they had. Creator only knew how much of the legends and the books were true.

Moray didn't look back at them as he walked alongside Gunnar. "Perhaps they are all in another place."

"Why?" Ama mustered.

"Could be preparing for something," Finnigan pointed out. "Moray, did... did they know your plan?"

Moray suppressed a laugh. "You think I told all the demons of Golgotha I was coming with gifts?"

"Don't—" Finnigan started to snap, but Moray cut him off.

"I have not personally contacted anything within Golgotha. Sadon and I spoke with our master. Sadon never mentioned if the spirits here were expecting us—Master probably alerted them, but not everything was my doing." Moray's voice dropped.

Ama didn't understand why Moray held so much anger within: His parents had been loving, they had raised him the same as Finnigan, and Finnigan had chosen the Light. What made Moray choose the Dark? How could he believe Abaddon loved him?

Her stomach churned, but she prayed through her doubts. The man in her dream... Who was he? He was one of Abaddon's, she knew that for certain. But who was he?

And what if the spirits that lurked here passed the rift and entered Mazzabah?

"Even if the demons find us, wherever they are, whatever they are doing, Creator will help us somehow."

THE PRAIRIE ENDED JUST as it began, like someone had cut the land's border and smashed the black forest on either side of the prairie. Finnigan blinked a few times. He was hallucinating again. There was no way they'd walked in circles. They stood still, staring at the forest, all at a complete loss for words.

Moray swore. "This can't be right. We're back where we started."

"Or," Gunnar mumbled, "we went straight through but the forest is just huge."

Finnigan gripped Ama's hand, hiding his own uneasiness. Ama and Gunnar had been in a red forest, similar to the black one, though they couldn't be sure where it had been. When they compared observations, the black forest was worse.

"It might be a pocket illusion," Moray muttered, voice firmer. "If it is an illusion, it can't exist alone. It would have to attach itself to a part of reality, something tangible. So we've... we've been in the black forest this whole time."

"We never saw any monsters. No rotting wolves, no tiger-beasts, just... just a bat creature once." Finnigan forced the words out carefully. They'd told Ama and Gunnar about Graft but hadn't allowed themselves any emotion doing so. Ama had cried a little but Finnigan had comforted her.

"Who knows why?" Moray shrugged. "Perhaps that bat thing was the king, so to speak, and no other animal cared to enter. Maybe the different ecosystem could kill them. I don't know!"

"Who made the illusion?" Gunnar watched the black forest. Nothing jumped out at them, nothing howled, nothing moved. The illusion remained around them, frozen in time as they stood at its border.

"A demon? The bat?" Finnigan sighed. "How can we know?"

Moray shook his head. "All that matters is we leave it behind. We need water. The ocean. At this rate, our best chance is to find a river and hope it leads us to the ocean."

"We go in?" Finnigan squeezed Ama's hand tightly. As tired and burnt as he was, he forced a courageous smile.

Without a word, they all stepped into the black forest. The branches fell behind them as if locking them in, once and for all.

THEY WALKED THROUGH THE black forest in a tight-knit line. Moray led them through the thick branches. Finnigan followed with Ama at his side, then Gunnar took the rear in case anything attacked from behind. The storyteller in Ama ran wild for a while, but she regretted it.

There could be killer birds. Big lions or bears. Hybrids of all types. Creatures with large claws, sharp teeth, lethal venom, anything. They'd faced ludicrous monsters thus far —what else could surprise them?

Ama's stomach twisted. She didn't want to know.

They walked in silence. If they talked, they'd probably bicker, and Ama didn't want to hear them argue or curse at each other. But she also couldn't stand the silence any longer.

Rubbing Courage's soft head, Ama spoke, her voice already sounding foreign. "This forest is heavy with spirits. We cannot see them."

Finnigan glanced at her. "It might be a mix of invisible spirits and those that are seen elsewhere. The sooner we get home to set this right, the better. Nothing about this place is good."

"Except Courage," Ama corrected.

"Except the rat." Finnigan mustered a smirk.

Gunnar spoke up sharply. "Anyone got answers as to why we were sent here? I get the whole 'send the ugly princes to their doom' idea, but me? What did I ever do to your precious wizard boy? He could've just tried killing me. That would've been fun."

"Would've saved us all the trouble," Moray mumbled.

"I saved your girl," Gunnar said easily.

"My name is Ama," she reminded Gunnar for the hundredth time.

Ama thought of Sadon's words before he'd cast her into Golgotha. He'd seen her dagger, said she'd cause trouble. Why did he think that? Why send her to the second realm just because of her dagger? It was a Gift from Creator—perhaps the wizard found fault in that.

"We're apparently paying you for doing such a morally correct thing," Finnigan said, voice cold. "Perhaps even a wizard was repulsed by your attitude."

Gunnar swore under his breath. "You disgusting little—"

"Perhaps it was a test," Ama interjected. "Moray, you knew the plan. Does this line up with anything?"

"You think this was my doing?" Moray snapped.

"No—"

"She was just asking a question, Moray." Finnigan nudged his brother's arm.

Moray relented but never looked back. "All I can think of is that if it's a test of sorts, I doubt it was Sadon's idea. He knows it was basically a death sentence. If Barric wanted us all dead, they would've gotten information from us and killed us. Sadon could visit me in my dreams, but he hasn't. He could see how we were if he wanted to."

Ama's stomach churned. She didn't comment on the dream fact. "Gunnar and me... He did not want us dead."

"Sadon didn't meet either of you or he would've." Finnigan eyed Gunnar with a frown, voice casual.

Gunnar glared daggers at Finnigan. "Maybe the wizard just wanted to get rid of us, didn't care if we lived or died."

"I suppose so," Moray said evenly. "And he definitely wanted us gone, just perhaps not dead."

Sadon had apologized to Ama and wished her luck. The wizard hadn't acted out of hatred or apathy. He'd wanted his plan, whatever it entailed, to work well but hadn't wanted her dead. Had he?

He'd sent them here, he was working with Lord Barric the murderer, and he was a wizard. Creator said to love those who hurt them... How could she love the magician who had sent her to her slow, painful death? She tried praying for the wizard. It wasn't much of one, but it would do for now.

"How's that supposed to work anyway?" Gunnar's voice jerked her from her prayers. "You just summon the ocean to send us back?" Sarcasm dripped from his gruff voice.

"Water helps me form a portal," Moray said, ignoring Gunnar's tone. "The more water, the stronger and bigger the portal. You don't think a warlock, well-practiced in the black magics, can summon us back to Mazzabah?"

Ama doubted Creator would truly allow them to free themselves by using something so wicked, but she held her tongue.

"Humph," Gunnar said with a chuckle. "Sounds like manure to me."

Moray pushed onward through the branches. "Do you have a better way out?"

"I think you're pulling our legs," Gunnar snapped, watching the woods alertly as they walked. Nothing jumped out to rip them to pieces. The trees grew narrower and further apart. Ama's chest tightened at Gunnar's words, but she focused on her steps across the leaves and needles.

"Because dragging us through hell on false hope is much easier than killing us all back when it started because it's hopeless." Moray laughed softly. "You're a joy at festivals, aren't you?"

"You can't deny it." Gunnar shook his head, hair ruffling, jaw so tight a vein bulged in his neck. "This is hopeless, and you're lying to us about a way out."

"We're getting out of here, no matter what it takes or how it happens," Finnigan interjected sharply.

"You don't trust him either, pretty boy! Don't pretend you do," Gunnar shot back.

"I don't see *you* finding a way out," Moray said with a snarl, but he hadn't stopped walking. "I have not dedicated years of my life to a magic that wouldn't be capable of such a crucial task."

Ama's heart pounded in her chest. Moray couldn't be trusted, but Creator would get them out. Before she could speak, Gunnar hissed, "I didn't see you stopping this to start with, your royal pain in the rear end! What fool thinks they could take on Golgotha? You're not a god. It's your fault we're all here—you expect us to follow you?"

Moray stopped in his tracks and whirled around, eyes flashing. His fists were clenched and he pushed past Finnigan.

Ama jumped out of the way, skin going cold. "Moray, stop—"

He reached toward Gunnar, but the mercenary punched him in the face. Moray stumbled back, swearing. Black magic grew around his palms. "You—"

Gunnar didn't back down, flashing a sharp smile. "Lay your hands on me and I'll cut them off, wizard boy. Use your words like a man."

"That's rich, coming from a killer!"

"Keep pushing and I'll show you what else I can do," Gunnar said. His face was set in a calm, almost waiting, grimace.

Look around, a voice that Ama recognized as Creator's whispered in her mind.

She gulped hard, palms sweaty as she obeyed. Her ears rang as the men argued.

Look.

The narrow brown trees reached high for the sky, disappearing before she saw the ends of them. These trees weren't red and weren't thick, and their bark was rougher, almost flaky.

A small breeze ruffled the branches, making them sway slightly. The narrow, bare branches creaked and moaned as they rubbed against each other.

Ama froze. There was no wind. She felt her hair, which clung to her head with sweat. Why were the trees moving, then?

She glanced back at the men, their angry voices jumbled. Finnigan pushed himself between Gunnar and Moray. "Fighting each other will get us nowhere," he said.

"Don't you feel that?" Ama whispered. "Don't you hear that voice?"

"What?" Moray wiped his bloodied nose.

"S-something is in the woods." Ama inched closer to the trees.

Gunnar unsheathed his long blades, expression growing hungry as he eyed their surroundings. "Demons or flesh?"

"I don't know." Ama gestured to the trees. "Look! They're moving. They shouldn't be moving! There's no—"

She never finished her warning. Something hard and long wrapped around her left ankle, biting deep into her flesh and bone. Ama screamed and struggled, then her feet were yanked off the ground.

"Ama!" Finnigan lunged, but his hand missed hers.

The ground and trees whirled up as Ama was yanked into the air. She screamed again, but her body didn't know where to move or what to do, like a ship tossing at sea. Her cry lingered in the thick air.

The next moment, she hung upside down, feet away from the open mouth of a tree. Thousands of sharp teeth-like splinters filled the human-sized hole in the tree's thick body. Blood rushed in Ama's head as she tried moving her limbs. Nothing happened. She screamed hoarsely, seized by fear and pain. Voices and yells filled her ears—the men were at least fifty feet below her.

The tree wrapped its branches around her body. The rough bark bit into her clothes and skin. Ama screamed and fought, wrestling for her dagger, but the wood creature restrained her. "Finn!"

The monster pushed her toward its mouth full of thousands, maybe millions of blood-stained teeth. Besides the mouth, the moving tree looked like any other brown tree. The hole was covered with different colors from the previous victims' bodies—red, black, and gold. Red blood would soon stain it afresh.

On her shoulders, hanging on tight, Courage's mouth was wide open, but Ama couldn't hear her. The little fluff's furious cries did nothing to deter the tree.

A sob rose in Ama's throat. She didn't want to die.

A blast of blue energy filled her vision before blackness engulfed her.

Twenty-Three

MORAY HADN'T TELEPORTED ANOTHER body before. He'd teleported himself a few times, but teleporting three other people along with him proved challenging. He pushed Ama off himself, but his body barely cooperated.

Moray hadn't known where he was going either. He'd gotten a brief picture of water in his mind, a hopeful attempt to reach the ocean. Thick, squishy moss shifted under his weight. He could hardly move, his entire body trembling. *Bad idea. Shouldn't have done that. No teleporting people again.*

Then again, he was rebelling against Abaddon. How long would his magic even last?

"Where are we?" Gunnar's voice boomed. "Moray, what the mother-of-pearl did you do?"

Water and mud soaked the back of Moray's tunic and pants, oozing against his skin. Staring up, he didn't see much sky past thick, heavy trees and vines.

Swamp. He'd teleported them to a swamp. That wasn't enough water to start a rift.

He took a deep breath and his body heaved and jerked. Something small and heavy slinked across his left leg. All of his senses screamed at him to move, but his body only shook.

"Ama!" Finnigan said. "I've got you."

Their soft voices followed, but Moray couldn't move.

"Moray?" Finnigan's voice shook. "Moray, what's wrong?"

Moray opened his mouth to talk, but nothing came out. *Help.* His tongue wouldn't work. *Help me. Save me. Something's wrong.* His legs jerked and he clamped his eyes shut. *Contain yourself.*

He was dying.

"H-he's hurting," Ama said, voice soft with worry. She'd always been so kind. And Moray had treated her like a dog. At least she wasn't dead—Finnigan had probably healed her, good as new.

None of this should've happened. He didn't understand it. All of this hell because he left Ama alone? Killing her now would do nothing. He wouldn't do it.

Pains jolted through his body worse than before, like pricks of iron tracing his nerves. Moray screamed in pain, writhing in the mud. His torso felt like a horse had planted itself firmly on his rib cage, draining the air from his body.

"Moray!" Finnigan grabbed his shoulders. He didn't sound confused anymore, like he knew now what was wrong.

"What is that smell?" Gunnar asked, his voice a dark snarl, followed by his daggers being unsheathed.

"A demon." Finnigan's grip on Moray tightened. "Moray, wake up! You're the only one who can fight it."

Moray couldn't tell them he was awake. He couldn't do anything but shake as the pain flooded his body. Would his Father kill him for disobeying?

He'd said so himself. That dark-eyed servant warned Moray that this would happen if he didn't repent.

"Open your eyes!" Finnigan shook him, causing another throb of agony through Moray's exhausted body.

He just wanted sleep. He wanted to leave this place. He wanted to be king.

Everything he had fought for was lost. Destroyed because of a traitor wizard and a bloodthirsty king. He was better than both of them. He had a good heart. What had he gotten for it? Death.

Finnigan's voice rose. "Moray! Open your eyes and fight."

Something snapped in Moray's head, yanking him back to reality. Or hell, since this wasn't any reality meant for humans. He almost wished he hadn't opened his eyes.

A large black figure with folded gray wings on its narrow back covered Moray's chest. Yellow orbs for eyes with narrow slit pupils sat in its dark face. Claws the size of small daggers protruded from its fleshy black hands, and the sharp edges dug into Moray's wrists. It pushed down hard, whimpering and weeping. "Everything is lost. You never should've trusted them. You shouldn't trust any of them!"

Moray froze where he lay, breath catching in his throat. A demon. He'd seen demons before but never like this. He tried sitting up, but the demon's claws dug deeper into his flesh. "Just go to sleep! It will be over if you give up," it moaned.

Moray lifted his head. Golgotha was supposed to be manifested by visible demons, but judging by the expression on the others, they saw nothing. "I'm fine..." He couldn't get the demon off. He couldn't shake the words it said.

Finnigan held him firmly, sweat trickling from his forehead. "You're the only one who can cast it out, Moray. Please—"

The demon groaned. "There's no hope. What's the use?"

Moray's brain whirled. He didn't dare voice a word or else Finnigan would hear. If he could somehow make sure the others didn't know what he faced, he could confront it easier. He could even ignore the demon.

He could handle this. He wouldn't give in to this demon, Despondency.

Its eyes flickered and it licked its lips, tongue forked. It whispered, "I am your friend, Moray. I care for you. I can help."

Moray struggled and sat up. The long, thin snake that'd been trailing over his foot lay hacked in pieces—Gunnar must've done that. The demon wrapped its arms around his shoulders, hanging off his back. Moray didn't know if he was simply strong enough to fight it now that he saw it, or if the demon wasn't putting up much of a struggle. *Abaddon is allowing this so I may suffer. I won't.* He clamped his jaw shut in pain as he pushed himself to his feet.

Finnigan pulled him up, his cheeks green. "Moray, the demon—"

"We can all bloody smell it," Gunnar growled. "What are you up to, Moray? Is it a friend of yours?"

Moray raised his voice. "Shut up!"

The demon hung on his back, whimpering. Gunnar, Finnigan, and Ama stood before him with wide-eyed frowns.

Control. Moray was in control. "It is fine."

Gunnar gripped his blades, as if willing to cut off Moray's head. "Did you accept the demon?"

"You cannot do anything," Moray said, voice devoid of emotion. "Put your blades away."

"I don't take orders from you, pretty boy!"

"Moray," Finnigan interjected weakly, "you are the only one who can cast the demon out. Please, let Elohai help—"

"Elohai is of no use to us now." The demon weighed him down, but Moray tried to act normal. They couldn't see it or hear it. He could keep it together. He would win. He would escape Golgotha on his own, without the help of his Father or Elohai. After all he had done to serve his Father, this was what he got in return?

Moray didn't need him. He needed no one. He would get them home and reclaim his empire.

And he would take Golgotha. He wouldn't accept defeat.

His people deserved a stronger empire and a brilliant leader, and claiming Golgotha would show how powerful Moray was without any god aiding him.

Finnigan's eyes hardened. "Elohai is the only way out of here, Moray. Look at you! Look what happened when you used the black magic here." He grabbed Moray's left hand. "Don't pretend to not notice the blackness staining your hands—the magic has consequences here. It is killing you!"

Despondency whimpered, "Just give up. You've no reason to do all of this. No reason at all."

Moray pushed Finnigan off. "I am strong," he said sharply. "I will get us out of here. I've counted on too many people and gods before—enough! What have they done for me?"

"Elohai has saved you!"

"Elohai would condemn me to hell for what I have done." Moray laughed bitterly, shaking his head. He eyed Gunnar and Ama. Ama's eyes glinted with tears, the rat around her neck trying to nuzzle her cheek. Finnigan had already healed the wounds the tree beast had given her.

Gunnar held his daggers, murder burning in his expression.

Moray shook his head firmly. "Like it or not, I will get us home."

Because no one else would. A holy God would never save a sinner. Moray wouldn't ask Him to. He would save his brother, his betrothed, and maybe the merc, and then they would see who the real God was.

Before they could argue further, Moray turned and headed deeper into the thick swamp, the stench of something rotting filling his nose.

Twenty-Four

SADON COULDN'T HEAL. IT was never a skill he could master. Had he tried healing the blind orphan, he probably would have burned the child's eyes out of their sockets. He kept Oliver in the cellar, fed him three times a day, and allowed him a bucket and a pitcher of water when Sadon wasn't there to babysit him. The boy couldn't have been more than ten years old, but he acted older. Despite his initial fear and crying, the boy hadn't shed another tear since. He asked many questions but never spoke willingly of his past. All Sadon could get out of him was that Shafiq had trained him, the boy had escaped, and a caravan of performers had taken him against his will. When the caravan entered Buacach, Oliver had escaped. "And the Voice led me here," he'd added softly.

Sadon didn't believe Elohai had led Oliver to his cabin, but he didn't have time to argue theology. Between trying to learn Oliver's purpose and help King Barric lead their new empire, Sadon was stretched for time. He hardly had time to eat meals, and now he ate them with Oliver, never getting a moment's rest.

"Eat, Oliver," Sadon said sharply.

Oliver sat at the kitchen table, his short, thin frame hunched over. He picked at his soup. "Why do you care if I eat?"

"Obey me." Sadon handled enough whiny children in the kingdom's counsel and court. As annoying as Oliver was, if Shafiq had trained him, the boy was a danger to society and a threat to Sadon. Oliver hadn't tried to kill him yet, but with his unharnessed skills, he couldn't be tossed out to the wolves. The timing couldn't have been worse, but he had to keep the boy here.

"You hate me. Why not kill me?" Oliver's tangled blond hair covered his forehead.

Sadon scoffed. "I do not hate you. Hate requires passion."

"You've no passion?"

"Of course I have passion." Sadon scowled. Why was speaking to children so difficult? "But I've no cause to hate you."

"You say I'm a liar. If you think I will kill you, you should kill me first. Why haven't you?" Oliver asked, voice heavy with defeat. And fear. Sadon had heard that tone many times before. He usually craved it. He wanted the fear and submission of others. Hearing it from a boy he could kill in a thousand different ways brought him no satisfaction. All Sadon saw in Oliver was himself.

He could not stand it.

Sadon finished eating, deciding he had figured out a good way to word what he wanted to say. "You will not name

Shafiq. You fear him. If you are telling the truth, you somehow escaped him all alone, even though you are not fully trained. I know you are not ready. But if you are lying, Shafiq let you come here to fool me."

Oliver's chin trembled. Tears dripped from his white eyes. "I am not a liar."

Sadon knew a liar when he saw one—and Oliver's broken heart was real. But Sadon could not let the boy know he believed his tale. "Perhaps not, but it is unlikely you escaped Shafiq and the caravan on your own."

"Elohai helped me. H-He came to me in the cell with Shafiq. He was kind. Sh-Shafiq is not kind." Oliver's voice shook, but he forced the name out.

"I am not kind either, but I have helped you." Sadon studied the boy's pale face.

"Elohai told me you would."

Sadon's anger flickered as he snapped, "Elohai knows nothing of me."

"You serve Shafiq's master, but it does not mean Elohai does not love you too. He has a purpose for you. For each of us," Oliver choked out, putting down his spoon and bracing himself for a blow. Sadon didn't strike him.

"Let's be clear, boy," Sadon said firmly. "I saved you to ensure leverage against Shafiq when I need it. You will explain yourself and tell me what Shafiq wanted. If not now, soon. That is why you are alive." Oliver claimed to have no idea what Shafiq wanted or what he planned to do to Sadon or Mazzabah. But Sadon knew the old wizard would have dire intentions.

He was the only one who could stop Shafiq.

He would do whatever it took.

Sadon led Oliver by his thin shoulders and guided him outside to the cellar. Oliver wept softly for the first time in two months. Two months had gone by since Sadon had sent the four outcasts into Golgotha. Two months of watching Buacach rise in King Barric's lethal grip.

Two months of doing his master's bidding. This boy could untangle it all.

Sadon could handle it. He would ensure his empire was secure.

War does not stop for weeping children.

KING BARRIC WASN'T A foolish man and handled the kingdom of Buacach with great care. Though a little abrupt at times, he was a fine politician. After only two months, he had a sizable number of followers. The kingdom was unable to mourn for their beloved king and queen much. King Barric pushed too hard for much grieving to take place. He rallied the troops and told the peasants and civilians how he could do their kingdom much good.

The people, thus far, had no choice but to follow him. They had been taken off guard, as a mass of people leading a resistance would be futile against Barric's best-trained warriors in all of Mazzabah. Not only did he have strong men behind him, but he also had paid off a few court men too. King Connall had never known of the traitors in his midst. Not even Moray had known the weight of the situation. Sadon had done a marvelous job at letting all of the tricky pieces fall into place without having to lift a finger to help.

Now, it was almost harvest time. He could take it all when it was ripe. He would kill Barric eventually, when the man had taken control of the lands and destroyed those who resisted. One day, the man's fleshly desires would take him too far, and then Sadon would put him out of his miseries. The empire would be too beautiful to be adulterated by Barric.

Until that day, Sadon would work alongside the man and be his right hand, his counselor, and his personal assassin.

It wasn't so bad, besides Barric being ten times more annoying than Moray. Sadon didn't let his emotions get in the way of his empire, however. It just became gruesome, facing arrogant peasants itching for peace and tiresome nobles aching for control.

Sadon teleported to the king's royal chambers. He hated traveling the castle on foot. In general, he just preferred avoiding any chance of human interaction whatsoever. Teleporting was a luxurious skill. He stepped up to the grand throne, where Connall used to sit, and bowed low. Barric insisted on pleasantries—something Moray never had.

"Etu will be here soon," King Barric said.

Sadon convinced Barric that the clan alliance must remain, even with Moray and Ama out of the way. As far as the clan knew, Ama had killed herself after hearing the news of the prince's death. Sadon didn't know if they'd believe the story, but the people of Buacach did. Word traveled fast across Mazzabah. Everyone knew what tragedy had occurred behind the giant stone walls.

King Barric couldn't waste time in setting his plans in motion. Keeping the alliance with Etu would ensure more troops and trade, and if it came to it, Barric could take their land as well. Things seemed relatively simple to Sadon—he'd even managed to fool the king into believing that Sadon couldn't hatch the dragon egg. That was a secret he kept close to his chest and would not reveal unless absolutely necessary. A wizard always kept a few risky secrets.

The guards alerted King Barric and led Etu into the royal chambers. Etu walked tall and strong, as any warrior would, but his eyes held exhaustion and pain that Sadon knew well. Something else glinted in them. Something brief and almost unnoticeable.

Hatred.

King Barric greeted Etu joyously, waving him over. "It is good to see you again, Prince Etu. Did the chief finally agree to our alliance?"

Sadon knew that the only reason Etu did not let his father come was because his father would start a war. If the chief were to raise a hand against Barric, there would be war, even if the father had a heart for revenge over his daughter's demise.

They could not afford that. No one had any choice but to obey Barric's commands or die, Sadon had made sure of it. Seeing his hard work in action sent a shiver of satisfaction through his spine.

Etu bowed low, jaw tight. "Yes, my king, all is well. Your alliance is even better than the previous pact. We are grateful... and gladly accept."

That much was true—the trade deal and the land agreements benefited the Wolf Clan more than Connall's had. But Barric would just as quickly turn on them and take everything away, something they'd never feared with Connall.

A brief taste of pleasure was nothing compared to bitter-earned freedom. At least the clan's trade tax would be low, and they would have more protection. While living like birds in cages.

King Barric beamed. "I'm glad to hear that your clan is appeased. Our alliance will build the future of Mazzabah."

Etu glanced between him and Sadon. Stoic expression unreadable, he said without hesitation, "Is there anything else I may be of service?" He spent his time playing mediator between the clan and the kingdom, a job he was good at, but by that brief look in his eyes, he was up to something else.

King Barric must've missed the sign because he laughed. "I think you've got your hands busy for now. It has been strong men's work, keeping the peoples at peace." Barric's motivations were fleshly—power, money, fame, greed. He wanted it all. His hatred for the royals stemmed from his envy—and that envy rooted his determination to keep every other civilization safe but not near as strong as his own.

"Word has it people will riot," Etu said.

Barric shook his head roughly. "They will not. Even if they do, in Buacach or another kingdom, they will not make it far. My men are by far the strongest. Any attempt at ruining our empire will be futile, will it not?" He shot a questioning smile.

"My men and I would gladly give our lives to this empire," Etu replied.

The empire that bound them all like slaves, but if they fought, they'd be slaughtered.

This was what Sadon fought for. A world order of peace and power.

"We will continue as planned with the alliance and trades." King Barric smiled.

"My king?" Etu asked.

"Hmm?"

"The caravans that enter Buacach... You bid them welcome?" Etu's strong jaw was clenched tight.

"Aye, they are beautiful entertainers. Shall I allow you to see a show?" King Barric's booming laugh filled the throne room.

Etu shook his head. "No, my king. There are children in those caravans. I fear they are using those children for vile things. I did not want to keep this from you."

Etu thought Barric didn't know the cruel things that the people of art and entertainment did...

Barric smiled. "Aye, I know of the children, but they are happy."

The children were tortured. Abused. Sold like tools. It was one thing about Barric that Sadon couldn't stand—his utter abuse toward women and children. Sadon might be a wizard, but unless his master ordained such cruelty, he despised it from any man that called himself strong.

Had Shafiq not treated him the way he did, perhaps Sadon wouldn't have even that sliver of humanity. It was a weakness.

Instead of shoving it away this time, Sadon gulped. Oliver had escaped from such a caravan. Would Sadon turn his back on children that were tortured the same as he was?

But why save them? He was a wicked man—that was how the world saw him. He would save the world, and they would all call him a demon.

Why save Oliver? No one saved me.

Twenty-Five

NO ONE SAW THE spirit clinging to Moray, but the three of them smelled it—a rotting stench like old eggs or something foul. Determined to protect Ama, Finnigan stuck close to her and followed Gunnar through the swamp. Gunnar hacked at thick vines and large wet plants, carving a narrow path through the thick trees. The swamp waters moved and rippled occasionally, but no one looked too close or for too long. The more they moved, the less likely they'd be eaten.

Or so Finnigan prayed.

If anyone spoke, it usually ended in an argument, so they'd given up on conversation. Finnigan didn't suppose there was much reason to talk besides the fact that he hated silence. What was there to discuss? Moray hiding and welcoming his demons? Gunnar refusing to have faith that they might be saved by measures besides their own? Or what of the fact that when they returned to Mazzabah, no one knew what awaited? Barric could be doing anything.

People could be dying. Everything could be ruined—and they might be too late to stop it.

Or they might never get home at all.

Finnigan took a deep breath, cringing at the stench that filled his nose. He chose courage and faith. Elohai would get them home by His means, not their own. They just had to go through the Place of Bones until Elohai saw fit to take them home.

He could not lose anyone else. Except maybe the mercenary. He was terribly infuriating.

Ama tripped on a tree root and stumbled a little. Finnigan caught her arm. "Careful."

"I'm trying."

Courage cast Finnigan a murderous glare and licked her fangs as if warning him to watch his tongue. Finnigan didn't understand how the creature could sense emotions so well. He wasn't even sure if the rat thing might turn on them. Ama was convinced good could exist in the Golgotha because Elohai had created it. Splitting the two realms had still left bad in Mazzabah, so she thought perhaps it had left good in Golgotha too. Finnigan didn't see it. Elohai was a God of mysteries, and Finnigan had too many of them to solve.

"Don't want you scarring your pretty face, Princess," Gunnar said sarcastically, eyeing the two of them.

Ama chuckled, the insult rolling off her shoulders. Finnigan glared at the back of Gunnar's head. "You're one to talk."

"I may look like a cut-up piece of pork, but I still like myself. That's all that matters, Finny."

Finnigan clenched his fists, but Ama grabbed his arm gently and whispered to Gunnar, "He's just hungry."

Gunnar gasped sarcastically. "He's just hungry," he repeated under his breath, cutting a large vine in half with one swipe of his blade. "We're all hungry! We'll eat again when we camp tonight. Only a couple more hours to go. Do your feet hurt, Finny? Do you want me to carry you, wee lass?"

"I'm about to sheath my dagger—"

Moray slowed his steps behind them, craning his neck toward the low-swooping trees.

Ama glanced back with a soft frown. "Moray?"

Finnigan followed their gazes but saw nothing. Just darkness creeping into the trees and snuffing out what little light they had to go by. "What?"

Moray didn't move forward. "Something is there."

"We'd best keep moving." Gunnar walked on without them, cutting away at a thick patch of vines.

Finnigan glanced between his brother and the mercenary.

"Something is in there," Moray repeated, frozen in place. "We cannot run from it."

"Sure we can," Gunnar snapped over his shoulder. "A short-legged princess won't stop us."

Ama scowled. "Being rude doesn't—"

Moray stepped toward the thick trees, slipping closer to the swampy waters.

Finnigan grabbed his arm. "Moray, you'll get yourself killed. Let's keep moving!" Elohai only knew how many demons Moray dragged along by now.

Moray brushed Finnigan off, expression cold as ice. "Something's here. All of you, go."

"We aren't leaving you here." Finnigan grasped Moray's arm tighter this time. "Come on."

Moray's dark eyes flashed with pure rage. "I will buy you time!"

Gunnar stopped a few yards away, facing them. "You are both going to get us killed!" he snarled. "Stop fighting like two dogs and let's move!" He lifted his two long blades and gestured to the tiny clearing he'd made.

Courage chittered on Ama's shoulder, jerking and rising on her tiny haunches. Ama stepped back from the princes. "What—"

Moray and Finnigan looked back to the murky, deep swamp. Past the leaves and debris, ripples pushed through the water. Finnigan held Moray and tried pulling him away from the water. "Moray, let's move!"

HE'D PROMISED TO GET them home. What king didn't break his promises? What foolish prince expected promises to be kept? Moray pulled away from his brother and mumbled something. The black magic came as he asked, but it drained him—a strange, hollow sensation.

Despondency moaned on his shoulders. "It's hopeless. Why have courage when they all view you as a monster? You're a monster. Nothing more, nothing more."

The voice carved deeper into Moray's mind.

I am more.

Finnigan tackled him backward. "No! Gunnar, help me!"

I am king.

Moray broke free from Finnigan's grasp with all the force he could muster and launched himself toward the waterside. The moment he did, the water surface burst open. Waves splashed and poured over the forest floor.

"You will become king of Golgotha and Mazzabah, and you will do so without the Light," Abaddon had said. But Abaddon had done nothing for him here.

Moray stood fast, the cool waters drenching him. Despondency screeched at him to give up, but Moray ignored the demon. He wouldn't need anyone's saving grace except his own. Never again.

"Moray!" Finnigan shouted over the ruckus. "Moray, move!"

The giant head of the beast plunged from the depths. Yellow scales covered its smooth, rotund body, and it was at least as thick as Moray was tall. It rose above him, the majority of its body still underwater. Two fangs stuck out from its pink mouth, and a hiss crept from its forked tongue.

Moray raised both hands and shot the large blast of energy he'd been summoning. The black ball hit the snake full on, burning through its smooth scales and flesh. Moray summoned more, stumbling to his knees weakly.

Get up. Be strong. You trained for this.

But Despondency pulled him down, the demon's claws digging into his veins again.

The serpent's tongue flickered as it dove for Moray. Moray rolled out of the way, body slamming against moss and sticks. A flash of blue light filled his vision.

AMA WATCHED THE SNAKE dive with uncanny speed. It missed Moray, then swung its head at Gunnar, opening its mouth wide and revealing gleaming fangs and teeth. Gunnar stabbed both blades into the creature's left golden eye. The snake jerked back.

Finnigan shot another blue blast of energy into the serpent's soft throat. The snake's body darkened, like the attack scorched it from the inside out.

Finnigan yelled, "Ama, run!"

Ama stood, her colored dagger drawn, but didn't dare go closer. She didn't run either.

She only had eyes for the monster as she prayed, voice firm. "Creator, You have given us the power to tread on serpents and scorpions, over all the power of the enemy." Her voice trembled ever so briefly as Finnigan dove out of the way from the serpent's jaws.

As soon as the words from the Letters left her lips, words she had memorized as a young child, another voice came from behind her. The voice of the man from her dreams. "You are mistaken, child."

Something sharp jabbed her neck, like a small needle tip, the type Mama used for sewing. Ama whirled around, gasping.

The man from her dream smiled at her, his cloak lowered. Short, wavy black hair framed his handsome face, and a thick, trimmed beard shaped his broad jawline. His eyes were light amber, twinkling at Ama with pure hatred. "You remember the offer I gave you?"

"I will never follow you!" Ama shouted, but panic rose in her chest as pain throbbed from her neck. What had he done to her? Courage tensed on Ama's shoulder and chittered away, but the man didn't react.

"Then you shall die here, Ama." The man lifted his black, serpent-head staff and looked past her to where the men faced the lethal water serpent. "You shall die, and your master shall watch."

Courage's mouth hung open as if yelling for help, but Ama heard nothing, darkness engulfing her.

THE SERPENT FLAILED IN the water like a crocodile. Water splashed, but through the murky waves, the snake's flesh and scales dissolved. Red blood turned the murky waters brown. The snake twisted and slammed its body through the large water hole—then it stopped.

Moray, Finnigan, and Gunnar stood watching and waiting at the edge of the swamp, but the waters slowly fell placid once again. Like the monster had never been there. As quick as it had come, it disappeared.

It was a trap.

"Move," Finnigan said, shoving Gunnar back. He must've figured the same as Moray. "It's coming back!"

"It's dead!" Gunnar snapped. "Between two blasts and my hacking—"

"Run!" Moray turned and ran but tripped on something soft. "Ama! Ama—get up!"

He yanked the princess off the wet ground. A small black bruise formed on her neck, a web of dark threads just beneath her skin. A poison... to kill a person slowly and painfully. A poison Moray had never used, by the looks of the Darkness mingling with Ama's bloodstream. It was an ancient poison for an elect few.

"Ama!" Finnigan ran over, grabbing her from Moray. "What happened?"

"Move!" Gunnar staggered away from the waterside, blood pouring from a gash in his arm. The monster had tossed Gunnar against a tree, but it wasn't slowing him down yet.

The wizard who came to them in the prairie had warned Moray to make the right decision. This was his punishment for not killing Ama. She would die anyway at the hands of Abaddon's servant.

The sound of water splashing the ground made Moray turn. The serpent changed—all flesh and scales melted away into the waters. All that stared Moray down was the serpent's stained skeleton, giant fangs still hungry for bloodshed.

Moray snatched up Ama's glowing, colored dagger from the dirt. "Run!" He urged the others down the tiny clearing. Gunnar tossed him a long blade, and they both tore a path through the vines and thickets. The serpent's massive skeleton didn't crawl out of the water.

They ran nonstop for as long as they could before Finnigan staggered to a stop. Breath heaving, he choked out, "Ama... Ama needs help. I have to heal her."

Gunnar leaned against a tree. The mercenary had more stamina than any of them, but the blood loss from the gash in his arm seemed to be catching up with him. Too many factors—exhaustion and lack of food, water, and sleep—wore on their endurance.

Moray breathed steadily and helped lower Ama gently onto a soft, dry patch of dirt. Ama's pulse raced, her paling skin hot to the touch. Finnigan pulled her close against his chest. His hands shook, but he healed her—or so it looked like he tried.

"Well?" Moray growled. "Heal her!"

"It... it..." Horror flooded Finnigan's eyes, and his face grew taut. "It isn't working." Just like with Graft, his healing ability didn't seem to remove whatever poison now rushed through Ama's blood.

"She's going to die," Despondency whimpered, still hanging on Moray's back. He'd shut up during the chaos but now whispered into Moray's ear when his guard weakened. "She'll die just like Graft. It's hopeless. Now you see that they will all die because of you. Hope kills the flesh."

Moray needed her as his queen back in Mazzabah. He'd need an heir. His master wanted her dead, but Moray needed her alive. "Try again, Finn!"

Finnigan's hands shook hard as he held Ama. Sweat poured from his temples. Nothing happened. Ama lay limp against him, her eyes closed and lips parted. Courage repeatedly nudged her master's head, but nothing woke Ama.

Moray paused. "I can try—"

"Your black magic will do nothing!" Finnigan practically shouted. "It is the cause for this hell to begin with! Your devil is a wicked master, Moray—he does not care who is lost. He feeds off death! Is that who you want to become?"

Moray flinched back at his little brother's harsh rebuke. "I do not serve the devil any longer." One disobedient choice, and Abaddon had stripped Moray of his home, his rank, and his dignity.

"Then you believe in Elohai?" Tears ran down Finnigan's cheeks. He rocked Ama against his chest, trembling like a man whose heart was being torn away, bit by bit.

"No," Moray said softly.

Finnigan lowered his head, mumbling weak prayers. "Save her," he choked out. "Elohai, save her. Please... save her."

Elohai did nothing. Hell wasn't a place for miracles.

"This is all wrong," Despondency groaned in his ear. "She shouldn't be dying. She wouldn't be suffering if you had given up!"

Moray closed his eyes briefly. In that split moment of exhaustion, two more claws latched hold of his back. A new voice whispered, "It isn't your fault. None of this is. You're clever, Moray, too clever for these fools. You need to keep going. You'll show them."

Moray didn't recognize the voice. He opened his eyes, and another demon peeked around his shoulder. Instead of Despondency's whimpering form, this demon scowled, anger twisting its black face. "This strife is not a burden. Let me guide you. You don't need anything else. You do not need Elohai."

Strife.

Moray gulped tightly. He could save them himself.

Gunnar stepped closer, kneeling beside Finnigan and Ama. He held his arm, blood pouring past his large, rough fingers. "I-I think we have something in the blasted bag..." He heaved it off his shoulders. "Look for yourself."

Moray snatched the canvas bag and dug into it hastily. He pushed past food, waterskins, and a blanket until his hand hit a small bottle. He yanked it out and uncapped it. One of Sadon's salves. The bottle was labeled *For bothersome supernatural antidote needs: 40% effective*. He swore at Sadon's cruel humor and slathered a large amount on Ama's swelling neck. The skin around her neck had cracked and darkened, her veins running black as the poison seized her.

Despondency tugged at Moray's head. "Too late, fool, too late! The poison is ancient. This will do nothing! Should've done it sooner. She'll die!"

Strife hissed, "She is your property. Don't wait on her god to save her like Finnigan. At least *you've* done something."

The salve soaked into the tiny needle mark. Ama shuddered. Her eyes flickered open, and she let out a moan. "F-Finn."

Finnigan laughed weakly and pulled her close against his chest. "Ama!" He kissed her head. "Oh, Ama, it's all right.

You'll be all right, thank Elohai!"

Moray's jaw tightened. "Elohai has nothing to do with this. I do."

Twenty-Six

FINNIGAN HELD AMA AGAINST his chest, shaking from exhaustion, but the relief and joy in his heart trumped the pain. He smoothed Ama's hair from her sweaty face. "It's all right now, Ama. Just relax." He gulped down the lump in his throat. She closed her eyes and leaned against him, unable to sit up, but her pulse steadied.

Finnigan turned and grabbed Gunnar's bloodied arm. He healed the deep gash in an instant. Gunnar swore in pain, and his eyes widened once the wound disappeared.

Finnigan grunted. "Don't read into it. We can't have anyone dying on us." Not again.

Gunnar rubbed his now perfectly fine arm, grinning like an imp. "You still owe me an island."

"Figured." Finnigan took the blanket from the canvas bag and wrapped it around Ama. She slept soundly now, Courage wrapped against her chest. Finnigan let himself meet Moray's cold gaze.

What if Moray was killed? What if Finnigan couldn't help his brother in his time of need—like he hadn't saved Graft or Ama?

He couldn't help him if he didn't want it.

"We should move," Moray said. "The serpents might follow us. There are probably hundreds more of them."

"It's almost nightfall," Gunnar said. "We will die if we do not rest, even in this godforsaken swamp."

Finnigan studied Ama's peaceful face. She needed sleep, and his drained body couldn't carry her any farther. "Please, Moray—"

"We camp, then." Moray worked his jaw. "If the serpents come to eat us, it's on your heads."

"A bone creature ain't got need for meat." Gunnar smirked, voice dry. "But I understand the resentment. I just doubt the immortal beings will crave our bitter, tough meat." He opened the canvas bag and distributed small portions of their precious rations. They wouldn't last much longer on the food, but they hadn't found any more yet. Finnigan doubted their chances of finding anything edible in the swamp, but they had found a good source of water.

Elohai's Letters reminded how the birds didn't sow or reap and He still fed them. Finnigan prayed Elohai didn't forget the fools He had roaming Golgotha. The forbidden realm. The other half of a world once proclaimed good.

Finnigan sighed, laying Ama gently onto the dry patch of ground. Using his Gift, he set fire to a small pile of dry and wet wood. It drained even more energy from his body, but at least they'd be warm.

He ate quietly. Gunnar sat against a tree, his keen eyes watching the swampland, as if he could see everything, as if nothing could harm him. Was he afraid?

Finnigan rubbed his head. He'd prayed nonstop for guidance, mercy, and courage. Perhaps Elohai truly was answering his prayers. But was he himself afraid?

He sat up for first watch while the others finished their food, drank some water, and curled up to sleep. He prayed and watched the looming trees, the fire offering little light to fend off the darkness.

MORAY WOKE FOR HIS watch shift and sat against a tree. Finnigan fell asleep beside Ama. The fluffy white creature rested on Ama's chest but watched the swamplands, licking her fangs. Gunnar snored softly, still leaning against a tree trunk, a dagger in his lap. Moray tended the fire while Despondency and Strife whispered in his ears.

"You will be the god to get them home," Strife muttered. "They'd never survive alone. They're too stupid."

"Why fight?" Despondency tugged at Moray. "There's no use. You should never have tried claiming Golgotha, never should've tried helping your people. All is lost now."

Moray glanced up at the treetops. The swamp was getting to him, biting away at his sanity. A king belonged in a land of vipers. Moray found comfort in the wet, dark grounds, but he knew it was all fake. Men of war never found comfort—comfort was an illusion. He wouldn't stay here. Nothing would stop him.

The looming trees and low-hanging branches hid far more than the naked eye could see. Every so often, a glimmering pair of eyes stared down at him. Red eyes. Gold eyes. White eyes. They scampered above the ground, never coming too close.

Too many eyes.

They peeked through the branches and wide leaves.

Too many faces.

Their whispers wafted through the thick atmosphere.

Too many, too many, too many.

Faces. Eyes. Everywhere. Coming closer in the dark. Voices rang in Moray's ears like a thousand knives piercing his rib cage.

They had followed him from the beginning.

Too much.

Moray stood heavily, legs burning from the exertion. Strife and Despondency clung to his back and he ignored them. He walked to the edge of the dry patch of ground where the others slept.

A soft breeze ruffled his black hair. He looked down at his hands, racking his brain once more for some way to escape the second realm. He didn't have the skills. He'd try using the water—if they found a big enough body of it—to create a makeshift rift, but he doubted it could happen. He needed Sadon's help, but Sadon was the traitor, the fool who'd cast them into hell. Moray couldn't trust him. But what choice did he have?

He sighed. He had to wait till he slept again before trying to reach Sadon in his dreams. He should have done it tonight.

Sadon could form the connection far easier than Moray could, but he hadn't. Even if Sadon betrayed them and wanted them dead, he would want information and updates on what Golgotha was truly like. He'd given Ama a bag of provisions, after all. But they wouldn't survive much longer. Moray needed to form the link with Sadon if the blasted wizard wouldn't.

Snap.

In the treetops above, the eyes all vanished from sight. The demons were hungry, and the group was without a doubt the first batch of human souls in a long while. Humans were the perfect prey for demons.

Two eyes appeared in the darkness. Big white orbs, but they stood eight feet off the ground and didn't float about like the other demons had. The eyes didn't move or blink. Moray couldn't make out a form in the blackness.

"I'm not getting eaten by a swamp monster," Moray muttered, kicking Gunnar in the leg.

Gunnar shot upright, lifting the dagger in his lap at the same instant he opened his eyes. Fighting truly was as natural as breathing to the mercenary. "What?"

Moray shook Finnigan awake and Ama too. Finnigan jumped to his feet, eyes widening when he saw the creature. "What is that?"

"Our grandmother," Moray said sarcastically. "Get ready to fight."

The monster came closer slowly. Trees creaked, snapped, and bent as the figure moved through them. The trees did nothing to deter it or even harm it, from what Moray could tell. A demon wasn't restricted by matter, but this monster broke tangible objects, so it had to have an embodiment of sorts.

Gunnar sheathed his dagger and drew his blades. Finnigan moved Ama behind them, and she held her strange dagger. Moray would have to ask about it. For now, he faced the monster and summoned black magic. The white eyes were all that showed in the darkness, moving closer, closer, slow but steady. Moray shot a blast of black magic at the creature.

Nothing happened. The black magic disappeared—as if the creature merely pulled it into itself. Perhaps fighting Darkness with Darkness was a foolish idea.

The monster stepped out of the shadows. It stood eight feet tall despite its hunched shoulders, and it was broad as a tree and pure black, like tangled, sinking flesh wrapped around a thick skeleton had been given life. The big white eyes hung from sagging black sockets. The monster's warped head was covered with small bugs and creatures that burrowed into its flesh as if avoiding the firelight. The monster's feet sucked into the ground as it pushed onward.

Moray stepped back, bumping into Finnigan. "Everyone move!"

Finnigan shot a weak blast of blue light at the beast's chest. The creature didn't make a sound as the light burned through its flesh. At least the light was doing more than Moray's magic had—but not enough. The monster pushed on, feet slipping through the muck like it was part of the earth. Finnigan let another ball of light surge into the monster's chest, but the creature didn't die. Black smoke wafted from its body.

Moray grabbed Finnigan's arm, steadying his brother's trembling body. "Kill it!"

Finnigan groaned. "That's... all I've got."

Gunnar stepped forward, expression grim. Without a word, he lunged for the monster, aiming for the head. His right blade struck the head in a swift blow but didn't cut through the neck. Gunnar's body jerked from the impact like he'd sliced into a rock.

"Gunnar!" Finnigan rushed forward, staggering. Ama pulled him back.

"Let him die," Strife murmured into Moray's ear.

Moray bit his lip and ran for Gunnar. The monster swung a large fleshy arm and hit Gunnar across the chest. Gunnar dropped but swung his other blade. It lodged into the monster's left leg. The monster never reacted like it was in pain, nor did it crumble. Before it could swipe Gunnar again, Moray shoved Gunnar out of the way.

The monster's jaws opened wide, revealing long, sharp fangs that practically covered the gap like jagged webbing. Moray jumped up, but the monster latched a hand onto his shoulder. The frigid flesh sent shivers down Moray's spine. He jerked, but the hand didn't move. Gunnar grabbed his blade, snarling, "Move!"

"I can't!" Moray used his other hand and sent a volt of black magic into the creature. Sharp sensations ran up his arm as he used the magic so forcefully. Strife moved away, but Despondency dug its claws against his skull.

"Just stop fighting," Despondency cried. "It's over... It's all over!"

GO FORTH.

The monster clamped down on Moray's arm and dropped its head, fangs hanging from its mouth inches from Moray's neck as he fought. Gunnar hacked at the monster's head, blades merely lodging into the flesh.

Ama pushed past the two men and plunged her dagger into the monster's burnt chest.

Time froze.

The monster stopped moving and lowered its head, fangs slowly morphing back into its gaping mouth.

The glowing dagger lodged into the ragged flesh. The darkness engulfed it, but Ama didn't let go or pull back. She whispered weakly, "The Darkness shall cover the earth, but the Creator's glory will shine upon you."

The monster's eyes widened. Bright white light seeped past the blade and burst from the wound. Ama held the dagger tight as light poured out. Big, strong hands grabbed her shoulders to brace her—Finnigan.

The monster never made a sound, but its white eyes practically twisted in pain. In an instant, it exploded. The ground beneath Ama was yanked away as Finnigan pulled her down, covering her with his body. Oozing black flesh splattered over them and covered the mossy swamp ground.

The dagger fell away from Ama's hand, glowing among the debris.

Twenty-Seven

BY MORNING, THEY TRUDGED through the swamps after a poor night's rest. They ate little and used the water sparingly. If they didn't find provisions soon, they wouldn't last long. Finnigan didn't intend to die from such a simple dilemma. Body weak from exhaustion, he kept Ama close, sometimes holding her hand. She moved slower, like her body didn't know how to push on like it had the day before. Her face was off a shade, and even Courage acted glum, like the creature knew her friend was feeling unwell.

After a few hours of agonizing silence and aching feet, Finnigan mustered enough courage to ask. "Ama, may I ask you something?"

"Yes." She focused on her footsteps that fell heavier than before on the mushy ground.

Finnigan gulped. "Where did you get the dagger?"

"Creator gifted it to me."

Gunnar scoffed from behind them. "You've got to be bloody pulling my leg."

"It is true," Ama said quietly. "Creator gifted my brother and me with the blades."

Finnigan smiled. "It is a beautiful dagger." Quite the understatement—the blade was the most skillfully crafted weapon he'd ever seen, yet Ama wore it hidden beneath the folds of her dress.

Ama hesitated, glancing up at him. Her heavy brown eyes pained him. "The sacred Gifts are precious to the clans," she said. "It has been many years since Creator gifted them to any of the clans. Our daggers are a secret."

Finnigan grimaced. "Oh. Sorry. You don't have to tell us if you don't want to."

"Why not?" Gunnar growled. "Ain't like we got anyone else to gossip with."

Ama chuckled and took a deep breath. "I'll tell."

Moray hacked away at the vines and created a rough, narrow path for them to walk along steadily. Gunnar kept close behind, watching their surroundings.

"Creator gives Gifts to His chosen. In olden times, after the Split, Gifts were not uncommon. But people stopped believing. Some clans even chose false gods, but we, too, began losing our closeness with our Father." Ama sighed. "Creator came to my father, the chief, and told him that He was gifting the Wolf Clan two daggers to be borne by Etu and me. When my father woke, he found the daggers where Creator instructed."

"Why did Etu get one? Isn't he a jackwagon?" Gunnar piped up, swatting a branch out of his way.

Ama's voice lowered. "Etu was not always so cold. He truly does care for the clan, but he comes across as... cruel sometimes."

Finnigan glanced down at her. Her expression fell, like the topic hurt her. It should, considering Etu hadn't seemed to really care for her much. "The blades have powers?"

"In a sense." Ama nodded, brushing her thick hair behind her ear. "They have immense Energy—with the right person."

"And with the wrong person?" Finnigan frowned.

"They could be killed by wielding it."

Gunnar laughed, shaking his head. "Why did your God gift them to you anyway? Some kind of 'good job following me, here are two useless weapons' gift?"

"When you obey His ways, He will bless you. You do not always understand the blessing, but it does not make it less precious." Ama spoke softly in such a way that made Finnigan's chest tighten—hearing her speak of Creator moved him.

He'd almost lost her—what if he failed her again? She deserved her family, her home, safety, and happiness... She deserved nothing that had happened. She was good, faithful, and bold.

If he failed again, she might die.

Gunnar followed them. "Sounds like a bunch of garbage. Your God let us come here to die."

"Our ways are not His ways," Ama said and sighed. "I do not pretend to understand. Having faith has not failed me. If I had no faith, I would lose nothing, and without hope, why fight?"

Gunnar didn't have any answer for that. Finnigan prayed that Ama's words were reaching the smart-mouth and his brother. After another long moment of silence, Moray's steps slowed and he glanced into the thick, tangled trees. "Do you hear that?"

Finnigan stopped in his tracks. If he heard that phrase again, he'd lose his mind. He glanced at Gunnar and Ama. Only Gunnar appeared to have heard the sound, his grip on his blade shifting.

Moray led them forward a few more steps, hacking a path. A soft cracking sound came from their right. Finnigan tensed. "I heard *that*."

They watched the woods closely but nothing happened. Another *crack* followed. They saw nothing.

Finnigan gulped. A monster or another snake or, heavens, a big bug? In Golgotha, who knew? He sniffed the air and took a steady breath. At least it wasn't a demon. Hopefully.

Gunnar moved them on a little, footsteps silent for such a big body. Something large jumped out from the treetops to their right, propelling itself toward Gunnar. Finnigan yanked the mercenary out of the way.

The creature hit the ground on two feet. It raised up, standing like a human would, covered in scales like a lizard. Its face looked like a blend of man and reptile, with large reptilian eyes and a short snout. It eyed them before lunging at Gunnar again, hissing. It was going for the kill this time.

Gunnar swung one blade and cut the creature's bare chest. Red blood splattered, but Gunnar pushed on, driving the blade deeper. The lizard creature screeched and staggered.

Another lizard creature dropped from the trees and dove for Ama, but Moray shoved her into Finnigan. The monster fell into Moray's sword and made him topple. Blood spurted from its opened gut.

Finnigan moved Ama behind him. "Moray!"

The monster bit at Moray's throat with sharp, tiny teeth as he wrestled. "A little help!" he shouted.

Finnigan shot a small blast of energy at the monster's head. The lizard creature crumpled.

Moray scrambled to his feet. Gunnar stood over his own kill, both creatures lying limp. Their blood seeped onto the soft moss. Finnigan's stomach turned at the sight, but there was nothing to be done now but move along.

"DID YOU KNOW ABOUT those things, Moray?" Ama asked quietly as they walked along. Moray wiped sweat from his brow while he cut them a path. Of all the things they had fought off and killed, nothing had resembled a human in the slightest, minus the demonic, white-eyed monster that looked more tree than human.

"All the legends I've heard, there's never been lizard people," Gunnar muttered under his breath.

"Yes," Moray said, not the slightest hint of emotion to his voice. He never looked them in the eyes—not since the demonic attack. Ama didn't know how many demons he now welcomed. She didn't know if he had a change of heart.

She knew no more of Moray than the first day she'd met him.

Ama gulped. "What are they?"

"Siiti." Moray swung his sword and broke through a thick vine, pushing onward. "They are basically lizard people. Not hybrid, per se, but they are capable of humanistic qualities."

"They have souls?" Ama gulped hard again, stroking Courage's head.

"I doubt it," Moray scoffed lightly. "Nothing has a soul here."

"Courage does."

Moray didn't look back, swinging his blade through the shrubs. "Consider her the one mishap out of a realm of monsters."

Ama didn't know why Creator would have left soul-beings in Golgotha to live in torment, but had He also not allowed Darkness to enter Mazzabah to test His people? She cradled Courage close. She didn't understand Creator's reasons, but He provided for them. Maybe... maybe He had cause for them here.

They trudged on for hours. The thick, dark swamp had a web of murky waters, but they avoided any body of water they could. Ama saw the waters churn sometimes—she never looked too long, so whether it was one of the giant serpents or some other monster, she didn't know.

If she could tell Finnigan of the wizard who hurt her... He needed to know. He acted as if he knew something was wrong with her. She also wanted to talk about what Moray knew of Golgotha, but he refused. She wanted to know where Gunnar came from, and why Etu, her cold-hearted big brother, had cared enough to send someone to rescue her. Ama figured Etu truly still loved her, even if he'd sent her off like an animal. She wanted to know what they'd do if Moray's magic didn't help.

Ama had no answers to most of her questions. None of them knew much, and even if they'd learned something from legends—or in Moray's case, some cross wizard—it could still be wrong. But she couldn't bring herself to talk about the wizard in her dream who had hurt her.

Ama studied the trees that draped around them. Just like the swamps in Mazzabah, this one held character—different types of trees, different plants, and definitely different creatures. She never liked the swamps in Mazzabah and this one was far worse.

Her neck ached softly, and she focused her thoughts again. Since the poison, the pain had grown almost insufferable, the fatigue draining her. It didn't matter, though. They couldn't stop and rest.

As Ama caught sight of a few narrow trees, something grabbed her attention. Carved gashes in the trees, one every so often. She shrugged it off. After half an hour, the gashes remained steadily present, one mark on one tree at every thirty yards. Ama gulped. "Does anyone else see—"

"The marks?" Gunnar chuckled. "Been there for over two miles. They're too precise and paced to be some angry animal."

Finnigan shook his head, glancing down at Ama. "No idea what it might be."

"Doesn't look like an animal did it," Ama said.

"Could be anything." Moray still didn't look back. Ama almost wanted to shake him till he met their gaze, but it wouldn't help.

They all wanted to get home and save their people. They couldn't win without each other. Why did Moray refuse them?

Ama sighed tiredly. "Guess it could be."

THEY HAD NO CHOICE that evening but to forage for food and search for clean water. The canvas bag had little water supply left, and the food was running out. Gunnar had a sense for foraging, but they were in Golgotha. Moray seriously doubted that their usual skills would prove reliable. Still, if they didn't try a few resources, they'd starve to death and die anyway.

Moray found a small plant that looked the same as one back in Mazzabah. He cut up the bark of the shrub and boiled it. Strife and Despondency nagged at his ears, but he focused intently on finding something edible. Gunnar had no interest in "peasant leaves," so he went into the nearby trees alone to hunt.

Moray had half a mind that any flesh in Golgotha would be poisonous or rotting from the inside out. But why not take the risk, especially if it got Gunnar away from him?

He didn't know why Sadon had sent the mercenary into Golgotha, besides offering Ama protection and hoping to get the merc killed. Gunnar would be too much hassle to take back to Mazzabah. Etu certainly didn't have the means to satisfy the big-mouth's bounty. Paying Gunnar would fall on Moray's shoulders. He'd be too busy restoring Buacach to bother with the mercenary.

Moray couldn't just cut his throat at night, so maybe the beasts would catch him while he was hunting alone.

Ama sat beside him, warming up beside the fire. She'd acted strange since the fight, most likely due to the poison. More quiet, less feisty, and her steps dragged. For a woman raised in the woods and skilled in working the land, she must have been sicker than she let on. Finnigan didn't ask about it, not yet.

Her eyes were heavy as she helped him peel the bits of bark off the thick branches. "Looks like the same thing at home," she said, sighing.

"Perhaps it never reached the swamps in Mazzabah, is all," Moray muttered. "Let's just hope it doesn't kill us." They could fight off fanged monsters and hungry demons, but without food and water, they'd be goners. But he wouldn't lose. He would get them through this.

Ama studied him, gulping. "Are you all right?"

"I'm fine." Moray eyed Finnigan, who searched for more firewood. He'd said he'd try to find dry ones so he wouldn't have to use so much energy.

"You've acted strange since—"

"It is fine." Moray stopped her. He didn't want to acknowledge the two demons on his shoulders, tugging at his mind, clawing at his body. He didn't want to acknowledge the eyes that hadn't stopped following them. He didn't want to risk being the only one losing their mind.

He was sane.

He was right.

He was king.

Truths were hard to hold on to when a person was drowning.

"I just want to help." Ama handed him a stripped piece of bark.

Moray took it, tossing it into the tiny pot they'd gotten from the canvas bag. He put the pot over the fire to boil. "You have acted strangely since the fight, too. What about that sting, or whatever happened to you? None of us have bothered you about it," he said tightly.

Ama's face fell, her tan cheeks littered with scratches and grime. "That's different."

"How?"

"I cannot be helped unless Creator heals me. You... you cannot be saved unless you choose Creator, yet you do not want that. We love you, Moray. We do not want to lose you to the Darkness." Ama's soft voice dropped as she looked away, her expression stoic. He knew she didn't like showing emotion in front of him.

"No, you love Finnigan," Moray said coldly. "You've loved him over me since Mazzabah. Do not lie to me. You are foolish, just as Finnigan, but I refuse to follow any master heedlessly. Never again." He stood and went to gather more branches.

Everyone was too hungry and exhausted to do much talking after that. Gunnar found a small spring a short distance away. They filled their waterskins, drank till they were full, and ate what little they had. Moray tried the bark first—and didn't die or burst into hives. They packed up as much edible food as they could find and hoped for the best.

Gunnar killed a helpless-looking creature that resembled a rabbit—it was twice the size and had no eyes, but it looked healthy. Or, at least, as healthy as anything could look in Golgotha. Gunnar gutted it, checking every crevice of the body, finally admitting it looked edible. He cooked up some strips of red meat. No one else offered to try it, but Courage hopped over and ate a large slab of meat. Ama cried out in dismay, but the little fluffball licked her bloody lips happily.

Finnigan groaned. "Well, if she isn't dead..."

They ate a little of the meat, fully expecting to die in the night.

Moray hoped for silence, but Ama would have none of it. His sharp retort earlier didn't shake her.

"We get plenty done when we work together," Ama said with a chuckle. "And without ripping each other's throats out."

Finnigan's cheeks reddened as he sat beside her, eating hungrily. "Guess we do make a good team."

"Team?" Gunnar scoffed, downing the rest of his meat and taking a swig of spring water.

"Yes. Whether we like it or not, we're a team, composed of three less-than-desirable men and a woman." Ama smirked. It was the first time Moray had heard her tease since he'd been with her in Golgotha.

Finnigan burst into weary laughter. Light crept back into his eyes. "I cannot argue, even if my ego is rather dented."

Ama laughed, lowering her head.

"I'm not a team player." Gunnar wrinkled his nose.

"Until we return to Mazzabah, we all are. And we will each be a good one." As if scolding a friend, Ama eyed Gunnar with a firm frown. Gunnar scowled but didn't argue further.

"What will this teamwork magically change, hmm?" Moray leaned back. "Shall we sing songs around the fire?" The sarcasm dripped from his tone like venom. They were far from a team, but if it helped the princess push on, so be it. In the end, he would rule, and Ama would be at his side.

"You gave them false hope," Despondency said and groaned.

I will get them killed.

"They know nothing," Strife growled. "You will win, Moray."

Moray gulped and pushed the voices aside.

"I'm not cozying up with him." Gunnar eyed him, apparently joining the teasing when he realized it annoyed Moray.

Moray winked and made a kissing sound.

"Nothing will magically change," Finnigan said. "Together we are stronger. Elohai has a purpose for us here. No matter what Sadon or Barric have done, no matter what any of us have done, we have hope. Elohai will save us if we repent and do His will."

Moray shook his head. "Look around you! Elohai made this. He ripped the realms and allowed Darkness to run rampant."

Gunnar spoke up sharply. "Aye, and your master is the bloody devil himself, Moray. I don't see him doing us much good either!"

"I have saved us. I will get us home. No one else. Like the black magics or not, it is the only way we get home." Moray ate some more.

"A lie," Despondency whispered. "You can't even do the spells anymore. Too weak! Should have given up."

Finnigan's expression darkened as he met Moray's gaze. "We have not had the energy to argue, Moray, but we are not stupid. You spent months—years, maybe—studying the black magics. You became a warlock! Our parents died having the hope you would repent, that you would choose Elohai."

"Elohai gave us no knowledge to survive here," Moray snapped.

"You are the reason we are here," Gunnar said, voice dropping dangerously low. "I have half a mind that you are lying to us when you say you have a way home. If you continue to lie to us, I will kill you, Moray."

"Do not threaten the king, Gunnar." Moray smiled coldly, rage burning in his chest.

Gunnar laughed. "You are not the king. And I am not afraid of your master or your demons."

Moray shot to his feet, throwing himself at Gunnar. Gunnar moved out of his way swiftly, and Moray fell into the dirt. Fury blinding him, Moray yelled and attacked again, chest burning and fists shaking. Gunnar unsheathed a dagger and stepped sideways, snarling like a dog.

"Moray, stop!" Finnigan grabbed Moray by his arms. "Look at yourself! What is wrong with you?"

Strife grabbed Moray's head, the demon's claws digging into his skull. Moray yelled again and pulled away from

Finnigan roughly.

Then he heard a voice, firm and steady, almost inaudible.

Ama praying.

Moray turned his fury from Gunnar's threat to Ama's pleas for peace. "How can you pray to a God that let us go?" he hissed. Finnigan held him back, but Moray glowered at Ama. "Why have faith in a God that never blessed your pure heart?"

Ama didn't stop praying. Tears ran down her face, glinting in the firelight.

Strife grew quiet, trembling with rage, his control releasing on Moray's mind. Moray stopped yelling. He stared at Ama in utter dismay, and his body slacked.

Finnigan slapped him across the face. "Demon or no demon, you ever speak to her like that again, I will gut you," he whispered darkly. He went to Ama and wrapped his arms around her as she collapsed. She slumped against Finnigan's chest, and he lifted her up.

The woman was ill. Dying, probably, since no good thing could last in this place. Gunnar was a toughened mercenary, a killer with the mouth of a sailor. Finnigan and Moray were trained, educated, prepared to be warriors ready for anything. Ama was by no means weak—but her heart was purer than theirs.

"She should've known, should've shut up," Strife whispered. "It's her own fault she's dying. Not yours. You're simply warning her to stop praying. You're helping."

Moray turned away and mumbled, "Enjoy being king here, Finnigan."

Gunnar took first watch as they lay around the crackling fire. A heavy tension covered them. The eyes, oh, the eyes, circling and fluttering about in the treetops. Moray attempted to watch the billions of stars that tried peeking through the thick treetops. All he saw were the eyes.

Moray took a slow breath and leaned his head back. He focused on the warmth of the fire, ignoring the hard ground underneath him.

BLACKNESS.

The world fell away, and Moray stood in oblivion, a place without light and without scent.

Sadon stood across from him, haggard as a wet chicken, unlike his usual rogue appearance. "Before you jump to conclusions, allow me to explain."

"You sent us here to die!"

"I sent you there to save you," Sadon snapped. "Barric would have you all killed. You and Finnigan were no use to him. Graft tried to find you in the castle. Barric would have killed Ama, and Gunnar was a nuisance to the plot."

Graft had tried to find him... Even from the start, his death was on Moray's shoulders.

"You betrayed me!" Moray screamed, slamming his fists down. "You sold me to our master."

"Your faith is your own struggle. I saved you from death. You wanted to explore the forbidden second realm." Sadon chuckled, eyes bitter. "How has the forbidden fruit tasted, brother?"

Moray struck him, but his blow didn't fall on anything solid. "You killed us."

"Oh? You seem alive to me."

"Graft is dead."

Silence. Sadon sighed softly and shook his head. "I am sorry. He was a good slave."

"He was a man!" Moray shouted. His chest tightened with fury. The image of Graft's wide, agonized eyes and convulsing body was etched in Moray's head. "A good man. Better than any of us. And he is dead!"

"The rest of you?" Sadon had never been one for emotions.

"We live."

"Continue to do so until I can get you out."

"I do not trust you, Sadon. No longer. You will leave us here like pigs, like one big experiment, while you play god."

"Isn't that what we intended?" Sadon scoffed. "I will get you all back. Trust me or do not, my plan will not be disrupted, and it is bigger than you or Barric. He will not see my betrayal coming. In a few months, but not yet."

Moray froze. "Months?"

"How long has it been there?"

"A... a week, perhaps. I am not sure."

"It has been over four months here."

"You're bluffing, Sadon. You have no plan. You betrayed me, and for what? Barric as your king? You made a mistake." Moray clenched his fists, head whirling. They were running out of time.

"I will handle this." Sadon waved a hand.

Moray snarled. "No. I will. Your master is a fake and so is Finnigan's god. No power, good or evil, can help a sinner. I will handle this, Sadon. I do not need your mock mercy to do so."

He ended the connection.

Moray thought of the wizard he had seen in the prairie. Sadon did not mention him. Why not, unless he hadn't known?

Twenty-Eight

THE KINGDOM OF BUACACH stood strong against the realm. After six months, no conspiracists rose their voices for danger, and no war raged over the deaths of the royals. The victories happened slowly, day by day, month by month, but Sadon had watched the lands change. They all ran on a healthy fear of the king that could rip their world into shreds if he wanted.

Barric would be the emperor, the man the whole realm feared, and he would love bloodshed—but not yet. Not when he could lose it all in the blink of an eye. So long as Sadon kept the rebels in their places and Barric built his army, they could eventually be ready for anything that lay ahead.

Sadon watched Oliver eat his breakfast, pushing his solemn thoughts aside. The boy never complained about his new life. No doubt he yearned to play, bound across the yard, and have his vision of course, but he never asked for those things. He was a prisoner and knew that asking for freedom would be useless.

"I will be back in a few hours," Sadon muttered.

"Yessir."

Sadon licked his lips and tied his long white hair back. Ever since his connection with Moray months ago, the plan in Mazzabah was going along almost flawlessly. Buacach stopped fighting and submitted to Barric. The lands agreed to trades and acknowledged Barric as a worthy ruler. Master had shown Sadon nothing but blessings and kindness.

Except the boy.

Sadon downed the rest of his water. Ever since Oliver had appeared at his doorstep, Sadon's inner struggles heightened. He was on high alert. Every shadow could contain Shafiq. Every man who looked at him for too long was a killer in disguise. Awareness was a safe trait to have, but too much could kill. After Moray's connection, that paranoia grew even more.

Sadon didn't have any intention to return the group to Mazzabah. They'd die in Golgotha. A tragic turn of events but not one his master said to change.

Moray's warning was more than an idle threat. Sadon's gut wouldn't let it go. "You made a mistake," he'd said. Sadon had prepared for every risk, and even the unexpected had been handled with utmost professionalism.

Still, something was missing.

Something was wrong.

It was because of either Shafiq or Barric. Neither man could be trusted. Shafiq was a ruthless warlock, his entire life dedicated to creating a legion of elect warlocks capable of conquering both realms, but he had never gotten far into that goal. Barric was a greedy king who would betray Sadon if it benefited him.

Sadon would have to find the issue soon or he'd risk losing his life's work. Unless he brought them back. If he actually found a way to open the rift and let them come home, they could stand a chance together, again. But Moray wouldn't trust him. Sadon couldn't repair that. He'd best focus on handling his own.

"Mind yourself, boy." Taking Oliver by the shoulders, he led him to the cellar outside. Sadon's master hadn't told him to kill the boy yet. But he was a risky loose end.

Oliver staggered down the stairs, grunting. "You still think I'm a liar?"

Sadon slammed the cellar door shut and teleported to the Buacach castle, which bustled with activity. Barric had the finest cooks and the most expensive slaves, and his foods were often imported. The people spoiled him. When one person had all the power, no one had any choice but to appease them for the sake of their families' lives.

Sadon bowed to the king in the throne room. The king was alone, his security detail standing guard in the hall.

"Sadon," King Barric said with a smile. "How are things beyond the walls?"

Sadon told him how the hostile clans had stirred trouble with rival clans. It had ended quickly, thanks to Barric's troops interfering, as per the alliance. Sadon also told him of the ocean towns doing all they could to make Barric's wishes come true, and how men were preparing to enter the desert and find lands to take over. "All is going as we planned."

"We must stay alert," King Barric said. "Any rebel might raise their head when we least expect."

"We can handle it." Sadon studied Barric, hiding impatience. "Was there something you wished to discuss?"

"Yes." King Barric leaned back into his large throne. He wore the royal king's attire, complete with robes and thick jewels that Connall had never worn. Despite leading and creating some of the finest troops the land knew, King Barric was not one to choose a life of hardship over fleshly desires.

"I wish to know what you expected when you betrayed Moray." King Barric's smile never faltered.

Sadon frowned. This was not good. "It has been the plan all along to betray Moray and rid the kingdom of the princes."

"After our time of planning and acting together to create the strongest empire this world has known, still it is not enough." King Barric waved a hand. "We need more than Mazzabah can offer us."

"We will conquer Golgotha in due time, my king, as we've discussed."

"The egg will not hatch for me." King Barric's eyes darkened. They'd discussed the egg before. The topic always made the king throw or break something.

"We cannot enter Golgotha before this empire is ready, my king."

"We can do what I wish!"

Sadon took a slow breath. "I wish to please you, my king, but hatching the egg now would cause only disaster. We have neither the provisions nor the troops to stand a chance in Golgotha."

King Barric leaned forward, eyes boring holes into Sadon's head. "I am king now, Sadon. You will do as I request or—"

"Or?" Sadon smirked. "You'll behead me? Hang me? I am your only chance of building the empire and conquering Golgotha. I'm the only warlock, wizard, what say you, in Mazzabah worth his weight in gold!"

King Barric stood up, a booming laugh shaking his broad body. "Shall I kiss your feet? Worship you?"

"A little respect would go a long way, my king." Sadon clenched his jaw.

"I have news for you, *Uriah*..." King Barric stepped off the throne and stood face-to-face with Sadon, his dark eyes raging with demons, a smile on his lips as his voice dropped. "You are not the only traitor in this throne room."

Twenty-Nine

AFTER TWO DAYS OF traipsing through the swamplands, they were all exhausted. They occasionally killed any furry beasts that put up little fight, avoiding the snakes and sting-worthy monstrosities when they could.

Ama's strength drained from her body. She prayed hard almost every minute as they walked. Creator was the only one she could confide in. Finnigan, too, but they didn't have any time alone, and she wouldn't voice her weakness in front of Gunnar and Moray.

"If we don't find the end of this blasted swamp, I'll kill someone," Gunnar growled as they walked along. Ama bit back a chuckle.

"Are you all right, Gunnar?" Finnigan suppressed a smile, his eyes shining with amusement.

"I'm as dandy as a cobbler in a centipede village," Gunnar said loftily. "Why do you ask?"

"You seem tense." Finnigan fought a laugh, meeting Ama's gaze briefly, eyes twinkling.

Gunnar guffawed. "Tense? Why would I be tense? We've only been surviving by the skin of our teeth!"

"We have found water and food," Ama said gently. "We're doing fine."

"Fine," Gunnar repeated. "Being hunted and attacked by monsters is not my ideal state of *fine*."

"What would you prefer?" Moray pushed on through the bushes. The swamp had grown thinner, and they didn't have to hack paths so much now.

"Any place but this."

Finnigan sighed. "Elohai will help us through. He has thus far."

Ama nodded, her heart pounding. Creator was showing them mercy—mercy none of them deserved. Seeing the monsters and demons and being attacked daily didn't help her nerves, but she chose faith. Creator had always been with her. She'd gone to Buacach to marry Moray and begged Creator for mercy. She did not understand it, but she believed that Creator would use all of this for good... somehow.

Ama gulped hard as they walked in silence. Their footsteps trod the ground almost without sound.

Courage nuzzled Ama's cheek with her fluffy head. Ama rubbed Courage tiredly, legs shaky, but she pressed on.

Even here in the place of death, You are in me, giving fire to my bones. I thank You.

She let her gaze wander about the trees. The marks on the trunks never disappeared. Some were old, and the bark had started growing over the fleshy white marks. Some were new.

Ama didn't say anything, but she gripped Finnigan's hand, uneasy. She wished they could talk alone. There was so much she wanted to say, so much she wanted to ask, but privacy was a luxury. Today, she'd been far too tired to talk anyway.

She didn't want to die here. She needed to tell Finnigan about that wizard.

Finnigan stopped in his tracks, bringing her to a halt beside him. "Does anyone hear that?"

Nothing good came from that question in Golgotha, this much Ama knew. "No..."

Gunnar stopped, scowling as he eyed their surroundings. "I don't hear—"

A scream.

A haunting scream that drifted through the swamp and hung there for seconds. Ama's skin crawled.

Moray gripped his sword without batting an eye. "Keep moving."

Finnigan gasped. "That's a woman screaming. We must help—"

"It's a trap, Finnigan." Moray shook his head, moving forward.

The scream came again, desperate and grievous. Ama had never heard such a sound. She never wanted to hear it again. It made her heart pound and her hands go clammy.

Finnigan left the tiny path they'd torn. "What if Sadon sent someone else?"

The woman's heart-wrenching cry filled the forest again. Ama tensed and watched Finnigan head into the thick trees before hastily following.

"Finn!" Ama begged. "Stop!" The hair on the back of her neck stood up. Her legs ached, but she yanked him by his arm.

"It could be a woman sent from Mazzabah. She sounds like she needs our help." Finnigan didn't shove her off, but his jaw tightened. "I can't take the risk and not help, Ama."

Gunnar guffawed and pushed past them. The cry came again. Louder. More urgent. Ama fought the temptation to cover her ears and break down. "Stop it! Both of you. It's a —"

"It can't be a demon," Gunnar snapped. "Let's go see what it is."

Moray's eyes narrowed. "It is a swamp monster or a demon, and either way, trying to find it will only get you killed."

"Finnigan, please, it's a trap." Ama held tight, but he broke free, his face pale, eyes almost dazed.

"It isn't a trap," he said firmly. "She needs help."

"We need to help her," Gunnar muttered. It was the first time he and Finnigan had agreed on something.

"No!" Ama pushed herself in front of them, desperate. Exhaustion crept through her bones. She was powerless against them.

No, she wasn't. But why couldn't she see the demons? Were they attacking her? Or was this her flesh speaking?

The woman screamed again. She—or whatever it was—was moving toward them, by the sound of it. Moray came over and slapped Finnigan hard.

Finnigan snarled. "Do not touch me! I won't be heartless like you." He tried pushing into the woods.

"It's a trap, Finn! This is not from Creator." Ama's anger rose as she fought fear. "Stop!"

Gunnar broke into a run, disappearing into the woods and thick swampland. Moray swore but held Finnigan tightly. "Gunnar, get back here!"

Another broken scream.

Ama took a few weak steps, but her legs throbbed. The unknown poison running through her veins was weakening her legs. "Gunnar!"

Losing sight of Gunnar, Ama glanced back at Moray, tears burning her eyes. Moray wrestled with Finnigan, knocking him out once he applied pressure to Finnigan's neck. Ama gasped and rushed to Finnigan's side, legs giving out. "Moray!"

Moray ignored her disdain, sheathed his sword, and fled into the trees. Ama held Finnigan, praying as hard as she could that Creator would open their eyes and make the screaming stop.

MORAY RAN THROUGH THE trees, heart thumping steadily in his chest. His boots barely hit the ground, and branches and thorns dragged across his skin and tore at his clothes.

He should've killed the dumb jackass.

Gunnar ran on like a wolf, but Moray gained on him. The mercenary was entranced by the screaming and ran into a thicket before tearing out with his blade, snarling.

The screaming was messing with Gunnar's mind. What monster was this?

Moray couldn't think of anything he had learned from the books and lore. He'd not heard of any screaming woman, unless it was a demon, but he didn't feel like it was.

Strife clawed at Moray's head, but he pushed on. "Gunnar, it will kill you! Turn back."

They ran, skittered, tumbled through the swamp. Tiny vipers and small furry creatures fled from them—or bit at them and Moray didn't stop long enough to fight.

"Let him die. He deserves death," Strife hissed.

Moray didn't stop running and he didn't know why. The woman's pained cries rang out in the heavy swamp atmosphere.

Gunnar staggered to a stop ahead of Moray. In the dark heavy-hanging trees, a woman hovered above the wetland. She glowed a pale white color, bare, her pitch-black hair cascading down her thin shoulders.

A ghost. She was a mere echo, no flesh or bone, no spirit left to save.

The ghost woman extended an arm. Her mouth gaped, opening twice as large as it ought to have. A broken scream tore from her lungs, no longer simply anguished. Instead, she begged for help—luring anyone who was foolish enough to come be killed.

Moray ran up behind Gunnar but didn't touch him. "Gunnar, she will kill you. Snap out of it."

Despondency whimpered, pulling at Moray's temples. "Give up and run!"

Moray grabbed Gunnar's arm. Gunnar stood dumbfounded, wide eyes watching the ghost scream. He shoved Moray off and reached out for the woman, who had large pleading eyes.

Moray swore. "No, she'll kill you! What is wrong with you? Let's go!"

If the ghost was casting a spell or something strange, it would be hopeless. He'd have to hit the mercenary and restrain him. A problem solved through violence, as usual.

"She's crying." Gunnar's voice was barely audible. "She needs help. She needs to be saved from this hell!" He struck Moray hard between the eyes, his blade barely missing Moray's skin.

Moray dropped like a rock, moaning. Mud soaked his pants and he groped in the moss, searing pain bursting through his skull. Face half-buried in slop, he barely made out Gunnar's figure moving closer to the ghost.

"Should've bashed his head open," Strife said, moaning. "Should've killed him before it got to this..." but the voice faded.

The last thing Moray processed was a large figure throwing Gunnar to the ground. The ghost woman screamed again, mouth gaping wide to reveal countless jagged teeth.

AMA HELD FINNIGAN'S HEAD out of the dirt, her dagger drawn in case any creature found them. Ama shook him gently but he didn't wake, and she stopped trying when the scream came again. Whatever the monster was, it had lured Gunnar as prey and was trying the same with Finnigan, no doubt.

Ama's stomach churned and she called for Moray. He didn't answer.

The scream sounded again and again. Ama gripped Finnigan tightly but pushed her shoulders up against her ears the best she could. Courage didn't seem bothered by the screams and put her long, lanky body against Ama's ears, helping block the sound. Courage licked her fangs and watched the trees.

Ama gulped hard, heart hammering as she waited, but the two men didn't come back. Only a few minutes had passed. She couldn't go search for them and risk leaving Finnigan behind. If she woke him, the screams might lure him again.

A cry echoed through the wetland once more—but this one wasn't heartbroken. The woman's cry shook with utter rage and pain. Ama jerked, fighting fear as she whispered prayers. Courage nuzzled her cheek. Had Moray killed it?

She sat still, shaking softly. Courage darted around Finnigan and chattered at him, almost angry-looking, but he didn't wake. Ama whispered, "Stop, Courage, he could—"

Out of the forest came a man. Around his broad shoulders, Moray hung like a limp rag doll, blood pouring from a gash between his eyes. Behind the stranger, Gunnar stumbled out, his head down. Blood gushed from a wound along his right forearm.

"Moray!" Ama laid Finnigan down and jumped up, rushing over.

The large man dropped Moray to the dirt. A long, tangled beard hung from his face, and his dark hair was streaked with gray. Ama grabbed a piece of white cloth from the canvas bag and put it against the wound to stop the bleeding. "Gunnar, wake Finn!" she ordered.

Gunnar knelt beside Finnigan, slapping him. "Wake up, princess."

Ama gripped Moray's shoulder, holding the rag steady. She didn't think the wound was too deep. Moray's chest rose and fell with even breaths. She glanced up at the stranger, heart in her throat. "Who are you?"

He was flesh and blood. Not a demon, not a spirit. He looked strangely like Gunnar. Same big build, same hair...

"Absalom," the man said, his voice slow and quiet, like he hadn't spoken in a long time.

Ama gulped hard. "Th-thank you for saving them."

Finnigan woke with a groan, shooting upright. "Ama!"

She gasped. "Easy. Can you heal Moray?"

Gunnar backed up, silent as death, keeping his distance from all of them. Finnigan dragged himself to his feet and knelt beside his older brother, healing the head injury tiredly. "Who is—"

"This is Absalom," Ama said. Absalom watched them closely like a dog watching prey. "He saved them."

Moray sat upright, rubbing his head with a growling swear. "Gunnar, you—" he stopped short when he saw Absalom. The man met his gaze and didn't speak another word. Moray sat up and Finnigan steadied him. Ama held on to the bloody rag as if for dear life, head whirling as they studied the strange man in Golgotha, the realm where no man was supposed to escape.

"Where did you come from?" Moray demanded.

"Mazzabah." Absalom turned to Gunnar, expression softening. "Why are you here?"

Ama's chest tightened. As gravelly as the man's foreign voice was, it was heavy with raw pain.

Moray opened his mouth, no doubt ready to wrestle answers from the man first, but Ama gripped his wrist. She shook her head, and for once, Moray listened and fell silent.

"We were sent here by a warlock. His name was Sadon." Gunnar couldn't meet the man's eyes. His empty, calloused hands trembled at his sides.

Absalom repeated the name. "Who are they?" His gaze fell back to the others, studying each of them intently. Ama held his gaze when he watched her.

"Um..." Gunnar stepped closer and gestured half-heartedly. "Prince Moray and Prince Finnigan of the Buacach Kingdom, Princess Ama from the Wolf Clan."

Absalom's shoulders drew back slightly and he knelt before them. He said something that Ama didn't understand.

Ama quickly stepped forward. "There's no need to bow before us. Please, you saved us, not the other way around." She didn't dare touch him.

Absalom lifted his head slowly, like her words took effort to process. Any part of his face not covered by hair was scarred—some scars looked like claw marks and some looked like he'd been gashed. Ama's heart dropped to her feet. How much hell had he faced in his lifetime?

"Stand, Papa," Gunnar said softly, touching Absalom's shoulder. Absalom pushed himself to his feet.

Ama froze. Papa? Gunnar hadn't said a word of his past to anyone but her. He had said his father was killed at sea. They'd never found the ship.

He was here... How?

"He's your father?" Moray asked. Finnigan moved to Ama's side and took her bloodied hand into his own.

"Yes." Gunnar set his jaw. "He is. And he saved us."

"The Swamp Woman has claimed lives before," Absalom said, voice quiet, grievous. "Not another."

Ama's skin crawled. "How long have you been here?"

Absalom met her gaze. "Over two years." He closed his eyes briefly. "Gunnar is not a child... He is grown. It has been much longer."

"Ten years in Mazzabah," Gunnar said, voice empty. Absalom had been stuck here. He'd missed Gunnar growing up.

Before Ama could speak, Moray asked, "Who sent you here?" It couldn't have been Sadon—Ama didn't think he was capable of casting out anyone a decade earlier. He was hardly Moray's age at the moment.

"Shafiq." Absalom's voice trembled with rage. "He was a part of our crew. He sent us all here... He sent us here to die. A portal appeared above the ocean, then Mazzabah was gone." He worked hard to make the words come out clearly.

Moray frowned. "Who is Shafiq?" He kept Finnigan and Ama close to him, but Gunnar stood beside his father, holding his arm like he might disappear.

"Shafiq is a great warlock. I was the captain, and he was part of my crew. I did not know of his forbidden magic." Absalom spoke like the words strained him.

Moray took a slow breath. "Captain Absalom of the *Königin*... I remember," he whispered. "Your ship was lost. Over thirty men vanished."

Gunnar's expression darkened. "Why would Shafiq send you all here?"

Absalom shook his head. "He told us he was experimenting for his master's plan. We could do nothing to stop him."

Ama didn't think it was like either man to admit defeat —but then she realized Absalom stood here alone. Over thirty men, a whole crew, had been sent into Golgotha with him. All dead now.

She worked her jaw to keep from crying.

Gunnar shot Moray and Finnigan glares. "I think we ought to keep moving. We're burning daylight."

"You are close to the desert," Absalom said, following Gunnar's change of topic quickly. "There are fewer creatures there but no water."

"Is there any ocean here? Have you seen any large body of water?" Moray asked.

Absalom studied him for a moment. "You're in a swamp."

Now they knew where Gunnar got his tongue.

"Yes, but a larger one," Moray urged.

"Yes, beyond the desert there is the sea," Absalom said, voice soft.

Ama's heart pounded. She didn't believe Creator would let them escape by Moray's magic method. But they couldn't just camp out in the swamp either, so she kept quiet.

"Then we go through the desert." Gunnar gripped his father's arm for dear life.

"We must make it through the swamp first," Moray mused wryly.

Finnigan, speaking for the first time, smiled gently and looked at each of them. "We'd best find more spring water and prepare."

Absalom's gaze lingered on Finnigan for a long moment before he turned and led them into the wetland without another word.

Thirty

FINNIGAN SUPPRESSED DOZENS OF questions as they moved through the thick wetland. Hours of walking left him bursting at the seams with curiosity—walking behind him was a man who had survived Golgotha for over two years. Absalom spoke in hushed tones with Gunnar, but everyone else kept out of it. Finnigan itched to ask the rugged man questions. How had he survived this long? Did he think there was a way out of Golgotha?

The way Absalom had looked at Finnigan when he said that Elohai would help them through... His expression had looked broken. Just briefly. Maybe he was overthinking it.

But Finnigan rarely overthought anything—in his humble opinion anyway—so he didn't think so.

He watched Moray lead them. Absalom and Gunnar had rotated that position with Moray—Absalom knew the swamp better than any of them and it showed in the way he led, but he gave Moray the reins so he could speak with Gunnar in the back of their trail.

Since the screaming Swamp Woman, Finnigan didn't talk much. Guilt ate at his gut over what he'd done. After all his prayers, he had failed Elohai and been so easily fooled. He'd failed Ama too. What was she feeling? She probably thought he was stupid or unworthy or... He gulped down the lump in his throat.

Maybe Ama didn't need him, but everything in him wanted to protect her. Finnigan would get her home to her family even if it killed him. She deserved to see her family, to see her clan, to be with the friends she held so dear.

Ama's hand slipped into his own—cold, trembling. Finnigan's step faltered, but he squeezed her tightly and let her lean on him. She was growing sicker. They had applied the salve twice daily, but the salve wouldn't last forever and wasn't helping much. Ama felt weaker, though she did everything she could to appear fine. She'd offered no explanation to what had happened.

"I will lead now, Moray," Absalom said. The man's revering attitude toward the royalty hadn't lasted when they told him not to bother. He was the best equipped to keep them all alive, so they would do best to just listen and obey.

Moray wasn't so fond of the arrangement. He scowled but let Absalom move to the front. "How much longer shall we walk here?" he asked calmly.

"Eight more hours at this pace." Absalom shot Ama a small frown.

Ama didn't seem to notice, but Finnigan's grip on her hand tightened. "We're making fine pace."

"She is slowing us down." Absalom walked onward, not looking back.

"It was a wizard." Ama didn't look up.

Finnigan tensed. "What? A wizard?"

He'd assumed the wound was from a snake or some other venomous creature. Whatever had happened, it obviously shook her, and he wanted to help her if he could. Ama looked down, but Finnigan gave her hand a squeeze. "You can tell us anything," he said gently.

Moray stopped in his tracks, watching Ama, eyes dark. "What do you mean, a wizard?"

Finnigan stopped and pulled Ama close. She took a deep breath. "I did not recognize him. H-he wore a dark cloak and held a staff with the head of a serpent. He stabbed a needle into my neck and was gone."

"What did he look like?" Moray pressed.

Ama described his face, but her voice grew strained. Finnigan placed a hand on her shoulder. "It was not Sadon?"

"No." She shook her head, thick dark hair falling over her cheeks. "It was not Sadon."

Absalom frowned. "Did he say anything?"

Ama hesitated but told them what he said, adding, "I-I do not know who he was, but he was there. Physically he was here in Golgotha. Somehow."

Absalom gave them a thoughtful frown, weathered expression hard and eyes cold. "The man you describe..." he trailed off. "That is Shafiq. The man who opened the portal and sent my crew here. I have spent all this time trying to escape, and he has been watching me all the while."

"I think between the five of us, we have something your crew never had. Black magic." Moray smirked. "I will get us home." He started walking, and the rest followed once again. They had no choice.

Finnigan led Ama on, praying hard over her shaking body.

THEY CAMPED IN THE swamp. Finnigan started a fire and Absalom tended it till it burned hot and steady. Absalom spent a short while scavenging for food—he knew more of edible plants and hunting meat. They ate a rather hearty dinner around the glowing fire. Ama helped the best she could, but Finnigan didn't let her do much. She ate quietly, hungry though her eyelids drooped.

Absalom didn't eat much, but he tried answering their questions. Gunnar asked a few, his expression heavy, constantly checking the surrounding trees for predators.

Ama watched Gunnar eat for a moment. He had spent a decade of his life without family, growing from a sailor's son into a top-notch mercenary. She gulped hard, pain growing in her chest.

"Over two years," Moray said quietly, "and you believe there is no way out. I will prove you wrong, but only if we get to the sea. We need your help to do that."

"I will help." Absalom gave him a cool smirk—he and Gunnar looked almost identical when they were being demeaning. "I've already saved your lives once, so do not treat me like a confused old man."

Moray frowned but didn't lose his temper again. They needed to pull together, and even he couldn't deny it at this point. He returned the smile and said, "At this rate, you say we'll reach the desert tomorrow?"

Absalom nodded once. "We will gather more supplies. The desert changes swiftly here. It might take us only a few days to reach the sea, or weeks, depending on the season. It is confusing." He glanced at Ama with a slight frown.

Heat flooded Ama's cheeks and she put her food down, losing her appetite. Was she weighing them down? Would she get them killed? She gulped down the lump in her throat. Her blood boiled, and the pain settled in. The antidote had only worked so much, and that was becoming clear—perhaps she wouldn't be all right.

"We will be fine," Finnigan said sharply. "Ama is strong and she's making fine progress."

Absalom sighed. "It will be different in the sun. We will need better coverings to survive the heat, and more containers for water."

"Where do you expect us to get those?" Moray raised one eyebrow.

"You're a wizard, aren't you?" Absalom smirked and leaned back. "I have a small shelter at the edge of the swamp—it has woven containers. We can make hats out of leaves and such tomorrow."

"A stylish plan," Moray muttered, standing. "I'll take first watch." He went to the edge of the tiny camp and faced the woods.

Gunnar shifted and finished his meal, sighing. "Ama is ill, and since there's no cure, we'll just have to do the best we can. If it comes down to it, we can always carry her."

"It will wear us out more, and we will never make it." Absalom shook his head.

Ama stared at her food. Finnigan kept a hand on her leg, but she found no comfort in his kindness.

Finnigan met Absalom's gaze, expression dark with fury. "Whatever you're implying will never happen. I will carry Ama to the ocean. None of us will be left behind." He spoke with utter conviction, and the image of Graft's burnt body filled Ama's mind.

Absalom studied her and looked away, face falling. "Forgive me. I did not mean—"

"You've done nothing but survive, Father," Gunnar intervened, voice taut and obviously angered by the conversation. Ama couldn't tell if he was angry at her or Absalom. Probably her. "We will make it through this—just slightly different than you have. You aren't alone anymore."

Absalom closed his eyes, moving closer to the warm fire. "I was never alone."

Ama's chest ached. She wiped sweat from her temple. "What do you mean?"

"I had my men. I had them until I lost them. Every one of them, gone." Absalom's voice broke. "But I still had Elohai..." He held his face, and his shoulders shook, but he never made a sound. Gunnar knelt and wrapped his arms around his father's broad body, face turned away.

Ama dropped her head and fought tears. "We have to have faith that Creator will get us home. None of this has been for naught. Nothing we have done is unforgivable, Absalom," she whispered gently.

It was the truth, but it hurt. Creator was a God of mercy and justice, and even when Ama didn't understand Him, He had cause. More importantly, He loved them.

She had made mistakes. She had fallen in love with Finnigan when she had to give her love to Moray. Tears ran down her face, and she gripped Finnigan's hand tightly.

"Ama..." Finnigan put his arm around her. "Ama, what are you saying?" His voice drifted, distant, like he was moving away.

Darkness overwhelmed her. Heat ran through her veins.

"She's delirious," Absalom said.

"What's she praying?" Moray demanded, voice just as far away as the others.

Forgive me, Creator.

Thirty-One

THE DEMONS CAME WHEN Ama slipped into unconsciousness. Black beasts with large wings and long claws, hanging in the trees like vultures waiting for meat. Moray grabbed his blade, Strife and Despondency hissing in his ears.

Finnigan held Ama's unconscious, trembling body in his arms. His eyes widened with rage as the demons circled. Almost as soon as he realized what they faced, he prayed—loud and hard, like his life depended on it, but Moray hardly heard what he said. Moray didn't care. He wouldn't sit around and beg some Creator to save him.

"Save yourself," Strife growled. "You have to."

One of the demons jumped from a tree, wings folded on his back. It had an impish grin as it studied Moray. "After all, you're righteous, are you not? A wizard, warlock, sorcerer, a man of many names and many skills... Are you not a god?"

Moray froze in place and stared at Self-righteousness. "I can get us out of here," he whispered. "I am no monster."

"No, you're a holy man." Self-righteousness gestured at the group that Moray couldn't seem to look at or hear. "They are all lost, Moray. Lost sheep must be saved by the wise."

"Don't listen to this," Strife hissed. "Don't save them!"

"If you don't save them, who will sing your praises? Who will kiss your feet out of reverence?" Self-righteousness whispered, stretching out a hand.

Moray stepped closer, heart hammering. Despondency moaned in his ear, begging him to give up and let the demons have their triumph. Moray looked Self-righteousness in the eye and choked out, "I welcome you. I always have. I'm no monster. I can save us." It was not a command so much as a plea. A desperate plea for help, and if a demon heard his cries, perhaps the Darkness held more mercy than the world believed.

Self-righteousness grinned and grabbed a hold of Moray.

FINNIGAN PRAYED ALOUD WITH all his might while the demons swarmed. One black body attached to Moray before disappearing out of thin air. It had latched on.

A winged beast jumped onto Gunnar, its thick claws digging into his temples. Gunnar screamed, reeling. He staggered, tumbling, half of his body dropping into the campfire. Gunnar tore at the demon on his body desperately, but the demon pushed him down as if it weighed a thousand pounds.

Absalom snatched Gunnar off the fire, rolling him into the damp ground. "Gunnar, fight it!"

"Gunnar!" Finnigan pulled Ama tighter. They wrestled not against flesh and blood but against principalities. Resisting the urge to run to the mercenary's side, he prayed. "I rebuke these reinforcements sent to destroy Elohai's chosen," he screamed. "I dismantle you all in the name of Elohai. His blood shields us!"

But Gunnar hadn't covered himself in the blood. The demons had not come tonight to haunt. They'd come for his bloodshed.

Absalom held Gunnar by his head, wrestling past the demon that he couldn't feel, but it was visibly fighting against Gunnar's body and holding him immobile. Absalom gripped Gunnar's face, voice urgent but eerily calm. "Elohai will save you. Repent, Son."

"I can't," Gunnar said, making a choking sound. The brutal, brusque mercenary was weeping and screaming. Another demon pounced from the trees and latched on to his head.

Gunnar cried out and tore at his shaggy dark hair. He thrashed, legs jerking, the left side of his torso singed from the fire. The stench of burnt flesh filled Finnigan's nostrils, but he pushed his nausea aside.

The demons watched from above. Their red eyes shifted and came closer. They bared their fanged teeth in wide grins. The demons jeered and snarled, the noises chorusing in the atmosphere. They laughed at Moray and Gunnar's agony, hissed and moaned when Finnigan prayed.

Gunnar thrashed beneath the demons and his father. Absalom held him, steadying his terrified son. Gunnar didn't stop convulsing and screaming.

Finnigan sucked in a breath. He prayed, and the demons screamed in fury. His hands shook and he wept over Ama's body, but he waged war with his Father like his life depended on it—because it did.

Elohai, Finnigan prayed, *I can't rebuke the spirits attacking Gunnar if I don't know them. Reveal them to me. For Gunnar's sake.*

Rejection, a demon that moaned in Gunnar's ears, weeping and panicking as it clutched his heart.

Revenge, a demon with bloodshot eyes and strong claws around Gunnar's hands.

Finnigan watched one more demon tormenting Gunnar in the dirt. He did not know what it was, but he knew the names of two of the demons. "Rejection and Revenge!" he snarled. "In the name of Elohai, be gone from him!"

Absalom continued to speak to Gunnar, who cried and screamed at him and Finnigan. "I cannot make them leave. Let me go. Let go!"

The demons screeched and warped his mind, thirsty for death, their bloodlust unquenchable.

Gunnar cried hard, eyes clamped shut. The demons kept speaking to him, though Finnigan didn't hear as he kept praying. Sweat poured from his temples and he felt Ama's feverish neck for a pulse. A soft thump met his fingers and he held on to hope.

Gunnar screamed again. The demons covered his body now. There was nothing Absalom could do.

Gunnar cried, just loud enough that Finnigan understood the choked words. "Elohai, forgive me." Fight lay in those words, but a heavy surrender too. Like he had given up a part of himself and held on desperately for the will to push on despite the demons holding him by the neck.

The demons clawing at his body screamed in outrage. "No!" Rejection snarled. "Elohai has done nothing for you. He does not love you. Who could love a killer? Who has ever loved you?"

Gunnar grappled at Absalom's arms, eyes still shut. "Elohai, save me!" he said, moaning. Revenge's claws sank deeper into his flesh. The third demon held its hands over his eyes, and he couldn't fight them off his body.

Absalom held Gunnar tightly and pulled something off his belt. A short, curved ram's horn. He held it to his lips and blew. A shrill, piercing sound burst through the swamp. As if fire poured from the horn's broad end, the demons screeched and took flight. They pulled away, cursing loudly.

Absalom blew again, the note long and crisp. The shofar's sound sent the demons in disarray. All Finnigan could do was pray and watch, astounded.

Finnigan breathed, glancing down at Ama's sweaty face and kissed her forehead. He was losing her. She wasn't breathing. "Elohai, heal her. Please... please heal her." His breath caught in his throat. "Absalom, help us!"

Thirty-Two

HANGING BY CHAINS IN a musty prison cell, on his knees and bare besides one undergarment, Sadon was alone with his demons. Every fiber in his being told him that he was a dead man.

King Barric knew his name. The name he had not used since fleeing Shafiq as a boy.

Uriah.

He had not been Uriah in a long time.

Sadon seethed, tugging at his chains. With the magic binding him against saying a spell or incantation, courtesy of Shafiq's abilities that Sadon hadn't yet mastered entirely, he could not free himself. He still prayed, but the questions overwhelmed him, and Abaddon probably didn't listen.

King Barric had betrayed him, just as Sadon had betrayed Moray. He hadn't trusted Barric but hadn't expected anything drastic so soon.

Shafiq was far more powerful than Sadon. If he combined forces with Barric, the realm could kiss its ass goodbye.

Sadon kicked himself for not expecting it when Oliver showed up at his door. He should have figured it out.

Where had Shafiq been? He'd disappeared, he had been gone for all this time, since Sadon had fled him... He should have hunted Shafiq.

A foolish thought. Sadon would never have faced Shafiq and survived. But now he had to fight or die, and he would not die on his knees.

Sadon closed his eyes. Oliver waited in the cellar in the middle of the wild woods. Without Sadon, he would starve, a meal for the rats. He was just a boy. The same helpless, terrified boy that Sadon had been. Back when he was Uriah. Back when he was human.

Back when he was capable of being saved.

There was a time when a monster could no longer be saved. No matter the person's origin, some lines were crossed and no redemption could be offered. Sadon did not think of himself as needing salvation—but Oliver was.

After all the years of hard work Sadon had spent building his empire, he would rather taste death than defeat. He couldn't save Oliver alone.

Abaddon would let Sadon die if he sought to make a future for the boy. If Sadon destroyed everything he had done... After all he'd risked and sacrificed for his master, this was the payment he'd receive?

You did not choose me. The voice was clear in his mind.

"I chose you," Sadon hissed. "I chose you over everything. Over my life, over my soul, over my friends—I gave everything. I turned into a monster for *you*!" His hoarse voice echoed in the damp cell.

His master replied, "You disobeyed me."

"Oliver could have been useful. We needed him alive."

"I told you to kill him. Remember that dream?"

Sadon had ignored it the moment he woke up. "He is no good dead."

"You are better off dead than come against me, Sadon."

Sadon laughed bitterly. "I am your most loyal, ruthless servant. When I step out of line, you kill me? I don't believe it." But fear grabbed a hold of his heart with both hands and clamped down. Hard.

"It is not your disobedience that must be punished."

"What is it?" Sadon snarled under his breath. He needn't talk, as his master could hear his thoughts, but Sadon wouldn't be a tight-jawed slave any longer. Speaking at least filled the shadows with his rage. He wouldn't bottle it up and whimper inside like he had when he'd been a child, chained and tortured. When he'd first been given the tattoo, he'd cried but never screamed.

"You have let yourself believe the illusion that honor may save this empire. I cannot allow my son to be so easily deceived." The voice dropped, frigid, sending shudders down Sadon's skin.

"How?" Sadon demanded. "I've done your will my whole life."

"Yet you were misled by a mere child. You have let love take root—and love cannot take root within a beast without a divine intervention. Tell me why this has happened."

"It has not."

Abaddon said coldly, "You chose to turn your back on me."

"What have you done for me?" Sadon whispered. "I loved you as my Father. You were my everything when I had nothing. But you let Shafiq win, over me. You promised me a life when I left Shafiq, but you have given me nothing but death."

His hands were heavy with blood. He saw all of it now. Dark red liquid fell from his fingers and crept into the cracks of the stone beneath him. He told himself it wasn't real.

Sadon groaned and clenched his bloodied fists. He didn't want this. He wanted Oliver to break free from the life of bones, demons, and Darkness.

Abaddon appeared before him, grabbing Sadon by his chin. Eons of hatred and pride burned behind Abaddon's eyes. He could take any form he wished. Sadon saw him as a handsome man, old enough to be his father, but Abaddon offered no comfort, no guidance. Only rejection.

"I made you a god," Abaddon growled, spittle flying into Sadon's face. "In the greatest time of trial, facing your mentor for the first time in years, what do you do? Did you call upon the magic? Did you call upon me? No!" he boomed. "You froze like a child. You are no warrior of mine. Not when you let that rat of a child live. You know the prayers he speaks to his Elohai." He smiled, dark eyes gleaming. "You let him pray in your home dedicated to me, your very own Father?"

"I failed you," Sadon choked out, anger rising, "but you left me."

Abaddon held his face tighter. "I was going to help you. I was going to let you rise above my servant Shafiq—and you were weak. You failed yourself... You failed the empire."

Sadon's heart hammered. He would not fail.

"I know you want to fix this, but nothing you do will save you." Abaddon let go roughly. "Remember that. Elohai will not lay His light upon you. I will kill you before He does. You are mine!"

Sadon set his jaw and didn't lift his head. He would get out of here. He would get the group of fools back to save Mazzabah. For Oliver.

The wooden door creaked open and light poured in, disrupted by a tall, broad, familiar figure. Abaddon disappeared into thin air.

"Hello, Uriah." Shafiq stepped closer, beaming. He ran a well-manicured hand through Sadon's long, tangled hair, stained with blood. "This brings you back, doesn't it? Chains, cells, demons, magic, and torture. Let's catch up, shall we? I know most of what's going on in the kingdoms, the tribes... but, hmm, you're full of knowledge pertaining to the royals lost in Golgotha. What have you and Moray exchanged during these months?" He leaned in, whispering into Sadon's ear, "Be a good boy again, Uriah. You're a dead one if you aren't."

Thirty-Three

THEY MADE SLOW PROGRESS through the swamp the day of the spiritual attack and camped in the wetland once more. They didn't reach the desert as they wished. Ama had been healed when Absalom blew his dark brown shofar and prayed over her, but her weakness remained.

The weathered seaman unnerved Moray, but after the attack, he rarely spoke. It was clear Absalom believed in Elohai. He just chose not to voice much else besides tart remarks and instructions on how they would survive.

Around the fire that night, after a day of walking and preparing for the sandy road before them, they talked. Moray focused on finalizing his own leafy hat that Absalom promised would help fend off the sun. Despite himself, he heard the others.

Ama, still weary and quiet but in much better health and spirits, sat beside Finnigan. They spoke about Elohai with Gunnar and Absalom. Gunnar was hungry for knowledge of the God he had surrendered to hours before.

Self-righteousness sighed on Moray's shoulder. "Soon they will be thanking you for saving them. They will see you as the man you truly are."

Strife groaned. "If you don't let a couple of them die first. They deserve it. They're weak and stupid. Look at them speak of hope."

Moray bit his lip, sipping from his waterskin. He laid the quiver of arrows down on the ground beside him, fingering the bow that Absalom had given him. Moray was an excellent marksman—a better marksman than he was a swordsman, while Finnigan could wield a sword better than Moray ever could. Absalom gifted Finnigan a large blade, and Finnigan beamed ear to ear.

"Thank you," Finnigan said firmly. "It will feel good to have something besides the Gift."

Absalom nodded once, eyeing Ama. "Your Gift, Ama. Have you seen it yet?"

"Yes." Ama didn't comment further, staring into the fire, the flames flickering shadows across her weary face.

Moray frowned at the strange question. She had the Gift of dreams—what use could that be here in Golgotha? Gifts of elements and powers were useful in the Place of Bones, but what could some dreams fix?

"She got us into this mess," Strife said sharply. "Her dream... Elohai warned her... This is all because of her meddling. Graft is dead because of her hunch."

Moray set his jaw. Perhaps the plan had been ruined because of her, but he didn't regret letting her live. He just ought to have taken better steps to keep her silent.

"Too late for that now," Self-righteousness murmured. "You did the best you could and you will continue to do so. It will be enough."

"It won't be!" Despondency said weakly. "It will never be enough."

Moray sighed and focused on his meal. For a moment, he wondered what it had been like for Gunnar, chasing those demons away and freeing his mind. "Gunnar?"

The merc lifted his head from studying the trees.

"What was it like, losing those demons?"

Gunnar eyed him wearily before answering. "I will not listen to you mock me."

"I am not."

"Why shouldn't you? You're carrying around demons, and I have a distinct feeling all you want to do is refute what happened today. You can't, can you? You, a powerful warlock, are not so powerful. Even here, in the darkest realm, the outcast region, the Light shines through. The Light is undefeated, piercing the Darkness and revealing truths that we don't want to face. We must face them if we want to escape alive. And you?" Gunnar scoffed and shook his head. "You would rather let all of us die here than admit you need saving, just as we do."

Moray's blood boiled, but he kept his head. "I have saved us, Gunnar. I have led us—"

"You think you are a god," Gunnar said and held up a hand. "But you are a sinner, just as we are. You cannot save us. There is no reason to reach the sea besides the fact the swamp is going to be our deaths. Ama had a dream."

Moray blinked. "What?" He studied Ama, but she stared down at Courage in her lap. "What dream?"

"A... a dream when I was sleeping, when Finnigan carried me after I was healed." Ama sucked in a slow breath. "We will reach the ocean, and Elohai will take us home." Her words were firm, but something lingered in them. Something she tried to hide. Something grievous.

What else had she dreamt?

Moray laughed. "Oh? That simple, aye? Elohai has let us face hell, face monsters, face demons, and lose a good man—His own servant—just so we can waltz home on His good graces?" He didn't mean to raise his voice, but he couldn't calm down. Not with Strife's claws pulsing at his temples, drilling him on, taking his tongue.

Finnigan shot to his feet. "Be quiet, demon!"

Strife hissed and his grip on Moray deepened. Moray's head throbbed. "How can you argue with me?" He smirked. "Elohai has done nothing for us. Ama's dreams mean nothing!"

Finnigan stepped forward, punching Moray hard in the jaw. Moray hit his knees and held his face, groaning. His vision danced and blackened.

"You will watch your tongue, Moray," Finnigan said vehemently. "Too long I have allowed you to treat Ama poorly. You will harm her no more!"

Moray held his aching jaw. He glared up at Finnigan, hauling himself to his feet. "She is my betrothed. When we return, by my doing, I will marry her and restore Buacach as the rightful king."

Ama stood up, legs shaking slightly, fists clenched. She looked Moray in the eyes and said, "Unless we turn to Him and repent, Creator will not bless our people."

"He will not get us home. He has caused this! I have done what I've done to help my people." Moray's heart grew cold, and the demons hissed in his ears.

Finnigan laughed bitterly, running a hand through his grimy curls. "You are lost. Elohai have mercy, I cannot... I cannot save you." His eyes moistened with tears, but he turned away from Moray and walked into the forest.

Ama weakly limped after him. Absalom watched them leave, then turned to Moray. His wrinkled, hairy face was hard with—what was it? Anger? No. The man didn't show a single emotion. He said in a low voice, "The demons you love now will love your death more."

FINNIGAN WAS INCHES AWAY from snapping his older brother's neck. They'd always bickered, always competed, but Moray wasn't even himself now. How many demons had he welcomed? If he didn't repent and surrender to Elohai, would Elohai shed mercy and take them home? Or would they stay here till they died?

"Finn." Ama's soft voice came from beside him. She touched his arm.

"I'm fine."

"You're not fine." She shook her head, giving his arm a gentle squeeze. "We cannot change him, but it does not mean Creator does not hear our prayers."

Finnigan worked his jaw. "Moray is no closer to salvation than he was when we were sent here. If anything, he's worse." Moray had gone from being cold-hearted to utterly intolerable.

Elohai had shown Himself to them repeatedly. He'd helped them, and Moray could not stand that.

"No one is so far that Creator cannot save them."

"If they repent."

She hugged him, small compared to his tall, lanky frame. Finnigan held Ama tightly, breathing in and out for a few moments, focusing solely on her heartbeat thumping against his chest.

"Then we pray he repents." She relaxed against him.

"I'm concerned that whatever it will take to change Moray will not be good." Even Graft's death had not softened him. It had made him harder, colder. What more could possibly shake Moray's heart?

Ama squeezed him, lifting her head and studying his face. Her deep brown eyes glimmered with hope. "Creator is for us. Why should we be afraid? Remember the Letters?"

Moray had come and sat between them as if they were unruly teenagers. Finnigan remembered Moray scoffing at the Letters and arguing over the heart of Elohai. Ama remembered the blessings and the good. All this time, Finnigan would've argued that no one could be more optimistic than he was.

A soft grin broke over his face. "I do now." Finnigan didn't let her go. He didn't want to think that their friendship would ever have to end. They'd only known each other—what, hadn't it been just over a month? "Ama?"

Her smile faded. "Hmm?"

"I know now how you feel about the wedding. How you feel about Moray. I should've stopped the ceremony before..." Finnigan gulped hard. He didn't allow himself to think of his parents' death. The image of his father's lifeless eyes burned in his mind. "I will not let Moray have you."

Ama was never one to complain, even when she'd been dying slowly, but she didn't refuse his offer. She opened her mouth when a loud, shrill scream came from the trees.

She jumped, pulling away from Finnigan and stepping toward the woods.

The cry came again. Almost childish—broken and sobbing but piercing the heavy wetland.

"Ama, wait," Finnigan said firmly. "It could be another trap, like the Swamp Woman." Definitely not one of his proudest moments, falling for a ghost woman's trap.

"N-no, that's a child!" Ama grew pale and her eyes hardened.

"It could be—"

"It isn't a trap." She stepped again, bound and determined to find the cause of the cries. Finnigan grabbed her arm.

"What is that?" Gunnar's voice came from behind them. "Is it another ghost?" One of his blades was drawn, as if he preferred something of flesh and bone that he could rip apart.

"No!" Ama insisted. The cry echoed again. "It's just a child. We have to find it."

Absalom stepped into the small clearing, shaking his head as he listened. "No, it is a siiti."

"One of the lizard people?" Finnigan hid his dismay. Nothing had made him feel dirtier than killing those monsters.

Absalom nodded.

"It's a child!" Ama yanked free, breaking into a run. She had the shortest legs of all of them but had one advantage—her small size. Before any of them could grab her, she'd ducked into a thicket and plowed into the darkness.

Moray swore as he ran over. "Ama! Get back here!"

Finnigan started after her, heart in his throat, but Absalom pushed him back.

"We go around," Absalom said. "Whatever monster has entrapped the child will want flesh. We must hurry."

AMA PUSHED HER FEAR away and raced through the branches and thorns, keeping just low enough that most of them grazed her back. Courage burrowed beneath Ama's chest and held on by her claws, growling at the ride she was on, but she didn't hop off.

The cries, such brokenhearted pleas in a tongue Ama did not understand, grew louder as she neared the end of the thicket. She slowed, vision weakened in the dark. She hadn't gone so far that they couldn't find her. They would bring torches. She had to find the child first.

She barely made out a large gathering of rocks near a small spot without any trees. A pond? Shuddering, Ama moved closer. Whatever was screaming lay in the boulders.

She sent up one more prayer before walking into the clearing. She pulled her dagger that glowed a soft red color, shedding light a few feet before her as she stepped over. Something small struggled between two large ragged rocks. It screamed and whimpered, flopping about like a fish.

Ama's heart twisted like someone stabbed a dagger in it. "Easy..." What was she supposed to say? It was a siiti—she could see the child's green face and scrawny tail hitting the rocks. In the red light of her dagger, she saw bright red blood coating the jagged rocks too. "Easy now. Don't be upset."

The siiti jerked its head up, eyes wide with fright. It whimpered and clamped its teeth-ridden jaws as if warning Ama to stay back.

She didn't budge, assessing the damage. "I'm here to help."

The young siiti's left foot was caught in a trap, like one a hunter might use to catch a bear back in Mazzabah. Ama wouldn't be able to remove it—not without someone to help keep the child from tearing her eyeballs out. Her stomach lurched.

"Ama!" Finnigan called. "Ama, get away from it. It's a trap!"

Flickers of glowing light moved quickly through the darkness—two torches and a big blue light from Finnigan's hands.

"I'm fine!" She wouldn't leave the siiti. Even if it were a trap, she had a dagger. And a lot of pent-up anger in a small body.

The siiti sobbed again, pushing against the rocks. Ama saw a spirit in its eyes—it was not a monster like the others they'd slayed. This one was not soulless. *How can this be, Creator?*

Finnigan burst through the clearing and gasped in relief. "Ama! Don't—"

"It is not like the others," Ama said firmly. "It's hurt—"

A low growl filled Ama's ears. She jerked, looking over the large rocks. A twisted face grinned, peering down at her with two crazed cross-eyes. The monster's pasty white skin had small acidic holes littering the flesh. A long, dripping tongue fell past its sharp fangs.

Ama screamed and shoved her dagger into the creature's left eye.

"Ama, duck!" Finnigan yelled.

She dropped, ripping her dagger free. The creature grabbed her arm with a bony hand, laughing in a wild manner. Ama tried shielding the siiti with her body as the monster jerked her arm.

Crack!

A large orb of blue energy shot from Finnigan's hands and hit the creature head-on. Its body crashed into a tree, the crack of its spine filling Ama's ears. The metallic taste of blood in her mouth choked her.

Finnigan wrapped his arms around her as she forced her eyes open. "It's all right, Ama."

"The siiti—" Her heart lurched when she saw Absalom pull a dagger, standing over the trapped child. "No!" she shouted, shoving herself in front of the ragged man. "Get away from him!"

"He is a siiti."

"He has a soul! Look in his eyes." Ama braced herself against the rocks, trembling with rage and fear for the child.

"There is not a monster in Golgotha with a soul." His words came hesitantly, like he remembered something, and it flickered in his old eyes.

"That isn't true and you know it," Ama mustered.

Gunnar rested a hand on Absalom's shoulder, gesturing with his burning torch. "Father, I think she is right."

Finnigan knelt down. "Moray, hold the thing. I'll get the trap off its leg. Gunnar, shed some light."

The men worked quickly, all because Ama had refused to let the creature be killed. Gunnar held his torch close to the rocks, shining light on them. Moray grumbled and swore, but he held the child down so it couldn't bite their fingers off.

Gunnar chuckled. "Feisty thing."

In a swift motion, Finnigan opened the trap and the little siiti jerked out. The child sobbed and licked blood from its snout.

Finnigan gently touched its scaly back. He healed the child's wounds and, energy drained, leaned against the rock. The siiti sat on its rear end, tail tucked about its legs, watching them with big eyes. It avoided looking up for too long but seemed obsessed with the fire. It jumped onto Gunnar, hanging off his shoulder to be closer to the torch.

Gunnar swore. "Get off—"

"Look," Ama said quickly. "It's cold."

"It's a reptile! It can handle itself!" Gunnar growled but didn't shove the siiti off his broad shoulder.

Absalom stepped back from them, silent as death. His rage practically radiated from him.

Ama took a shaky breath. "Absalom—"

"They were all supposed to be dead. It was best that way." Absalom eyed the siiti child as it watched the fire burning intently.

"What?" Moray scowled. "The siiti are soulless, aren't they? Like everything else?" He eyed Courage testily, but Courage just bared her perfect sharp teeth at him.

"There were few... There were few that were not." Absalom's voice grew hollow. "They helped us."

"Helped?" Gunnar stared at his father in dismay.

"You best explain, Absalom." Moray stood and hauled Finnigan to his feet. "Should we kill this thing or not?"

Absalom didn't speak or move for a long moment. Despite her anger, Ama couldn't blame him—agony wrestled in his eyes. He didn't know what to say so he would not rush to speak, unlike Gunnar's personality. None of them said anything. Waiting. Watching. All the while, the siiti sat on Gunnar's shoulder and watched the torch burning as if the fire was its life.

"There were few siiti from the Split. A clan... that survived the craze. Hundreds of years ago, a settlement of people was outcast from Mazzabah. The Crow Clan was very deep in the magics back then. They sent a settlement of their enemies into Golgotha. The people survived here years and years ago. The siiti they met all those decades ago, they had souls and they learned... but the rest of Golgotha picked them all off. One by one. I knew of three siiti with souls and I saw them die." Absalom's voice was low and empty, but tears trickled down his brown cheeks and disappeared into his beard. "This child should not exist."

Silence.

"How many other creatures had souls but died here like animals?" Finnigan whispered.

"Many." Absalom gestured to Courage.

Ama cupped the fluffball close against her chest and fought sobs. Surely, there was cause for these heartbreaks and horrors. Could they not undo what was done in the past?

"So this," Gunnar said, frowning down at the creature on his shoulder, "is the last of its kind?"

Absalom nodded once.

Moray stepped toward Absalom, fuming. "Why not tell us any of this sooner?"

"Did you not know of that legend?" Absalom frowned.

"No!" Moray shouted. "I didn't. I should have, but I didn't. Why would you keep that a secret?"

"It does not benefit us." Absalom paused and closed his eyes. "It did not help us get home, which is what you all wanted. Now it matters, so I speak. Do you not lie and hide things on purpose, Moray?"

The verbal slap made Moray fall silent, his face red with pure rage and hatred. Ama bit her lip. "There is no way we could all share every story we know of. We are surviving, not here to tell every tale that comes to mind," she said in Absalom's defense.

Finnigan took her hand. Ama sheathed her glowing dagger and sucked in a deep breath.

"The siiti have humanistic intelligence. They can speak, walk, reason, as a human does," Absalom continued tightly. "If it has a soul— and it seems to—we shall continue our journey with it."

"Aye," Finnigan agreed quickly.

"Oi, then one of you take it," Gunnar growled. The siiti's tiny rib cage heaved with breath, and it cocked its head at Gunnar. "Don't you dare bite me, you little—"

"Gunnar, it obviously loves you." Finnigan grinned wryly. "You carry it."

"Ama saved it first!" Gunnar argued, picking the siiti up by one hand. The child wrapped its arms and legs around Gunnar and hung upside down, tongue flopping.

Ama laughed softly, relief flooding her. Some good had come from Golgotha, after all. "If it wants me to carry it, I will... but I do not think it does."

"It will kill us." Moray grumbled something else under his breath. Finnigan glanced back to the dead monster that had set the trap.

Ama gulped hard. "Finn?"

"Hmm?"

She squeezed his hand. "We haven't gotten eaten yet."

Finnigan laughed and shook his head. "Not yet. Let's go sleep."

They reached the campfire. Gunnar complained and swore, sitting down near the fire, but the siiti curled up in his lap. "The others of its kind are dead? You're certain?" Gunnar asked his father.

"All of the ones with souls were lost. I do not know how this one survived. The soulless of its kind are ruthless hunters." Absalom stared at his blade. Ama's heart ached for him. He had almost killed a child without giving a moment's thought to seeing if it could possibly have a soul.

Gunnar grunted. "Lucky little rat."

"Not luck. Elohai had a reason for its life," Finnigan said quietly. "As He has a plan for each of us." He leaned back against the dirt, sighing.

Moray turned his back to them and the fire, showing his absolute disgust at their conversation. Finnigan squeezed Ama's hand and she lay beside him, praying that they would reach the desert tomorrow. That Creator would bring them home. That they could help heal the broken realms, even if she didn't know how that might look.

Thirty-Four

THEY REACHED THE PALE, scorching desert the next day. Moray paid close attention, the illusion of the prairie in his mind, but the desert wasn't any illusion. If they continued to drink water, keep their skin covered, and stay aware of body temperatures, they would be fine. Moray had seen people dead in the sandy deserts of Mazzabah with water still in their waterskins. The desert, like any other terrain, had its own set of challenges, but the terrains they faced in Golgotha had heightened trials: monsters and whatever else Elohai felt like tossing at them.

Absalom led them onward, most of his body covered. None of them looked very intimidating with their handwoven hats and pathetic attempts to cover their bodies with what clothing they had. Moray carried the canvas bag of supplies, but each of them carried their own waterskin, in case they got separated. Gunnar walked on with the siiti hanging from his shoulders most of the time, but the child occasionally walked. The sun had already burned the child's scales, but the creature didn't cry.

Ama and Finnigan were like disgustingly hopeful peas in a pod. Finnigan was overly protective of her, though he hadn't quite come out and told Moray to go pound sand. Yet.

No one—not his righteous brother, his brave betrothed, the smart-mouth merc, or the wise sailor—could change Moray's plan. Sadon had changed some of it, but Moray would also handle him accordingly once they returned.

Sadon had formed a connection last night too. He had promised a way to bring them all back. They'd been exchanging information over connections since the first time, but there was the possibility they were both lying to each other. Moray had told most of the truth, avoiding some details so he could have the upper hand, not telling too much of the state of Golgotha to make it easier than he had to. That way, if Barric sent his men, they'd be ill-equipped and be slaughtered like flies, but there was just enough truth in what he said to be believable.

Sadon had told Moray of Buacach's submission, of the state of the clans and civilizations, of Barric's intentions. Sadon never let the connections last long, but he had never been cryptic, so Moray assumed their links were not being supervised. Sadon hadn't said if he was telling the news to Barric.

Sadon had also never mentioned Shafiq, and Moray never brought up the wizard.

Moray pushed the thoughts aside promptly. Thinking of Barric fueled his rage, but not having a proper outlet made his temper flare. With no one conversing, he had nothing to snap or retort, and the anger kindled like a black tar around his rib cage.

Sometimes Ama and Finnigan whispered, and sometimes Gunnar and Absalom would speak in their low voices. No one brought him into conversations. He didn't join in. All they spoke of were tragic pasts and their love for Elohai anyway.

At the end of the day, when the sun sank and the temperature cooled, they set up camp. They drank water and ate some cactus fruit that Absalom prepared. The siiti sat at Absalom's feet and watched him, licking its drying snout. He sighed as he watched the child with eyes like a hawk and his worn face scrunched.

"I wonder if he has a name," Ama said and smiled sadly.

"Why is it a *he*?" Gunnar grunted, leaning back against a boulder they had checked for unwanted creatures. So far, nothing living had found them in the desert.

Ama turned to the child and asked, "What's your name?"

Moray rolled his eyes and opened his mouth to berate Ama, but the creature hit its tail against the sand. In an almost childlike growl, the siiti said, "Tanka!"

Gunnar's jaw dropped. "Blast it all. The bugger can talk!"

Tanka licked his tiny teeth and crawled into Gunnar's lap. "Tanka!" he repeated, puffing his light green chest. Gunnar burst into laughter.

Ama smiled, finishing her water and falling silent. She also gave some water to Courage, who remained buried beneath her clothing. Moray sighed, the thought rising in his head of how he would transport them all home. He didn't know how he would with his draining magic, but he'd find a way.

Absalom took first guard. Moray closed his eyes and felt Sadon making a mental connection as he fell asleep.

The connection was like any other, besides Sadon's change of heart and offer to get the group back to Mazzabah. The first time he'd suggested it, Moray had laughed in his vision.

"You're lying through your teeth, Sadon. After all we have done together, all we have learned, you allowed Barric to trump me like dirt. What has he given you that I have not?"

"It is not about that—"

"Aye, I suppose it doesn't take much for a traitor to make such rash decisions," Moray jabbed.

"I shed mercy upon you, Moray." Sadon glared at him with burning eyes and clenched fists. The wizard had never intimidated him. His skills might have been more honed than Moray's, but they didn't scare him.

"How?" Moray would kill him with his bare hands, even if it took the last bit of energy he had to summon the magic in Mazzabah. For whatever reason, his magic ability was weakened in Golgotha—but he'd hidden it.

"Barric insisted I kill you and Finnigan. He was going to rape and abuse Ama. He was going to kill innocent civilians. And who saved you? Who has kept the peace? Me." Sadon shook his head, his usual smooth, silky hair now tangled. The dream flickered slightly as if he lost control of the connection, but then he continued, "You and I are men of business. I bid to the highest bidder, yes. I had a brilliant plan and I made the mistake of offering it to Barric. I am aware of my mistake. I am aware that I should not have done this... but it cannot be undone. It is up to you and me to fix this." The connection flickered.

"Where are you?" Moray snapped. "We have no time to waste. Strengthen the link."

"I cannot."

"Why not?"

"I will right my wrong. I will help you restore Mazzabah in the only way I can. Be ready, Moray. Bring them to the sea and try to make the connection yourself then. I have... I have just enough strength for three of you. And if Ama has another dream, heed it."

The connection broke. Blackness surrounded Moray and he jerked awake.

Pray.

Abaddon did not hear him any longer. Sadon might have believed in their Father, but his master had made it painfully clear he wanted Moray dead.

"You are capable of surviving alone. You are wise. You do not need any god besides yourself," Self-righteousness said firmly in his ear.

Moray shifted in the sands and faced the heavens. Billions of stars lit up the black sky that hung low in the desert. The sky in Mazzabah was ugly compared to this one. How could such beautiful things exist in a Place of Bones? How were the souls in Mazzabah any more deserving of life than those here? They weren't. He would not be so heartless as Elohai or his master. He would be better.

"You do not need the help of these people," Strife mumbled.

He would not need Ama's dreams or kind heart. He would not need Finnigan's Gift or courage. He didn't need Gunnar or Absalom.

He needed no one.

FINNIGAN DIDN'T LIKE DESERTS and hated sand with a burning passion, no pun intended. Sand had a ridiculous knack of getting into every crevice of the human body. He hated it but figured he didn't have much to complain about. They were all alive and hadn't faced a single monster since arriving in the scorching place. Maybe even the monsters were smart enough to avoid the sands. Or maybe something worse awaited them.

As hard as it was to believe, Finnigan couldn't save them all alone. They needed Elohai. *The righteous are as bold as a lion... We can make it through.* Finnigan squeezed Ama's hand gently before releasing her. He hoped that when they returned to Mazzabah, she could rest. He wanted rest, too, but he hadn't survived being poisoned, so she deserved it more. He'd have plenty to do, saving his kingdom. That'd keep him busy.

He hadn't let himself think about his father's last request. *You will be king, not Moray.* Moray was not fit to be king, but he would never listen if Finnigan announced such a ludicrous claim.

They stopped for a bit, drinking water and resting in the shade of some large rocks. A small snake writhed across the sand and fled, but nothing else bothered them. Finnigan suppressed a laugh. All the things they'd fought—four-eyed, rotting wolves and serpents made of bone and strange bats with stingers—and this little snake fled them.

He'd killed so much here, yet the fight wasn't over. He'd have to fight in Mazzabah too.

Would he kill a man? He had no answers, and Moray didn't speak to him about the large issue they had yet to face.

Finnigan was too exhausted to push his brother. Perhaps he was a coward. It was taking all his strength to keep hope and get through Golgotha alive, protecting the ones he cared for. Moray wasn't helping matters with his cynical attitude and cruel words. If Moray didn't repent, Finnigan hadn't a clue what he could do to fix things alone.

Finnigan rubbed his head as they started off once more. Absalom said the trek to the sea might take only a few days or weeks based on how the season was—whatever that meant. Finnigan couldn't imagine such a strange ecosystem. He had studied the weather and the lands in Mazzabah. Seas and deserts changed, but so quickly?

It *was* Golgotha, after all.

Thirty-Five

THICK BLACK STORM CLOUDS rolled in from the horizon, the thunder filling Ama's ears and making her heart hammer. A rainstorm in the desert didn't sound safe. It wasn't the most threatening thing they had faced, but she had a terrible feeling. "Absalom? Will the rain reach us?"

Absalom barely eyed the horizon. "Aye."

"Will it be dangerous?"

"Aye."

Ama gulped and fought desperation over his characteristic one-word replies. "Is there any shelter before we reach the sea?"

"Shelter out here won't save us," Gunnar said. "We must reach the sea before it comes, or we're sitting ducks."

"What if the ocean is days away?" Finnigan trudged along behind the two men. Moray took up the rear and kept silent. Finnigan usually wasn't one to voice the worst-case scenarios, but the heat was getting to them.

Another groan of thunder rushed over the desert. The storm growing in the distance filled Ama with wonder—but the beautiful sight could be her demise.

In the desert, a rainstorm might not be so nice if it brought lethal lightning with it. Ama had heard stories of people killed by such storms. Gulping hard, she prayed under her breath as they walked. The sand slowed them but they trudged on, Absalom moving them at a strict pace. Ama could only imagine what the captain had seen during the years he'd survived here. He'd probably lost men to this very desert, yet he led them on like a steadfast shepherd.

Ama prayed they could give the man what he deserved once Creator got them home. He deserved a home, money, anything he wanted. They'd have to pay Gunnar for his help, but unlike Gunnar, Absalom had no interest in worldly possessions. This showed in the way he spoke, the way he told stories of Elohai. He never spoke of his family or crew around the others, but Ama heard him whispering with Gunnar. The two men held personal matters close to their chest.

She didn't blame them. Ama would've kept silent like a mouse had Finnigan not been there alongside her. While they had the time and energy to say little, she trusted Finnigan with everything in her, even if she didn't always understand him.

Finnigan said he wouldn't let her marry Moray. Did he simply want Moray to not get the throne for the safety of his people? Or did he...

Maybe Finnigan loved her. He'd shown her great care. Of course, he was also a kind-hearted person.

Don't be ludicrous, Ama. He can't love you.

She held Finnigan's hand tightly, hoping that the sea was close. Even if they found the sea before the storm arrived, Moray couldn't get them home. He lied when he said he had the magic to do so.

Ama looked at the men. Moray, with his trudging steps, his hunched shoulders that'd been straight with pride before entering Golgotha. Finnigan, his gentle grip on her hand and his eyes watching the horizon. Gunnar, holding Tanka close against his broad chest as the child slept. Absalom, holding a staff of thick pale bone in his right hand as he led them through the yellow sands.

None of this would have happened if they had not gone through hell. No good would have come without the bad. Ama smiled softly. They would go home. Perhaps Creator did not reveal every detail and every explanation, but He always showed just enough. There was always cause to hold on to faith.

THE RAIN FELL IN heavy torrents, blackness engulfing the sands like the sky had burst open. In a strange way, it had. The pouring rain blinded Finnigan, but it didn't take long to see the lights in the darkness.

He squinted, rain muddling his visions. Scattered like sentries, radiating figures stood in the distance. Finnigan couldn't see much, but they looked human-like. Each figure had great, glowing wings that pushed the darkness back.

Slowly, the figures moved closer and surrounded the vagabonds at a distance, but they were just close enough for the shelter of their wings to block the dark. The rain hit the group, but the suffocating darkness couldn't pass the radiant angels.

Angels.

What were they doing in Golgotha?

Finnigan pulled Ama on, panting for breath. Courage huddled against Ama's neck and Tanka cried softly as if sensing their somber mood, but they ran onward. The child burrowed against Gunnar as the mercenary moved through the soaked sands.

The thunder droned on and the lightning wasn't far behind. The first strike of lightning hit far to their right. Finnigan didn't know exactly what lightning did when it hit sand, but he knew what it did if it hit a person.

Too close. That was too close. "Move!" he yelled. But there was no end in sight in the darkness. They couldn't run forever.

Finnigan didn't have time to gape at the winged sentries guarding them, shielding them with hidden faces. They had to take this chance and flee.

Absalom never faltered and led them. He didn't look at the angels either. Had the angels appeared in Golgotha before? Finnigan hadn't thought of such a thing. Golgotha was a place of death, demons, and monsters. Not angels. But Elohai could do as He pleased. He must've decided they needed drastic help. Finnigan wouldn't argue.

They were not so gone that the Light could not save them.

Finnigan tore his gaze from the angels and focused on moving the others along through the blinding rain. Lightning struck the sands around them, but nothing hit them.

What did he have to be afraid of when he was being shielded by an angel and guided by Elohai Himself?

Ama's dream said to keep going till they reached the sea.

They wouldn't stop, no matter what.

Rain soaking him to the bone, Finnigan kept a hold on Ama. Moray stumbled, but Gunnar shoved him along. Tanka's tail wagged as the water drenched him. The poor child probably delighted in the storm—his scales had been cracking in the horrid heat.

Always a silver lining.

For at least an hour, they walked. The rain pounded, thunder clapped, and lightning struck the desert like a raging beast. The angels shielded them from the demons racing and sweeping across the sky. Finnigan steeled himself when the demons dove low, clashing against the angels with their claws and fangs bared.

A few of the angels drew swords, bigger than any weapon Finnigan had ever seen. One of them grinned almost eagerly as a demon jumped toward him.

Sling!

The sword cut the demon in half. Black blood splattered the wet sand, and the demon shrieked before fading in a puff of smoke. The burning smell of rotten eggs filled Finnigan's nostrils. He pushed Ama on quickly.

The demons attacked, screeched, tore at the angels with all their might. The angels never broke their positions. The

Darkness didn't harm the five as they walked through the desert of death.

Finnigan lost all track of time after that. While the angels fought the demons off, he prayed that Elohai would let them get to the water. Before Ama's dream, he hadn't cared if they reached the sea. Finnigan didn't doubt her connection to Elohai, though she had struggled to voice what Elohai told her to. Moray, Gunnar, and Absalom were not exactly a loving bunch.

She had chosen to be brave anyway, and her voice was going to save them all, if they could battle the storm.

They climbed up a hill and staggered in the wet sand, rain wearing them down. At the top, breathless, Finnigan looked down across the desert. Heavy sheets of rain plummeted endlessly, unleashing upon the sand and the sea.

The sea.

Finnigan winced. "Does anyone see that?" Maybe the heavy rain was pulling tricks on him. As soon as he'd gotten the brief sight of the body of water, the rain blacked it all out again.

"We made it to the sea!" Ama cried, voice strained but heavy with joy.

A clap of thunder rang in Finnigan's ears.

A demon pushed at the angel to his left, hissing, snapping, cursing at Finnigan. He refused to let his focus waver from the mission before him—but a flash of lightning filled his vision. Everything went black.

Thirty-Six

MORAY HAD BEEN RIGHT all along. The Light had no mercy for sinners. It was a sick joke—the angels fending the army of demons off their backs, the Darkness at bay as they trudged through the drenched desert. But the Light had limits to its kindness. They'd reached the limit.

The bolt of lightning struck Finnigan down. He fell face forward into the sands, the left side of his body singed black. Moray yanked him up. "Finn!"

Ama, somehow unharmed as if Finnigan had let her go before the lightning hit, grabbed Finnigan's other arm. "Move!" she yelled.

Move forward.

"What for? Their God doesn't care about you," Despondency said with a moan. Despite the wicked storm, Moray's demons still clung close. He eyed the angels before helping Ama pull Finnigan onward. Moray felt for a pulse in his brother's neck and found it, however faint it was.

He would get them home.

"Yes, you can. No one else can but you." Self-righteousness pushed him on.

His master had forsaken him. How could he rule the realm if it rejected him?

"You can show them all." Strife pushed his claws into Moray's head.

I'll show them all. I will win this.

Ama tripped, bringing Finnigan and Moray down with her. They staggered and tumbled like sheep down the hill. Moray spit up wet sand as he dragged himself to his feet, tossing Finnigan over his shoulders. "Go!"

"Just reach the sea," Self-righteousness muttered. "The magic will come. The magic obeys you. You are holy. You do not need the master's blessing." The demon's voice continued in his ears. Moray had no choice but to listen to it.

They pushed on as the heavy rain threatened to drown them like rats and the demons swore they would die. The angels never let the demons come close.

Except for the demons that Moray wouldn't let go. No angel could save him from what he'd welcomed.

At the end of the hill, the desert dwindled into the ocean that churned like the waters would overflow. In Golgotha, anything was possible, but Moray hoped the sea held back the flood. They couldn't open the rift if they drowned.

Moray struggled to see through the torrent and kept his eyes on the sea. So close, yet so far. Ignoring his demons as they overwhelmed him with voices, he held Finnigan tightly and moved ahead of Ama. Gunnar, Tanka, and Absalom would slow him down—he couldn't save them.

He would have just enough strength to save Ama and Finnigan and himself.

Anything more would be suicide.

"Moray!" Gunnar's voice roared over the thunder. "Moray, watch out!"

Moray didn't turn back or slow down. Footsteps sinking in the sand, he pulled his left leg out of the muck—it held fast. Swearing, he tugged harder.

"Moray!" Ama screamed.

He looked down, water blinding his vision. Something had his ankle—a hand, only its grip was iron. Out of the sands, a hand of white, sun-bleached bone held on to his leg. Moray wrestled his leg free, balancing Finnigan's heavy body over his shoulders. "A little help!"

Gunnar swung his blade at the skeleton arm. It snapped and fell on the sands. The rest of the skeleton's arm pushed up through the ground.

"Skeleton army!" Absalom snarled, just loud enough that Moray could hear the man's fury above the storm. "Run!"

Run. Easier said than done in a downpour, in wet sand, with angels fending off demons on all sides and, apparently, with skeletons rising from the earth.

Moray ran the best he could, Ama close by his side. Finnigan didn't wake up, and Moray fought the fear that he might be carrying his little brother for nothing.

Gunnar, with Tanka hanging off his back, kept his blade in hand as he ran. Absalom pulled his shofar and blew it as they sprinted—how the man found the air in his lungs to do both at once, Moray hadn't a clue. Surviving in the Place of Bones must have given him immense stamina. Or perhaps the man truly believed that the war horn offered more protection than a blade when going into battle.

Skeletons erupted out of the sand, mass numbers pushing themselves up like daisies. Daisies of bone in the valley of death. Moray grit his teeth. *I'm losing control.*

The skeletons staggered toward them from all directions. The angels never wavered, slicing the onslaught of demons. The demons vanished in dark puffs of smoke, but they never stopped coming.

"Run!" Absalom shouted once more, lowering his war horn, leading them toward the ocean.

Ama's dream had foretold a fate where Elohai took them home when they surrendered themselves to the bitter, salty waters. Moray didn't expect Elohai to save them, but at least the others had come here. After days of hardships, they had made it to the sea, only to find hundreds of skeletons hungry for blood and demons who had been awaiting their arrival.

When they reached the shore, the skeletons flanked them. They staggered and stumbled, their white-bone figures just visible in the dark storm. Closer they trudged, hollow eye sockets never looking away from the group that fled them.

Moray scanned the ocean. No turning back now. There was no way they could fight off thousands of dead with some swords and magic. He lowered Finnigan to the shore.

The storm thundered and the rain blinded Moray, but there was plenty of water. If he could summon enough black magic, he could open the portal.

The angels spread out just enough to give the group room to fight. They radiated a warm golden light, the shield they created keeping the Darkness from engulfing the humans. The angels could handle the demons, the humans could handle the dead.

Or so he hoped.

"Moray!" Ama grabbed his arm. Her dark hair clung to her cheeks, her clothes hung off her. She looked like a wet rat. "Wait! Don't try to open the portal."

Moray eyed the ocean. Through the rain hammering the churning waters, something else moved beneath the black waves. Large scales appeared and disappeared—coming closer, as if a great beast had been awakened from the depths.

A Leviathan.

He shoved Ama off. "I have to!" he shouted over the storm and the crashing sea. "I have to save us!" Gesturing to the sea, though he doubted Ama could see what he did, he yelled, "We're surrounded!"

Thirty-Seven

THE PRISON DOOR CREAKED open. Jerking awake, Sadon lifted his head, the movement sending bolts of pain through his body. The chains held him up, dried blood covering the stone floor.

Blood he had shed for the sake of saving Oliver. Blood brought by his true master, Shafiq.

The ways of torture used by the brilliantly cruel wizard were lethal for most. Not for Sadon. He had been tested, trialed, immunized from a young age. This time had been different. Shafiq had tortured him in ways he had never before.

Sadon struggled to adjust his eyes to the sudden burst of light. His body trembled—all injuries had been healed, but Shafiq's healing had been just enough for Sadon's survival. The torture would not end until he told the truth about the chosen four and the reason why he had betrayed Shafiq.

Or so Shafiq said. Shafiq might want those answers, but he would also torture and kill Sadon, all because Sadon had fled him and created his own empire. Such betrayal required death.

He had brought this on himself.

A figure peeked into the room, then rushed in. "You're the wizard who sent Ama away?"

Sadon blinked. Sucked in a painful breath. "Etu?"

"Keep it down." The Wolf Clan warrior picked Sadon's locks in a matter of seconds. His tan face and eyes—eyes as dark as Ama's—were tight with concentration. Etu caught Sadon as he fell and hauled him to his feet. "The warlock must hate you. I've seen dead rodents more handsome than you."

"We have to get them back," Sadon choked out. He'd never shown such weakness before. No one had ever seen him broken besides Shafiq—but he couldn't waste time feeling shame. Not when lives were at stake.

He had to undo what he'd done. If the prophecies Shafiq had taught him as a child were true, then the group in Golgotha could be the Remnant from the legends of old. The only ones who could restore the kingdom and save Oliver.

Etu pulled him out of the cell, into the narrow stone hallway. He whispered, "Can you transport us out of here? No one's waiting for us outside. It was hard enough getting in here."

Sadon glanced down at his naked body, the black tattoos on his skin reminding him of all the years he had wasted serving a cruel master. "I can try."

And he did, but the magic had gone from him.

Etu groaned. "You're supposed to be a warlock."

"I... I betrayed my master. He promised me death. I have to fix this before—"

"You mean you can't do black magic?" Etu hurried through the corridor, half-carrying Sadon's limp body.

Sadon forced a breath. "No."

"Why? Because you disobeyed your master?"

"Yes." Rebelling against Abaddon would be his end, but he wouldn't repent. Not with Oliver's life at stake.

And he desired to be forgiven by Elohai.

But wishes were futile.

Etu glanced down at him. "Have you repented?"

"W-what?"

"Creator is the only way we will make it out of this. I was ignorant before, but it is true—and I won't be weighed down by a wizard without magic who still thinks he can save the world without Creator on his side." His tone grew taut.

"I'm interested in saving only one." Sadon's breath caught, chest burning with agony.

"Then pray and repent now. We have one shot at this. We need to reach the castle and bring them all back through the portal. I need your help."

How could a clan warrior, a man unlearned in the Golgothan legends and magics, open the portal? Sadon's legs ached as he walked, forcing out, "Of course. But there is no way to open the portal without the dragon, and I cannot make it hatch now."

"We won't need the dragon." Etu grunted, rounding the corner with Sadon. A few torches on the stone walls lit their path. "I've got a plan."

Sadon followed, but fear held on tight to his heart. They wouldn't escape the prison. Shafiq would find him and kill him for his disobedience.

But he was alive now. Not by his master's mercy or his own power.

Was this why he was alive? To save Oliver? No more, no less?

Thirty-Eight

AMA'S LEGS BUCKLED BUT she managed to hold her feet beneath her, gripping Finnigan's unconscious body for dear life. The waves tossed over the shore in violent drafts. She feared it might all pour out, covering the desert and leaving everything destroyed by the bitter waters. That couldn't happen, could it?

Gulping hard, Ama turned to face the skeletons. Their eyes glowed a strange white color that wisped through the blackness.

Ama didn't understand. They were surrounded by skeletons, demons, and something coming at them from the ocean. Elohai had told her they would all be saved if they repented. Had she misunderstood her dream? A sob choked her, rainwater burning her eyes.

Even after seeing the angels covering them and the pathetic demons screaming in agony every time Absalom blasted his shofar, Moray refused to admit the Light was prevailing.

Gunnar gave Ama the child, face heavy with rage. "Hold them," he ordered. "We must fight." A fierce determination laced his words—no fear, no anger that Elohai hadn't taken them back home.

Tanka sobbed and shook against Ama's shoulder. She held the child close, pushing Finnigan's head into her lap. "Creator, help us!"

Gunnar, Absalom, and Moray faced the skeletons that came too close. The skeletons had no weapons, but anything could be dangerous in many numbers. They attacked the group, their jaws and teeth clicking and chomping. At the same time, countless demons swarmed them, blocking out the world in a dark cloud. Rain passed through them and lightning continually struck the desert.

Moray cut down a few skeletons, trying to edge his way closer to the churning waters. Gunnar and Absalom fought side by side, their styles of battle similar, their blades sure. Absalom tossed his shofar to Ama. He didn't try yelling over the wind—she knew what to do.

She couldn't save them all from the evil. She couldn't save her people from Barric. She was powerless.

In her surrender, Creator could lift her up. If she had faith, she could do His will.

Ama blew into the rough ram horn that was heavy in her hands. Prayers burned straight from her heart, which hammered as she glanced at the ocean. They couldn't kill the horde of walking dead. They couldn't survive the tumultuous waters.

As Ama rocked Tanka and held on to Finnigan tightly, she kept blowing the war horn and praying in her heart for protection. The angels fought the demons with stunning accuracy, the stench hard to stand as the demons vanished in smoke, over and over. The skeletons bit and ground their jaws at their prey. They swarmed Absalom but he fended them off with his blade, never staying still for longer than necessary.

They pushed Gunnar away from Absalom. Their bony arms grabbed at him, tore at his clothes. Gunnar yelled—a piercing cry Ama barely heard.

"Gunnar!" she shouted.

Absalom slashed through the skeletons, cutting them down. Skulls fell to the sands, rain pelting the bones that littered the dark ground. He broke through and covered for his son while Gunnar wrestled with a few giant skeletons that seeped from the Darkness.

"Creator, please save us," Ama said, shaking. She glanced at Moray. "Moray, you have to surrender! If you don't surrender, we all die!"

He didn't seem to hear her. He cut the skulls off a few skeletons that bit at his neck.

Courage jumped down from Ama's shoulders and sat protectively on Finnigan's chest, chattering at the rain. She turned toward the skeletons, then faced the ocean, her tail shaking.

Ama's chest tightened. Courage saw something out there. Letting her gaze linger, Ama strained to see something in the sea.

Large, dark shapes stood out against the rain, coming closer. Scales? Ama sucked in a breath. "Moray! Look!"

He didn't turn around—he still couldn't hear her.

Tanka lifted his head, watching the men fight the skeletons that gained ground. Gunnar fell to his knees as skeletons clambered and bit at his flesh. Ama tried covering the child's eyes, but in a frenzy, the siiti boy jerked away from her. He ran for Gunnar.

Ama laid Finnigan on his side in the sand. "Tanka!" She ran toward the fight, stomach twisting. "Tanka, come back!"

She couldn't look where Gunnar had fallen.

Tanka got a few yards away from Gunnar, his short legs unbelievably fast, before Absalom snatched him off the ground. He held the child by the back of his neck and ran to Ama.

Ama snatched the child from him, rain blinding her as she glanced back to Gunnar. He'd broken free and ran toward them, yelling, "Move back. Back!"

The angels still stood around them like a barrier between the Darkness while the demons raged. The skeletons crawled and staggered closer, dragging across the sands.

Moray led them back to the shoreline where Finnigan lay. The skeletons gained on them slowly while the angels warded off the screeching demons. The sounds grated Ama's nerves, but by now they all faded into nothing. A strange peace settled over her.

Creator wouldn't forsake them. The screams, the monsters, the demons, the roaring sea—nothing stopped Creator's mercy.

Ama held Tanka tightly and skidded to a stop beside Finnigan. He stirred, coughing as he inhaled rainwater. She dropped beside him as thunder clapped in the heavy sky above. She pulled him up weakly and the others surrounded them, still protected by the angels, but the skeletons were nearing.

Ama picked up the war horn, fighting sobs. She loved them, all of them, in different ways—but she couldn't save them.

Gripping Finnigan's hand, she held the shofar to her lips with her other. Tanka held on to her neck and buried his face against her chest. He was too weak to do much else. They had all been running low on stamina to begin with.

Even in the Darkness, even with the demons raging, even with the dead hungry for destruction... They were a light in Golgotha.

They were the Lights that shone in the Place of Bones. Elohai was always with them.

She blew the shofar once more and didn't let herself look at the chaos around her.

THE FIRST THOUGHT THAT entered Finnigan's mind was, *She's so beautiful.* The nonstop storm had drenched them all like ducks, but Ama still radiated a beauty Finnigan had never seen before. He gripped her hand as his second thought came: *We're in trouble.*

The skeletons hadn't been there before he'd been struck by lightning. The creatures hurried through the sand like a swarm of flies—their eye sockets full of white mist that illuminated in the dark storm. The sound their snapping jaws made sent shivers down Finnigan's spine. The rain added to the dramatic, horrendous effect.

He sat up, glancing down at himself. He was burnt from the lightning strike but not too badly—his Gift had helped his body heal itself to some degree. Even when he was almost dead, he could make a pun. "Ama?"

She huddled close. Finnigan wrapped one arm around her and the child, drawing Energy with his other. Moray, Gunnar, and Absalom fought off the walking monsters. The demons and angels raged in their war.

Ama blew the war horn. The demons withdrew at the long blast—momentarily. One of the angels turned and, for the first time, made eye contact with any of the humans. The angel looked like a man—dark hair, solemn eyes—but was still large and radiated supernatural light. He pulled a small shofar from his belt and pushed it into Finnigan's hands.

"Do not be afraid." The angel looked down at Tanka, voice low but crystal clear through the tumultuous world around them. "Elohai is with us. You will return home if you stand boldly in the face of your adversaries." He joined the other angels in the fight once more.

The angel's words were the final push in Finnigan's spirit. He got up, left leg burning, and held the shofar in his hand. As blue energy burned in his other, Finnigan blew the shofar with all his might. The sound of the war cry pierced the thunderstorm.

Ama pulled herself to her feet and joined him, Tanka holding on to her tightly.

Hundreds of the demons withdrew, pulling away from the angels. Some screamed or swore, and some cried and begged the noise to stop.

As they headed toward the sea, the skeletons moved faster, skittering onto the running sand. Moray never used his magic, counting on his sword and struggling against the hungry creatures. Could he still wield the dark magic? Absalom protected Ama, Finnigan, and the child.

Gunnar moved away from the beasts, blood pouring from multiple gashes along his arms. Finnigan lowered the shofar from his lips and shouted, "Gunnar!" He shot a blast of blue fire at a small group of skeletons that ran at his friend.

It wasn't enough.

More skeletons grappled with Gunnar to the sands. Absalom ran for him, gusts of wind pulling at the survivors.

And the sea burst open.

A serpent, the largest creature Finnigan had ever seen, ten times the size of the serpents back in the swamp, rose from the foaming waters. The beast's jagged teal scales shimmered a soft light. It watched them with large golden eyes before opening its jaw wide. The sea waves lapped violently at the shores.

Finnigan grabbed Ama and Tanka away from the shore, moments too late as water gushed over them. Blackness engulfed him. He fought hard to keep his grip on Ama and Tanka, the shofar lost somewhere in the waters that churned around him. His lungs were filled with burning, bitter water—the kind the people in the Letters had used to cleanse themselves.

Up. Finnigan had to pull them up. Ama struggled at his side. They needed air. His lungs burned for it.

Which way was up?

As the bitter water ran down his throat, life burst into Finnigan's veins. His aching body filled with new zeal. Pulling Ama with him, Tanka clinging to his neck, Finnigan swam through the raging sea until they reached the top.

They crawled onto the sand, away from the churning waters. Skeletons tossed and turned in the sea behind them, but hundreds still remained on the sands. Finnigan coughed up water, Ama and Tanka lying in the sand beside him. He groaned. "Elohai..."

He watched the sea. Moray, Gunnar, Absalom—they were gone.

"Finn!" A familiar voice shouted over the thunder.

Finnigan lifted his head. Down the shore, Moray and Absalom ran toward them. Where was Gunnar?

Moray screamed again, "Move! Run!" He gestured to the skeletons that clambered toward the shore.

Finnigan jumped up, helping Ama to her feet. She held Tanka on her back, and Courage burrowed under Ama's neck. The Leviathan rose once more in the sea, its great body nearly vanishing in the storm before it brought itself crashing down against the sands.

They ran, barely escaping the serpent's crushing body. The ground broke apart beneath them. Somehow they kept going, but Finnigan hadn't a clue where they were headed. The skeletons surrounded them and would kill them. The Leviathan, too, was breaking the world apart to kill them.

The demons swarmed high. Where were the angels?

He yanked Ama on. "Run!"

The angels reappeared in flashes of light before them. Finnigan and Ama stumbled to a halt. Absalom and Moray weren't far behind.

The same angel that had spoken to Finnigan before lifted a hand. "Stand and fight, and Elohai will bless you." He didn't sound patient, but he hadn't used the giant sword in his hands on them either. Finnigan clenched his jaw, every heavy breath burning.

"That's the Leviathan! We'll be crushed!" Moray shouted. "Move!"

The angel met Moray's gaze. "Your little faith will be your demise if you do not repent." With that, he joined the other angels, and as before they held the demons at bay.

Finnigan didn't understand—why didn't they kill the Leviathan? Why didn't the angels fight the skeleton army? The group had battled demons before.

Then he realized it didn't have to make sense. They had to have faith.

Finnigan looked to his older brother, the man he had always loved, always looked up to. "You have to surrender, Brother. If you do not choose Elohai, we will all die. Please —"

"I do not need your God!" Moray gestured toward the Leviathan as it disappeared under the sea. "Where is He? Elohai is gone! Every master leaves in the end!"

"No!" Absalom grabbed Moray's arm. "He loves you, Moray. More than anyone can possibly love—He loves you."

Moray screamed in rage, face red. He held his sword and ran toward the ocean.

Finnigan ran after him, but Absalom stopped him. "We must stand."

"He'll get himself killed!" Finnigan struggled against the man weakly. The surge of strength and clarity the water had given him remained, but not as strongly. His mind and body had been healed and rejuvenated, but just enough for him to press on.

Ama grabbed his hand, shaking hard, but she jutted her chin. "We can't save him," she choked out. "We can't save him, Finn."

Finnigan didn't know if it was the rain, but she looked like she was sobbing.

"Be still." Absalom released him, and they stood in the sand, between thousands of skeletons coming for blood and the Leviathan that wanted them dead.

Was it possible to do the things the Letters spoke of during battle? They had fought tooth and claw, till nothing left remained in their bodies. Could he be still and believe that Elohai would save them if they merely trusted Him?

Finnigan watched Moray leave and sobbed. "Elohai, save us."

He could not lose another brother to this realm. Graft and Gunnar were gone. And he could not save Moray either.

He lifted his head weakly to the horizon, where the rain pounded against the sands that split and shifted. Among the dark jumble of shrieking demons stood Shafiq the wizard, his staff in hand. The top of the staff glowed a dark red that etched up into the sky. The demons swarmed around the energy and sprang toward the shoreline where their prey sat.

Shafiq had been here the whole time, Finnigan realized, watching and waiting for them to fail, ready to snatch them up for his cruel master.

Finnigan's broken sobs ceased. An enraged cry rose from his throat and he lifted his fist into the air, standing close to Ama and Tanka. "*Cha trèig Dia sinn!*" he screamed toward the wizard, voice almost lost in the thunderous storm. *Elohai will not forsake us.*

Thirty-Nine

SADON AND ETU HURRIED through the prison corridors beneath the castle. Shafiq never stopped them, but Sadon's fear didn't leave. He paused sluggishly beside the stone walls. "In here," he whispered.

Etu snapped, "We need to move. We hardly have the chance of escaping without the guards seeing—"

Sadon pushed against one of the stones. A secret narrow door slid open.

"Oh." Etu pushed him in. "Hurry!" Their footsteps landed hard on the stone floor, and Etu shut the door behind them. He sniffed as if fighting a sneeze.

"Be quiet," Sadon whispered. "This will lead us out of the underground to the servant chambers."

"How do we get to the dragon egg?" Etu pushed Sadon in front, supporting him the best he could in the cramped, dark place. The rotten smell of dirt and mold filled Sadon's nose, but anything smelled better than blood and Shafiq's expensive colognes.

"It's still in the vault chamber," Sadon said, panting. "We can reach it." If they kept to the secret passageways, all they'd have to do was take out the guards at the chamber doors. "How many men are with you?"

"Within the castle walls, twelve."

"Inside the castle?"

"Three."

Sadon moaned. "You tribes know little of force in numbers."

"We know much in stealth and skill," Etu bit back. "You know this war will never be won if the people stand and fight. They will be killed like sheep, which is why they have submitted to this traitor king. The very king you have served."

"I know my wrongdoings." Sadon's throat went dry. He would die for what he had done. Abaddon would end him. He didn't need to be reminded.

Etu and Sadon hurried through the stuffy passageways. They slipped out near the great hall and, without getting caught, ran to the next secret door. This door led to the chambers, if Sadon's weary mind proved correct. Etu helped support him, but the darkness and the lack of clean air worsened Sadon's senses. He pushed his legs on, trailing a hand on the stone walls for support.

He began to pray to Elohai but stopped short. He would not repent and pray to a god who had never saved him before. He was broken but not that broken.

Silent as mice aside from Sadon's heavy breathing, they went up narrow stairs and down long stretches of passageways until Sadon slowed to a stop. "Here. The egg is in the chamber right outside this door."

"As are the guards." Etu pulled an arrow from his quiver and nocked it on the bow he carried across his back. "I'll handle them." They were most likely replaced by some of Barric's finest, and Sadon didn't care if the guards lived or died.

Sadon sucked in a weak breath before pushing the secret door open. Sure enough, two guards stood outside the strong wooden doors across the hall. They immediately lowered their spears toward them.

Etu released his arrow, piercing the skull of the first guard. In an instant, he'd nocked another arrow and shot the second man before he could throw the spear at the intruders.

Both bodies hit the stone floor, spears and armor sending soft, resounding thuds into the corridors. Etu pulled Sadon over and, like the king of all locksmiths, broke into the doors. Sadon followed him on shaky legs. Etu tossed the bodies into the room and shut them in. He took the pants off one of the guards and threw them at Sadon, who got dressed weakly.

Just a little more. Sadon rushed to the dragon egg that sat safe and sound on the pedestal.

Etu dragged a large piece of furniture over, blocking the door. "That'll buy us some time." He came over, a smile flashing over his face. "The fun begins." The warrior pulled a long, jagged blade from his belt. The blade glowed an array of bold colors. Despite his years of being a wizard and dealing with all sorts of supernatural weaponry, the daggers

Etu and Ama carried were unique to what Sadon had ever seen.

"What is that?" Sadon asked.

"I'll explain later. Now start praying, little child. You are new in Creator, and you have a hell of a journey ahead of you to healing, but right now, we are brothers. And we will open the portal."

"That's rich, coming from the warrior who hated me only weeks before now." Sadon held his aching side, vision blurring.

"Creator told me that Ama and I can open the rift using these daggers He gifted to us." Etu grinned and the blade glowed a brilliant white that pierced the room. "Simple decisions can change everything. A surrendered heart can move mountains. Now pray."

"No way in hell, pretty boy. Your God can't hear me."

Forty

"I LOVE YOU, CHILD," said a voice.

Moray ran through the sands, the merciless rain against his back like a wall between the last of his kin and his fate.

But that voice, vastly opposite of Abaddon's, whispered in his mind, "Will you choose your brother's death over your kingdom?"

He pushed on harder. The Leviathan thrashed about in the sea, occasionally, bringing its giant head down against the shore to cause an uproar like an earthquake. Moray narrowly avoided the head as it hit to his left. A torrent of sand ripped beneath his feet, and he was thrown sideways. While the Leviathan recoiled, Moray staggered upright and ran on. He didn't want too much or too little distance between him and the beast at first. All he had was a blade and the echo of his black magic.

"You will be enough," Self-righteousness whispered.

The new voice was quiet and unyielding, almost like Ama's nagging. "Would you lose them all simply to win one last fight? It does not have to be this way. Come to me."

"I won't lose them," Moray growled. All of his training in Mazzabah had prepared him for endurance. He hadn't passed out from exhaustion, but he was running out of time. The monster would kill them all if he didn't stop it. He was the only one who could, and the others knew it—that's why they stood like cowardly dogs on the shore, far behind him.

Strife laughed. "Let them cower. You will win this alone."

A second voice spoke, starkly contrasting the first foreign one in tone. "You can use the magic. It is a part of you now, and you will be the god of Golgotha, a god of your own making."

Too many voices.

Too many eyes in the heavens, watching him like prey.

Too many people expecting him to change, when they should know what he was.

A king.

A liar.

A monster.

The Leviathan lifted its head and upper body—or part of its body, since Moray had no idea how large it was overall—and watched him. Its two golden eyes never wavered, peering into Moray's very soul. A hoarse roar erupted from the serpent's mouth, fangs flashing through the storm, as if it didn't like what it saw.

One last monster.

One last battle.

Then they could go home. It was up to Moray, once and for all.

He racked his brain for memories of what the legends told of the Leviathan, but legends had made it clear that the beast of destruction could not be killed by mortal hand.

Unless we turn to Him and repent, Creator will not bless our people. Ama's words.

Moray growled under his breath. He had to focus. He had to summon the magic.

The Leviathan trembled, preparing itself for another bash against the ground. The animal didn't behave in a frenzy like the serpents in the swamps. This one calculated, watched, waited for Moray to make a move, like it had challenged him to a fight and he was slacking.

Moray stopped and faced the giant serpent at a somewhat safe distance, though how safe could a person get from a monster? He sheathed his blade, knowing it wouldn't do him much good if he didn't see a soft spot through the thick blackness and the rain. Stabbing the beast would be the equivalent of poking it with a stick, if a blade could even penetrate those thick blue-and-green scales.

"Magic can," the second, cold voice whispered. "You can defeat anything with power and knowledge."

But he had neither of those things.

Moray held his hands together. Hands that had killed. Hands that had practiced forbidden magic for years. Hands that had worshipped the very devil that had promised him nothing but death.

Moray had already proved disobedient, and he did not want Abaddon to take him back. He could make it alone. He did not need a master. The magic obeyed him.

His chanting growing louder and stronger as he fought against the storm, Moray summoned black magic. As the ancient spell left his lips, the first, firm voice crept into his mind. "You can do all things through me. Repent, and I will save them."

Moray shouted at the top of his lungs. "I do not need a god as cruel as You, Elohai. I do not need anyone!" Adrenaline surged through his body. He stood tall and strong, like a king ought to in the face of an adversary.

"You will be left in the Darkness if you do not choose the Light."

Moray lifted his hands, aiming at the Leviathan while it watched him as if in amusement. Rage burned in his chest. The Light had no mercy for sinners. All he was to the Light was a beast in need of saving.

"The Light has a place for all who love it, my child," the gentle voice said.

Love. The word churned in Moray's mind, his insides seething like the storm and sea before him. He didn't need love. A king did not need love. What did love do for his father? It got him killed. The finest man in Mazzabah, slaughtered like an animal.

Summoning every fiber of energy in his body and spirit, Moray unleashed the black magic.

When Moray first came to Golgotha, his magic had been strong, nearly as strong as Sadon in some divisions. It was no longer his to control.

The air ripped from Moray's lungs. His knees buckled and he fell into the wet sand, feeling like his organs had all lurched, like invisible hands tried pulling his life out of him as the magic left him.

His demons laughed in his ears, hissed at him, swore at him. Despondency grappled for reach, but all Moray heard were Self-righteousness and Strife pushing him on.

A third voice came, unknown but familiar, one he'd heard ever since he'd been young. "You can win this alone. Now get up. Become god of the realms. Rise from the ashes. Kill all who laughed."

Rage-fueled stamina coursed through his veins. Moray staggered up, but the harm done to his body wasn't so easily undone. Part of him was gone. The magic had taken part of his spirit. Abaddon was right.

The Leviathan thrashed in the water, foam spurting across the shore. Moray turned, shaking like a leaf in the horrendous winds. Had Finnigan seen his shame? Had the others seen how weak he had been?

Skeletons flocked the shore, coming straight for him, the demons screeching as they followed in a scattered cloud.

Finnigan, Ama, Gunnar, Absalom, and the child were nowhere in sight. A small, glowing streak pierced the storm clouds above—a closed rift.

Moray's heart lurched to his throat. That wasn't possible. Only he could open the rift.

The passionate yet gentle voice came again. "You knew the truth and you hardened your heart."

"No!" Moray screamed, backing away from the ocean, legs shaking. "No! I was the one to open the rift. Me and my magic—no one else!"

But they were gone. His family had vanished to Mazzabah. Safe and sound.

He was alone.

Except for the wizard that stood in the sands, the skeletons avoiding him as if he were their master. Shafiq watched Moray, the hood of his cloak lowered, his glowing staff in hand. "Come to me!" he called, voice ferocious, rising above the ruckus.

Moray faced a monster that wanted him dead, an army of skeletons on his back. His magic had departed—he tried summoning more, his voice cracking with rage, but the spells did nothing.

"I will never come to you!" Moray yelled, salt water burning his eyes.

Nothing.

He was nothing.

"No," the second voice implored. "You are king, you are a god. You have not come all this way for nothing! You did not begin this empire to surrender everything so easily. Fight or die!"

What was his empire if he had no family to prosper with?

Shafiq laughed. The cold sound pierced Moray through like a dagger. "Then perish here, son of Connall! Face your demons and lose, like so many others have before you." The red energy from the ancient staff burst, engulfing Shafiq's body. Just like that, he disappeared.

Moray would not bow to any god who deserted him. He lifted his head as the Leviathan did the same. It would slam against the sands, and this time, he wouldn't flee it. He'd let the monster kill him. Let his blood be shed on the bitter water's shore. Let himself die like Graft had. Graft, the brother who had deserved a happy life, killed by Moray's pride.

Pride.

That was the voice.

But Moray remembered something else: Graft's voice. *Elohai is the only way.*

If Graft had died for Elohai... if Finnigan and Ama believed so much... if Absalom survived here for two years... if his parents had adored him despite his flaws...

Moray could not do this alone. He did not want to survive here alone if it meant he'd lose everything else and keep his pride. This was not what he wanted.

Not anymore.

Because of his greed, Graft had died in his arms. His closest friend had suffered for Moray's sins. Because of his selfishness, his parents had been murdered.

Moray had never intended for any of that. He'd never meant for his brother and betrothed to suffer for his doings. It was all his fault. Every life lost, every life harmed, the blood was on his hands. What could he do to fix his friends and his kingdom, if all he'd ever done was destroy?

I'm hopeless.

The words carved into his mind. Helpless. Powerless.

There was nothing he could do to bring Graft back, nothing he could do to bring his parents back. The others, too, would be better off without him.

What did he have left? Nothing. He'd fought for everything and now had nothing.

The first voice whispered in the raging storm, "Repent and you shall be saved. Trust Me and I shall be your strength."

Moray didn't deserve the strength. He didn't deserve to be saved.

But he didn't want to die. He didn't want the life he'd fought for. He wanted something more. Something like Finnigan and Ama had.

Hope.

Moray balled his fists and screamed at the demons in the sky, screamed at the hungry skeletons, screamed at the Leviathan, screamed at Elohai. "Cleanse me!"

The salty water poured over him joining the tears running down his cheeks, but he didn't back down. It burned his eyes, his lungs, even his skin as it struck like a thousand little blades. "Cleanse me from what I have chosen!" Moray had nothing to give but his broken soul. Would it be enough?

The demons on his shoulders pulled him down into the sand again. Their claws dug into his skull, his chest, ripping him apart with their bodies and voices. They were liars, just like he was, but he didn't want them anymore.

He didn't want Pride to be the death of him. Pride had killed enough good men already.

Moray shouted those two words again, and a cracked plea followed as water rushed down his throat. "Please!"

He didn't deserve love. He had lost the others—they were good, they were faithful, deserving of love and redemption. They had not sold their souls. They had not played god. Moray had played a part in Abaddon's plan all along. Abaddon would destroy the realms. How could he have been so fooled by love? By fear? By pride?

Moray wept hard, curling up in the sands as his demons tore into him. The Leviathan came crashing down, and the ground beneath Moray dispersed in a fury. He hit the sand a distance away, and the demons remained. The skeletons ran for him, teeth gnashing.

"Elohai, forgive me!" Moray begged. Water filled his lungs, sand blinded his vision. He'd brought this on himself. He had cursed Elohai for how long? Why ought a holy God save a monster from his own self-inflicted destruction?

"You do not need Him," Pride snarled. "Be silent and die like the king that you are, or get up and end this on your own."

"I can't. I can't end this. I couldn't control it, and I was a fool for thinking I could." Moray clutched his head. "Get off me!" he begged the demons. Utter terror clutched his heart, closed his lungs. He couldn't move any part of his body now. Everything piled over him. Water filled his nostrils.

Elohai, please!

The darkness wanted him dead for his sins. Moray couldn't fight it any longer. He could not win. "Elohai!"

The scream was the last thing to leave his lips.

After a moment of eternity, the waters stopped thrashing. The demons hissed and screamed in fury, but they fell away from Moray's body and he struggled, opening his eyes.

The Leviathan vanished. The churning sea rolled and shook as the serpent disappeared from the battle.

Forty-One

"OPEN THE RIFT AGAIN!" Finnigan shouted at Etu with all his might. He didn't react to being in the dragon egg chamber, nor did he question why Sadon the traitorous wizard was in the same room as Etu the cruel prince. None of that mattered. All that mattered was that they had left Moray behind in the second realm of death and he was facing a Leviathan that wanted to eat him.

Ama held Tanka against her chest. Her blade glowed a brilliant white—same as Etu's. Somehow, they had opened the portal with the sacred blades. It had been a blur and a flash, and Finnigan could hardly process it.

Absalom knelt on the floor by a body—Gunnar. Blood pooled and mingled with the water that their drenched bodies poured onto the floor near the dragon egg pedestal.

Finnigan stopped mid-shout and ran over. Dropping beside his loud-mouth, boisterous friend, he laid hands on him wearily.

"He—" Absalom began, but Finnigan tuned him out.

Near death, holding on by a string, Gunnar was covered with bruises, bites, and bloody gashes. He'd inhaled enough water to kill anyone. Hands trembling, Finnigan grabbed his arms and healed him, begging Elohai to save Gunnar as he did so.

After a long, agonizing minute, Gunnar's chest jerked with a big breath. His gashes and bites healed, the skin where they'd bled turning a soft pink. Absalom rolled him over and Gunnar violently coughed up water.

Finnigan pulled away, tears in his eyes. "Moray needs us," he forced out.

Ama gently put Tanka down, and the siiti ran for Gunnar, mumbling incoherently. Tanka crushed Gunnar in a hug. The mercenary swore, pulling the boy close and leaning against his father weakly. He took in his surroundings with wide eyes.

They had endured Golgotha and made it home. Without Moray.

Ama staggered to Etu, knees buckling. Etu caught her and sat her on the floor, his expression taut with rage. "We cannot open the rift again. Elohai blessed us once. A second time would drain the life from Ama. She is the only other one who can bear the blade's connection and power. It is her Gift and no one else's."

Finnigan pushed forward, kneeling beside Ama—his friend, his beloved. The woman he had fought for and tried to protect. After all of the hell they had faced, she would die if they saved his brother. He couldn't ask it of her. Sobs choked him, but he pulled her into a tight hug, unable to speak.

Ama gently pushed him away. "We're bringing Moray back," she said firmly. "Creator told me we would. Moray has repented. I know he has." She met her brother's harsh gaze. "We do it again. Elohai will give me strength."

THE PORTAL RIPPED OPEN the dark sky. The demons fled but couldn't pass through the portal opening. Piercing white light scattered the shadows below and stilled the sea.

Moray lifted his head, sobbing. Before he could take in the extravagant beauty, Golgotha disappeared. The prevailing light flickered in his vision before a new, familiar setting engulfed him. The chamber room of the sacred artifacts. He breathed in like he might be dead—but air filled his burning lungs.

Alive.

Elohai... You let me live, Moray thought.

I breathed the breath in your lungs, Moray. I love you, came the reply.

Sobs racked his body as he tried moving, but his body didn't work. He couldn't feel a thing now.

"Moray!" Voices chorused—victorious, familiar voices. Finnigan wrapped his arms around him and pulled him upright gently. "Moray, it's all right, we made it to Mazzabah. Elohai saved us!"

Moray held his brother for dear life, unable to hold the flood of tears back. Fear clutched his heart. "Abaddon said I would die if I did this," he choked out.

"Did what?" Finnigan held him upright.

Moray spotted the others then. Ama, passed out in Etu's arms and Courage chattering in her ear. The warrior kneeling on the ground like a cougar ready to pounce Moray the first chance he got. Absalom helping Gunnar sit up, with Tanka curled up beside them.

Elohai had shown mercy once, but nothing could save him from Abaddon. His previous master had been worse than the Leviathan. Elohai was not that powerful.

"Nothing," Moray answered his brother, taking a shaky breath. The voices all tumbled in his head now. Not all of the demons had left, but he hadn't a clue which ones he wrestled with. In the moment, he didn't care—they were alive, in Mazzabah. If he could get his senses back, he could press on in his fight.

Sadon stepped closer. He was bare besides a pair of pants, which looked to be stolen from one of the guards knocked out and tied up in the chamber corner.

"I hear shouts." Etu eased Ama onto the floor near Tanka and Courage. "We will be discovered—"

Finnigan lifted a hand. "Listen."

The shouts passed outside in the hall, jumbled, panicked. No one broke into the chamber room.

"Something's wrong," Moray said. "We need to get out there." They needed to kill Barric. Restore the kingdom. It couldn't be done in a day, but whatever was happening now was going down quickly. He drew himself up, legs shaking as he stood with Finnigan's aid.

Etu hesitated. "It... it may have been the rift."

"What?" Sadon snarled. "What happened? It worked perfectly both times!"

"The second time was difficult." Etu glanced down at Ama. "She wasn't able to hold the rift steady. Something might've been able to slip through."

"Abaddon..." Sadon paled. "Moray—"

"Abaddon was going to unleash Golgotha into Mazzabah all along," Moray said, voice hoarse. "We cannot let him." He eyed Finnigan.

Finnigan didn't look at him, however. His attention was on the egg. The giant shell had started to glow.

THE DRAGON EGG HAD always called Finnigan. Never before had he had the courage to allow himself such a claim, but it'd been true. The white egg with brown webbing covering the tiny scales almost hummed to his spirit—speaking something only he could understand. Calling him closer.

While the others spoke, Elohai directed Finnigan's attention to the egg. Wiping rainwater from his eyes, boots sopping on the marble floor, Finnigan approached the egg. His ears rang as he closed his eyes briefly. *If it be Your will, Elohai, let it be done.*

He reached out, touching the dragon egg of legend.

It hummed softly at his touch. The egg shook, shuddered, and a small crack traveled down the top.

"You broke it!" Etu said.

"No," Moray whispered. "The dragon has chosen Finnigan."

"It can only choose a king." Sadon leaned against the wall, pale as a ghost.

Finnigan's chest tightened. His father's words ran through his mind, but he couldn't speak. Pain clawed his heart, and every breath felt as if shards of glass dragged against his lungs. He thought of his father and mother, of Graft, and Elohai only knew of the innocent lives lost under Barric's rule. They had all deserved life. They had deserved happiness.

The egg cracked, and another low growl came from it. Finnigan would not flee from his fate. He glanced back at Ama, who hadn't woken. Her beautiful soul had saved them—she'd followed Creator from the beginning, and He had blessed them for it. It was his turn to save her. It was his turn to love her with everything in him and pray it was enough. If he could help Elohai's people be restored, Ama could go home to her clan, if she so wished.

Maybe... maybe she would stay. But he wouldn't ask it of her.

He kept a firm hand on the egg as it glowed softly. "We need to get Ama and Tanka somewhere safe before all hell breaks loose."

Forty-Two

"WE NEED A PLAN," Etu said sharply. "We cannot face Barric and whatever may have entered through the rift without a plan." The Wolf Clan men were always prepared for battle, but this one would be unlike any they had faced before.

Moray didn't know how they would survive the chaos ahead of them.

He had to save his people.

He had to save Mazzabah.

Moray gulped down the lump of dread forming in his throat. His father had raised him to be a fighter, a strong man, a courageous one. But he knew his fate: He and Sadon would die at the hands of the master they'd once adored. Abaddon would not let them survive after their betrayals. But no one else had to know that.

The ancient dragon had chosen Finnigan. Finnigan had always been everything Moray couldn't be.

No... Moray had worked for it, saved them, done everything in his power to be a good king. He'd fought for the crown. It was his.

Moray stared at his brother, heat flooding his cheeks.

Pride. Pride still plagued him. The voice flickered in his spirit and he couldn't shake it. "You deserve to be king, Moray. Why shouldn't you be?"

Moray sucked in a sharp breath. He couldn't hear the others speaking around him. His vision blurred. The voice overpowered every sense, shaking him to his core. Pride grabbed hold of Moray's heart with both hands and held fast, voice sharp, firm, familiar.

He focused on his surroundings, shaking softly. Absalom looked at Finnigan with a solemn expression. "We must move fast. We may be unnoticed if the others are panicking."

Ama groaned, eyes opening as she stirred on the floor. Tanka grinned a toothy grin. "Am-Am!"

"Ama!" Finnigan exclaimed. "Are you—"

She sat up, eyes dazed, staring at him and the egg. "Finn? What are you doing?"

Etu dragged her upright. "The egg chose him. He's going to be king. Because these people are fools and leave such things to ancient dragons. But none of that matters if we don't get out of this castle."

Pride kept wrestling in Moray's spirit and harsh words echoed in his mind as he reached the door. A way out—they needed to get out, unseen, and figure out what was going on out there. Over six months had passed in Mazzabah, if Sadon had told him the truth in his dreams. Moray had no clue if anyone would follow him now. Loyalties might all be destroyed. Chaos lay beyond these doors.

Being back in Mazzabah hadn't magically solved every issue. Maybe Barric had taken over everything. Maybe there was no return.

No, he would help restore his father's empire.

"You will be king, Moray," Pride said.

"No!" Moray growled under his breath. The others spoke rapidly, his brother and his friends, the people he had come to love more than his own blood. Voice low, Moray whispered, "In the name of Elohai, I rebuke you, Pride. I will not allow you to control me. No more." His voice cracked as the last words left his mouth, but he squared his shoulders. Perhaps his demons would never leave—but he'd never give up the fight. Not when he had family depending on him.

"Let's move," Gunnar snapped. "Ama, take Tanka and hide."

"No," Ama said firmly. "I will not hide now. Not after all of this."

Tanka jumped onto Gunnar's shoulders and snapped his jaws, as if showing he wanted to join in the fight too. The rains in the desert had healed his scaly body, and his eyes glimmered mischievously.

Finnigan gulped hard. "Ama, please listen."

"I'm following." Ama stepped closer to Finnigan, jaw set with unyielding determination.

Absalom pulled a blade. "No time to waste arguing. We leave the castle and see what has been done. Royals first." A smirk lit up his features. The man hadn't been in Mazzabah for many years, and he had a world to see and take in. He was home, but the first thing that awaited him was another battle. It seemed that he preferred it that way.

"Let's go." Moray flashed a grin. As long as he focused on the others and what he could do before his death, the fear didn't suffocate him. Yet.

THE GROUP ESCAPED THE castle through secret passageways that Sadon led them through. The wizard moved like a wounded wolf but didn't speak besides whispering an apology before he opened one last door. Blinding sunlight poured from the outside world into the dank underground corridor.

They flooded out of the castle wall—right onto the great wall that surrounded Buacach. Finnigan breathed in sharply. It felt surreal to have been in such cramped quarters, fleeing for their life in the castle he'd grown up in, and suddenly be overlooking it all like a hawk.

The euphoria did not last long.

The skeleton army had entered through the rift.

Thousands of skeleton dragged themselves across the Red Forest floor, screeching and crying out. Finnigan didn't understand how the rift had allowed them into the chamber room and a skeleton army into the forest, but after time in Golgotha, some questions were best left unanswered.

Along the wall overlooking the forest and the world beyond, soldiers scrambled to prepare for the battle ahead.

Men gathered bows and arrows, rushing to light the torches before the sun set. Dark streaks of red and maroon lit up the sky, like Elohai was painting a picture based on the mood of the kingdom.

Soldiers in uniform collected barrels of spears and swords and stationed them along the walls. Those would do no good against monsters of bones. Finnigan ran over to the nearest man who looked like a general and grabbed his shoulder. "Hey!"

The man whirled around. "Who do—" he froze, eyes growing wide. "P-Prince Finn—" He gaped at the dragon egg hatching under Finnigan's arm.

Finnigan spoke quickly, Elohai giving him what to say. "Those skeletons are only killed when they are decapitated. We need more weapons and more men. And we need worshippers—we need people singing and blowing trumpets throughout the fight. Hurry!" He wasn't a general or a captain or even the king yet. As far as this man knew—a man he'd never seen before, as Barric seemed to have changed the lead warriors—Finnigan had been dead.

The general, a man put into his rank by Barric, turned and obeyed Finnigan's instructions. He called out the orders, barking at anyone who didn't move fast enough.

Finnigan thanked Elohai that it worked. He gulped as he eyed the skeletons. What else could go wrong? Barric could come and find them alive if one of the soldiers snitched. But there was no use being paranoid. They had to focus on this fight first.

Ama gripped his hand tightly, always at his side, ready to face the world. "Let's find positions. The monsters won't be much farther now."

"You—"

"I'm going to worship with Tanka." She smiled, eyes heavy as she picked up the shofar Absalom had given her. Without a care of the soldiers racing around them and the fact that all hell was soon to break loose, she hugged him tightly. "Creator is with us. I'll see you when it's over, Finn."

Ama turned, taking Tanka closer to a brick room where the exit to the wall was. There were many stations along the wall.

Finnigan hoped the soldiers and singers hurried— whomever they were. No one in Mazzabah had worshippers among their warriors. He knew the clans sang and danced before fights, but not simultaneously. Elohai had instructed him, and he would listen.

He ran to the others. Moray took over a large group of men that immediately began obeying his orders. Finnigan assumed they'd been soldiers Barric hadn't swapped out or trained. Absalom and Gunnar never left each other's sides. Finnigan would've done anything to have his father beside him then. He would make his father proud. He would do his kingdom good.

The skeletons beat on the stone wall. They were too weak to break it, but who knew what else they were capable of? They could clamber up it, stack atop each other, or worse, break through the gate somehow. They were from a realm where Darkness reigned and anything was possible.

But they were in Mazzabah now, and Elohai was with the righteous.

PERHAPS ELOHAI DID ANSWER some prayers. Moray hadn't expected anyone to obey their warnings. Really, he'd expected the soldiers to kill them all on sight, considering they probably knew Barric's barbaric intentions. No such thing happened. In minutes, the troops were rallied along the walls and in the city at the foot of the wall. Men with swords, bows, spears, and cannons stood at the ready.

Among the warriors and soldiers on the kingdom wall, the worshippers sang. Moray hadn't a clue where the general had found them. They played instruments and blew trumpets like a miniature army. Their voices carried through the heavy, dark atmosphere like swords through veils. The Light would prevail, by the hands of warriors and the voices of praisers.

Moray never would have thought he'd have stood where he did then. He stood as a prince, not a king. A dead man, not a god. He'd go down kicking, either way. He'd die for the sake of his brother and his empire.

The voices in his head argued. The demons whispered lies. He blocked it all out, focusing on the Voice of Elohai.

"Go for the heads," Absalom said to them, voice firm. He met Gunnar's gaze, a small, almost melancholic smile tugging his lips. "Do not brutally outdo the lot of them, Son."

Gunnar laughed a booming laugh. "Of course not, Father."

Moray eyed his brother at his side. Overlooking the world, he felt a strange sense of fellowship—like they belonged here, at the edge of it all, facing the Darkness with the Light within. Perhaps his Light was far from as great as Finnigan's. But it was something to keep him alive until fear and Abaddon took Moray's last breath.

His flicker of hope in Elohai was smothered when he saw five giants of bone and sharp teeth wander out from the Red Forest. These were at least twice the size as the other skeletons. In the setting sun, mist surrounded the skeletons. To the soldiers, it was simply the dew, nothing supernatural about it.

Finnigan swore. "Let's move!"

The leaders of the soldiers—or half of them, as Moray noticed a few had disappeared, which didn't sit well in his gut—shouted for their men to begin waging war.

The cannons and arrows sent their assaults over the wall and into the skeleton army below. Moray's ears rang, but he watched closely. He had shot the monsters with arrows and killed them, but it took a perfect shot. They didn't have that time. They needed an army of men below to fight outside of the walls. It would cause more deaths, but if they didn't take control quickly, who knew what might happen? If the giant skeletons got too close, they could bring down the wall or smash through the gate.

Moray glanced at Finnigan and Gunnar as they unleashed arrows below, both taking critical aim. He ran from the edge and hurried to the general. Grabbing his arm roughly, Moray snapped, "We need men out there. We're losing time like this. Look at the giants! The large ones will break through the wall, we must take them out first. Lock the gates behind us."

The general watched as the giants came closer. The rattling jaws and gnashing teeth of the skeletons beyond the wall filled the air like a symphony of bones. The man eyed Moray and said in a sharp voice, "I trust you to lead them below. We'll shut the gates and handle the rest."

Moray's chest tightened, and he steeled himself with all he had left. If he was going to die, at least it would be for his people. He would die humble—as a royal ought to be, crown or no crown. "Aye. I'll lead them past the walls, and we will kill the giants."

Forty-Three

THE DRAGON EGG HATCHED beneath Finnigan's feet, the shell shattering to the stone floor. Finnigan wrestled between shooting arrows at the skeletons below and keeping the dragon from leaving. He didn't expect the little creature to sit still like a trained dog. What if it blew someone to smithereens? Caring for a dragon during a battle against monsters wasn't ideal.

At his side, Gunnar laughed. "Ugly little thing looks just like you, Finny." He let an arrow loose at the beasts below. Skeletons dropped one by one, but the soldiers' progress was slow compared to what they had left to destroy.

"Shut your trap," Finnigan snapped.

They weren't going to make it. Finnigan didn't know if the skeletons could become bored or reasonable, but if they decided to hunt another civilization, one without walls... He gulped. No, they'd end it here, no matter what. He stepped back, yanking the dragon off the ground.

The hatchling was as big as his chest. He didn't like the thought of being cramped in an egg like this thing had been. Covered in tough yellow scales, it flicked a tongue over Finnigan's face, hot saliva dripping down his chin.

He groaned. "You're awfully warm. Legends say you can breathe fire." He glanced down at the skeletons. "Wonder if you can do so this young." Doubtful. The thing probably couldn't even fly.

Of all the times to hatch, of all the kings to choose, this dragon had picked him, in this moment. Finnigan didn't have time to sit around and wonder why. There was a reason though, and he had to trust Elohai that he could do what had to be done.

He put the little beast on his shoulder—it felt twice as heavy as it ought to—and hurried down the top of the wall. He needed to be on the ground below. He needed to face the enemy head-on, like a true king. Gulping down bile, he stepped into the guard station.

Halfway down the stairs, he saw the back of Moray's figure in the torches' light. "Moray?"

Moray glanced back, scowling. "What are you doing?"

"Same as you." Finnigan caught up with him. The dragon flapped its big wings and nearly knocked Finnigan over, but Moray grabbed his arm.

"Fall down these stairs and you won't help the battle anymore."

"You think?" Finnigan pushed on. "We have to stop the giants before they break through."

"Aye and they might have magic, powers we just haven't seen. We're wasting time throwing arrows at bones."

"We need—"

"I have a hundred men waiting for me," Moray whispered. "We will do what we can to kill as many as we can, perhaps enough so the cannons can handle the rest. Or perhaps someone will murder Barric—wherever he is—and the other soldiers will be free to do the right thing. You're the king. Get up on the wall and show the troops hope."

Moray didn't want him to die.

Finnigan gripped Moray's arm with all his might. "We're brothers. We fight side by side. No matter what."

"And if we both die and the kingdom falls into the hands of Barric?" Moray snarled. The dragon hissed back, tail flicking as if in disgust at Moray's tone.

"Elohai will not let it happen." Elohai would protect them. After all they'd faced in Golgotha, nothing scared Finnigan on his own turf.

Moray eyed the dragon and started down the stairs. "Perhaps He won't."

Finnigan flashed a grin. "Let's go face some giants."

AMA STOOD WITH THE men and women who were worshipping. They sang of Elohai, of His strength and shelter, while the shouts and orders of the soldiers roared. Their bold, fiery voices joined the clamor. The booms of the cannons, the shouts and screams—the singing rose above it all. She'd lost sight of Finnigan and Moray. She'd overheard that men had gone on foot to meet the giants head on to buy the men on the walls some time.

Gunnar darted for the stairs, blades in hand. Ama called out to him and he glanced up, shouting, "Real war's on the ground! Some of the buggers are startin' to glow." He vanished down the stairs. Absalom followed closely after his son.

Glow?

Ama turned back to the edge of the wall, looking down. Her knees shook at the drastic height, but she pushed away her fear. The hundreds of skeletons swarming the castle walls had dark red mist pouring from their hollow eye sockets. Their jaws chomped the air. The largest of the skeletons moved toward the walls.

Ama took a shaky breath. "Oh, Creator, help us." She gripped the shofar tighter, blowing it with all she had left in her spirit.

The skeletons clustered together at the gate below. She knew the soldiers had sent a large group down to face the army head-on. The men she'd traveled with through Golgotha were about to enter the heat of it all. Her chin trembled, but she kept blowing the shofar.

They had survived Golgotha. Together. They wouldn't stop now, not with Creator on their side.

Tanka clung to Ama's legs, shaking with anxiety. He growled and hissed at any soldier who got too close to her. Under his breath, he begged for *Papa*, whom Ama figured meant Gunnar now. She comforted the child, sheltering him from the battle raging around them.

In a sudden flash of red, the gates burst opened and skeletons swarmed toward the city. An army of men following their true, beloved princes met them head-on in flashes of light. The mist burst from the skeleton army like a streak of red lightning.

Blue light covered the warriors in a massive shield the same instant—Finnigan using his Gift to ward off the Darkness. Their Gifts might not save them alone, but with Creator, they could defeat anything. They'd defeat Barric and the traitors who'd hungered for war. There was hope as long as there was breath.

DESPITE KING BARRIC'S MURDEROUS rule, many of the soldiers followed Finnigan and Moray, regardless of the lethal consequences. The men who did not follow did not stop them, and no one called for Barric—Finnigan guessed that the pile of dung was probably hiding in a castle chamber. He didn't care who died protecting him.

Farmers, traders, and any able-bodied peasants came to join them with their shovels, blades, and axes. In total, about three hundred of them stood against the hundreds of skeletons pushing through the opening. The clinging and clamoring of metal and voices pierced the evening, sending shivers down Finnigan's spine.

He wasn't just fighting for his people. His people fought for him. Some still remained loyal to the royals, even if it might cost them their lives.

He shouted as he ran to the front, using all the Energy he could muster to shield the men and kill the first wave of skeletons. The dragon left him and flew above the destruction. Finnigan supposed its ability to fly was instinct, like a foal walking on wobbly legs minutes after birth.

He kept his Energy pulsing like a shield, protecting as many men as he could. When the blue light hit the skeletons, their bodies exploded, sending bits of sharp bones in all directions. Finnigan hated the idea of the shrapnel harming his own, but he couldn't stop it from reaching some victims. Their cries burned in his ears.

The red glowing mist that wafted from the enemy army raged hot and united, every one of the skeletons pushing on harder. Whatever the red stuff was, Finnigan figured it was their life source. Destroying their bodies only caused the mist to move to the next of their kin.

"Target the giants!" He glanced up briefly, watching the giant skeletons approach the gate. Red mist glowed from their eye sockets and gaping jaws.

Elohai, save us.

The skeletons pushed forward. The cannons sent heavy artillery and killed dozens of the monsters, but they couldn't pick off all of them. The men on foot pushed back with all their might. Severed skulls scattered the soft dirt, and broken bones littered the grass. As the battle raged—blades against bones, Light against Darkness—blood coated the piles of bones. Bodies of men lay scattered.

In war, focusing on the Darkness did little to save the living. Finnigan felt the battle that was clashing in the heavens—between demons and angels. In Mazzabah, he couldn't see it, but he had seen enough in Golgotha to understand that this battle was bigger than flesh against bone.

"LONG TIME NO SEE, Ama," a familiar, weary voice came from behind Ama. She lowered her shofar and gaped at the sight of a bloodied, haggard Hasa. He grinned at her and hugged her quickly.

"Hasa, what—"

"I came with Etu to save the wizard," he whispered. "Long story, but a few of us Wolf men are out here fighting, and Sadon is with us. Figured I'd come up here to help watch your back." Her friend eyed the shofar. "You ought to be singing. I know your voice could defeat this disaster."

Ama gulped hard. "The others—"

"They're making progress below. The giants are moving in." Hasa laughed wildly. "Best fight I've ever been in. Riveting! You keep singing. It is helping." He rushed off, presumably to find Etu, his commander and friend.

She held Tanka close and watched the skeletons crumple in masses beneath the thick trees. Darkness settled over the world. Ama sang with all the energy she could muster—which wasn't much—and when that was gone, Creator breathed more voice into her lungs.

Forty-Four

FIGHT.

Tooth and nail.

Spirit and body.

Flesh against bone.

Moray didn't know what to think. In his spirit, he knew what was true. All he had done, every sin he had committed, every demon he had loved—he wanted none of the Darkness anymore.

Despite the blood on Moray's hands, Elohai still wanted him. Elohai would not forsake him or destroy him as Abaddon had.

He would die here because of what he'd done. Elohai would not be able to save him from a fate he chose. A fate Abaddon chose for him.

The skeletons piled up, bones rolling in the dirt, but the troops pushed onward. The great gate was shut again. They were on their own. All or nothing. If they couldn't stop the monsters, they'd lose everyone, everything, and there would be no return for Mazzabah. Not with Shafiq out there, waiting to unleash his own hell.

End the army.

Moray swung his blade skillfully, severing two skeletons in one go.

Kill Barric.

A skeleton lunged at him with outstretched arms, fingerbones grabbing him with steel-like grips. Its jaws gnashed inches from Moray's face, and the red mist seeping from the monster's eyes made his stomach twist. Moray cut off its head.

Kill Shafiq.

Rage fueled Moray's movements as he fought alongside his brother and friends.

Restore my father's kingdom.

Moray couldn't win alone, but Elohai was with him, and he would walk in that truth. Even if he'd known and learned of Elohai and the Letters, living in rebellion had destroyed him. Now, with his eyes clear, he could do his best and hope Elohai understood his effort.

Screams tore through the heavy atmosphere as men fell, clutching their bloodied necks where the skeletons had hit the mark with their hungry teeth. Moray pushed further. "Cut them down!" he screamed. "Cut them all down! Reach the giants!"

The men followed him. A man at his left was attacked by a handful of the beasts. Moray hacked at them ferociously, but the man clutched his neck as blood spurted. He was just a farmer—probably had a wife and children beyond the wall.

Moray ran on, cutting down any monster that crossed his path, aiming for the giants. The man had died because of him. Just as Graft died. This was all his fault.

He had to focus on the tasks. He could not listen to the voices of doubt.

One of the giants reached them. Sweeping out with one hand, it knocked a few soldiers down as the rest attacked with blades. It bit a man's head off before they killed it.

Finnigan's shield held fast, but Moray caught sight of the dragon flapping around the giants. A grin lit up Moray's face. The little bugger wasn't so useless after all. "Finn!" he yelled over the screams and shouts of men.

Finnigan looked over, drenched in sweat and trudging along, but each step seemed to take energy he could hardly expend. "What?"

"Your bloody dragon's distracting the giants!" Gunnar yelled from Moray's right. He was splattered in blood—someone else's, most likely—and wore a bloodthirsty expression. Many Goidelic warriors told tales of men that turned almost rabid during war. Gunnar didn't come from Moray's blood, but he was still bred for war. It showed in the way he wielded the blades in his strong hands and the way his eyes took in every bit of movement, all while speaking and maintaining his wits. His father was almost identical in his animalistic style of fighting, but instead of conversing, the old man focused on slaying the skeletons around Moray and Gunnar.

Moray gulped, grateful the two men were on their side.

Finnigan watched the dragon, face grim. He didn't slack the shield, and the blue energy throbbed around the men that kept tucked close, weary of accidentally slipping beyond the light. Arrows streaked the sky, hitting their marks most of the time, but the help from the wall wouldn't be enough.

The cannons weren't enough either. The giants saw every attack and moved out of the way. They were now too close to the fight to be struck without the fodder causing friendly fire.

Was I wrong, Elohai, to lead the men on the field?

Moray's heart hammered and his stomach twisted as he fought hard. More men screamed as their lives were ended by brutal bites and strangling hands. Three hundred men against countless skeletons weren't good odds.

Something Finnigan had said many times when they'd been children popped into Moray's mind. A piece from the Letters. "When thou go to battle against your enemies, and see horses and chariots and people more than thee, be not afraid of them, for Elohai is with thee, and will not forsake thee."

Moray pressed forward, Gunnar and Absalom at his side as they faced the second giant. It swung a large arm toward them, but they lunged low, cutting it down at the legs. Absalom swung the final blow, severing the monster's head. Moray wasn't sure how long their blades would hold against bones.

As if on cue, a familiar roar came from behind them—Etu and his clan members. They ran through the dark like a wolf pack hungry for blood. Loud thuds followed as they dismembered skeletons to Moray's right and tore through the minions. Etu's blade showed a bright yellow color as he ripped it through every skeleton he ran upon. They attacked him, but his blade wreaked havoc. His men carried axes that chopped the skeletons' heads off with precision.

Moray groaned as he staggered away from the defeated second giant. Pieces of rotting flesh hung off the giant's dark bones, filling Moray with slight nausea.

The voices came again as he stumbled forward.

"You will die."

"That is your fate."

"You will die a liar, a traitor, a monster."

"Abaddon is coming."

A LONE WOLF SURROUNDED by packs of rabid dogs, Sadon fought alongside the royals, the soldiers, and the clan warriors. Screams rang in his ears, and the melody of crunching bone rattled in his head. This was what he had welcomed into Mazzabah.

Where was his victory after years of planning and obeying his master?

If he failed, Oliver would be found by Shafiq and slaughtered. All that mattered was Oliver. The princes might decide to hang Sadon for what he had done, but he would go down fighting. He would die for that child who believed that Elohai loved even the most broken souls.

He would die to ensure that Oliver could live in a kingdom where he was embraced. He would live, and Ama would care for him. The boy would not die for Sadon's sins.

Sadon swung his sword, beheading two skeletons in one slice. Another cry rose, young and piercing. The battlefield reeked of blood and fear, smells he knew all too well. Would his scream join the others, to be forgotten in the symphony of war, an echo in time? He jumped over a pile of bodies, pushing deeper into the raging war, closer to the hungry skeletons.

"Pray," Etu had said.

"Believe," Oliver had begged.

Abaddon's words burned in his mind: "You are mine."

If Sadon chose Elohai, he would surely die. But he could not die here. He had to live, for Oliver. No matter the cost.

A skeleton grabbed him from behind, dragging him down to the dirt, chomping jaws lunging for his throat. As soon as it tried, its skull tumbled from its body as a blade swung through its spine.

Moray stood over Sadon, yanking him to his feet, blood and sweat smeared over his face. He said nothing but plunged back into the battle.

Sadon did the same and beheaded another creature with a furious yell. But he couldn't shake the fear from his mind.

Even Moray had made a choice. He had turned from Abaddon. What would befall him now?

Too long, Sadon had submitted to a god who had let him fall. No more.

He chose the Light. For Oliver... He chose the God who gave him Oliver.

OUR BONES ARE FULL of life, unlike the monsters we rage against. Finnigan repeated the truth inside his head over and over as his body threatened to give out. He had never used this much Energy before in his life. After the fight in Golgotha at the seashore and now this, his soul hung on the verge of utter exhaustion—but adrenaline drove him forward.

His shield weakened and grew smaller, protecting only the farmers and younger boys, the well-trained men going out in front and slaughtering as many skeletons as they could. The shield now slowed the speed of the skeletons that passed through but didn't break them apart.

Before him, the warriors fought hard. But the numbers of skeletons were still great. It would take a miracle to win.

Finnigan kept his arms raised, trembling. He itched to fight alongside his brothers—but Elohai told him to stand still and hold the shield.

Etu fell as a giant skeleton swiped his legs. Hasa and the others hacked the giant down. Hasa dragged Etu across the bloodied, bone-covered forest, dropping him behind Finnigan's shield.

Etu screamed and clutched his broken legs, blood pouring from a gash in his head. He held his glowing blade tightly. "I'm the only one who can wield this! I have to get out there. This blade is—"

Hasa slapped him lightly. "Give me the blade."

"It is bonded only—"

"It is a Gift from Creator, and right now, I believe He will allow me to wield it." Hasa held Etu by his shoulders.

Etu shoved the blade at Hasa. "Wield it well, brother."

Hasa smirked and then glanced at Finnigan, calling, "Stay in one piece, King! My friend is waiting for you with open arms!" And he ran into the thick of the fight with Etu's glowing blade in his hand.

MINUTES TICKED BY. HALF an hour. Moray lost count of time. All that mattered was that they'd downed three giant skeletons and the numbers of the minions trickled. Men continued to die, but they still had a chance.

Fight.

Flesh against bone. Truth against principalities.

As the demons assailed Moray's mind, words of truth spoken by his parents, Finnigan, Ama, and Absalom filled his head. The words fueled his righteous rage as he fought.

Men had followed him into battle. He would not fail them. With Elohai, they would be saved.

But could he truly be saved from the death that awaited him?

Gunnar, Absalom, Moray, and a few others attacked the final giant. It moved swiftly, snatching one of the men off the ground. The others attacked with all their might, but it was too late. The giant took a bite before Hasa cracked its leg bones open with Etu's blade.

The giant fell, swinging both arms to catch itself. It snapped its jaws, reaching toward the nearest man. The beast grabbed Absalom by his torso and slammed him down against the ground, red mist engulfing Absalom's body.

"Father!" Gunnar screamed, digging his blade into the giant's neck.

Absalom swung his sword but couldn't move, chest crushed by the giant's tightening grip. The giant snapped its jaw, lunging one last time. It bit down on Absalom's neck before its skull popped away from its spine. Blood spurted from Absalom's neck and he fell limp onto the forest floor, blood pooling.

Gunnar yelled, dropping beside his father in the midst of the battle. He held Absalom close, weeping as blood soaked his shirt.

The final giant lay slain, but not without a high cost.

As Moray turned away to help slaughter the rest of the skeletons, he saw a hooded figure at the edge of the giant tree line. The familiar serpent-headed staff glittered in the smoke that engulfed the wizard's body. Moray froze in his tracks. "Gunnar..."

Gunnar lifted his head, choking back a ragged sob. Moray moved in front of his friend, but the wizard lowered in a mocking bow, voice calling through the chaos, "May my old friend rest in peace, Gunnar, son of Absalom! And may you hear his blood cry from this ground till your own dying breath."

A scream of fury escaped Gunnar, but Shafiq disappeared into thin air.

The war raged on like nothing had happened. Breathing hard like his entire body might explode, Moray shouted into the pandemonium before him, "I choose Your fate for me, Elohai. Not Abaddon's!" He would not choose the path Shafiq had.

The voices wrestled and argued, threatening to choke him to death.

"Elohai!" he shouted. "We repent! We turn to you!" His sword struck the back of a skeleton's spine, severing it in two.

He did not want to die by Abaddon's hands.

Come to me, the voice said.

"We will not die. We will live and praise You!" Moray never looked back, fighting with all the breath he had left. The warriors followed his lead until every last skeleton lay in a heap. Bones mingled with the blood of the fallen as the torches on the walls cast shadows over the forest. Shafiq had led the skeleton army into Moray's homeland, but never again would such tragedy occur. Moray would die before that wizard harmed his family again.

Forty-Five

THE WARRIORS STOOD SILENT on the crimson-stained forest floor, surrounded by crumbled skeletons. The cannons and the shouts and the skeletons' chomping teeth —everything fell eerily silent like a dome had been placed over the forest, blocking all noise. The worshippers on the wall ceased their singing.

Finnigan dropped the shield and wept as he saw the destruction. Two clan men carried Etu through the gate. The wounded cried for help, shattering the silence, but the sinister atmosphere remained.

Oh, Elohai, what has happened?

Finnigan stepped through the dead bodies, heartbeat drumming in his ears. Soldiers tended the wounded. Young boys, farmers, and traders lay injured. Boys who'd never deserved this chaos wept, a few over the bodies of their fathers. Some retched and some just stood there as if waiting for someone to tell them what to do. A few men took over and started orchestrating the cleanup and the moving of the wounded.

Finnigan pushed on. Under the thick trees, amid a small group of dead and with a giant skeleton sprawled to their left, Gunnar held his father's body. In the darkness, it was hard to see them, but Finnigan heard them. Like nothing and no one else in the world existed, Gunnar sang an old sailor's song over Absalom's broken body. His voice, soft and hoarse, wavered every so often.

Finnigan crashed down beside him, resting a shaky hand on Gunnar's shoulder. He didn't say anything. No words helped a man when his father was gone. Finnigan knew that better than anyone.

Gunnar rocked back and forth, voice low. "It is what he wanted." He said nothing more, gently laying Absalom on the dirt. Gunnar removed his own shirt and covered Absalom's upper body before turning to Finnigan. "But I will hunt the wizard who caused this."

"Sadon has repented—"

"Not Sadon. Shafiq will die for all he has caused. It was he who led the army here. It was all him. I saw him." Gunnar pushed past Finnigan as if the whole battlefield held no concern to him, his sight focusing on the next kill, the next fight. It was his breath. It was his life. "Let's kill Barric before he flees."

MORAY STAGGERED AND FELL into a puddle of blood and bones, retching. Too many bones. Too much blood. Too much, too much, too much. The eyes watched him from the trees—just like in Golgotha.

Abaddon is coming.

He screamed, dragging himself backward, the bodies all around. He didn't want to die.

"Finn!" he yelled, voice cracking. "Help me!" All worries of how he looked as a prince were gone. Let the men hear him beg for help. They didn't see the demons. They didn't know what he'd brought on himself.

They didn't see what he was. Not truly.

Abaddon is coming.

"No! Don't kill me. Don't take me. I did good. Please!" Moray clutched his head, feeling over his body for lethal wounds—but he was alive, in one piece.

"Moray!" Two hands grabbed his shoulders. He jerked, looking up into Finnigan's face. In the faint light of the torches on the walls, Moray saw no fear in his little brother's eyes. Immediately, Finnigan prayed, voice firm as iron.

Moray didn't hear all of the words over the voices in his head. His demons did. Screams tore his throat as Finnigan helped him rebuke the demons he'd so hastily welcomed in. It drained him—his lungs heaved, and fear clawed its way out of his chest like a kraken. He couldn't stand up, and Finnigan held him by his arms.

Finnigan kept praying. Moray weakly did the same, until Elohai engulfed him in His arms and Moray collapsed— free from the Darkness he had created, free from the fear that promised death.

I choose Your fate for me, Father. Not Abaddon's.
No matter what becomes of me. I am Yours.

Finnigan called for help as Moray fell asleep, blackness engulfing him.

AMA HELPED TEND THE wounded in the barracks. Tanka followed her closely, hissing if anyone complained or tried touching him. She insisted the child was fine—she wouldn't let him get three feet away from her as she worked. All the while, she prayed quietly, exhaustion creeping in. Her muscles burned, her eyelids drooped, and her heart ached. Hasa had sworn he'd seen Finnigan, Moray, and Gunnar alive, but they'd disappeared with a group of soldiers and the dragon.

She knew they were going to kill Barric. She shuddered, remembering the way the man had touched her, remembering what he'd wanted from her. She briefly prayed protection over them and placed a blanket over one of the injured men who slept on a pallet.

What if Shafiq was there? And where was Sadon? As much as she wanted to go find answers, she didn't dare drag Tanka out into the mess.

And Absalom... She choked back a sob, moving on to the next man who begged for a drink of water. Ama got it for him and helped him down a few swallows.

Absalom, their friend. He deserved life, life at peace after years of fighting the second realm. But he was dead, at peace in heaven. Tears ran down her cheeks.

Tanka tugged on her arm. He mumbled something and Ama knelt down, knees buckling. "It's all right, Tanka. Let's get you to sleep."

He wiped at her wet cheek with his tiny claw, gentle as could be.

Absalom fought for each of you, Creator whispered, *and I will bless my faithful servants.*

In that moment, Creator's voice was all she needed. Ama's body racked with sobs as she pulled Tanka against her chest and held him.

She would see her people again. She would hold her family once more.

BARRIC HID IN THE underground, and it took them all night to find him. He'd escaped out of the same passageway Ama and Gunnar had tried escaping from. The soldiers chased him out, and at the end of the tunnel, Finnigan and Gunnar stood ready. The dragon, which Finnigan hadn't named but needed to, perched on his shoulders, talons sinking in a bit too deep.

Barric stumbled, his wife behind him. They'd both grown robust, their eyes even darker with demons than the last time Finnigan had seen them. Barric lifted up both hands. "Finnigan, allow me—"

"You murdered my parents!" Finnigan roared. "Every death is on your hands!" Rage obscured his vision. He didn't intend to kill Barric. He'd keep them alive and make an example out of them before the court, but he wouldn't murder them.

Even if he wanted to.

Gunnar gripped his blade in crimson-stained hands, stepping closer to the traitors. He said nothing, like an angel of death.

"It was for the good of the empire. Your father's compassion and his devout religion was weakening the kingdom. The people deserved greater!" Barric didn't back down, voice firm. "I—"

He never finished. The dragon leapt into the air and dove onto Barric like a banshee. Barric screamed, wrestling at the beast on his head. He dropped heavily, his wife screeching and backing away.

Finnigan's gut dropped. "Stop!" he shouted. "Stop it!"

The dragon didn't listen. It took one snap to break Barric's neck, and the little hatchling did nothing more. Shaking itself like a dog, it turned to Finnigan, smoke trailing from its nostrils. Its gold eyes burned with anger. Finnigan felt the same anger in his spirit. The bond was there, even if he didn't understand it. Yet.

"It needed to be done," Gunnar said sharply. "A pity a dragon had to do it."

Finnigan shakily knelt and touched the dragon's scaly head, breathing deeply. Two soldiers ran over, one carrying a torch. They restrained the screaming wife and marched her off. Finnigan hadn't a clue what they'd do with her yet. And right now, he didn't care.

"It is over," Finnigan whispered to the dragon. It pushed its head against his chest, warmth flooding him like a new fire had entered his body.

However, something in Finnigan whispered to him that it had just begun.

Forty-Six

One Week Later

THE WEDDING CEREMONY WAS small, far smaller than the first had been. Ama's clan was invited to the Buacach castle. Her parents, a few siblings, and a few nieces and nephews stood among Finnigan's people—united. All Ama had done had been for Creator's will, even when she hadn't understood, or had feared and doubted.

Heart swelling with joy, she gripped Finnigan's hands and listened as the ceremony closed.

The grueling week hadn't been without hope. They had buried their dead, with strangers attending Absalom's funeral. Gunnar hadn't spoken much since his father's death, but he helped where he was needed. Shafiq had disappeared, but Sadon—or Uriah, as he was now going by his true name—had pledged his loyalty to the princes once more. His heart had changed because of the blind boy who stood near him at the edge of the gathering.

Ama's heart had changed because of the little siiti boy hanging off Gunnar's broad shoulders. She believed that good could be anywhere now—and that everyone had a place, even if they made mistakes.

Finnigan grinned at her, holding her hands gently as the wedding ended. He had taken the lead as king quite well, but Ama knew his struggles. His grief over losing his parents and friends ran deep. Ama would be there for him. Through hell and through heaven, they would be together, till death did them part.

Over the week, they discovered a great deal. Much of Buacach was in turmoil, and other lands despised what Barric had done. Restoring peace and order would be difficult, but they hadn't endured Golgotha for naught. Creator would bless them and their peoples if they obeyed Him. He would help them uncover the traitors.

Ama and Finnigan went to dance to the music played by her people. Joy ran through her veins as Finnigan learned the dances of her clan, his face flushed with laughter. He wasn't a good dancer, but it didn't stop him. He sang off-key and danced with her like no one was watching.

As the song changed to a softer, slower one, Ama leaned against Finnigan. She watched her parents dance among the others. Gunnar wrestled Tanka out of the dessert table. The mercenary had congratulated Ama on the wedding earlier. Uriah whispered to Oliver as if describing the scene to the boy. Oliver grinned wide and hugged the ex-wizard with all his might.

Ama gulped hard. "Finn?"

"Hmm?"

"Would it be strange of me to ask Oliver to dance?"

Finnigan laughed. "I think he'd love it, my dear." He followed her over to the corner where Uriah sat with the boy.

"Oliver?" Ama asked. The boy lifted his eyes, face red as he realized who was speaking. "Would you like to dance with me?"

"I-I don't—"

"Don't worry," Finnigan interjected. "She's a good dancer. Hasn't stepped on my toes once tonight."

"You stepped on mine," Ama said, chuckling. She gently took Oliver's hand. "Well?"

"Yes!" Oliver cried, and Ama led him to the dance floor.

The song of her people drummed in her soul as she led him in dance, and he beamed wide the entire time. Once the song ended, she walked with him to the dessert table, whispering into his ear her secret plan.

Oliver grinned and nodded. When Gunnar stepped over with Tanka, Oliver casually said, "Gunnar, what do you think these things are here? I smell something weird." Oliver pointed at the foreign Goidelic food.

Ama's heart hammered but she kept a straight face, hand trailing to a piece of cake as Gunnar moved closer to Oliver.

Gunnar frowned, holding Tanka close. "Looks like a dog vomited on a silver platter."

Splat! The second the words left Gunnar's mouth, Ama smooshed the piece of cake onto Gunnar's back.

He jumped, swearing. "Why, you little—"

"That's for calling me stubby." Ama laughed, licking icing off her fingers. She caught sight of the other men laughing. Gunnar's face went red, but he smiled.

"You win this round, Princess."

Ama looked forward to a life spent as queen if it meant being surrounded by the hooligans she called family.

FINNIGAN WATCHED THE WEDDING ceremony like it might be a dream. The past week had been hellish and there was much to be done, but he couldn't seem to think about any of the bad things. Not when Ama was his wife and she was laughing like all would be just fine.

"Hmm." Gunnar sidled up to him and Uriah.

Finnigan frowned. "Hmm what?"

"I called it."

"Called what?"

"You two." Gunnar eyed Uriah. "Did you?" While Gunnar didn't talk much, when he did, his smart remarks and annoying jabs had doubled. Finnigan couldn't be angry at him. People had strange ways of coping with grief and anger.

Uriah nodded once. He spoke even less. Maybe because of his guilt, though Finnigan didn't doubt for a second the man had given his heart to Elohai. He still struggled the same as Moray did, but they were trying wholeheartedly to do Elohai's will after years of serving the Darkness.

"Well, you tidy up very nicely, minus the cake splatter. How's it feel being beaten by a woman?" Finnigan teased back.

Gunnar scowled as if insulted.

"We're never letting you live that down," Moray piped up, coming over with a slice of cake. "But Gunnar has you beat with scars, Finn. Women like scars."

"I have some!"

"Real scars, not paper cuts," Gunnar scoffed. He picked up Tanka and held the tired boy close. Tanka yawned and leaned against Gunnar's chest, tail flicking. No one for a second doubted the mercenary's intentions of keeping the child. Finnigan knew nothing more of the man's plans. He had asked but gotten no answers. Maybe Gunnar would work in the city and raise Tanka. Finnigan hoped he settled down, as Uriah was going to.

"I have Ama," Finnigan said, as if sealing the matter. "You three can fight over the rest."

Moray rolled his eyes and watched the people dance slowly across the marble floors. He'd never been one for dancing, but it'd never broken Finnigan's spirit. "I wouldn't act so tough."

"Huh?"

"I hear you screaming in the morning—Courage has taken to hiding in your closet, hasn't she?" Moray raised one eyebrow. While his brother had apologized to Ama and Finnigan for all of his wrongdoings, his teasing didn't cease.

Heat flooded Finnigan's face as he burst into laughter. "Aye, the little rat has. Loves scaring the daylights out of me."

Gunnar chuckled. "Serves you right, ugly."

Uriah laughed, but Gunnar eyed him. "You're not one to laugh, jackass."

"I am a bastard who's worse than a jackass and ten times as striking." Uriah grinned cheekily and grabbed a glass of punch, lifting it into the air.

Finnigan sighed, watching Ama. Etu sat at the edge of the dancing room. Ama's parents hadn't entirely forgiven their eldest son, but they would. They were kind people. Etu had sacrificed Ama, but he'd done everything to make it right. The Light had mercy if one repented.

None of this would have happened without Elohai. Finnigan was thankful for every trial and every blessing.

I will make You, my parents, and Graft proud.

MORAY SLIPPED OUT ONTO the balcony as the ceremony ended. Finnigan and Ama would whisk off to their chambers for the night, and the feast would end. Work would begin in the morning—the long battle of alliances, peace treaties, trade deals. They had to find the traitors and the spies. And Moray still had to face plenty of demons and nightmares himself.

He tugged at his shirt collar. The sweet smell of flowers filled his nose—someone had replanted the garden below. The deep black sky glistened with millions of stars and one perfect moon. The silent night soothed his very bones.

"Isn't quite as beautiful after seeing the skies in Golgotha." Finnigan's voice came from behind him. His little brother walked over and leaned against the marble railing, watching the sky.

"This is home. Beauty isn't something you can compare." Moray sighed.

"Aye, it isn't. Moray, I…"

"You don't have to say it."

"I do. He was my friend too."

"Gunnar lost his father, and he has not spoken a word of it or Shafiq." Moray just wanted peace. And silence. Two impossible things to gain at a wedding.

"Grief is not something to compare either, Moray. Everyone grieves differently. No one's pain is worse…" Finnigan trailed off, tears falling from his eyes. "Not that I can say anything you don't know."

Words didn't soothe the pain. Words didn't bring their parents, Graft, or Absalom back. Life and death were two things unfathomable by humans.

"There is a time for death, a time for miracles…" Moray shook his head, running a hand through his hair. "I listened to you and Mother at night, you know. When we were children, and you read the Letters aloud. All through this journey, I remembered the Letters, the things you spoke of, the things Ama said." He paused. "Elohai was fighting for me the whole time. Or waiting, at least. I'm not sure which. The Darkness was strong, so strong, and I wanted to be as powerful as Elohai. As powerful as my master. But I wasn't. I failed, again and again. I failed everyone." His shoulders sagged and he covered his face.

Finnigan put his arm around Moray's shoulders. "Don't let the spirits torment you even if you cannot see them now, Brother. Have peace. We're all doomed if we don't have the

Light." He smiled sadly. "There is a reason we went to Golgotha. I do not believe it was all a mistake."

"Lives were lost."

"And lives were saved. Tanka, Uriah, Oliver, and you... all saved from the Darkness. I weep over the lost, but we must fight on for the living. We must focus on the Light, or the Darkness will win," Finnigan whispered hoarsely.

"We know of the unseen, the Darkness, but how can we fight without focusing on it all?" Moray gulped hard, voice breaking. "I do not want to end up like Absalom."

"To fight the Darkness and not be lost to it, we must focus our hearts to the Light and fight when Elohai tells us to. We will make it, Brother. We will fight together. We already did Elohai's bidding once. We saved Mazzabah."

"Fight for our people, our family, to help the lands..." Moray lifted his head. "Or fight to win Golgotha?"

Finnigan didn't look away. "If there are souls that need saving there, I... I cannot turn away from that."

"You think Elohai wants you to take such a mission?" Moray set his jaw hard, studying his brother in the pale moonlight.

Finnigan nodded. "Not just now, but... Well, Elohai created the realms, and if He wants me to help save Golgotha from the Darkness, I must do so when He bids."

Moray chuckled weakly. "Is saving Buacach not enough for you?" But he knew his brother's heart, and he would follow him through anything. The time of fear had ended. The time for war had started, war against the Darkness, and they would win.

URIAH.

Elohai is my light.
That is who I am.

Something changed when he welcomed Elohai into his heart. Uriah busied himself working, trying to regain the princes' trust and help the people he had ruined. They let him—he didn't understand why, but they let him help.

Perhaps Elohai's mercy and redemption were more powerful than he'd believed.

But Shafiq was out there somewhere, and one day he would kill Uriah. Until that day, Uriah would serve the Light, and he would raise Oliver.

Oliver fell asleep after eating too much cake and dancing with the new queen of Buacach. Before passing out, he'd whispered, "This has been the best night of my life, Father."

The words struck hard in Uriah's heart.

Father.

He didn't deserve that title now, but one day he would, with Elohai's help. His demons, his past, his struggles—they couldn't hold him back from what Elohai had in store for him now.

Until Shafiq won.

Uriah gulped, carrying Oliver into the halls. He didn't miss his magic. The nightmares that raged and the demons that visited him in his cabin at night made sure of that. He busied himself with work, and the men did the same. They all had demons they faced at night. They all had the faces and screams of the dead lingering in their memories. Such was war.

Elohai, if I must die to save the others, to save my boy, I will. If I must die to defend against Abaddon, I will.

Forty-Seven

GUNNAR WATCHED THE MORNING sunrise peep above the horizon, purples and yellows staining the dark sky. He remembered when he'd been a child living on the edge of the sea. Absalom would rise early, take Gunnar to his ship, and work as the sun crept into the sky. Gunnar could picture the scene perfectly, complete with the strong smell of Absalom's morning coffee and the stench of crewmen as they rallied. Those sunrises had been tastes of heaven.

Those days were over. Gunnar had no yearning to see the ocean again. He had done his time as a sailor. He had done his time as a mercenary.

But there was one last thing he had to do.

Absalom had told Gunnar of what had happened in Golgotha. His father had one of the finest crews in the land, and because of Shafiq the traitor, they all lay to rot in the cursed second realm.

Shafiq had taken everything from Gunnar. His father. His crew. Shafiq had tormented his friends.

He turned from the castle's window overlooking Buacach. Tanka slept on a small bed beside his own, snoring loud enough to wake the dead. Gunnar hadn't expected to love the siiti child, but he hadn't fought it. After Absalom's death, the child was the only thing keeping Gunnar sane. Ama had tried speaking with him, as had Finnigan, but nothing helped.

He would set things right. Shafiq would not harm another.

He sighed and pulled his shirt on to hide his scar-covered torso. In a few more months, the kingdoms, clans, and masses of annoying people would be at peace again. A new normalcy would be achieved. They would not need him for much longer. Then, he could hunt down the man who had sent his father and his crew—Gunnar's family—into the second realm to die.

Vengeance is yours, Elohai, but where is the harm if I do Your bidding?

Acknowledgments

This novel was unlike any I've ever completed. Without the following people, it wouldn't be in your hands.

Thanks to...

To my parents, for helping me brainstorm, teaching me how to study God's Word, and reminding me that I have to eat meals. Thank you, Mom and Dad, for everything.

To Tory and the kiddos, thanks for supporting me and giving me lots of laughs when I needed them most.

To Kody, for TV binge-watching, long walks, and helping out with the pup when I needed it most. (PS. Yes, I can drag my brother across the floor.)

To my beta readers who enjoyed this novel and gave suggestions that made it even stronger. You guys rock!

To you, epic reader, for picking this book up. Thanks for taking the ride, it means more to me than you know.

Most of all, thanks to the Lord, for picking me up when I broke and guiding me through thick and thin. It was a blessing to write this novel with You.

About Author

Angela R. Watts is the bestselling author of The Infidel Books and Golgotha. She's been writing stories since she was little, and when she's not writing, she's probably drawing or working with her amazing editorial clients. You can join her newsletter or connect with her on social media.

https://angelarwatts.com/

Newsletter: https://www.subscribepage.com/v7y6ro
Facebook: Angela R. Watts. Author and Editor
Amazon: https://www.amazon.com/Angela-R-Watts/e/B07F97JNMY/ref=dp_byline_cont_ebooks_1
Twitter: @PeculiarAngela
Instagram: @angelarwattsauthor

Made in the USA
Coppell, TX
18 April 2022